A fusion of thrill, fear, and passion,
masterfully woven together . . .

———————————

Each page serves to pull you further
into the heat of the action . . .

———————————

The Spill is more than a page-turner—
the gripping narrative invites you to eagerly
discover what happens next. *The Spill* is undoubtedly
an essential addition to your reading list.

D1523027

THE SPILL

For more information or to book an event, contact:
kealawoil@gmail.com
www.keithabbott.com

Cover design and art by Jeff Brown Graphics, www.jeffbrowngraphics.com
Interior design by Liliana Guia

ISBN:979-8-8547-104-42 (Paperback)

First Edition: July 2023

THE SPILL

KEITH ABBOTT

TABLE OF CONTENTS

TABLE OF CONTENTS

ACKNOWLEDGMENTS

Writing *The Spill* has taken much longer to finish than it should have. My excuse is that life kept getting in the way. But because it has taken so long, I have a long list of people who have encouraged and inspired me throughout the years.

First, I wish to thank my family, children, and even grandchildren, some of whom were not yet born when I first began this book; my significant other, Charlotte Mitchell, the Southern Belle of my life, who has read the manuscript almost as many times as I have, and, yes, thanks to my ex-wives for putting up with me as long as you did.

Thank you, Chip Monk, my good friend, for allowing me to use your unique name as one of the good guys. You rock! I foresee a future for Chip's character.

Thank you to my friends, writers, lawyers, and friends in the oil and gas industry, including the Denver Association of Professional Petroleum Landmen, the American Association of Professional Petroleum Landmen, JRC Oil and Gas, and RA Resources, Inc.

Thank you to my writing/author friends, including members of the Rocky Mountain Fiction Writers, the Writers League of the Villages, the Wine & Words Social Club, the Working Writers Workshop Group, especially Phil Walker, Jack O'Brien, Shirley Jones, Eric 'Doc' Honour, Susan Delay, Carey Winters, Leon Gottlieb, and Rich Friedman.

A special thank you to Linda Keenan of Pen, Paper & Pals Writing Club for your motivation at a time when it was needed.

Thanks for the excellent cover by Cover Design and Art by Jeff Brown Graphics. Brett Savory, thank you for your editing skills. Thank you, Liliana Guia, for your interior design and putting up with my thousand questions.

Thank you to Michael Warren and Mary Massucci at Brick City Digital Marketing for my website, www.keithabbott.com.

Thank you to the Florida Writer's Association and the Royal Palms Literary Awards, a fabulous group of writers helping writers.

Finally, thanks to Jon and Elaine Singer and Jeff and Lisa Rhoades, my beta readers.

I'm sure I have left out many but thank you to all.

PROLOGUE

Jules Washington, reeking of whiskey, bursts into the oil terminal control room. A young woman trails him through the doorway; her laughter echoes in the tense silence of the room. As she steps into the dimly lit room, the laughter fades, her gaze captured by the pulsating lights from the computer consoles.

Jules Washington looks disheveled, evidence of a tumultuous evening. His formal black tie, once neatly tucked under the collar of a crisply ironed white shirt, is now absent. Beads of sweat are rolling down his glistening ebony face. Looking at the girl in anticipation, he runs the back of his shaky hand across his lips.

The sweet sound of the young woman's laughter rouses a slumbering man nestled in an oversized reclining swivel chair in the heart of the room. Startled, Kuno lifts the baseball hat off his nose, revealing a youthful face on the edge of manhood. Kuno is accustomed to his American supervisor's fondness for entertaining the local prostitutes, inviting girls to the control room for a nightly rendezvous. As was his habit, Kuno first ignores the laughing woman but then takes a closer look at her.

Compared to other female visitors Washington has brought back to the control room, this girl's beauty is striking. Her flawless, light olive skin is set off by strands of blonde hair, giving her a very European look. She is wearing form-fitting black pants and a sparkling top that reveals her cleavage. Staring at her, Kuno is reminded of pictures of women depicted in high-end fashion magazines.

Spying Kuno, a sudden scowl crosses the girl's face, diminishing her beauty. Compared to Washington, she now appears sober and in control, her eyes sharp and alert.

Washington lets go of the girl's hand and swaggers toward Kuno. "This is my man, Kuno, fresh out of the jungle," he tells the girl. "I'm teaching him how to load oil onto these big ships," he boasts with slurred words, pointing out the window at the outline of a massive ship tied up alongside the pier. "We're loading these boats with Nigerian oil, which is being sent all over the world."

"Ahh," the girl nods, making the appropriate "I'm impressed" response.

"I'm going to go lay down for a few minutes," announces Washington to no one in particular. His words hang awkwardly in the air. Licking his lips, he gives Kuno a knowing wink. "Wake me when it's time to switch to the forward hold."

Washington staggers toward the back room, pulling the girl behind him. He closes the back-room door without so much as a glance at the monitoring gauges.

Kuno sighs and settles back in the captain's chair, where he can get a panoramic view of the computer screens. An array of gauges and dials measure the flow of the Nigerian black gold pouring into the colossal holding tanks of the oil tanker Desert Rose. He tries to ignore the sounds from the break room.

A fog bank is rolling in, cooling the otherwise hot African air. Mesmerized by the constant hum of the computer fans and the rhythmic blinking of panel lights, Kuno begins to nod off. Shivering in the air-conditioned control room, he pulls his sweatshirt around his neck and snuggles into the captain's chair. The flickering green lights on the computer panels indicate the oil is flowing as it should be. With a final glance at the blinking gauges, he closes his eyes. The back room is silent. Through the fog, he hears the hypnotic clanging sound of the rocking navigation buoys in the harbor. . . .

As Kuno slips into the world of dreams, his mind wanders back to his village, bringing up painful memories. The dreaded disease, AIDS, swept through his tribe, claiming the lives of his family. Ultimately, only he and his brother, Fanan, remained, . . . and Busi, the love of his life.

Two years younger than Kuno, but many years wiser in the ways of the world, Busi didn't tell Kuno she was infected until after they had slept together. At that point, it no longer mattered to Kuno. He loved her. The new European medication held promise and, according to the mission doctors, could turn the tide in the disease. The only barrier to their survival was the costly price tag of the drugs.

After their mother is buried, Fanan suggests Kuno come to Lagos to live with him. Leaving the jungle he loved and moving to Lagos had been daunting, but Kuno knew it was his only option. Fanan offered Kuno a bed in his small hovel in a Lagos shantytown, and they agreed there would be no rent until Kuno could find employment.

On his second day in the city, Fanan came home from work with good news. "You're in luck, little brother. The American oil company I work for, Americo, is hiring. I have spoken to the office about you. They know you are smart because you speak and write English and French. You have a good chance of being hired."

The following day Kuno applied for a job at the Lagos Oil Terminal. He was given a written test and, to his surprise and delight, offered a position working the night shift in the oil terminal control room, the strategic hub coordinating the loading of the giant oil tankers.

Although Fanan worked in a different area of the terminal complex, they both worked the night shift and shared their walks to and from work. The two brothers had begun to forge a new-found bond, chatting about their day-to-day experiences and memories of family and Kuno's new love, Busi.

Kuno loves his job working for the oil company. Despite being on the job for over six months, each night, as he approached the terminal, he was filled with awe and wonder at the scale of the operation. The massive tankers appearing out of the darkness, the constant hum of machinery, and the immense responsibility of the control room are in stark contrast to his previous life.

Kuno wakes with a start. The sweet memories of Busi and the jungle disappear, replaced by the naked American looming over him like a wild beast. Washington's bloodshot eyes are bulging with rage. Instinctively, Kuno raises his hands to defend himself, but Washington kicks the chair, sending it crashing to the deck. Kuno gasps as the back of his head slams against the floor's hard surface, sending a jolt of pain through his body.

"Fall asleep on watch, will you!" Washington is screaming, seething with anger and clutching his fists in fury. The veins on his sweaty neck stand out, glistening in the dim lights. He points to the flashing red light warning that the aft holding tank is over-flowing. "You're causing an oil spill, you idiot!"

"Please, I'm sorry," Kuno manages to say, his voice trembling. He lifts his hands to protect himself from the enraged man.

"Sorry, doesn't cut it. You forgot to switch the loading tanks. The oil is overflowing." The American is beyond reason. In a drunken rage, he kicks Kuno in the face, leaving a bloody jagged wound above Kuno's right eye.

Rubbing blood from his eye, Kuno is rolling away. He stumbles to his feet but slips, falling backward. He tries to push Washington away, but the drunken American is too strong.

Through the haze of pain and confusion, Kuno sees the silhouette of the girl standing in the back-room doorway. She is wearing only underwear, her top discarded. In her right hand, she is gripping a gun, her face expressionless.

Grabbing Kuno by the throat, Washington lifts him off the ground. "You little bastard, do you know what you've done?" he bellows, his rage showering Kuno's face with putrid spittle. "I'm going to kill you for this."

Kuno struggles to free himself, but his efforts only make Washington squeeze his throat tighter. Helpless in the rigid grip and unable to breathe, Kuno squirms like a fish caught on a hook. On the verge of blacking out, he sees the girl point the gun and fire. The flash lights up the room, but the sound is muffled, only making a dull thud when the bullet tears through flesh.

Washington jerks in a spasm, releasing his grip on Kuno's throat as fragments of Washington's skull and brain matter splatter on Kuno's face.

Kuno collapses to the floor, free of Washington's suffocating grip. Washington crashes on top of him. Hot blood runs out of the American's skull, cascading over Kuno's face and chest, mixing with his own. Kuno stifles a gag, swallowing the bile surging in his throat. With quick, shallow gulps, he pushes the large man off him and struggles to get up, slipping on the pool of blood.

"Get out of here." The girl's voice is cracking like a whip, bringing Kuno back to his senses. Her gun now points at Kuno. He nods, feeling a mixture of fear and gratitude toward the girl. Then, stumbling toward the door, he stops, eyes fixed on the flashing red emergency button on the panel.

"Get out of here if you want to live," she repeats. "Don't ever come back."

Nodding toward the flashing red button on the control panel, Kuno coughs. His voice is hoarse, and he can only whisper. "I need to stop the pumping."

"Touch that, and you die," says the girl, her ice-cold eyes bore into him. She gestures toward the door with the gun. "Go!"

Kuno coughs and rubs his throat. "What about him?" he says, nodding toward the dead American.

She glances down at Washington's body while pointing the gun at Kuno. "I'll take care of that pig. Go now!"

Kuno glances at the clock and the flashing lights on the control panel. He fights to speak without coughing, "The next shift

won't be here for over seven hours. I need to turn the valve off."
He takes a step toward the control panel.

"You are an idiot, aren't you? Touch those switches, and I
will kill you. This is your last warning." From her snarling, wild-
eyed look, Kuno knew he would not have a next.

Kuno's eyes are on the dead body lying on the floor. He
shakes his head in disbelief. Despite his faults, he had a grudg-
ing respect for Washington. He doesn't deserve to die like this.
He turns toward the blinking red lights, a bewildered expression on his face. The blinking means something, a warning. He's
confused. Everything is a blur. He hears movement behind him
and turns toward the half-naked girl, but his eyes only focus on
the gun in her hand. Now he remembers—the red lights are a
warning. He needs to stop the pumping.

"I need to shut off the valves. The oil will spill into the ocean."

She looks at him, then shrugs. "Suit yourself." Pointing the
gun at Kuno's head, she pulls the trigger. A lifetime of living in
the jungle combines with a rush of adrenaline as he springs to
his right, but not quickly enough.

The bullet finds him, grazing his head just above his left ear.
With a yelp, he whirls, throwing his body on top of her. Both fall
to the ground, wrestling to get the gun. Kuno smashes his fist
into her mouth while trying to twist the weapon from her grip.
She is surprisingly strong and wiry, kicking at him and pounding
his face and head with her free hand. She struggles to get to her
knees, still clutching the gun.

She snarls like a wounded animal. "You bastard, I will
kill you."

Dazed from his wound, Kuno rolls away while twisting the gun in her hands. With a surge of fear, he yanks on the weapon. Her finger is still on the trigger. The gun explodes and falls to the deck.

Kuno opens his eyes. Crimson blood spurts out of the black hole in the middle of her cheek, streaming down her once-beautiful face. Silently, she falls onto the blood-soaked deck, mixing her blood with the dead American. Her lifeless eyes are open, still staring at Kuno.

Kuno staggers to his feet, squeezing his eyes shut, hands clutching his head. His brain isn't working. What to do? He begins to shake and tries to stand but slips on the bloody deck.

What have I done? His voice screams in his head. A wave of panic followed by nausea sweeps over him. Incapacitated by fear, he gasps, leans over the two bodies, and vomits.

Kuno grabs the chair for support, attempting to stand again. He staggers to his feet, eyes fixated on the door. He knows that, if arrested, the authorities will blame him for the death of the two foreigners. He will be executed, or worse, spend the rest of his life in a Nigerian prison.

In a panic, he stares at the gun, picks it off the deck, and shoves it into his pants pocket. With a final glance at Washington's body, he rushes out the door into the night, all thoughts of the flashing shut-off valve forgotten.

Two men stand in the darker shadows on the loading pier, watching the oil flow over the side of the massive oil tanker, Desert Rose. Both crouch lower when they see a flash come from the control room. They back farther into the shadows when

THE SPILL

Kuno bursts out the door and dashes down the stairs. He looks up and down the pier and begins running toward the city, his feet pounding in the night.

"Track him down and kill him," the smaller man whispers in French to the larger, nodding toward the fleeing Kuno. "I'm going to see how she is doing. Meet me at the hotel."

At the rate of thirty thousand barrels per hour, the backbone of the Nigerian economy runs into the dark waters of Lagos Harbor. The fog becomes thicker, helping to deaden the sound. All is quiet. The course of human events is changed.

CHAPTER 1

THE CALL

Late-night phone calls are never a good sign. The piercing ring-tone jolts me awake. With a groan, I stretch, roll over, and glance at the clock. It's midnight.

I cough and pick up the phone. "What?" I answer, bracing for bad news. "What is it?"

"Jesse, we've got a problem." The tense voice on the other end belongs to Kim Carson, my lead attorney. "We need you at the office now!"

Her tone worries me. Something must be seriously wrong for her to call me at this ungodly hour. "Give me a hint," I mumble.

"I just got off the phone with Dan Farmer. There's an oil spill in Lagos. A bad one."

Oil spill. An oilman's worst nightmare. The words jolted me awake. "Have you told Hammer?"

"Yeah, I just got off the phone with him. He wants everyone in his office ASAP."

It must be bad for her to call the company's president before contacting me. After returning from Russia, I was named Vice-President of Production for Americo Oil & Gas, the US's fifth-largest independent oil company. Unofficially I was the company's troubleshooter. All calls go through me first, before anyone.

"Why didn't you call me first? What time is it, anyway?" I scolded her.

"Hell, I don't know," she snaps. "It's the middle of the night. Maybe I was dreaming about what an asshole you are."

I ignore the comment. "Okay, I'll be at the office in thirty." I roll over and lay there, replaying the conversation in my mind, abruptly halting at the words . . . "Oil Spill."

The words echo in my head, sending a shiver down my spine. I spring out of bed. Not bothering to comb my hair, I slip on jeans, boots, and a flannel shirt.

As I stand in front of the mirror, pulling on my clothes, memories flood my mind about my last visit to Lagos. My team was putting the final touches on a natural gas pipeline agreement between Russia and Chechnya. At the time, tensions between the two sides had been high, with each side despising the other. Convincing them to work together toward a mutually beneficial agreement was a delicate task.

As a half-Navajo Indian who grew up on the reservation in New Mexico, I had a unique perspective that allowed me to build a good rapport with both parties. Over many bottles of vodka, I told them stories of the Wild West, Geronimo, the Apache war chief, and battles between cowboys and Indians. Most, but not all, were fictitious. They liked it when the Indians won.

Negotiations had gone better than expected, and we secured a lucrative pipeline contract that benefited all parties, including Americo Oil. Our team was on our way home when we were unexpectedly diverted to Lagos, Nigeria.

That was two years ago, and I still remember the heat—the poverty of Lagos. The Nigerian Oil Minister had been impressed by the successful Russian agreement. In the aftermath of years of civil war, Nigeria found itself standing amidst the ruins of what was once a thriving oil industry – the very lifeblood of its economy. The Nigerians were desperate to get their oil wells pumping. I knew how to make that happen. Discussions were quick and went better than expected.

One lesson I have learned in the oil business is that disagreements can be resolved by issuing a substantial payment and being generous on the terms. In Lagos, I was given the authority to "make it happen."

When I left Lagos, Americo Oil & Gas of Denver, Colorado, was Nigeria's exclusive oil and gas producer. Naturally, the country would make trillions of dollars from their share of the production, but of course, Americo got a healthy piece. Since the Agreement was signed, my company has made billions from the deal.

When I returned from Nigeria, John Hammer, President of Americo, nominated me to be the Vice-President of Production, which meant I negotiated all Oil & Gas lease agreements on behalf of the company. Despite some initial hesitations from the Board of Directors, Mr. Hammer made the final decision. I was promoted to Vice-President of Production with a substantial pay increase.

Despite the blinding snowstorm, thirty-five minutes after Kim's phone call, I step off the elevator at the office on the 32nd floor of the Americo Building. Kim greets me with a cup of black coffee.

THE SPILL

Long-legged and slender, she is nearly as tall as me, and I'm an inch under six feet. Her highlighted brown hair is pulled back in a ponytail, but strands escape and dangle over blue eyes that show signs of fatigue and worry. Apart from her appearance, her most valuable quality was her intelligence, making her one of the smartest people I've ever known.

"You look like shit," she says, handing me the coffee.

"You don't look much better," I answer, unconsciously running my fingers through tousled black hair.

"Screw you," she sniffs. "John's waiting for you in his office." Then, brushing loose strands of hair out of her eyes, she turns and marches down the long hallway.

In the background, the phones ring incessantly. People, some still half asleep, are on computers or phones—a few both at once. I can sense an escalating tension, teetering on the edge of panic permeating the office complex.

Combat Central is the President's corner office. John Hammer stands silhouetted against a floor-to-ceiling window with an unobstructed view of the majestic Rocky Mountains. Moonlight reflects off the cold beauty of snow-covered peaks and blinks through fast-moving storm clouds.

Hammer nods to Kim and me as we enter the office. He continues speaking to the half dozen people already gathered.

"Listen up!" His voice is raspy. "As you all know, Dan Farmer oversees our operation in Lagos. A good man."

Heads nod in agreement, including mine. Farmer had been offered my Vice President job but turned it down, preferring to be in the field instead. He was the first to suggest me for the VP position.

23

Hammer continues, "Stay with me on the timeline, folks. Lagos is eight hours ahead of Denver, so right now it's . . ." he pauses to look at his watch.

"Nine a.m.," someone yells out.

"So, about seven a.m. this morning, Lagos time, an oil spill was discovered alongside the terminal pier where an oil tanker, the Desert Rose, was tied up and being loaded. The Desert Rose is a new breed of tanker that can cut the speed of crossing the Atlantic in half.

At seven a.m., it's still dark this time of the year, so the full extent of the spill wasn't realized for over an hour." There is a collective sip of coffee in the room as people struggle with the time shift.

Hammer continues. "One of the workers at the terminal complex has a brother who works in the control room; I think his name is Keeno or Kuno—not sure exactly how it's pronounced. They live together, but this Kuno is a no-show after their shift ends at seven. His brother contacts security, who checks out the control room. They find two dead bodies and a flow valve cranked wide open. Terminal security and Lagos police are investigating."

The room goes dead silent.

"What was the flow rate?" I ask, breaking the hypnotic trance in the room.

"About thirty thousand barrels an hour," Kim answers.

"Does anyone know when the spill started?" I look at Kim. The question is answered with silence in the room.

Kim shifts in her seat. "With Dan's help, I've run some numbers. Shifts are twelve hours, from seven to seven. The storage tank farms are checked at the end and beginning of every shift. So, we know how much was in the tank farms when the evening shift started."

Several people nod, running an internal calculation in their heads.

Kim went on to explain her logic. "I compared the reading at the beginning of the shift at seven p.m. with the reading when the valve was shut off about thirteen hours later. There was a difference of about four hundred thousand barrels. The ship, Desert Rose, had filled its forward hold during the day shift. The night shift only filled the aft hold, which had a capacity of a hundred and seventy-five thousand barrels. Subtracting the hundred and seventy-five thousand from four hundred thousand tells us about two hundred and twenty-five thousand barrels were lost or unaccounted for."

There is shuffling in the room. I glance at Kim and wink. Then, finally, someone mutters, "Good job, Kim."

"At forty-two US gallons in one barrel, over nine million gallons of crude overflowed from the ship." Hammer shakes his head in disbelief.

He leans forward on his dark cherrywood desk, glaring at the group. "How in the hell did this happen? I thought we had all these safety measures to prevent something like this. The Board is going to go ballistic."

The room goes dead silent again. Most of the gathered group looks down at the ground. The corporate world is famous for finding a scapegoat when things go south. But unfortunately, a catastrophe like this reflects on everyone—not only the company but the entire oil industry itself.

"Jesse," barks Hammer, turning to me, "I need you on-site as soon as possible. I want eyes on the ground. Dan Farmer is managing the situation until you arrive."

He turns to Kim. "Ms. Carson, please call the airport. Tell Ron to get the jet fueled up. Wheels up by six."

"PR people," he calls out, "get geared up. No leaks to the press. Keep a lid on it. If contacted, the standard response is 'We are investigating.'" He pauses and looks around. "Let's move, people. I don't need to tell you jobs are on the line here." He didn't. There is a scramble to get out the door.

Hammer stares at me. "Take whomever you need; every resource we have will be made available. But I want you to take Chip for security."

"I want Dr. Ramos, also."

"Why Ramos?"

"Hector worked on the Deepwater Horizon oil spill in the Gulf. He's familiar with containment techniques," I answer. "I need him." Hammer nods in agreement.

Kim interrupts by stepping forward. "I think I need to go!"

Hammer glares at her. There is a brief flash of anger in Hammer's gray eyes. "I don't see any reason for you to go. We need you here to help coordinate."

There is an awkward pause. "Kim was in Nigeria a couple of years ago," I remind Hammer. Then, I look at Kim, "If I recall, you worked with their Federal Ministry of Petroleum. That could be helpful. You know the oil minister, don't you?"

"Yes, I do," Kim responds firmly, brushing a loose strand of hair from her eyes. "Nasir Gambasha and I worked together on the Nigerian Operating Agreement, and he was quite instrumental in closing the deal for Americo. I was a year ahead of him at Harvard.

I glance at her but keep my mouth shut. She's being modest. Her contacts were a major factor in getting the deal done.

Hammer hesitates. "Alright, Carson. You're in. But I want a daily report from both of you."

I take a quick peek at my watch. "When you call Ron, let him know we take off at six," I tell Kim. "Also, contact Hector and Chip. Have them meet us at the airport at five-thirty."

I am pleased Kim is going with us. She is highly competent, organized, and intelligent—a combination I greatly appreciate.

Despite that one night in New Orleans when too many rum bushwhackers blurred our judgment, we both try and keep our relationship strictly professional. As I watch her giving orders to others in the room, the echo of that night catches me off guard. I remembered in the morning sun, how we had tried to blame the intimate encounter on the rum, promising it would never happen again. Yet, sometimes the memory of the passion, like the echo of a haunting melody, slips back into my mind.

The room clears out, leaving only me, Kim, and Hammer behind. Alone in Hammer's office, the gravity of the situation settles in. We're dealing with a disaster that could potentially ruin the company and impact countless lives.

"There's a lot on the line here," Hammer states. "I'm counting on you. Stay safe."

With that, we depart for the other side of the planet.

***

Snow is falling faster when I stop at my house for some quick packing—just the basics. My Ford Bronco hugs the snow-packed road like it has glue on the tires, easily navigating the icy highway to Centennial Airport. Four-wheel drive is essential in the Colorado winters.

I am getting close to the Airport when I see the flashing blue lights of the Colorado State Patrol reflecting off the falling snow. Downshifting the Bronco to a near halt, I briefly look to my right at a car turned sideways on the shoulder of the road. As I creep by the accident scene, I slam on my brakes. A man is standing with both arms spread, leaning against the roof of the accident vehicle. A police officer has his hand on the man's shoulder.

I pull off the road, sliding to a stop. Zipping up my jacket, I open the door and step into the brutal cold and blinding snow, hurrying back toward the accident scene.

"Officer," I call out, "what's the problem?"

The patrolman turns to me and drops his hand to his sidearm. "Sir," he barks at me, "you need to get back in your car."

I halt and put both hands in front of me, ignoring the order. "Officer, my name is Jesse Ford. I am the Vice-President of Americo Oil. This man is Dr. Hector Ramos. Not only is he a friend of mine, but we are catching a flight to Africa. We have somewhat of a crisis and need Dr. Ramos's expertise to help us."

The patrolman shines his flashlight on my face. "What did you say your name was?

"Jesse Ford. Dr. Ramos and I work for Americo Oil." I glance around, not seeing any other vehicle involved in the accident, and say, "Look, officer, this is a single-car accident; no one is injured. How about letting him slide on this?"

"Mr. Ford, your good Dr. Ramos has been drinking. If I took a blood alcohol test on him, I'm guessing he would be well over the limit. Good thing I stopped, or he would've probably frozen to death."

I shrug. "Maybe, but I can drive him to the plane. It's not far—just over here at Centennial Airport. He won't be returning for several weeks. I promise to give him a good lecture. Can you let him off the hook? Dr. Ramos is the Director of our research lab. He's doing important work for the company, and we need him tonight."

The cop flashes the light in my face, looking closely at me. "Did you go to law school at CU?"

I pause, looking at the cop. The face under the wide-brim hat seems vaguely familiar. "Yeah, I did. Graduated about ten years ago."

"We had criminal procedure class together. Unfortunately, I had to drop out after my first year, but I remember you."

"Well, officer, you made it into the legal field. Good for you. I sure would appreciate it if you could give us a break here," I plead. "I'll make arrangements to get his car towed."

The patrolman sighs. "All right. Get him on that plane, but I'm giving him a warning."

"Thank you, sir. Can you send the warning ticket to my office at Americo? We're running late and can't miss this flight."

The cop nods. "Get him out of here."

I grab Hector's bag from his back seat, take him by the arm, and steer him toward the Bronco. "How're you doing, Hector?"

Hector's speech is slurred. "Thanks, Jess. Went to a party last night. May have overdone it." He staggers, steadies himself, then swivels towards me, slinging his arm over my shoulders.

"Jesse," he murmurs in a whisper, "we're close. Yesterday we ran a test with a rat. It's gonna blow your mind. One second it was there, then—poof, it's gone."

His words are cut short by the Highway Patrolman's voice, interrupting any further conversation. "Hope he's not the pilot." I chuckle and wave as I help Hector into the Bronco.

The snow is easing as we drive past the gate onto the tarmac of Centennial Airport, a small county airport the company uses on the outskirts of Denver so we can avoid the hassle of Denver International. Hector is asleep when I pull into a large hanger bay where a Gulfstream G550 with the Americo logo on the side is in the final stages of refueling. The posh fourteen-passenger capacity jet with dual Rolls Royce engines can easily handle a trans-ocean flight.

"I'm cold. What's going on? I don't feel good," Hector slurs. I unload the bags, leaving them on the hanger floor. Hector is stumbling as I help him out of the Bronco.

"Let's get you on the plane so you can get warm," I said, supporting him while he leans on me. The pilot, Ron, grabs the two bags, loading them on the sleek jet.

The flight attendant, Yvette, married to Ron, supports Hector up the stairs. "A little too much partying," she says with a twinkle in her eye.

I give her a quick smile. Hector grins. "Help him grab a seat and throw a blanket over him if you would, please, Yvette."

As we climb the stairs, a black GMC Suburban pulls into the hanger. Charles "Chip" Monk steps out, giving Jesse a quick wave. He opens the back hatch of the Suburban, grabs two large nylon duffel bags like they weigh nothing, and walks toward the jet. Ron offers to stow the bags, but the tall, former Navy SEAL refuses. I have to smile. No one touches Chip's weapons but Chip.

Over some beers one night, Chip told me how he was forced to choose between a juvenile detention center and the military during his last year of high school. Chip chose the Navy. In boot camp, he decided to try out for the Navy SEALs. After undergoing a grueling six months of "attitude adjustment" in the BUD/S training program, Chip proudly called himself a "frogman."

Fast forward ten years, boasting a Navy Cross and two Purple Hearts later, but now an unemployed civilian, Chip was hired as a security consultant for Americo Oil. He is currently the Director of Americo Oil security and one of my closest friends. His bravery and skills saved my ass a couple of times when we were in Chechnya working on the pipeline deal.

Kim is already waiting in the jet. She flashes me a smile but quickly hugs Chip and Hector, waving her hand over her nose after hugging Hector. "Whew," she says. "Hector, you've been doing some partying."

"Hey, beautiful," Chip says with a boyish grin. "I knew you would be on this trip when I heard we were returning to Lagos." He shakes Hector's hand, pats him on the back, then waves his hand in front of Hector's face. "Hec, you need some mouthwash."

Chip turns to me. "Yá'át'ééh," he says, carefully enunciating the Navajo greeting. There is a satisfied smirk playing on his face.

"Hello back to you, white boy," I retort with a grin. "Glad to see you've been brushing up on your Navajo."

"I speak five languages, but I'll be damned if I ever learn that language."

"Keep practicing." I laugh, recalling my childhood upbringing in a household where my Navajo mother staunchly insisted my brother and I speak her native language. "Your grandfather was a code talker, a 'Wind Talker,' during World War II," she would sternly remind us whenever we grumbled about speaking Navajo instead of English like our schoolmates. "He's a hero you should be proud of. He saved many lives by passing secret messages over the radio in Navajo."

By 6:30 a.m., the aircraft levels off at twenty-seven thousand feet. Ron strolls back into the cabin, leans over, and whispers in my ear. "A minor mechanical issue popped up. I need to land in Atlanta to check it out. Normally I wouldn't be too worried about it, but I want to have it looked at before a trans-Atlantic crossing. Also, as long as we're in Atlanta, I can refuel."

"How long?"

"I'm not sure. The mechanics will have to answer that."

I study my watch, calculating the flight time from Denver. A non-stop to Lagos would have us landing when it was still dark.

"I want to do a low flyover of the Lagos harbor area after sunrise and get a bird's eye view of the spill area. A layover in Atlanta might work out. It'll give us a chance to grab some breakfast."

Ron nods. "I'll keep you updated."

Hector is awake and working on his third cup of coffee as the group gathers around a small conference table in the rear of the plane. I roll out a city map of Lagos, lean forward on my elbows, and look at my team.

"Lagos is the fifth largest city in the world; some twenty million plus live there. As you know, it has one of Africa's busiest oil terminals. Most of the oil is pumped by Americo. So, here's what we know." I turn my head from Hector to Chip; Kim had heard it all in the office.

"This morning, about eight, Lagos local time, security at the terminal received a phone call from an employee. He said his brother, Kuno Targba, who works in the control room at the terminal, did not show up at his normal time after work. They both work the night shift from seven to seven and walk home together after work. Security called the control room but got no answer, so they sent a couple of guys to check it out. At about the same time, oil was seen overflowing from the deck of the Desert Rose, one of our ships being loaded. The police found two bodies in the terminal control room. Dan Farmer is working with the police and will keep us updated on the investigation."

Hector squirms in his seat. Chip's unblinking eyes narrow but never leave my face.

I shoot a glance at Kim, who doesn't move. "According to Terminal Security, one of the deceased was the control room supervisor, Julius Washington. He's worked for Americo for about fifteen years. The other body was a young female. So far, we know nothing about her other than she is not Nigerian."

"This guy Kuno was a recent hire about a month ago. He's now disappeared. Local police are looking for him," Kim adds.

"Sounds like a mystery," Chip says. "How were they killed?"

"Bullet wounds to the head. But no weapon was found at the scene. Lagos police are investigating but aren't being very helpful," answers Kim.

"How bad is the spill?" asks Hector.

"Over two hundred thousand barrels released, based on the time and rate of flow."

Ramos does a quick calculation and lets out a low whistle. "Damn. Over eight million gallons. More than the Exxon Valdez."

I nod. "According to Dan Farmer, the spill has been stopped, but two hundred thousand barrels makes for a major spill. So our immediate concern is containment. Hector, you worked on the Deepwater Horizon spill. Any thoughts?"

Everyone turns to Hector. Taking a sip of black coffee, he runs a hand over his shaved head, sits up straighter in his chair, leans on the tabletop with his elbows, and crosses his arms.

"The Deepwater Horizon spill was the worst in US history. Eleven workers died, and over eight million barrels were released into the Gulf; there is evidence that leakage continues to this day. But as terrible as the loss of human life was, the long-term damage to the food chain and marine life along the Gulf was an environmental disaster."

The group went silent. They had all seen the impact of an oil spill, either on TV or in person. The Deepwater spill had been on the news daily, and millions lived along the Gulf Coast.

Hector continued, looking at me. "From what you say, if the leak is stopped, containment to limit the damage is the highest priority. First, we get booms on the surface around the spill area. The surface area of the spill on the water will nearly double daily from tides and currents. In the Deepwater Horizon spill, we built berms along the coast twenty-five feet wide, rising at least six feet above the highest water tide. Unfortunately, they did not keep the oil from migrating onto the beaches. This process must begin immediately."

Hector sits back and takes a breath. "Once contained, the oil must be removed from the water and the coastal area, but this remediation process is expensive and complicated. There is currently no efficient way to get rid of the oil."

Hector pauses and asks for a refill of his coffee. Yvette brings a pot and leaves it on a side table.

Hector looks around the table. "Here comes the bad part," he says, leaning forward on his elbows again. "On the Deepwater spill, we tried an experimental dispersant called Corexit. It was effective and worked fast, but subsequent analysis showed it contained cancer-causing agents, hazardous toxins, and chemicals, increasing the threat to marine life."

"Wow!" Kim exclaims, sitting back in her chair and brushing back the hair falling onto her face. "I guess we can rule that out."

Jesse and Chip nod their heads.

"Well, not so fast," said Ramos. "The failure of dispersants in Deepwater has discouraged most research into that area but not all. For example, I heard of a company in France called CIVO, which claims they have developed a genetically designed micro-organism dispersant. They call it *Denz* and claim it can reduce or even eliminate the environmental impact caused by oil spills, breaking down the petroleum into a substance consumed by the organism then digested as a form of harmless, biodegradable waste."

Kim opens her laptop, searching for information on CIVO.

Chip shakes his head and looks at Hector, asking, "How'd you learn all this shit, man?"

Hector gives a knowing smile. "A Ph.D. in microbiology and quantum physics from MIT doesn't hurt, my friend. There are other things besides breaking things and killing people, you know."

Chip shrugs nonchalantly, leans over, and playfully punches Dr. Ramos in the shoulder. "We each do what we do best, doc." Ramos gives a nervous grunt and clears his throat.

"I found something," says Kim, breaking the uneasy silence. She slides her laptop over to me.

I look at the screen. "Let's take a break," I suggest, glancing around the small compartment. "I want to do some research on this CIVO company. It might be a good time to get some shut-eye until we get to Atlanta. We'll eat breakfast at the Sky Club and relax until the jet is ready."

For the next three hours, I am engulfed in searching and reading. Except for the whine of the dual jet engines, all is quiet as we began our descent into Atlanta.

As we disembark, I catch Ron's attention. "Don't forget, a daylight flyover in Lagos. We'll be up in the Sky Room Lounge."

"Yes, sir. I'll keep you updated."

Breakfast is complete, and I'm working on coffee and orange juice when my cell phone goes off. I take a quick look at the screen. "It's Dan," I say to the curious eyes around the table.

"Hey, Dan. What's up?"

"More bad news, Jesse. Harbor authorities have shut down the terminal, claiming it is too dangerous to load tankers until the spill is contained and the pier cleaned up. The government is pissed. But worse news," continues Dan, as if it could get worse, "there are reports of an explosion at the tank farm where the oil is stored. At least one of the storage tanks has ruptured. Right now, a tsunami of oil is surging into a residential area of Lagos. The Nigerian military suspects terrorism."

CHAPTER 2
LAGOS

"We're fifteen minutes out." Ron's voice announces through the speaker. "Almost seven a.m. Lagos time. Better grab your seats and buckle up."

With a lurch, the descending jet drops through the light cloud cover revealing gleaming beaches and modern skyscrapers in the distance.

I pick up my handphone buried in the back of the headrest. "Ron, don't forget to make a low pass over the harbor."

"No problem. We'll be following the coastline over Lagos." The jet dips to the right, still dropping.

Below us are at least fifty anchored oil tankers dotting the Lagos harbor, waiting to fill their empty storage tanks with precious black gold. The thirst for oil is never quenched.

"Looks like rush hour in New York City," scoffs Chip.

The sparkling turquoise water looks pure and inviting. "It's so beautiful from up here," whispers Kim.

As the jet drops lower, a fluorescent-colored sheen on the water can be seen around the pier area. "Kim," I ask, "can you get me the weather forecast—wind and ocean current? It looks to be migrating toward the south beaches from up here."

"Ron, one more favor," I say to Ron through the phone. "There are tank farms just north of the harbor area. They may be hard to recognize from up here, but I would like to pass over that area if you could."

The jet drops lower with a noticeable reduction in speed. From the air, the giant crude oil storage tanks look like rings on the ground. I point through the windows at the tank farm as we pass overhead. "These tanks have a diameter of about ninety meters and are about twenty meters high. They can hold up to sixteen million gallons of crude. In the US, the EPA requires a large berm around storage tanks in case of a rupture. Not so much here in Nigeria."

"There," points Kim, her voice animated. "You can see a washed-out gully from the tanks into the streets."

"Yeah, a flood of oil," frowns Chip. "I bet that's a mess down there. It looks like a dam broke."

The cabin is silent as we view the tragic scene.

"Was anyone killed?" whispers Kim. There is no reply, but in looking at the gruesome picture below, the answer seems obvious.

"We've seen enough. Take us down," I tell Ron.

Local time is a few minutes after seven a.m. when the wheels of the Gulfstream touch down at the Lagos Murtala Muhammed International Airport.

Dan Farmer, the acting point man for Americo in Lagos, is at the airport to greet us. He is beginning to show his age; his hair is grayer and thinner, and he has put on some weight.

When the hatch is opened, a blast of heat sweeps through the cabin, reminding me of a hot, wet army blanket wrapped around you. A big difference from the weather we left in Denver, where it was snowing.

"Leave your bags," Dan says after the greetings are done. "They'll be waiting for you at the hotel. I figured you might want to see the oil terminal and pier area first, at least as close as we can get. Unfortunately, we won't be able to get near the tank farm because the military has cordoned off the area."

We squeeze into his Land Rover, thankful for the AC; the heat is oppressive, even with the air at full blast. I pull the sticky shirt away from my chest and wipe the sweat from my brow.

"Turn up that damn air conditioner," Kim quips. "A few hours ago, we were in a blizzard. This heat is killing me."

Dan glances at her in the rear-view mirror but leans over and turns the AC on max.

"We flew over the harbor coming in," I tell Dan. "There are plenty of ships anchored in the bay. We could see the oil sheen drifting south toward the tourist beaches."

He twisted his face toward me, his eyes reflecting concern. "Jesse, this is a disaster waiting to happen. It's going to be a lot worse than we think. The tourist industry is already in the toilet because of the civil war. The spill could easily make it crash. Just the overpowering stench will keep people away from the beaches, not to mention the dead marine life washing up on the shore."

"How bad is the pier?" I ask, not sure I want the answer.

"Port authorities won't allow new ships to dock until the pier area is cleaned. The fire danger is too great. Plenty of those ships out there are Americo ships. The company is losing millions every day until the pier, at least, is clean."

I wipe sweat from my forehead. "How did the spilled oil get on the pier?"

"The ship, Desert Rose, was tied up alongside the pier. Oil flowed over the side, spilling onto the pier and into the water. It's an unbelievable mess."

Two guards at the gate into the pier area stop us. Each carries a military-style rifle slung over their shoulder. One guard shifts his rifle off his shoulder, holding it with both hands as he approaches the Land Rover. He bends down and looks inside. His eyes freeze on Kim.

Dan flashes his ID, not looking at the guard. "Company executives."

The guard's face contorts into a scowl as he locks eyes with Jesse, a mixture of suspicion and simmering anger evident in his gaze. His finger hovers close to the rifle's trigger, a silent threat. The unsettling glare pierces each occupant like icy daggers as the Rover moves past the gate.

"What's his problem?" Chip says through narrowed eyes.

Most people here blame the company for the spill. People can't work with the terminal closed. No work, no money."

Chip shrugs. "Guess you can't blame them."

Farmer stops the Land Rover at the start of the pier, which extends over the water and is rumored to be the longest loading pier in the Lagos harbor area. "We don't want to go any farther," he warns, staring up at the giant ship. "The pier is soaked with oil."

The hull on the port side nearest the pier—from the deck to the waterline, beginning midship aft toward the stern—is covered with shiny black oil. The water around the ship appears sluggish in the small waves and has a lustrous iridescent sheen, constantly changing from florescent brown to rainbow colors on the surface.

There was silence as everyone stared at the grimy sight.

Massive in scale, the Desert Rose is one of the newest oil tankers in the fleet. Built with the latest evolutionary design, significant engine and hull structure changes are groundbreaking. As a result, the time needed to cross the oceans has been reduced from weeks to mere days; in the oil business, time is money.

The gigantic ship, when empty, sits four stories above the water line but is now low in the water from the weight of full storage tanks. Black in color, the massive structure casts a giant shadow over the pier, giving the scene a surreal appearance. Across the stern, the name Desert Rose in white letters stands out against the black. Below the name is the home port, Lagos.

"Oh my god," says Kim, covering her nose and mouth with a scarf. "That smell is disgusting. It makes my eyes water."

Workers wearing masks and rubber boots walk down the pier, glaring at our vehicle as they pass.

Dan points to a gray two-story building on the far side of the pier. It appears tiny in comparison to the ship. "That's the Terminal Control Room." The entryway to the building is blocked by yellow police tape.

"More bad news about the tank farms," Dan continues. "I spoke with a government engineer who verified a rupture in one of the oil holding tanks, but thankfully, there was no explosion. The oil breached the berm around the tanks and flowed into the streets and houses. So far, we don't know what caused the tank to burst, but guess who's getting blamed? All that oil on the ground is highly flammable. All it would take is one little spark to set it off."

I shake my head in disbelief, wondering what else could go wrong. "Hammer's going to love hearing this," I say sarcastically. "Keep me updated."

Kim's eyes are watering, and Hector begins complaining about a headache and nausea. "Those poor people who have to smell this in their homes," says Kim, shaking her head. "I feel so sorry for them. Let's get out of here." Hector and Chip nod in agreement.

***

The portal to the Lagos Continental Hotel exudes an air of grandeur and sophistication, designed to captivate visitors. The towering glass doors, framed by sleek, polished metal, greet visitors into the world of luxury beyond.

Stepping out of the Rover, I'm immediately engulfed in a world of chaos. Lagos street noise is overwhelming, with the continuous roar of speeding cars joined by the high-pitched whine of motorbike engines.

Drivers swerve, horns beep, and curses fly. Added to the mix are the thousands of bicycles dodging traffic to stay alive. From my former time in Lagos, I know this is the norm—just another day. The foul odor of exhaust fumes is mixed with the scorching heat, making the air nearly as unbreathable as the pier we just left.

Relief washes over me as I enter the double glass doors, a refuge from the pandemonium outside. The hotel has a reputation for extra comforts and is the preferred place for guests in Lagos. The cool air surrounds me in the grand lobby, decorated with marble flooring reflecting the soft glow of elegant chandeliers hanging from the high ceiling. The walls are adorned with intricate art-work and colorful tribal tapestries. Stylish African furniture and plush seating areas invite guests to relax in lavish comfort.

My phone makes an annoying buzz demanding I answer, but I wait until I am well inside the air-conditioned lobby, away from the outside noise, before connecting.

"What?" I shout into the phone, covering my free ear with a hand.

"I said the Board is going apeshit!" yells John Hammer into the phone.

Perching my sunglasses on my head, I lean against one of the massive marble columns in the lobby.

"Okay, I hear you now," I say calmly. "You don't need to yell." The noise from outside is subdued but still annoying. Distracted by the frantic tempo of the boulevard, I am reminded of a popular Lagos saying I never forgot:

> *"A gazelle wakes up knowing it must outrun the fastest lion, or it will be eaten. A lion wakes up knowing it must run faster than the slowest gazelle, or it will starve. It doesn't matter whether you're the lion or a gazelle; when the sun comes up in Lagos, you'd better be running."*

"I received a call from a guy named Dr. Aran Lassiter in Paris," Hammer says. "This Dr. Lassiter claims someone with the company contacted him but didn't mention a name. Probably a Board member. If I were to guess, I would say that asshole, Verne Sheldon. Lassiter operates a company in France called CIVO International. He says he has a solution to our problem in Lagos. I didn't care for the guy. He reminded me of a snake-oil salesman."

At the mention of CIVO, I put my hand back over my free ear. "That's interesting. We were discussing the cleanup on the plane. Hector mentioned CIVO, who claim they have a new bioremediation process."

"Call this Dr. Lassiter and see what he has to say," Hammer orders. "Call me back after you speak with him."

I nod. "I'll call as soon as we hang up. By the way, we just finished a tour of the pier area. Afraid there's more bad news," I say, dreading what I'm about to tell him. "One of the storage tanks at the tank farm ruptured. Dan has engineers looking into it. The berm could not contain it, and oil flowed into the streets of the nearby suburbs. Dan said the oil minister is so pissed, he's ready to have us arrested. . .."

"Oh, for Christ's sake! Can anything else go wrong?" Hammer exclaims. I can hear the worry in his voice. "We need to act fast to clean up this goddamn mess. The pressure is on. The Board is losing its mind. They're breathing down my neck, demanding results, like, yesterday."

I take a deep breath. "It's not just the Board. To make matters worse, the media is snooping, starting to ask questions. So far, we've managed to keep a lid on it, but when they get wind of the spill, they'll pounce on it like rabid dogs, blaming Americo. Our public image will be taking a serious hit."

"And," I continue, wanting to get all the unwelcome news out there at once, "port authorities are refusing to let ships dock until the pier is clean. So there are a lot of pissed-off, unemployed Nigerians walking around, looking for someone to blame."

Hammer grunts. "I had accounting run some numbers. We're losing nearly fifty million dollars every day the port is closed."

"I have Kim researching this CIVO company," I tell him. "Their website claims to have designed a newly developed micro-organism that cleans up the oil by eating it. Could be interesting if it works and they can move quickly."

"Lassiter wants a hundred and fifty million dollars to clean up the spill," says Hammer, still focused on the money. "There is no way in hell we'll pay that much. Lassiter says he wants his people to inspect the site. He assured me he could have people in Lagos within eight hours, maybe less. Let me know what you think after your phone call. If it sounds promising, I want you to go to France and check it out. Take Hector with you."

"I'll have Hector on the phone with me when I call. The science part is more up his alley. How soon can we get our containment people here?" I am gripping the phone, thinking about the oil seeping into the streets. If this isn't handled quickly, it will be an environmental disaster.

"I've got the response team and equipment coming from Saudi Arabia," Hammer tells me. I can hear the stress in his voice. "But it'll be at least twenty-four hours before they're on site." Hammer's irritation cuts through the phone like a switchblade.

"CIVO could be our solution for the cleanup."

"Maybe," says Hammer. "Lassiter claims decontamination time can be cut in half or less with this new micro-virus. He calls it *Denz*."

"Has it been used before?" I ask. Cutting the cleansing time by half would be significant.

"That's the downside," answers Hammer. "This spill would be the first real-life test case outside the lab. However, Lassiter swears the virus has been fully tested and assures me it is safe, with minimal environmental impact."

"I wonder if the EPA has approved it?" I can feel the frown lines on my forehead. The EPA is our nemesis.

"This is Nigeria," Hammer says and snorts. "Who gives a shit about what the EPA says here?"

"There could be some violations under EPA guidelines. We're introducing an untested, synthetic organism into oil that will end up in the US market. That's an argument for EPA jurisdiction," I warn. The idea makes me uncomfortable. If it ever got to court, I fear it would be a loser for us.

"Right now, I don't give a shit about the EPA and their regulations. Let's get this area sanitized and deal with the fallout later. But I'll have our Washington attorneys check it out," Hammer promises. "Make sure you keep a lid on our plans. The last thing we need is the EPA in the picture or some Congressman freaking out because we introduce an untested germ. Africa is full of bugs; most don't even have names."

I disconnect and walk toward the elevator but stop when I hear someone shout my name. "Mr. Ford, how will you clear up the mess your company has made in our city? Do you know our water system is now polluted?"

Surprised, I see a gaggle of reporters holding microphones and cameras walking into the lobby toward me. Great! I think, running my fingers through my sweaty hair and wiping the damp rivulets from my brow.

"What will it cost Americo to remove the oil and compensate us?" shouts one reporter. "Is Americo going to file bankruptcy? Are you going to settle the threatened lawsuits? Did terrorists cause the spill?"

That question sparks a frenzy of terrorist-related questions, including shouts of names of known terrorists and whether they were involved. I hold up my hand and glare at the obnoxious reporter. "We are investigating the incident to determine who's at fault. But it's true; we have reason to believe foul play may be involved."

This sends the reporters into a frenzy. "What kind of foul play?" asks three different correspondents, all at the same time.

I raise my hand again, signaling for quiet. "As I said, we are investigating and working with the police. We will be holding a briefing once the facts are uncovered."

I spot the shadowed silhouette of Kim standing near the elevator entrance. I swiveled mid-stride, steering toward her, relieved to escape the madness.

"What a clusterfuck," she mutters, holding the elevator door open until I arrive.

"I couldn't have said it better," I say, stepping inside the elevator. The door hisses shut, cutting off the gang of reporters shouting unintelligible questions.

"How did the press find out I was here?" I ask, looking at Kim.

She shrugs, handing me a room key. "It's Lagos. Who knows? Hector and Chip are in the room waiting for you."

As the elevator silently rises to the penthouse suite, I give Kim a quick replay of my conversation with Hammer. "Somehow, CIVO found out about the spill and contacted the office. Hammer thinks we have a Board member leaking information."

"Hammer is paranoid. If CIVO can do what it says, they might be our best option out of this mess."

"Maybe." I give a slow nod, my mind recalling a question from a reporter. "I heard a reporter mention a lawsuit. Get in touch with our local firm. Have them check into it. I want to nip any legal action in the bud before it goes viral."

We both know an oil spill means lawsuits. Environmental groups seem to have unlimited funds and jump at any chance to destroy the hated oil companies. For them, it is a wish come true. But they are the first to bitch about high gas prices. Of course, the lawyers loved it.

***

The woman's voice was professional and smooth, with an accent I couldn't immediately place.

"CIVO International. May I help you?"

"Yes, ma'am, my name is Jesse Ford. I am with Americo Oil. May I please speak with Dr. Aran Lassiter?"

"Please hold, Mr. Ford. I will check and see if Dr. Lassiter is available." Hector, Chip, and Kim are gathered around the speakerphone. I glance at Kim, who raises her eyebrows and tilts her head slightly.

After a minute of silence, Chip begins to tap his foot, stopping when a man's voice answers. "Mr. Ford. This is Dr. Aran Lassiter. I was expecting to hear from you." There's a trace of a French accent mixed with an underlying tone of arrogance.

"Yes, Dr. Lassiter. Thank you for speaking with me. I'm told you contacted our office. It seems you may be able to assist us with the problem in Lagos."

"Ah, yes, the oil spill. I believe I can provide the service you need. CIVO has developed a solution to assist in the bioremediation scrubbing of oil spills. What is the current situation in Lagos?"

Before we get into that, tell me how you discovered the spill."

Lassiter clicks his tongue. "Ah, Mr. Ford, I cannot give away my trade secrets. But suffice it to say, I know you have a serious problem in Lagos. Has it been contained yet?"

He does have someone feeding him information. "We'll have our containment people on site tomorrow, but, as you know, the cleanup will be the major problem. It sounds like you may be able to contribute to that issue."

Lassiter sighs. "Well, Mr. Ford, I don't know if I can 'contribute,' as you say. But I can 'solve' your problem. I took the liberty of beginning preparations after I got off the phone with Mr. Hammer. With your permission, I am prepared to have our people in Lagos within eight hours. In the meantime, I understand you may want to see our facility in Paris, and you are welcome. It is about a six-hour flight, and by then, we should all be in a position to see if an arrangement can be reached."

I hit the mute button and glance at Kim. "Call Ron," I tell her. "Tell him to prepare the plane for a quick trip to Paris. I want to be there in the morning." Kim nods and steps out of the room.

I unmute the phone. "We can be in Paris by morning."

"Excellent. I will arrange to have you picked up at Orly Airport."

"Sounds good, Doctor. I'll see you tomorrow."

As I disconnect, Kim walks back into the room. "Ron said it would take about an hour to get the plane ready. Six-hour twenty-minute flight time to Paris," she tells me. "So what's the plan?"

"We leave for Paris in an hour. I'm going to grab a shower. Meet down at the bar in an hour."

"I think I'll jump in the shower also," says Hector, now sober, with a sheepish grin.

Kim wrinkles her nose. "Don't know if I can be ready by then."

I give a nonchalant shrug. "I'll send you a postcard and tell you what you missed." Our eyes meet for a brief second. "All right, let's move. One hour."

"I was planning on sleeping," moans Chip.

***

I have always enjoyed the dark and cozy lounge at the Hotel Continental. The bar is made from exotic African zebrawood polished to a high gloss. It is one of the most beautiful I have ever seen. Walking into the lounge, I am greeted with the familiar smell of liquor mixed with cigarette smoke and the unusual scent of the zebrawood. It brings back memories of the hours perched at this bar while Kim and I hammered out the terms of the Nigerian Operating Agreement two years earlier.

I spot Hector and Chip sitting at the bar, but not together. Hector is at one end by himself, nursing a drink. Chip, always the ladies' man, is talking to an attractive redhead smiling at him. She looks at me out of the corner of her eye, then turns her attention back to Chip. Kim is nowhere to be seen.

I sit next to Hector, who lifts his drink in greeting. "Soda water," he says, giving me a look over the top of his glass. I order a whiskey on the rocks. "Another soda water for my friend," I say to the bartender, looking at Hector, "and whatever that happy couple is having." I nod toward Chip and his newfound friend.

Hector and I look at each other as the woman sitting by Chip giggles. "He never quits," Hector says with a chuckle and rare smile.

Sitting at the bar, I wander back to how I first met Hector. I was in my third year of law school. Hector's sister, a classmate, cornered me at an otherwise boring party. "Hey, Jess. I want you to meet my big brother, Hector," she grinned. "He just graduated from MIT and is back in Colorado to find a job."

Hector seemed shy and quiet at first. "Big brother here is the first in the family to graduate from college, a Ph.D. from MIT no less," she said proudly, wrapping her arm through his.

That earned a second look from me. "Impressive. What are your plans, Hector?" I asked.

Hector shrugged. "I have a few offers on the table. Exxon, maybe."

As the night wore on, Hector and I spent most of the party talking. We discovered we both had mixed parents. Hector's father is white, and his mother is a native of Columbia. He was fascinated by my life in the Southwest, growing up on the Navajo reservation. By night's end, we laughed about each of us being "half-breeds."

Hector's degree is in quantum micro-engineering, specifically nanotechnology. I was impressed with him. We stayed in touch, and several years later, when an opening became available in America's new research lab, Hector was my first choice to fill the position.

"There's only one condition to you working for me," I told him as we toured the lab. "I want you to think outside the box in terms of alternative energy."

A grin broke out on Hector's face. He waved his arm around the lab. "Oh, hell yes, boss. Wait until you see what I can do with a place like this. Remember the TV show Star Trek? My thesis was on quantum technology, the future of artificial intelligence, and teleportation. How's that for thinking outside the box? One of these days, we're going to run out of oil. Then what?"

That was all I had to hear. When Hector came onboard, America's research lab, located an hour's drive north of Denver, was in the beginning phase of a major overhaul and upgrade. Thanks to Hector's recommendations, the initial cost estimate for the makeover more than doubled. However, by the completion of the project, the costs had escalated to double that again. It had been a hard sell for me to the Board of Directors, but according to those far more knowledgeable than myself, there is nothing quite like it, at least in the private sector.

"We are dealing with a finite source of energy in petroleum. The Saudi Arabian oil fields are already showing signs of depletion," I had argued to the Board. "New technology is on the horizon. We need to plan now for tomorrow. If not, Americo will eventually be gobbled up by major companies having the foresight to invest in the future."

"I think we should just sell now and take our profits," argued Vernon Sheldon, the Board member who led the opposition to the expansion.

By a vote of four to three, John Hammer being the deciding vote, the Board reluctantly agreed to the expansion.

It is thirty minutes later before Kim breezes into the bar, looking fresh and alert. "Gee, look who decided to show up," jokes Chip. She ignores him.

"I'm ready," she says, glancing at me. "Off we go to gay Paree."

CHAPTER 3
LASSITER

Aran Lassiter was not always evil.

Born in Paris, Aran was raised in the Islamic tradition, as defined by his Saudi Arabian mother, Leya. However, her nurturing of Aran was brutally discouraged by his alcoholic French father, Henri.

Henri and Leya met when he was serving in the French Foreign Legion. After twelve years of service in Africa and the Middle East, Henri received a dishonorable discharge from the Legion, the reasons for which he never revealed and refused to discuss.

Under his mother's gentle teaching, Aran became a fluent speaker of French, Gulf Arabic, and English by age five. Happy and intelligent, Aran was outgoing and had a large circle of friends and family.

At the age of eight, Aran's innocent life took a dark turn the night Henri, in a drunken rage, violently raped Aran for the first time. Henri's drinking got worse, as did the sexual abuse Aran suffered. The boyhood innocence that defined his childhood was never recovered. Attempts by Leya to stop the abuse merely resulted in her being severely beaten by her husband.

Cast out by her Arabian family when she married the foreign infidel, Leya's only family contact remained her younger brother,

Saad Kalb. Growing up in Saudi Arabia, Leya and Saad remained close, despite the family's contempt for her French husband.

Wealthy and well-connected, Saad claimed to be distantly related to the Saudi Royal Family. Using his connections, he had the enviable position of investing oil money on behalf of wealthy Saudi families. Saad excelled at making money for his clients, who overlooked his skimming.

Saad despised Henri. On his frequent trips to Paris, he arranged to meet Leya and Aran at his hotel or a restaurant rather than the family home. Leya was reluctant to disclose the nightmarish life she and Aran lived, fearful of what her brother would do. Her young son did not share her reluctance.

It was late afternoon at the hotel restaurant. Saad was laughing as he told Leya the latest gossip from the Kingdom.

Aran interjects, turns to his uncle, and says, "I love my mother but hate my father. I wish he were dead."

Startled, Leya glanced at her brother, then dropped her eyes to the ground. There was a stunned silence at the table. Finally, Saad tilted forward toward Aran, which caused Aran to cringe and lean away. "Tell me, Aran . . . tell me why you wish this of your father?" Saad asked in a soft voice.

Aran begins sobbing, and his pent-up emotions pour out like a dam breaking. His voice shakes as he spills the horrid details of their home life. Saad said little but listened intently to the sickening stories.

Saad sat back in his chair, long suspecting Leya's life with Henri was bad, but he was stunned by the sexual abuse of Aran. His eyes filled with tears, followed by a rising tide of fury.

"He is nothing but a French pig," Saad swore with a curled lip. "I am going to kill him. Leave that bastard and come back home," he begged his older sister.

Leya sadly shook her head. "Please, Saad," she said, still refusing to look her brother in the eye. "I cannot. Aran has opportunities here he would never have in Saudi. In the Kingdom, he would be labeled as an infidel half-breed child, lucky to end up cleaning toilets."

She shook her head again. "No, I cannot do that to Aran. The whispers, the shame it would bring to our family . . ." Leya lifted her head and stared into her brother's eyes. "I will not let that happen."

Aran scooted off the chair and ran to his mother. Wrapping his arms around her, he buried his head in her neck. "Please, Mother," he sobbed. "I can live anywhere with you as long as you are safe from Father."

Saad nodded in understanding. He knew Leya spoke the truth. He had seen it happen to other women who married foreigners and bore their children. "You know the family can protect you both."

She reached out to take her brother's hand, her pleading eyes looking up into his.

"You know they can't," she said bitterly. "Even the royal family could not protect me from the humiliation and dishonor."

Saad stood. Walking around the table, he encircled his arms around his sister and nephew; his eyes closed in pain. "I have an idea," he whispered. "Let Aran return to the Kingdom with me until you get situated. He will attend the finest schools. No one will know about his past."

Aran jerked away from Saad, clutching at his mother. "No!" he shouted. "Mother, please don't abandon me," he begged as tears flowed down his cheeks. Leya was silent.

She turned toward her son. "Aran," Leya said slowly, looking into his tear-filled eyes, "it might be good for you to see your family . . . but only until your father and I work out our problems. Then you come back, and things will be much better."

"Aran," coaxed Saad, "you have cousins and uncles who want to get to know you. It will only be for a brief time."

Saad sat back in his chair, staring at both with narrowed eyes, his face hard. "I promise he will never hurt you again. I will never let him touch either of you—ever."

He gave his sister a knowing look. "He will be taken care of." Leya lifted her eyes, slowly giving her approval.

Aran and his uncle left the next day for Riyadh, Saudi Arabia.

Four days later, in the early morning hours, Henri's body was discovered in an alley outside La Bar Chez, in a seedy cesspool area of Paris slums. His throat had been slit, and what few valuables he may have had were missing. The crime site was in a Muslim neighborhood labeled by the police as a 'No-Go Zone.' After a half-hearted attempt at an investigation, the police ruled the death a late-night robbery gone wrong and closed the case.

***

It is six years before Aran tells his uncle he is returning to Paris. It isn't the first time he has expressed his desire to return to France, all of which has been discouraged by his uncle.

Contact between Aran and his mother grows less and less. Twice she promises to visit Riyadh, and twice she fails to show.

Her seeming lack of empathy for his feelings leaves him feeling abandoned, unforgiving, and angry, sending him into black despair and thoughts of suicide. Aran becomes bitter, but even worse, he becomes vulnerable.

His uncle Saad attempts to comfort him by introducing him to other young family members. Through this family connection, Aran is introduced into the world of religious fanaticism—Islamic extremists who hate and fear the West, specifically America. These zealots recognize and use Aran's anger and feed it to promote their own goals. From there, it is only a small step for Aran to enter the ruthless world of terrorism.

"Why go back to Paris?" Saad challenges when Aran tells him of his decision to return to Paris. "You have studied at the best schools in Riyadh and could attend any university."

"I have applied to the Paris Institute of Molecular Biotechnology and have been accepted. I start classes in the fall." Aran turns to face his uncle, "I am eighteen. I can do as I please," he says defiantly.

Grudgingly, Saad agrees, and arrangements are made for Aran's return to Paris. Upon his arrival, he is greeted by his mother, now a thin, sickly woman.

Leya's skin is pale and gray. Aran hardly recognizes her, remembering her long beautiful black hair, now streaked with gray. Her dark eyes no longer sparkle and are bloodshot. The thick makeup cannot hide the sagging, wrinkled skin on her jowls and neck.

"You have grown so much!" she exclaims, standing back and admiring her son, who was now a slender six feet, with straight black hair and dark eyes. Aran's thin lips are accented by a pencil-line mustache and sharp goatee. "You are a man now and so handsome," she says, ignoring the acne scars covering his face and neck.

"Thank you, Mother," replies Aran, avoiding eye contact.

Linking her arm through his, she proudly guides him toward a taxi. "Your room is ready. I have not made many changes."

"I will be getting my place near the institute as soon as possible," says Aran.

Leya nods. "I expected you to. But try and stay close to me if you can."

That evening, Aran sits back on the terrace with his mother. Aran drinks a soda while casually watching his mother put down her third gin and tonic.

"You are not aging well, Mother," he tells her as she stumbles back to her chair after refilling her fourth drink. He stares into her bloodshot eyes. "Are you using drugs?"

In a slurred speech, Leya denies taking drugs. Aran's face is impassive, but he recalls the signs of drug use and the ever-present smell of alcohol from childhood memories of his father.

"Don't lie to me, Mother. I see it. You forget your husband. I don't!"

Disappointed in his mother, Aran becomes cold and withdrawn. Then, one night in a fit of rage, he strikes her while she is in an alcohol- and drug-induced stupor. The following day he moves out.

After the incident, Aran rarely sees his mother. His focus is on his studies at the Institute. He grows particularly fond of chemistry—the school and internet supply food for his curious and increasingly cruel mind. Aran is familiar with the power of pain, a lesson well learned as a child.

Chemistry pleases him, a pleasure he takes to new heights as he discovers certain chemical mixtures create pain, fear, power, and control.

A neighbor's annoying cat is his first victim. The reaction from two drops of a homemade potion on the unsuspecting cat's tail is swift and severe. Aran watched in fascination and pleasure as the poor animal screamed while trying to bite its tail. He never sees the animal again.

It is six years before Aran graduates near the top of his class with honors. His mother and Uncle Saad are present for the graduation ceremony. Both watch with pride as he receives his Ph.D. in molecular engineering.

The evening after graduation, Aran and his uncle sit outside on the second-floor terrace of his mother's apartment. It is a warm spring evening. Each man drinks a glass of wine from the Grand Cru region of France, home of the world's finest Bordeaux.

The rich aroma of hot bread and pastries drifts out of the ovens from local bakeries preparing for the morning rush, combined with the savory smell of roasting chickens. They sit quietly, taking in the smells and looking down at the avenue traffic. Couples walk hand in hand, their laughing conversations interrupted by bell-ringing cyclists.

"I love Paris," says Saad with a sigh. Aran nods in agreement. "You have done well, Aran. Your family is pleased with you."

Saad looks at his nephew with pride. He has grown into a handsome man, tall like his French father, combined with the beauty of a younger version of his mother. Saad likes the goatee, which gives Aran an Arabian look.

"Thank you, Uncle. I could not have done it without your help. I am grateful and will always be in your debt."

"You have enormous potential, and I will be there to help. What are your plans now?" Saad smiles as he reaches over and pats Aran's knee. Aran stiffens, and Saad quickly removes his hand. "Why don't you come back to Riyadh with me?"

Aran raised the wine glass to his lips. "Thank you for your offer, Uncle, but my future is in Paris. This is where I want to live." Aran pauses and glances up at his uncle, then continues.

"During the Deepwater Horizon oil spill in the Gulf of Mexico, British Petroleum contacted one of my professors at the Institute. They wanted him to research micro-organisms that could be used to clean up the spill." Aran's eyes sparkle, and he begins to speak faster. "I was his teaching assistant at the time and had the opportunity to contribute to that research."

Saad sits up straight in his chair, silent. His calculating eyes are glued to Aran's face. Sitting his half-filled wine glass down, Aran leans toward his uncle and looks up into the night sky.

"If there is one weakness in the petroleum industry, it is cleaning up oil spills. The process is expensive, difficult, and not always successful, no matter how much money is spent. But on the other hand, the bad environmental publicity can cost an oil company billions of dollars." Aran sees his uncle nodding and continues.

"My professor has discovered a way to grow vast quantities of a micro-organism, a micro-virus, that consumes oil, but after digesting the oil, it disposes of the remains as a waste product and then dies. The organism cannot reproduce. The leftover waste product, which my professor calls 'virus shit,' is water soluble and biodegradable. Over time, the waste, with nature's help, will naturally dissolve into the earth. Thus, the oil spill disappears, the beaches are clean, and the environment is back as before the spill."

Saad nods, looking at Aran but not seeing him as he considers the possibilities. "You could become very wealthy with this organism."

Aran takes a sip of wine and shakes his head. "But there is a problem."

Saad's eyes narrow to slits. "What?"

"Even though I am his teaching assistant, he will not show me, or anyone, his formula. He keeps it locked in his office safe. I could create and copy the design if I had the formula." Aran pauses. "Uncle, a micro virus is a biological catalyst that speeds up the rate of a specific chemical reaction in the cell. The virus is not naturally destroyed during the reaction and continues to live and grow. My professor discovered a method to kill off the virus after each chemical reaction, eliminating the risk of environmental contamination.

Saad nods his head. "That's a good thing, is it not?"

"Yes, it is . . . for the greedy giant oil companies. They produce more oil, reducing the need to import oil from us. Good for them, bad for the Kingdom. The Americans will then control our lifeblood, way of life, and religion. Those infidel bastards will squeeze our people until we die or become their slaves."

Saad looked hard into Aran's eyes. "So, I suspect you have a plan. What is it?"

"I can stop the virus from dying. It will consume everything and anything with a petroleum base. But I have discovered a chemical compound that will act as an antidote and stop the micro virus when needed. With proper funding, I can start my own company and develop mass quantities of this organism." Aran watches his uncle's eyes. "But there is one problem."

Saad hesitates, then asks, "So what is the problem?"

"I need that research my professor keeps in his safe."

Saad sits back in his chair with closed eyes. Even though it was against the advice of the family when Saad brought Aran into his home, he is pleased that his investment with the young man is beginning to pay off. The smells and sounds of Paris wrap around him as Saad imagines what the future may hold.

The two sit on the terrace, talking until the early morning hours. Then, as the first rays of the sun start to creep across the rooftops of Paris, they crawl off to bed.

Two days later, Aran's former professor is found hanging from a rope in his office. Nothing appears to be missing. When the police open the office safe, they find papers, money, and a passport. They are unaware that three notebooks have disappeared. Several of the professor's students, including Aran, are questioned. Finding no evidence of foul play, the police ruled the death a suicide and closed the case.

A month after the professor's death, Aran receives a phone call from his uncle Saad late one evening. "Aran, I have a gift for you. It will be delivered tomorrow."

Aran, who had been sitting, slowly gets to his feet, keeping the phone glued to his ear. "Thank you, Uncle. What gift is that?" Aran recalls his uncle warning him that the French police were notorious for listening in on phone conversations, especially those from the middle east.

"My gift to you is a sword. This sword can be honed to a fine edge. Only you can wield this sword. Use it to finish what we spoke of. There will be instructions coming along with three notebooks you will find interesting. We want you to start the company you dreamed of. Funds will be available. Build whatever research facility you need. People will be available to assist you. Be smart about how you build."

The phone line goes dead. The following morning a private courier delivers a box filled with three notebooks.

Dr. Aran Lassiter spends the next four months in Saudi Arabia, renewing old acquaintances and cultivating new ones. Discreet meetings are arranged with those 'sympathetic' to a cause and way of life Lassiter has come to embrace.

At one such meeting, Saad introduces Aran to a slender man who appears to be about Aran's age, known only as Faisal. "Faisal will be your shadow. He will have access to everything," Aran is told. "And he will also be in charge of your security."

Aran argues with his uncle about Faisal's role in his plans.

"Faisal will be there," states Saad with a clenched jaw. "He will not only protect you but will protect our interests, as well. Don't be stupid, Aran. Do you think we will write you a blank check without control over where our money is spent? Faisal is well qualified. Not only does he have a background in chemical engineering, but he is with the Ministry of Saudi State Security. You have no choice in this matter; it is settled." Saad glares at Aran while Faisal remains silent, watching the two men.

Aran throws up his hands in a fit of rage. "I don't like it!" he screams. "I don't need a babysitter." Then, he turns to Faisal and points his finger. "Stay out of my way."

Faisal's face remains impassive, but his eyes narrow. Faisal walks up to Aran, staring into his face. Then in a lightning-fast move, he reaches out and grabs Aran by the throat. Aran begins to struggle. Even though Aran is larger, Faisal easily lifts him off the ground.

"Listen to me, you impudent child," Faisal growls, "you will do what is asked, and you will do it without any argument. Do you understand?"

Unable to speak with the hand on his throat, Aran struggles to nod his head. Faisal lowers him to the ground, much to the relief of both Aran and Saad.

Like a jigsaw puzzle, the pieces come together. Thanks to a Paris law firm with close connections to the Middle East, CIVO was created. A team of scientists and researchers come together from the Middle East, all devoted to the cause of Arabian superiority.

***

After over a year of demanding work, testing, failure, frustration, redesign, and retesting, the research team is gathered in the large CIVO lab, as they had done numerous times in the past year. Once again, all eyes are glued to the airtight box. Cameras are focused on the glass box, recording every detail.

THE SPILL

Lassiter stands in front of a monitor, wringing his hands. On his right is his uncle, Saad Kalb. On his left is Faisal. The room is dead silent as the seconds tick by. Inside the glass enclosure, oil has been poured on the floor, a puddle the size of a golf ball.

"Three . . . two . . . one," the technician counted down. "Start the spray."

A red aerosol spray containing the virus is introduced into the glass box. No one breathes; all eyes rotate between the monitors and the glass box.

"Oh my God," someone says. "It's like a monster."

"It's working," whispers the technician, his eyes fixated on the screen. After a few seconds, he repeats in a loud voice that can be heard throughout the lab, "It's working . . . IT'S WORKING."

There is a collective sigh of relief in the room, and scattered clapping, mixed with shouts of "Allahu Akbar."

The puddle of oil in the glass container begins to shrink in size, replaced with a dark, green-colored dust that gently blows across the glass floor. The lab becomes silent once again. Under the original design, the micro virus would die after ingesting the petroleum and digestion process. Under the new design, if successful, the virus will survive and multiply as long as there is oil to consume—not dying until there is no longer oil.

The technician held up his hand. "Insert additional oil."

At the bottom of the glass box, a small puddle of oil begins to appear. "Stop," orders the technician.

A murmur of voices spreads across the room as the virus breaks down the newly inserted oil.

They watch the hideous-looking organism begin to grow and multiply under the electron microscope while, at the same time, the freshly inserted oil shrinks in size. The cell quickly divides, becoming two, then doubling again within seconds.

After two minutes, the technician looks up at Lassiter, standing behind him, giving him a tense smile. "It is working."

Lassiter nods his head in satisfaction, remaining speechless.

Saad stares at the monitor with a mixture of horror and admiration. "We have invented a terrifying new weapon," he says darkly.

Faisal opens his mouth to speak, but nothing comes out. He takes a step back from the monitor. A shudder sweeps through his body. He unconsciously begins chewing on the fingernail of his index finger as his lips tremble.

They named the superorganism *Denz*. *Denz* performs even beyond CIVO's wildest expectations. The accelerated bioremediation process consumes petroleum hydrocarbons in minutes instead of days. Further testing reveals that the appetite of *Denz* is not limited to petroleum hydrocarbons. It destroys any substance with a petroleum base and is especially fond of lotions. One unfortunate research assistant discovered *Denz* also has a unique appetite for the oil on human skin.

Through inadvertence and failure to follow protocol, an assistant's finger comes in contact with the deadly virus on a microscope slide. Within seconds the assistant begins scratching and rubbing her thumb, which is turning red, as though from a rash. Minutes later, the woman is sobbing and screaming in pain. Her entire hand had turned a bright red. A shot of morphine does not eliminate the burning pain as the rash begins creeping up the woman's wrist.

"We have to amputate," the CIVO doctor tells Lassiter. The infected woman screams in the background.

Lassiter reaches out, touching the doctor's arm. "Wait," he says, licking his lips. "I want to see what happens."

"Make it stop," pleads the horrified woman, staring at Lassiter with terror-filled eyes. "It's eating me alive."

It is an hour before the screams stop. Layers of bloody skin peel away from the woman's body. In her throes of pain, she rolls off the bed, now an unrecognizable mess of skin.

There is a deathly silence throughout the room. Finally, Lassiter shrugs, a cruel smile on his face. "It appears *Denz* enjoys the taste of human flesh." He pauses in thought. "People consume food, and most commercially grown food is sprayed with fertilizers and insecticides with a petroleum base."

His black eyes turn to Faisal. "Find another subject to test," he orders, "but this time, use the antidote. If it works, we are ready to release it."

It is late evening when Lassiter meets with his uncle and Faisal in the corner office at CIVO headquarters. Together they finalized the details.

Lassiter sighs in satisfaction and sits back in his chair, staring at the other two men. "We are ready. All the pieces are in place." He turns his head to Faisal. "Contact our people in Lagos." He turns to his uncle. "Tell our friends at Saudi Aramco to shut down all production and cap the oil wells."

Lassiter licks his dry lips. Then, leaning forward, he glares at the two before him. "We are about to set off an earthquake felt around the world. It is time."

CHAPTER 4
CIVO

"News of the spill has been leaked to the press. We're taking a beating. As usual, the press is like dogs in a feeding frenzy." Kim declares as she sits across from me on the flight to Paris.

"We knew it was only a matter of time," I respond. "All the more reason to get the spill cleaned up quickly."

Kim scoffs, a touch of amusement in her eyes as she fixes her gaze on me. "You are way too optimistic. This mess will stretch out for months, possibly even years. We're in the crosshairs of allegations of price gouging, anti-trust violations, and the biggest ecological disaster since the extinction of the dinosaurs. There are rumblings of congressional hearings. Senator Henshaw of California smells blood and is circling like a shark that's caught the scent of blood. But like the true politician he is, he's using this as an excuse to push a bill to shut down drilling on federal lands 'to protect our pristine wilderness' and punish the 'greedy oil companies' because of soaring oil prices."

"Sounds like Henshaw is doing a good job pushing the prices up. Should we pay him a promoter fee?" I smile sarcastically, shaking my head in disbelief. "All this fake news is making our Nigerian oil more lucrative. Thank you, Senator Henshaw."

Kim pats my knee. "Funny boy." She stands and returns to her seat.

I had instructed Ron to take his time on the trip to Paris. "We don't want to arrive too early, about seven o'clock. Take your time, maybe once around the park."

Ron shrugged. "It's your gas," he said, laughing.

I recline my seat back, letting my eyes drift out the window at the clouds below us, bathed in the glow of moonlight. I shut my eyes, but sleep evades me. My thoughts wander, drifting, recalling the past—memories of Libby.

I can still visualize her seated in the front row on the first day of Evidence class. Fully intending to sit in the middle of the stadium-style classroom where I could remain indiscreet, I saw Libby as I walked down the steps. Seeming to have a mind of their own, my feet propelled me down to the front row. I dropped into the seat beside her, struggling to come up with a clever opening line.

Finally, I swallowed and turned to her. Then, giving her my best smile, I say, "I think you're in my seat."

Turning her ponytailed head, she smiled at me with those sparkling blue eyes. And just like that, we clicked. The connection was instant, like a bolt of electricity. From the look in her eyes and the coy smile, I sensed the feeling pass between us.

The relationship quickly developed into a steamy romance, then into a fiery love affair. Within two weeks, she spent most of her time with me in my tiny one-bedroom apartment near the Pearl Street Mall in the historic heart of downtown Boulder.

The cool fall evenings were spent strolling through the outdoor mall, and despite cool evenings, still colorful, bright flowers, street performers, and dogs, not to mention the best street bars west of the Mississippi. We usually ended up in one of the local breweries, spending hours just talking over a custom-crafted brew. Good times.

Our backgrounds could not have been more different—Libby, from Austin, Texas, was the daughter of an oilman who owned a Landman Service company, while I was half Navajo Indian and half Irish, born and raised on a trading post in the deserts of New Mexico and Arizona.

"What's a landman?" I asked. "I've never even heard that term before."

Libby's voice became animated as she explained. "A landman works for various oil companies. The oil company geologists locate potential areas of oil and gas using seismic surveys, like sonar underground. If the site looks promising, the oil company hires my father's company to search land records to see who owns the mineral rights."

"Sounds like you know the business."

"Oh yeah, I've worked for my dad since I was a teenager—all over West Texas, Oklahoma, and Colorado. I love the oil business. If the mineral owner signs the lease, the oil company can move a rig onto the property and start drilling. I've seen dirt poor farmers get forty to fifty thousand dollars a month if a well comes in."

I told her about my life. My father, Brian Ford, immigrated to America from Ireland after World War II, seeking the American dream. He fell in love with the wide-open deserts of the great Southwest, eventually ending up on a trading post near Window Rock, Arizona, working with his first love, horses. The trading post was built in the late 1800s and was one of the first in the area, serving as a trading area for the local Indian tribes and the first white settlers.

My younger brother, James, and I were both born there.

"I bet your parents are proud of you," she said with one of her easy laughs. "Jesse Ford, the almost-lawyer."

"Yes, but the family is also proud of James. He's a corpsman with the Coast Guard stationed in Pensacola. It wasn't always easy. Being half Navajo and half Irish made life difficult for us at times. Behind our backs, we were called 'half-breeds,' an insulting term, by both whites and Indians.

Libby loved the stories of my childhood on the trading post. "Please take me there sometime," she begged.

There was talk of marriage. But as time went by, cracks began to appear in the relationship. It was not all roses for two "Type A" lawyers. Reluctantly, we both realized it was not working, and by mutual agreement, the relationship ended. After graduation, Libby moved to Washington, D.C., accepting a job with the Environmental Protection Agency.

It had been Libby who suggested I apply to Americo Oil in Denver as a landman. "A law degree is the perfect background. My father also knows John Hammer, the President of the company. He would put in a good word for you."

In my third year of school, I applied for a position with Americo Oil and began working as a landman under Dan Farmer, now Americo's representative in Lagos.

Every year, Libby sent a Christmas card with a note asking how I was doing. My reply was usually a couple of sentences.

When my father died, I was surprised to see her at the funeral in Window Rock, Arizona. She asked if she could see the trading post she had heard so much about.

She was surprised at its size. Giant cottonwood trees made up the valley surrounding a two-story building built with sandstone rocks. A streambed, dry six months a year, ran near a corral with a barn, serving as a home for three horses and three head of cattle.

We rode horses, talking as our mounts strolled down the sandy bottom of a dried-up arroyo. The conversation flowed back and forth like old times. I built a small fire as the sun vanished behind the western horizon.

"Has it been hard? Going from this life on the reservation to the life you have now?" she asked.

"When I lived here, my skin was brown from the desert sun. I was an Indian. Now I live in the mountains. I sit in an air-conditioned office all day. I wear business suits, and my skin is turning pale. But in here," I said, pointing to my chest, "I will always be an Indian."

The firelight flickered off our faces when Libby leaned over and kissed me. Then, as the sun set, we made love in the desert. The next day, she returned to Washington.

***

Bitter cold greets us when we land at Orly airport outside Paris.

"Just bring your briefcases," I tell my companions. "No need for luggage. We're headed back to Lagos after our meeting."

"Fine with me," says Chip, pulling a beanie hat over his head as a blast of winter air rushes into the plane through the open exit hatch.

A black Mercedes SUV, motor running, is parked near the front of the plane. As a group, we begin walking toward the vehicle. A man with middle eastern features leans against the hood, one hand in his coat pocket, the other holding a cigarette. His breath, mixed with the cigarette smoke, forms a cloud around his head. Taking a final hit off his cigarette, he casually flips the butt as we approach.

"I'm your driver," he says to nobody in particular.

"CIVO?" I ask. The man nods, reaching for my briefcase.

"No," I say, shaking my head and pulling my case out of his reach. "I carry this."

The driver shrugs and climbs behind the wheel of the Mercedes, not bothering to open or close the doors for his passengers.

"Rude asshole," says Chip, glaring daggers.

We are driven over to a small Customs building for private aircraft. "All out. Customs," says the driver.

The small room is warm, and our passports are quickly stamped, except for Chip, who is singled out.

Chip is given a full body scan followed by a pat down. "Open your briefcase," says the customs agent, his thick French accent accompanied by a smug grin. "Take everything out. Turn your computer and cell phone on and off."

"I don't know what the fuck you said, but I don't like your tone," growls Chip, turning to face the agent with narrowed eyes.

I corner our driver, nodding at Chip. "Why are they hassling him?"

"They think his name is fake, named after a cartoon."

I have to chuckle. "They think you're a cartoon," I explain to Chip.

Kim pats Chip on his shoulder. "Poor little chipmunk." She teases with a laugh.

"I'm starting to not like this place," Chip says loud enough to be heard ten feet away.

CIVO headquarters is located fifty kilometers north of Paris. As we drive through the brown winter countryside, broken up by the small villages and the occasional grand French Chateaux slipping past the windows, there is silence in the SUV. Only Chip's keen eye notices the microphone disguised as an air vent in the headliner of our vehicle. He nudges me and points. Silently he mouths the word "surveillance" to me.

I acknowledge with a nod.

Two stone columns supporting a massive front gate signal we have arrived. A small sign with "CIVO International" is attached to one of the columns. Security cameras are visible on each side of the gate. Two uniformed security guards armed with military-style rifles and sidearms stroll toward the vehicle.

Chip nods in the direction of the approaching guards. "Those are the new Beretta ARX100 tactical combat rifles. A little over-kill unless they're expecting a war."

One of the guards stops at the driver's window, his blue steel handle pistol is still in the holster, although his hand is resting on the sidearm. He exchanges words with the driver while his companion stands back from the Mercedes, gripping his rifle and watching. The guard bends down and scowls. His eyes linger on Kim. She flashes a smile, but the guard's face remains stoic.

Speaking a language I didn't understand, the guard calls out toward the guard house, where the outline of a third guard can be seen. Finally, the gate opens, and we proceed down a cobblestone driveway.

"Those guys don't look French to me," Chip says in a low voice.

Hector shrugs. "Arabs. A lot of them have immigrated to France."

Barren trees line the cobblestone driveway curving toward a large building at the top of an incline. Brown grass lines the road but is immaculately manicured, like a championship golf course in the dead of winter.

Reaching the top of the hill, we get a full view of the massive four-story CIVO complex. On the road from Paris, the estates we could see through the trees had primarily been the classic European architecture. But the CIVO building is futuristic, laced with black-colored steel beams intertwined with chrome and narrow vertical windows. The driver stops at the front entrance and immediately opens our doors.

Chip gives a low whistle as he steps out. "Damn, this place looks like a fortress."

As we step out of the SUV, two large chrome doors at the front of the building open automatically, revealing a middle-aged woman wearing a snug-fitting pantsuit of black leather accenting an already flattering figure. Her blonde hair is a short pixie cut. Black patent-leather stiletto heels with red soles make her taller than either Hector or me, but not Chip. She gives me a brief smile, steps forward, and extends her hand.

"Mr. Ford, welcome. My name is Carla. Doctor Lassiter has asked me to be your escort." She turns to look at Hector. "Dr. Ramos, welcome."

Chip receives a nod of acknowledgment, while Kim is completely ignored. Kim shoots a piercing glare at the woman. Stepping forward, Kim touches the arm of the blonde woman. With more than a hint of irritation, she introduces herself, emphasizing her name.

"Oh, by the way, Carla, my name is Kim Carson, and this is Chip Monk." Kim extends her hand. There is a surprised gasp from the woman, and Carla responds with a look of contempt, refusing to acknowledge the gesture. She looks down at Kim's outstretched hand, ignores it, and continues into the building. "Please follow me," she says, leading the way through the entrance.

Kim looks up at Chip and mouths the word, "Bitch."

The decor in the reception area mirrors the outside of the building but is softened by artwork, paintings of horses, Arab buildings, and battle scenes. Despite the early morning hour, the building seems busy. People, primarily women, scurry in and out of connecting doors. Chrome desks are strategically located throughout the reception area.

All the women are dressed in the same fashion as Carla, the black patent-leather pantsuits with stiletto heels. With few exceptions, all have their blonde hair cut short.

"They look like clones," Kim smirks.

Three closed doors lead off the main reception area. Middle Eastern motif artwork and pictures of vibrant colors of rich red, blues, greens, and gold dot the room, conveying a sense of opulence and luxury. Much of the artwork depicts Islam religious themes.

In front of each doorway is a chrome desk with a computer monitor. Each desk is staffed by one of the women, who ignore us.

Double doors at the far end of the room open into a wide hallway. We follow Carla down the corridor lined with the same style of pictures on the walls, which ends at a large solid door polished to a high gloss black. Carla opens the door and ushers us into a spacious office with furniture matching the same style as the front reception area.

In the center of the room lies a circular floor rug, its intricate design depicting a vibrant crescent moon and star in vivid shades of green and red. The room has no desk, but instead, a polished conference table rests in the far corner, surrounded by high-back leather chairs. The smell of freshly brewed coffee permeates the office. I can't help but wonder what has been discussed around this table.

"Please make yourselves comfortable," Carla says, indicating the chairs around the conference table. "Dr. Lassiter will be with you shortly. May I get you anything? Water, coffee, or a latte if you desire?"

I glance at a coffee bar in the corner of the room as I sit. "That coffee smells good. I'd take a cup with cream, please, ma'am."

Hector raises a finger. "Cream and sugar, please."

"Latte, please," says Kim, sitting next to Chip.

Chip shakes his head. "I'm good."

I continue to explore the office as Carla walks to the coffee bar. I see nothing hinting at the personality of the mysterious Dr. Lassiter—no pictures, trophies, or personal mementos.

Carla returns carrying a tray of filled cups on saucers. I am taking my first sip of the brew when a tall thin man enters. He has jet black hair, stylishly long, combed straight back, thick dark eyebrows that accentuate black eyes, and a black goatee streaked with gray that comes to a sharp point. Acne scars sprinkle both cheeks and neck on his olive-colored skin. He wears a black European-cut sport coat and pants, contrasting with the white sweater underneath. His shoes are polished to a high gloss.

He strides straight toward us, hands at his sides. "Mr. Ford, Dr. Ramos, Mr. Monk, and Ms. Carson." He greets each of us by name and with a nod but makes no effort to shake hands or introduce himself.

"Thank you for coming. I hope your journey was uneventful," he says, sitting in a leather chair. He is smooth-spoken and speaks impeccable English with a trace of an accent I cannot place. Carla backs out of the room, slightly bowing in Lassiter's direction as she closes the doors.

I keep my eyes locked on Lassiter, studying his eyes, expressions, and body language, searching for any sign of deception or hidden agenda. I see none, yet an unexpected shiver runs through me. My initial impression of Lassiter leaves me feeling uneasy, matching my impression of the building—a fortress on the outside but luxurious inside, shielding its secrets from prying eyes. Like the building, Lassiter hints of concealed power and hidden depths.

I sit my cup down and lean toward Lassiter, anxious to get to the purpose of our visit. "As you know, Doctor, we have a situation in Lagos. We would like to hear about your research on bioremediation."

Lassiter drops his gaze, inspecting his fingernails.

I pause, annoyed by his apparent lack of indifference.

Oblivious to the break in the conversation, Lassiter lifts his head. Then, in a slow, measured tone, he says, "I'll do better than tell you, Mr. Ford; I will show you. Come with me." Without waiting for a response, he stands and walks toward the door.

I look at the others. Kim shrugs and begins to stand, followed by Chip and Hector. We follow Lassiter through a side door into a long hallway.

While leading the group down the corridor, Lassiter turns to me. "Mr. Ford, I understand you are half-native American Indian. What an interesting background."

Caught off guard by the comment, I stutter, "Ah . . . yes, I am. My father is Irish, and my mother is Navajo Indian." I pause, then continue, "Her tribe can trace their roots back before Muhammad." I stare at Lassiter. "I understand you also have an interesting parentage."

There is a look of unease on Lassiter's face. "I see you have done your homework. Yes, I do. My father was French, and my mother is an Arabian of the House of Saud. So it appears we do have something in common."

"Yes, sir, it does."

We stopped at a solid door with no windows. Lassiter enters a code on the wall plate, and the door swings open into a small room containing a bench and lockers. There is a second door at the far end.

"This is an airlock chamber," Lassiter explains, opening one of the lockers. "We strive to keep any contaminates out of the research area and request everyone put on coveralls, gloves, feet coverings, and face masks." He looks at Kim. "Ms. Carson, would you be so kind as to wear a hairnet? The air must be purified before the door will open," he said, pointing at the airtight door at the far end of the chamber.

As I enter the research lab, I notice people scattered throughout the room, all wearing red coveralls. Some sit at banks of computers and monitors, while others gather around large barrels stacked along the back wall. In the center of the room is an elevated stage, upon which sits a small glass box. A cylindrical object hovers directly above the glass box, resembling a large microscope. Cables emerge from the microscope and disappear into the overhead ceiling. Bright lights are aimed into the box.

Lassiter points to the large containers at the far end of the room. "Those large vats contain our product, which we have named *Denz*. It must be kept at a certain temperature. The application at a contaminated site is simple. Our technicians spray *Denz* in an aerosol directly onto the petroleum. It will begin breaking down the oil, expelling it as a digested waste product. This process begins immediately. The waste product is a form of dust that does not harm the environment and will be absorbed into the soil through natural weather. After the waste product is dispelled, the *Denz* dies and is absorbed."

Hector is nodding. "I would like to see a demonstration."

THE SPILL

"I anticipated you might, Doctor, and we have prepared a presentation for you." Lassiter signals a technician. "Let's introduce our guests to *Denz*."

Lassiter points to the small glass box in the center of the room. "Our presentation will take place in the glass container. First, we will add a small amount of petroleum to the box, then introduce *Denz*. Above the glass container is an electron microscope. A beam of electrons will magnify the image of *Denz* by twenty thousand times. We will be able to view the process on this monitor. Please step over here," he says, pointing to a spot near the monitor.

"The image on the screen is the petroleum in the glass case. It is scanned by the electron microscope and transmitted to this monitor," explains the technician.

Everyone gathers around the screen, staring at a stringy image with a florescent green hue. There was silence in anticipation. Kim grabs Chip's arm, squeezing it tight. Hector and I lean into the screen while Lassiter stands back, observing his guests as they watch the monitor.

"Proceed," orders Lassiter.

CHAPTER 5
DENZ

"We're going to introduce *Denz* now," announces Lassiter, directing his gaze toward us. A delicate pink mist gracefully floats onto the iridescent green petroleum in the glass container.

"Watch closely," he whispers.

I find myself holding my breath as the pink mist descends.

An amplified image of the fluorescent oil is displayed on the screen, magnified ten thousand times to the cellular level by the electron 3D-colored microscope. As we watch, the oil becomes shrouded by the *Denz* pink mist.

"Now we zoom in to twenty thousand magnifications." Lassiter gives the technician the necessary command. Our view reaches deeper into the microscopic world, revealing a horrifying sight. The pink cells come into sharp focus, their circular appearance distorted and misshapen. Tentacles, resembling wriggling worms, extend from their bodies, each tipped with fang-like claws.

I watch in horror, unable to tear my eyes away as *Denz* encounters the petroleum. The tentacles squirm faster as they come in contact with the oil. The fluorescent pink tentacles pulsate, surrounding the oil cells, like a predator feeding on the flesh of its prey. Gradually, the oil cells vanish into the pink haze of *Denz*.

THE SPILL

Hector gasps as the fangs begin pulling the fluorescent crude into the main body of *Denz*.

"Holy shit," whispers Chip, inhaling sharply. "That thing has eyes." Kim grabs Chip's arm but keeps her eyes locked on the monitor.

Fine black dust with a green tint is expelled from the *Denz* main body, moving gently with the airflow.

There is stunned silence. Hector is the first to speak. "Very impressive, Doctor. The claws at the end of the tentacles suggest these cells are mutated or abnormal, similar to a virus or pathogen. Clearly, there is a biological process taking place."

Lassiter gives a hurried glance at the technician, who immediately freezes the picture on the monitor. "As you just witnessed, the oil and *Denz* are gone, turned into fine dust, which is biodegradable and harmless." No one notices when the technician turns off the monitor.

Lassiter turns to me. "This technique was tried back in the days of the Valdez spill but was only ten to fifteen percent effective, even under the best circumstances. Here at CIVO, we have genetically redesigned the micro-virus to the point where they are ninety percent effective."

I find myself becoming excited about this new technique. In theory, it would be perfect for our situation in Lagos.

"I am happy to let you tour our facility now. But as you may guess, the process of creating *Denz* is highly classified. Since we are the only company that has perfected the procedure, we are reluctant to give away our secrets, and there are certain areas that I must insist are off limits." Lassiter waved to a man who

85

had been following the group. "Faisal, come here, please," he calls out.

As Faisal walks toward the group, Chip locks eyes with him. There is a flicker of recognition. "Hey, Faisal, long time no see," Chip says slowly, lowering his arms. I recognize Chip moving into a fighting stance.

Faisal meets Chip's gaze. "Mr. Monk."

Both men stare at each other in unspoken recognition.

Noticing the interaction between Faisal and Chip, Lassiter gives Faisal a frown coupled with a hard stare. "Faisal, please take Dr. Ramos to the research staff so he can review the test results."

Faisal ignores Lassiter, instead keeping his eyes glued to Chip. Then, without breaking his gaze, he says, "Dr. Ramos, please follow me."

"If you don't mind, I would like to tag along," says Chip, glancing at me.

"Please understand, Mr. Monk, there are some places we cannot allow you to go for the reasons I earlier stated," repeats Lassiter in clipped and precise words.

Chip shrugs. "Got it. No problem."

Lassiter turns to Kim and me. "There isn't much more I can show you. I would suggest we retire to my private dining room. We can eat something and meet up later with Dr. Ramos and Mr. Monk."

***

The dining room is laid out with tablecloths. "So, what do you think?" I ask Kim as she returns from the buffet line.

She is about to bite into a tuna sandwich but stops before answering. "I thought it was pretty sick, but the demonstration was impressive, and, let's face it. It works!" she takes a bite of her sandwich and swallows before answering. "Lassiter seems anxious to impress us. If we don't use CIVO, we'll spend a hell of a lot more than a hundred and fifty million dollars." She pauses to take a swallow of water. "I can tell you one thing; the oil minister is under severe pressure to open up the port. And something else to consider, the Chinese are just sitting on the sidelines, hoping to take our spot in Nigeria."

Lassiter enters the dining room and takes a seat at our table. "You are all welcome to spend the night. We have rooms for overnight guests."

"Thank you for the offer, Doctor, but we'll return to Lagos. I have some meetings I must attend tomorrow morning," I answer. I don't want to spend the night.

Hector enters the room as Lassiter begins to reply, followed by Chip and Faisal in conversation. As he walks, Hector looks at the ground, deep in thought. Faisal stops speaking when he sees Lassiter sitting at our table.

Hector sits down and sighs, looking at Lassiter. "The process seems like it could be risky. What if the virus doesn't die off as designed? How do you terminate the process?"

Lassiter gives a dismissive wave, frowning at Hector. "We have removed *Denz*'s ability to reproduce. The process is eighty-five to ninety percent efficient, but there is a certain amount of risk involved, as with any leading-edge technology.

You must weigh the risk related to the spill's catastrophic environmental and financial damage."

I sit back in my chair, watching the exchange. He's avoiding the answer. How does he know the extent of the damage in Lagos? My mind flashes to a picture of oil bubbling to the surface in the streets of Lagos. The environmental damage has already surpassed catastrophic.

"Why hasn't *Denz* been used in the field?" I ask.

"This is a new process. We required a spill to test *Denz*. Americo is the 'lucky' victim, in a manner of speaking. I wish to emphasize that *Denz* has been thoroughly tested in the lab and remarkably successful, as you just saw."

"I would like to have a word with my people. Do you have someplace we can meet in private?" I ask.

"What he means, Doctor, is no bugs," clarifies Chip, with a glare at Lassiter.

There was a slight upturn in Lassiter's thin mouth. After a hesitation, he nods, leaning back in his chair. "The only place we have security cameras is in the lab itself, strictly for our security, of course. However, you can rest assured there are no listening devices or cameras in my office, which you are welcome to use."

"I wouldn't mind stretching my legs," Chip says, standing and looking down at me. "Anyone else want to go for a walk?"

"Thanks for the offer, Doctor," I answer, "but we're going to take a stroll outside." I glance around my group. "Get your coats."

Lassiter shrugs. "I quite understand, Mr. Ford. That door leads directly to outdoor seating. I assure you it is totally private."

I motion for my companions to follow me through the exit door. Leaving the warmth of the CIVO dining room, we step outside. I immediately turn up my collar. The cold, dry air reminds me of a Colorado winter day.

As the door closes behind them, Lassiter turns to Faisal. "Make sure the cameras are turned on. See if you can pick up their conversation."

Kim and Hector pull knit hats over their heads as the frigid north wind carries the swirling snowflakes. Pockets of sun rays break through the wintery clouds waltzing across the frozen ground. In single file, we follow a stone path leading away from the CIVO building, stopping at a bench where we gather in a semi-circle. Our exhaled breath forms a misty cloud inside the circle.

"Should've brought gloves," says Kim, shoving her hands deep into her coat pockets.

Chip's sky-blue eyes scan the nearby area for cameras. "I'm not seeing anything, but let's assume we're being watched."

Stamping the light dusting of snow off my feet, I turn to Hector. "So what do you think?"

Hector shrugs. "Let's face it, as we just saw, it works. This is a major breakthrough for the petroleum industry. From what I saw, the science is solid. I wish I had more time to dig deeper into the process. CIVO has developed a bio-enhancement process in a micro-virus with degradative characteristics." Hector sees the blank looks on his companions' faces.

"Simply put," he explains, "*Denz* organism absorbs petroleum and turns it into a waste product. *Denz* merely speeds up the natural biological process to eliminate waste. The concept has been around since the Exxon Valdez spill. CIVO has dramatically increased the speed of the breakdown. What used to take weeks or months, *Denz* does in minutes—immediately. What they have accomplished is very impressive."

Hector pulls his beanie hat over his ears. "The lab is state of the art, almost as good as ours. I have some ideas for improvements we can make in our lab. The scientists seem to know what they're doing and, in some ways, are beyond me in this field. But based upon what I witnessed, I think we should go with them."

I nod, turning to Chip. "You and that Faisal seemed pretty chummy. What's up with that?"

Chip exhaled, watching his breath in the cold air. "Faisal is, or was, in the Saudi Security Agency. I worked with the guy about five years ago in the Navy. I liked him. Very cool, very efficient, a detail guy." Chip pauses. "I don't think he's here voluntarily. He seems to despise Lassiter, so I'm guessing he still works for the Saudi government, probably on loan to beef up security. Lassiter must have some high connections with the Saudis to get him. He's done a good job. This place would likely stand up to a full-on assault. I saw things I would do differently, but overall, they have a first-class security system."

"Any concerns or red flags?"

"Yeah, a few. First, every square inch of this place is probably under surveillance. People don't have that kind of security unless they are hiding something or paranoid. I think we have a little of both here.

Second, I noticed there is a basement section to this building. I asked to go down there but got brushed off. I'd love to see what's down there. That's usually where they keep weapons and good stuff like that."

I nod. "I agree. This place is like a fortress, but for now, I want to stay focused on our issue." I turn to Kim. "What are your thoughts besides their fashion?"

Kim pulls her coat up around her neck. "I'm not real crazy about his employees. They're cold and emotionless, like robots. It's creepy. I wonder why most of them are women. I never saw anyone laughing or talking to each other—unusual for a group of women employees—but they appeared very disciplined and efficient. They're not just window dressing."

"Speak for yourself," says Chip, with a chuckle.

Kim ignores him. "I'm curious about the money trail and want to research the funding source. Somebody has put big bucks into this place. Considering Lassiter's background, I'm guessing there's a Saudi link. I have some connections in Riyadh. I'll see what I can find out.

"I can't speak to the science part, of course, but we all saw the same thing. I agree with Hector. It works! The demonstration was impressive. CIVO wants to use us as a test case, which makes sense. If it works in Lagos, other oil companies will beat down their door.

Our options are very limited at this point. I can tell you that the Nigerian Oil Minister is catching heat from his cronies. I guarantee they'll see this mess as an opportunity to line their pockets. We can't rule out China putting pressure on the oil minister to shit-can us so they can step into the picture. It almost makes me wonder if China isn't behind the spill. The bottom line is that we can't afford to wait and do nothing. I don't see that we have much choice here."

I want to think. "Okay, give me a few minutes. I'm going to call Hammer. Some privacy, please. Go inside and warm up." No one argues. I turn to continue walking down the stone path, pull my phone out, and hit the speed dial.

Hammer answers on the first ring, sounding nervous. "Jesse? So what do you think?"

"Hey, John. We toured the lab. It's impressive. According to Hector, the science is top-notch. Lassiter treated us to a demonstration of his product, which he calls *Denz*. It performed as advertised, ate the oil, and turned it into a cloud of dust. Very effective, almost unbelievable. Hector says their lab easily compares to ours. I think he's jealous.

"That said," I continue, "something about Lassiter rubs me the wrong way. I kept thinking about your comment about the 'snake oil salesman.'"

John gives a low chuckle.

"Very appropriate. He is one cold-blooded son of a bitch and somewhat bizarre, which means he's probably a genius. We all have concerns but agree there are no good options at this point." I pause. "I think we should move forward. All I need is the green light from you."

There is a pause. "Dammit, Jesse! He wants a hundred and fifty million dollars. The Board is going to have my ass if this doesn't work. What about payments?"

"He wants it all upfront. When word gets out about this process, assuming it works, CIVO can easily ask for triple that amount."

"No way we are paying it all upfront. We're the lab rats here. Lassiter should do it for free." Hammer hesitates. "Okay, we pay half first. The balance won't be paid until we ensure this process works."

"I don't know if he'll buy that, John. He seems like a greedy bastard, and he knows he's got us by the short hairs."

"A hundred and fifty million dollars is extortion."

"I agree," I interrupt. "However, keep in mind we're producing ninety thousand barrels of oil daily in Nigeria at a hundred dollars per barrel. That's about two weeks of production—a small price to pay. I'm surprised he's not asking double that, even for a test case like ours."

"I'm not sure the Board will look at it that way."

"It's going to get worse every day we delay—not to mention we're running a risk of losing the Nigerian lease if we don't get off our ass. Hell, John, you're the President and CEO. It's your company. You started it from scratch. As CEO, you make the day-to-day decisions of the company. According to the bylaws, the Board has no legal right to interfere in those judgment calls unless it is gross negligence. In this case, we all endorse CIVO and ratify your decision to hire them. It's your call and yours alone. You don't need their stamp of approval. Let them bitch . . . so what? We need to move on this."

"Thanks for the lecture," Hammer says sarcastically. "Is that your legal advice?"

"It is!"

"See if Lassiter will take half now. Tell him the second half is subject to Board approval based on results. If this goes south, we're screwed."

"John, I know what's on the line here. I can get this done. Just give me the go-ahead."

Hammer sighs in resignation. "Okay! You have my authorization to proceed. Then get back to Lagos as soon as you can. You and Kim need to meet with the oil minister."

"I'll keep you advised."

"I've been called to Washington. Leaving early in the morning, but I want to hear about the terms before I get there. Call me anytime."

"You're not meeting with the EPA, I hope," immediately thinking about Libby. I want to keep her as far away from this mess as possible.

"I wish that was all I was doing. But no, Senator Henshaw is having a hearing about the gas prices going up. I suspect he will blame us, so it will be a fistfight tomorrow."

I laugh. "Well, good luck with that. I'll keep you updated. Have fun."

I return to the dining room table to the searching stares of my colleagues. I refuse to meet their eyes. Glancing up at a corner camera, I remain silent, keeping my poker face.

I only look up at the sound of approaching footsteps when they stop at the table. "I need a few minutes with Dr. Lassiter," I say. My companions stand in unison, moving to a table in the far corner.

Lassiter looks down at me with an annoying smirk on his face. "Well, Mr. Ford?" he says, sitting down. I regard him silently, refusing to let the man push my buttons.

"I'm afraid we're going to pass."

Lassiter gives a quick gasp. The annoying smirk disappears, replaced by a look of panic.

I shrug easily. "We're talking with Monsanto."

I study Lassiter's darting eyes and clenched fist. His forehead starts to glisten with tiny droplets of sweat. Welcome to my world, asshole.

"No one in the world has the process CIVO has," he protests, an edge of desperation mixed with anger creeping into his voice. "You're making a huge mistake going with anyone else."

I shrug again. "The spill's not that bad. A hundred and fifty million dollars is too much."

Lassiter pauses, wiping the sweat from his brow. "We'll agree to modify the terms. Half upfront with the balance due upon the successful cleanup of the spill."

I shake my head. "Sorry, Doctor; it isn't going to happen. We're concerned about being your 'guinea pig.' Sorry to have wasted your time." I begin to stand.

Lassiter reaches out to touch my arm, stopping me. "Wait, Mr. Ford. As you so eloquently pointed out, you are my guinea pig. My primary goal is to get *Denz* out of the lab and into the field. I am willing to make concessions on the price to accomplish that goal. I'm sure we can come to some arrangement."

My gaze sharpens, fixating on Lassiter. Got you, you bastard. "Twenty-five million dollars upfront, with the balance to be determined upon completion and based upon the results," I say coolly. "In other words, if the results are unsatisfactory, we owe you nothing. I can speak for the Board. They'll accept those terms."

Lassiter sits back in resignation. I almost feel sorry for him. "Mr. Ford, I understand your position and want to work with you. Since this will be our first test case in the field, I'll agree to accept twenty-five million dollars upfront. However, upon the successful completion of *Denz*, a second payment of a hundred and twenty-five million dollars will be due."

I shake my head. "No deal. Twenty-five million dollars upfront. The remaining balance will be determined by our engineers based upon satisfactory completion. This is a take-it-or-leave-it, Doctor. Otherwise, we walk."

A glare of hatred crosses Lassiter's face, but I am surprised when his loathing is unexpectedly replaced by a momentary look of triumph. Neither man blinks.

Sighing, Lassiter drops his gaze to the floor. "Agreed," he murmurs. "We accept those terms."

I breathe an inward sigh of relief but can't shake the annoying thought in the back of my head. Why the look of triumph? I hold out my hand. "We have a deal."

Lassiter looks down at my outstretched hand, ignores it, but lifts his eyes. Once again, a gloating look stares me in the face.

A flush of unease tingles through my body, and I slowly drop my outstretched hand. Something feels wrong.

"My lawyers will draw it up," says Lassiter with a tight-lipped smile. Then, turning, he storms out of the room.

CHAPTER 6
POLITICS

Hammer steps off the elevator to the main floor of the Dirksen Senate Office Building, feeling like Daniel stepping into the lion's den.

Although he has appeared at a half dozen hearings in the past, the butterflies of anxiety are always present. Hammer takes a deep breath, grips his briefcase, and wipes the dampness from his brow. As he walks through the double doors into hearing room 226, the media types and news cameras turn to focus on him. The large room grows decidedly quieter.

Faced with the threat of a subpoena if he refused the demand of the Senate Energy and Natural Resources Committee to appear at the hearing, under the advice of Americo's law firm, Hammer decided to face the committee head-on.

"They're out for you, John," warned Americo's D.C. attorney, Bob Coleman. "Be prepared for a dark ages-type inquisition."

Senator Chad Henshaw of California is the Chairman of the committee. He and Hammer had clashed in the past, and it was no secret they were at opposite ends of the political spectrum.

With a bang of his gavel, Henshaw brings the Committee to order.

"Ladies and gentlemen, I am hereby convening this investigative hearing into the current situation of energy resources of the United States, the prices being charged by the oil companies to the consumers of oil and gas, and specifically, to the alleged reports of a massive oil spill in Lagos, Nigeria by Americo Oil & Gas of Denver, Colorado. We are fast-tracking this hearing on the Lagos oil spill that reportedly occurred due to its potential impact on our national security and the environmental damage to Nigeria.

There are six committee members present," continues Henshaw. "Although each member is entitled to a five-minute opening statement, I request that opening statements be waived in the interest of time. Any objections?"

There are none. Henshaw looks down at Hammer over his glasses. "Our first witness is John Hammer, who appears voluntarily. Mr. Hammer is the President of Americo Oil & Gas of Denver, Colorado. Mr. Hammer, do you have any introductory remarks?"

Hammer lifts his eyes off the papers on the table before him, takes a sip of water, and looks up. "No, sir."

Senator Henshaw leans forward from behind the dais, staring down at Hammer. "Mr. Hammer, how many barrels of oil does Americo produce daily?"

"Exactly what do you mean when you use the word 'produce,' Senator?"

"I mean, how much do you sell on the marketplace?"

"So you mean how much oil does Americo sell per day, not how much we produce per day?"

"Okay, Mr. Hammer. You want to play word games. First, I want to know how much oil does Americo 'produce' daily—however you define the word?"

"Daily 'production' varies. There is no set number. Wells and pumpjacks go down—they are, after all, high-maintenance equipment. While equipment is being serviced, it will, of course, interfere with daily production from that specific well. The oil and gas industry is very complicated, Senator." Hammer's words carry a hint of condescension, calculated to divert attention from the real issue at hand, the oil spill and environmental disaster in Nigeria.

Henshaw leans back in his chair, his expression mirroring his frustration. An aide steps over and whispers into his ear. Henshaw nods while gazing at Hammer.

"Mr. Hammer," the senator's voice resonates with a hint of frustration, "Can you tell me the number of oil and gas wells Americo operates?"

Hammer's response carries a trace of defiance as he seeks clarification. "Do you mean nationally or internationally?"

The tension in the hearing room intensifies as the senator becomes impatient. "No, damnit, I mean, how many oil and gas wells does Americo operate? I don't give a damn where they are."

"So you mean globally? Well, once again, Senator, you are asking me about a constantly changing number. As wells dry up, we plug and abandon them. On the other hand, we are constantly drilling new wells. You will have to give me a specific date to answer that question truthfully."

"So I take it you have no idea how many oil and gas wells Americo operates. I think the shareholders of Americo would want a CEO and President who is a little more knowledgeable about the company's operations."

Hammer directs a steely gaze at Henshaw. "Senator, that comment simply underlines why you're a politician instead of a businessman."

The aide was back at Henshaw's ear. The Senator covers the mic with his hand, and a short discussion ensues.

"Isn't it true, Mr. Hammer, that the oil industry in general, and Americo in particular, has conspired to increase the gas price at the pump?" Henshaw leans back in his chair, a smirk on his face.

Hammer's attorney shakes his head, reaches out, and covers the microphone. Then, leaning over, he whispers into Hammer's ear. "Careful, John, he is trying to set you up with anti-trust violations.

"Senator," answers Hammer in a slow, measured tone, "you are accusing the oil industry of criminal violations, implying the industry sets the oil prices without taking into account supply and demand. I cannot speak for the entire industry, but I can speak for Americo, and the answer is absolutely not. While it is true that gas prices are rising, if you want to blame someone, blame this government's energy policies. The government bans us from drilling on public lands and shuts down our pipelines, which prevents the oil and gas supply from getting to the market. Oh, hell yes . . . those actions will impact the price of oil. It's simple supply and demand, Senator. Yet while our demand increases, the government reduces supply. The result is that prices increase. So who's really conspiring to increase the gas price here?"

Henshaw had been whispering to his aide, ignoring Hammer's answer. "Isn't it true, Mr. Hammer, a massive oil spill in Nigeria, caused by your company, is not only a monumental environmental disaster but will cause the United States to lose future oil rights in Nigeria?" Henshaw looks down over his glasses, glaring at Hammer.

"The answer is no and no," Hammer says, focusing on Henshaw's glasses.

"Oh, is that right?" thunders Henshaw. "I understand your company has spilled over nine million gallons of oil. In fact, oil is even seeping into the streets of Lagos, creating an economic crisis for Nigeria. And yet, while this is happening, you continue to line your pockets with the working person's hard-earned money. As a result, today, the average gas price at the pump is over thirteen dollars and fifty cents per gallon."

Hammer starts to speak, but the Senator holds up a finger, cutting him off while he shuffles through some papers. Then, with a look of triumph on his face, Henshaw waves a piece of paper in the air. Both men glare at each other. Hammer feels his heart race and braces himself. Uh-oh, here it comes.

"And . . . oh yes, coincidentally, while this price gouging is going on, Americo had the highest quarterly earnings in their history? Mr. Hammer, why don't you tell us the truth?"

There is dead silence in the hearing room.

Hammer slams his hand on the table, startling everyone in the room. "Senator, with all due respect," his voice dripping with sarcasm, "I'm not going to sit here and listen to your exaggerations and innuendos. Americo's earnings are high because we are good at what we do, despite this government's energy policy. You don't have a clue as to what you're talking about."

A line from a movie flashes in his head. He can't resist. "Senator," he growls, leaning forward, "you want the truth, but you can't handle the truth. I'm done here." Hammer stands, peels the mic off his jacket, and tosses it on the table.

The hearing room erupts in laughter and scattered applause. Henshaw pounds the gavel, demanding silence. His glasses slide off his nose, hitting the sound block as the gavel comes down.

Calm and composed, Hammer turns and smoothly walks out of the hearing room, followed by reporters, some on their phones, some still laughing as they shout questions.

"Mr. Hammer, are you saying it is the government's fault that gas prices are so high?"

"I'm saying our government leaders do not understand business, which is the engine that drives this country. Sadly, their ignorance is being paid for by the consumers."

As Hammer walks down the steps of the building, a black limo pulls up to the curb. Hammer doesn't wait for the driver to open his door. Getting into the back seat, he slams the door. Hammer pulls out his phone as the limo pulls away from the curb.

"Ben, let's get some lunch. I need a drink," he says into the phone.

"I only caught the tail end on C-SPAN," says the smooth voice on the phone. "Good exit, John. Meet you at Ruth's."

THE SPILL

John Hammer and Ben Thompson have been friends for over forty years, since their youthful days as roustabouts in the oil fields of Colorado. The two decided to take a chance, consolidate their funds, and rent a drilling rig. After leasing the oil and gas rights in an area with potential, they drilled their first hole. It had been an all-or-nothing gamble for both. Lady Luck smiled, the well hit big, and both men became wealthy overnight. Hammer continued in the business, eventually forming Americo Oil of Denver.

Ben Thompson took a different direction. His good looks, natural speaking ability, and oozing charisma led him to hear the call of politics. With the generous financial assistance from his friend, most of it above board, he easily won the open senate seat in Colorado. Despite going in a different direction, Ben Thompson remained on the Board of Directors of Americo.

Still reflecting on the hearing, Hammer follows a smiling maître d' to the back room of Ruth's Chris Steakhouse on L Street. Ben, sitting at the table, stands as Hammer approaches. The former partners shake hands, followed by a quick hug and pat on the back. Whenever schedules permit, the two friends meet at their favorite restaurant. Two glasses of bourbon on the rocks magically appear at the table.

Glasses clink, a nod, and both drinks disappear.

"How's the family?" asks Hammer.

A proud-father smile erupts on Ben's face. "Couldn't be better. Bennie has just been accepted as a freshman at MIT. He's a whiz in science and math—so unlike me."

"Very good. Tell him congratulations from me," says Hammer. "He'll end up with a real job, unlike us digging holes in the ground."

Both men laugh.

Ben nods. "Mary would have been very proud of him. God, she loved that boy." There is an awkward silence. "It's been three years now, and I still miss the hell out of her."

Hammer swirls his ice cubes, breaking the uncomfortable silence. The waitress steps into the room and nods at the empty glasses.

"A couple more, please," Ben says, nodding at the waitress. As she leaves the room, he turns to Hammer. "Your little ruckus with Henshaw is all over the news."

Hammer shakes his head, a shadow of a grin on his face. "You know, the sad thing is, I actually like Henshaw. But I'll tell you, he gets in front of a camera and turns into a pompous asshole. He's so in the pocket of the White House, he can't think straight."

The redheaded manager brings their drinks. "The usual?" she asks, flashing a smile at Ben.

"No potato on mine, please," says Hammer.

Taking a sip of the bourbon, Hammer gives his friend an abbreviated version of what transpired at the hearing. Ben sits back, silent and listening. Finally, he leans in toward Hammer, staring with piercing blue eyes. "John, what's going on in Lagos?"

Hammer looks up over the rim of his drink. "It's a mess over there. Two people were murdered. We're dealing with it, but I may need your help on this one. We're working closely with the police to find the killer, but he seems to have disappeared. The spill should not have happened—too many safety features were built into the system. I think it was intentional."

The conversation stops while their medium-rare steaks are served. After dropping off their orders, the waitress nods toward the empty glasses on the table. "Another?"

Both men shake their heads. "Just time," says Ben. "We'll let you know if we need anything."

Once the waitress has closed the doors, Hammer continues. "Henshaw's blaming Americo for the spill, the high prices at the pump, and every other woe facing the country." Hammer rolls his eyes in frustration. "It didn't help that Americo's quarterly earnings just came out—a record high."

"Good news, but bad timing," said Ben, taking a bite of the steak. "You know what politics is like in this crazy town. . . ." Hammer's phone goes off, interrupting Ben.

Hammer glances down, "It's Jesse," he says, holding up a finger. He puts his phone on speaker so Ben can hear.

"Jesse, what's happening? Ben is here with me, and we have you on speakerphone. Did you get it?"

"Hey, John. Hello Senator," says Jesse. "It's a done deal. Paperwork is drawn up and inked. The bastard wanted a hundred and fifty million, half paid upfront with the balance due upon the successful completion of the spill. I told him that was unacceptable. The final terms are that we pay an initial twenty-five million, with the final balance to be based on the results as determined by Americo engineers. In other words, if the results are unsatisfactory, we owe CIVO nothing."

"Damn, he agreed to that?"

"I think he was happy to get it. We're going to be his test, baby. If it works, he'll be one rich son of a bitch."

"If it doesn't?"

"We're screwed, but so is he. Lassiter says his crew can be in Lagos tomorrow. We're taking off from Paris this evening. Should be in Lagos by early morning."

"Good job, Jesse, to you and your crew. You're still in Paris, right?" Hammer asks. "By my reckoning, it should be about dinner time there. Why don't you let Americo take your crew to one of Paris's fine restaurants as a small reward for a job well done? Maybe even spend the night and fly back tomorrow," Hammer finishes, glancing at Ben.

"Dinner sounds good, but we'll pass on spending the night. I want to return to Lagos as soon as possible and closely monitor the CIVO operation. You two have fun. I'll call when we arrive in Lagos."

Hammer frowns as he disconnects. "That was almost too easy," he says to Ben.

"Jesse did his job. He negotiated a hell of a deal. We're lucky to have him. He might be taking your spot someday if you ever retire."

Hammer nods. "Days like this make retirement sound good."

Ben takes another sip of his drink and watches his friend across the table. "The President is slated to make an announcement on this tonight," he shares. "He's going to order the release of the Strategic Petroleum Reserves to drive down gasoline prices."

"Gee, what great timing," snorts Hammer sarcastically, shaking his head. "Just before an election. A lot of good that's going to do. Releasing the reserves will stabilize the price for about a month. Then they'll shoot up higher than now, except our reserves will be gone. What a fool."

"John, some advice," Ben hesitates, toying with his empty glass. "This spill in Nigeria, get it handled. Quicker the better. Washington is looking for a scapegoat, and their crosshairs are aimed at Americo. If there is anything I can do . . .." Both men nod in silent understanding.

***

Worry had made sleep impossible on the red-eye flight back from D.C. to Denver. Even though he was tired, Hammer drove straight to the office from the airport. Now, in the quiet early morning surroundings of his office, he leans back in the custom-built chair, resting his boots on the highly polished desktop.

Hammer can't resist a smile as he watches the early morning sun hit the eastern slopes. The sparks had certainly flown in the marble halls of the Dirksen Hearing Room. He shakes his head, wondering how politicians, with few exceptions, could even look at themselves in the mirror without cringing.

Rubbing bloodshot eyes, he tries to make the pounding headache disappear, shifting his gaze to the large windows framing the snow-covered peaks of the Rocky Mountains. I need a drink. This headache is killing me.

Pulling the desk drawer open, he removes a glass and the bottle of Knob Creek bourbon. Pouring a healthy shot, he downs the whiskey in one gulp. The fiery liquid ignites a trail of warmth down his throat. Feeling slightly out of breath, Hammer takes several deep breaths.

As he pulls the drawer open to return the booze, he spies the small container of his forgotten medication, reminding him of his high blood pressure. Taking another deep breath, he pops the lid and dumps two pink pills into his hand, one more than usual. Pouring another shot, he tosses the pills into his mouth and washes them down. The last thing I need now is another stroke.

The heavy pain in his chest comes out of nowhere. Clutching his chest, he slumps over in the chair, head on his desk, trying to take short breaths. He turns his head, staring out the window at the mountains he loves. Drool trickles out of the corner of his mouth, and a tear runs down his cheek.

Please, God, not like this.

CHAPTER 7
HEART ATTACK

We are pleasantly full and content from a delightful meal at Monsieur Bleu restaurant, basking in the warm afterglow of several bottles of exquisite French wine, as we take in the view of the Eiffel Tower from the restaurant's vantage point.

It is nearly midnight before the jet lifts off the runway. We should be back in Lagos by early morning. But as our plane lifts off, my mind begins to drift. I recall my phone conversation before dinner with the Nigerian Oil Minister, Nasir Gambasha.

"Mr. Ford, I told your Denver office to give you my private number so we can speak   *gap*

about the oil spill in Lagos," the smooth, oily voice of the oil minister explained.

"Can you please enlighten me on your plans to clean up this disaster? It is costing my government a great deal of money to provide security and evacuate that area where oil is leaking on the streets, not to mention the loss of income from all those poor people who cannot return to work at the oil terminal and piers."

I shook my head. As if you care, you greedy bastard. "I understand your situation, sir," I answer. "Kim Carson and I are on our way to Lagos as we speak. Would it be possible to meet with you tomorrow so we can update you on our plan? We anticipate the spill will be cleaned up shortly, and everything will return to normal. It has our fullest attention."

"Lunch tomorrow. I'm looking forward to seeing you and Miss Carson." The phone went dead.

***

The shadows from the morning sun were becoming defined as the jet's wheels kissed the runway at the Lagos airport. Although I had planned to sleep on the plane, sleep only came in fits and starts. I struggled with conflicting priorities and a lack of clarity on the best course of action. On the one hand, the urgent need to deal with the disaster requires swift and decisive action, which must be weighed against bold and risky steps. Even though I have reservations about using the CIVO *Denz*, time constraints leave me no choice. This is a high-stakes game, but we must move forward.

The thrill of victory I had initially felt has been replaced by a feeling that CIVO's agenda was not in Americo's best interest. It is the uneasy feeling about Lassiter I can't shake. What really trouble's me is that I can't put my finger on the reason for my unease.

The look of victory in his dark eyes haunt me. The man had given up millions to make a deal with Americo. Granted, Americo will be the first test case, but so what. If the test fails, CIVO stands more to lose than Americo. We can just go hire another company to clean up the spill.

Americo is committed now. If I wanted out of the deal, I needed something solid and tangible. An ill-founded feeling is not enough. The answer eludes me, but the feeling bounces around in my head like a pinball.

I am reminded of Kim's observation: Somebody has put big bucks into this place. Kim had nailed it. How did a man raised in the ghettos of Paris, whose father was a dishonored former French Legionnaire and whose Arab mother was cut off from her family, put together a multimillion-dollar research facility? Lassiter struck me as a smart man but not intellectually brilliant. There had to be a connection I was missing.

At the bottom of the stairs on the tarmac, I wait for Kim. Touching her elbow, I take her aside.

She reads the look in my eyes. "You look tired. It's Lassiter, isn't it?"

"I can't shake the gloating look on his face when he agreed. The key must be the money trail."

Kim looks at me through her sunglasses. "Always is. Money or power."

"Lassiter didn't care what we paid him. He had a separate agenda. I'm not sure what or why. Do some digging and see if you can come up with anything. Look into the mother's family."

Kim nods. "Give me a few hours."

I turn to walk away, then stop. "It would be nice to have some answers by the time we have lunch with Gambasha."

Kim groans. "I was trying to forget that."

I shrug. "I feel the same, but we must deal with him."

As Hector comes down the plane's stairway, I stop him. "On your tour of the CIVO lab," I ask, "did you notice anything that didn't feel right? The process, research . . . anything?"

Hector thinks for a moment, then shakes his head. "CIVO has created a protein shell that surrounds and protects the virus and allows it to attach to a host oil cell. The virus gains entry into the host cell and, once inside, hijacks the process to reproduce. This leads to the assembly of the virus particles to then infect neighboring petroleum cells.

The process has been around for a while, at least since the Exxon Valdez spill. Lassiter has found a way to dramatically speed up the absorption time. As I said in Paris, *Denz* turns absorption time from weeks and months into minutes. This isn't voodoo science. They've just made it faster. I don't care for the man, but must admit, the process works."

"What happens to the micro virus after the absorption time?" I ask. "Did you actually see the virus die?"

Hector drew a breath to answer just as a black Land Rover screeches to a halt ten feet from the group. Dan Farmer jumps out and rushes over to me. "Have you heard from Denver?" he asks, breathing hard.

"Not since leaving Paris. What's up?"

"Just got a call from Denver. Hammer had a heart attack." There is stunned silence from the group.

I take a sharp breath and feel a chill of dread wash over me. "Is he . . . alive?" I ask through trembling lips.

"Still alive but incapacitated. Hard to get information at this point. I thought maybe you had heard more."

My head sways in stunned disbelief. "I just spoke with him as we were leaving Paris." I hesitate, uncertain of what to do, caught off guard by the sudden turn of events. "I'm going back into the plane to call Denver. Stay put," I tell the group. My fingers are moving over the speed dial of my phone as I hurry up the aircraft stairway.

"Deirdre, this is Jesse," I say, recognizing the sleepy voice of Hammer's secretary. "Sorry to wake you. We just landed back in Lagos and heard about John. How is he?"

"Oh, thank God you called. We were trying to reach you on the plane. It's crazy here. John is in the hospital, stable but still unconscious. They don't know how bad it is yet. I came to work early and found him at his desk. I know he got in early this morning from Washington. Probably came straight to the office from the airport." Her voice begins to choke up. "I'm home now. It's been a long day."

"Deirdre, I'm counting on you to keep things under control until I get back. How are things with the Board?"

"Jesse, the sooner you get back, the better," Dierdre pleads in a strained voice. "I feel overwhelmed with John in the hospital and you and Kim on the other side of the world. We're just drifting. The Board is in an uproar, and Vernon Sheldon is a major pain in the ass."

I hesitate. My initial thought is to send Kim back to Denver, but she lacks the experience in dealing with the Board. Vernon Sheldon would eat her up. It will have to be me.

"I plan on getting back there as soon as possible, but we have an emergency over here, as you know. Let me sort things out. I'll be back to you," I assure Diedre, trying to calm her.

Disconnecting, I walk up to the cockpit where Ron, the pilot, is going through a checklist. "Ron, how long before we can be underway for Denver?"

He hesitates, running calculations in his head. "We could be ready in about an hour, a couple of hours at most," he says. "What's up?"

"Make it one hour. Hammer had a heart attack." His mouth drops open. I walk back to the exit hatch and call down to the group standing in the shade of the aircraft wing. "Quick meeting. I need a word with you all."

I can feel the nervous tension as everyone enters the aircraft. "A change of plans," I say. "I'm going back to Denver. Kim, you're in charge until I return. That means lunch with Gambasha is on you. Hector, you and Chip keep an eye on the CIVO operation. Their planes should be landing later today."

***

The grandeur of the Oil Ministry's offices has never impressed Kim. To her, it is wasteful and extravagant, especially in Nigeria where the money could be better used for other critical needs.

As she strides through the reception area, the click of her high heels on the marble flooring, coupled with her figure-flattering pantsuit, draws attention from both men and women. She learned at an early age to take advantage of her physical presence and confident demeanor as tools to assert her authority and influence.

When he dropped her off at the hotel, Dan Farmer had offered to go with her to the palace. Kim quickly shot down the idea. "Believe me, Dan, I can do much better solo. That reminds me, I need a set of wheels. Can I use the Rover?"

Farmer nodded, handing her the keys. "I'll be at the airfield to meet the CIVO planes, which should arrive later this morning. Give me a call when you're done. I'll catch a taxi back to the hotel."

"Give CIVO whatever they need . . . within reason. Don't mention Mr. Hammer's condition," Kim cautioned.

"I've located a vacant warehouse near the pier for them to set up. It has a large parking lot for storage and equipment," said Farmer. "The CIVO crew can use it as a base of operations. It's dark and nasty, but it's big and air-conditioned." He turned to go, then paused and turned to face her. "Remember to call me when you're finished," he reminds her again.

The woman sitting behind the small desk glances up at Kim, a mannequin smile on her face. Kim looks down at the secretary-doorkeeper. "Kim Carson here to see the oil minister."

"Are we waiting for Mr. Ford?" the woman asks with a smile and quizzical look.

"No, we are not. It's just me."

The woman looks Kim up and down before picking up the phone.

Within a minute, a tall, athletic-looking woman comes down the stairs. Her black skin is perfect and unblemished, and her big, bold eyes are done with just the right amount of makeup.

"Ms. Carson, we were led to believe Mr. Ford would also be in attendance."

"Mr. Ford will not be in attendance."

"I'm so sorry. I hope everything is okay," she acknowledges in flawless English. "My name is Zuri. Please follow me." Without waiting for a response, she turns and returns up the stairs.

Kim follows, recalling the last time she had been in this building. She and Jesse had just finalized the agreement between Russia, Chechnya, and Americo over a gas pipeline. They had boarded the plane and were homeward bound when Denver requested they detour to Nigeria.

The country was emerging from ten years of civil war and chaos. The war paralyzed the economy and brought oil and gas production in the country to a standstill. The Nigerian government, aware of the success of the Russian/Chechen agreement, had requested that Americo use its negotiating skills to assist in getting the oil flowing again.

There had been a ruthless political tug-of-war between the Nigerian President, a Christian, and the oil minister, Nasir Gambasha, a Muslim. Negotiations were at an impasse, and the country was on the verge of falling back into civil war, a situation neither side wanted. Jesse, Kim, and a few other staff members had spent a grueling six weeks dealing with tribal, religious, and, most importantly, money issues.

Finally, after years of conflict, an agreement was reached, along with a lucrative oil and gas drilling program for Americo. Although Jesse had been the point man for Americo, Kim had played a central role in negotiating the agreement.

Kim is ushered through the double doors into a spacious office. A rotund man, as round as he is tall, beams a smile and walks toward Kim with open arms. Kim braces herself, knowing what is coming.

Nasir Gambasha gives Kim a tight squeeze, reaches down, and pats her butt. "Is Mr. Ford not coming?" he inquires, a flicker of disappointment crossing his round face.

"Hello, Nasir." Kim smiles dryly. "Jesse has been called back to Denver on an emergency." She shrugs her shoulders. "Looks like you're going to have to deal with just me."

"That is good. You are much easier to look at than him," the oil minister says with a laugh. "I have taken the liberty of ordering us some lunch." He points toward a large table in the corner of the room.

Two hours later, with a full stomach and a million dollars richer, the oil minister gives Kim a goodbye hug, followed by his customary pat on her derriere. "If you ever decide to marry, I would love to have you as one of my wives."

"Thank you for the offer, Nasir," Kim replies and smiles on her way through the double doors, "but I don't think my boyfriend would approve."

Sitting in the Land Rover, waiting for the air to cool, Kim calls Jesse on the satellite phone with an update, knowing he should be well over the Atlantic at this point.

In answer to his question, she says smugly, "Oh, you know, he pats my butt, and I give him a million dollars. What could go wrong? He initially wanted five million for reparations to the people; any state-owned company impacted, the cost of cleanup, and all security, including new weapons for their army."

She pauses while Jesse tells her the highest priority is to get the pier cleaned up so ships anchored in the harbor can begin docking.

"Gotta go. Dan's on my cell phone. By the way, Nasir Gambasha sends his love. Says he's sorry he missed you." Kim chuckles. "I'll keep you updated, and you do the same."

CHAPTER 8
REPORT TO THE BOARD

Standing outside the double French doors of the Board Room, I hear the dull hum of conversation from within. I always get butterflies before speaking to the Board of Directors. Today will mark the first time I have addressed the Board in a crisis situation.

The grandfather clock chimes six times as I step into the room. All conversation stops. The weight of the silent stares and unspoken questions from the four men and two women hang heavy in the air.

The company is facing a critical moment. As the Vice-President of Americo Oil and Gas, the world's fifth-largest independent oil company, the task of presenting a plan to steer us in the right direction has fallen on me. The future of the company will hinge upon this encounter.

I am oblivious to the stunning night view of the floor-to-ceiling windows from the fiftieth floor of the Americo Building, nor do I notice the sculptures and artwork depicting scenes from the old west. I take a deep breath and focus on the key points I must convey.

I summarize the issues in my head. Our company is facing an environmental disaster that could potentially force us into bankruptcy; our public image has been shattered, and while we face these challenges, our leader, the President and Chairman of the Board, has a life-threatening heart attack. What else could go wrong?

I take a deep breath and clear my throat. Nods and greetings are exchanged with those seated around the oval table, except Vernon Sheldon, who ignores me. Cell phones are turned off, an absolute rule enforced by John Hammer's tight rein. International deals are finalized and approved in this room, some earning billions of dollars, some not. Interruptions are not allowed unless it is life or death.

Ignoring the microphone, I begin to speak. "Thank you for coming this evening. First, along with you all, I want to send out my prayers for the speedy recovery for John. His leadership is missed."

There are murmurs of agreement throughout the room.

"You're all aware of the serious situation in Lagos. I'm here to update you. We're being attacked by the news media, social media, and politicians;—present company excepted," I say, turning to Ben Thompson on the monitor, who is attending the meeting from Washington on Zoom. "Thank you, Senator, for all you do and your willingness to serve on the Board without compensation."

Colorado Senator Ben Thompson and John Hammer started Americo Oil from scratch twenty years earlier. After Ben was elected to the U.S. Senate, according to Senate Conflict of Interest Rules, he was required to surrender his ownership and seat on the Board of Directors while serving as a Senator.

However, the politicians conveniently wrote an exception to the rule, allowing Senators to retain board positions so long as they were not compensated. Ben gladly made the trade-off.

My eyes search the board, coming to rest on Marci Stone. I focus on her as I begin to speak. "The media has decided to make Americo Oil the scapegoat for the oil spill in Lagos. We are not going to let that happen. We will set a textbook example for oil companies worldwide on how to deal with an oil spill. The situation in Lagos is being resolved, even as I stand before you."

Vernon Sheldon, a large man with a shaved head, squirms in his seat. Sheldon, the newest member of the Board, is a self-made millionaire, owning three auto dealerships and a significant interest in the Denver Broncos NFL football team.

Sheldon can't contain himself. I almost expect him to raise his hand to get permission to speak. "Mr. Ford, I'm wondering what the hell you're even doing here. Shouldn't you be in Lagos, dealing with the spill? If you need to update us, you can use Zoom like Senator Thompson here instead of wasting time and money to appear in person. Maybe someone more mature and experienced would be better suited to lead the company until John returns." Sheldon wipes a droplet of sweat off his forehead.

"And just whom would you suggest?" Marci Stone interrupts before I can reply.

Marci is the largest shareholder next to John Hammer and Ben Thompson. The slender, middle-aged woman is heir to serious money rumored to go back to the Rockefeller fortune. In her youth, she had been a high-profile party girl, and for years her wild sprees and affairs had been steady fare across the cover of the supermarket tabloids. Back then, she was an embarrassing figurehead on the Board, which was overlooked because of her family's high-profile name and huge investment.

But that changed after her marriage to a Saudi Arabian prince. The prince kept a tight rein on her. She dropped off the social circuit, even converting to Islam. The prince died several years ago. After his death, she remained a Muslim and never remarried. She still wore a khimar headscarf in public.

Sheldon scowls at Marci. "I . . . I think someone such as myself, with a good head for business, maturity, and a proven track record could handle everything."

She dismisses his claim with a laugh. "And I think we need to hear what Mr. Ford has to say."

With a hint of a smile, I acknowledge Marci's support. "Mr. Sheldon, I'm here because of sensitive issues I want to make the Board aware of. I believe this is best done in person. I want to give the Board the details of our plan for cleaning up the spill. I will also answer any questions you may have. Mr. Hammer and I believe it is important to keep the Board advised on events impacting the company."

I wrap up my presentation to the Board with a summary of the negotiations with Lassiter in Paris and the major details of the agreement reached. After an hour spent answering questions about CIVO's plan for cleaning up the spill using the *Denz* virus, the room goes quiet. "Any more questions?" I ask.

Shelton breaks the silence. "Do you mean to tell me we have agreed to pay CIVO millions of dollars, and we don't even know if this *Denz* works yet?"

"That's correct," I answer. "Americo will be the first company to test *Denz* in a real-world situation . . . one of the reasons we're getting it so cheap. The price would be triple if it were already proven to work. And when you consider *Denz* will cut the cleanup time in half, it would still be a good deal, even at that price. But make no mistake, Mr. Sheldon, time is of the essence here."

"I don't like being the guinea pig and will vote that we not go with CIVO until we see actual results in the real world," Sheldon states flatly.

Two Board members mutter their agreement.

"I support going with CIVO and approve the actions John Hammer and Jesse Ford have taken in dealing with the spill's cleanup," says Marci.

Senator Ben Thompson and one other Board member nod their approval.

Marci turns to me. "Looks like we have a tie, Mr. Vice-President. According to the bylaws, it is up to you to break it, one way or the other."

I hesitate, recalling my unease about Lassiter. This will be my only legitimate opportunity to get Americo out of the CIVO agreement. I swallow. "We go with CIVO."

As the meeting breaks up, I stand near the video screen, able to speak in private with Senator Thompson.

"Good job in Paris," Thompson says. "Have you seen John yet?"

"Not yet. I'm headed to the hospital now. Thank you, Senator. I appreciate your support," I add.

Ben smiles at the screen. "John and I trust you but keep your eye on Sheldon. Get back to Lagos as soon as possible and take care of this mess. Call me if you need anything."

"I will. Thank you, sir."

***

The corridor of the cardiac unit at Denver's St. Joseph Hospital is busy. I dodge medical personnel wearing pink, blue, and green scrubs and the occasional white-coated doctor. The people and staff rushing about remind me of my father's last days in the Gallup Indian Medical Center.

As I walk past the rooms, I hear TVs, the murmur of low voices, and muffled groans. In the background, the smell hints of blood, vomit, and feces combined with disinfectant cleaners—all familiar smells in any hospital—smells I will forever associate with the sick and injured. I hate hospitals.

John Hammer looks frail lying in the hospital bed. Oxygen tubes come out of his nose, and there is an IV in each arm. Wires disappear under his gown, attached to electrodes on his chest, arms, and legs, monitoring irregular heart rhythms and potential complications. I reach out to touch the unconscious man's shoulder, leaning on the bed's cold metal railing.

I turn at the sound of rapidly approaching footsteps behind me. "Mr. Ford? My name is Doctor Richards. I am Mr. Hammer's cardiovascular surgeon." A tall man in a white gown extends his hand. A mask covers his nose and mouth. He is clearly in a hurry and speaks in short, clipped bursts.

"He's in a coma. Drug-induced. It allows us to evaluate brain activity. He may have been deprived of oxygen during the stroke.

However," he raises his hand in my face, interrupting the question I am about to ask, "he has good cerebral activity. We feel confident he'll recover but maybe not a hundred percent. Only time will tell. If you have any questions, contact my office." He hands me a card before rushing off.

I turn back to Hammer's bedside, looking down at the immobile man. His skin is pale. Saliva is running out of one corner of his mouth. I take a corner of the sheet and wipe the dribble away. Then, reaching out, I squeeze Hammer's hand. No response. Leaning over, I pat his head and squeeze his shoulder. "Get well, my friend. I need you," I whisper.

***

Uber drops me off at my place. The house is cold and dark, unwelcoming. I flip on the lights and fireplace. Taking off my coat, I toss it on the couch, grab a drinking glass, and fill it with ice, a little Coke, and a lot of Jack Daniels. After a large sip, I lean back in my favorite recliner, sigh, and hit my phone's speed dial.

"Sorry to call so late," I say when Libby answers.

"Jess, where are you? Are you downstairs? Come up." Libby Burns mumbles, half asleep.

"I'm in Denver," I say with a laugh. "Sorry to wake you. I keep forgetting you're on the other side of the world."

She hesitates, still waking up. I can hear her breathing softly into the phone. "Oh . . . I thought you were downstairs—what a dream. Please don't tell me you're calling about the oil spill this time of the night." She gives a soft squeal as she stretches, followed by a drawn-out yawn.

"I'm glad you still have your sense of humor." I smile into the phone. "I'm stopping off in D.C. tomorrow on my way back to Lagos. Are you free?"

"Maybe. I'll check my busy social calendar. Tomorrow is going to be crazy for me. How about dinner? I know a good place. I'll text you the address."

"I'll be there . . . I promise."

"You better be."

CHAPTER 9
DESERT ROSE

Chip Monk's eyes narrow as he watches a Russian Antonov An-24 twin-prop cargo plane magically drop through a hazy mixture of fog and Lagos smog. With a screech and puff of smoke, the wheels of the aircraft touch the runway of the Lagos Murtala Muhammed International Airport. Why is a Russian aircraft transporting CIVO equipment?

He pulls the brim of his Tilley hat down on his eyebrows as the morning sun blasts over the horizon. Chip, Hector Ramos, and Dan Farmer watch in silence as four more cargo planes land, stopping just feet from the hanger where they stand.

Behind the men, lines of Americo Oil trucks wait to transport men and equipment to a warehouse near the oil terminal. The location is perfect and has a large parking lot used as a helicopter landing pad.

"Let's head back to the warehouse," Chip says, jumping into the waiting jeep.

By noon, crews dressed in red hazmat coveralls begin installing large drums filled with the *Denz* virus on the undercarriage of a helicopter. Workers wear fully enclosed helmets, reminding Chip of NASA-developed space gear.

The Desert Rose is given a high priority so it can get underway. Since the President released the Strategic Petroleum Reserve, the need to deliver oil to SPR in Louisiana has taken on a new urgency.

Chip peers out through dark sunglasses at the activity. "I've seen armies that could take some lessons from this crew," he says to Hector, an unusual compliment coming from Chip, who is not easily impressed.

"You think we need some protection from this *Denz*?" Hector asks, a concerned look on his face. "This stuff could be hazardous if we come in contact with it. Maybe we should at least be wearing a mask."

Chip mumbles in agreement. Spotting a large box of paper masks near the warehouse entrance, he grabs a handful. Stuffing one into his pocket, he hands one to Hector, who hurriedly puts his on. Dan puts his into the pocket of his cargo pants.

A group of red-clad workers, wearing helmets and loaded with backpacks, climb into the roaring helicopter. Chip holds onto his hat as the engine gears up, and the aircraft lifts off the parking lot. The sound of the chopping blades becomes more distant as it flies the quarter mile to the end of the pier. A fine red mist sprays from the attached drums as it passes over the ship.

"The spraying is done from an altitude high enough so the vertical lift from the blades doesn't blow the spray away from the targeted area," says a voice behind the men. Turning, they see a giant of a man. He smiles at them as the sound of the helicopter grows distant.

"If you follow me, Mr. DuVal would like to introduce himself," says the man, returning toward the warehouse.

"You two go ahead. I've got my car here," Dan says. "I'm going to clean up and grab a bite. Kim should be done with her oil minister meeting soon. I'll meet her back at the hotel. We'll see you two back at the hotel after you're done here."

"You think he and Kim have something going?" Chip wonders out loud, staring at Dan's retreating figure.

"He wishes," Hector answers. "After being stationed in Lagos for a year, Kim is a treat for the eyes."

Chip grunts, turning to follow the tall man toward the warehouse.

It takes several minutes for their eyes to acclimate to the dim light in the large, air-conditioned warehouse that serves as the operation center. A mixture of fluorescent lights, some of which are burned out, combined with the glow of blue screens from a half dozen computer monitors, provide the only lighting.

The computers line the walls, each with a technician watching a monitor. None of the technicians wear red suits, but all wear masks. In the background, low-pitched voices mix with the whirring of the computers. Two well-lit offices are part of a side wall. In the larger office, a crowd of people mill about, some on phones, some looking at maps rolled out on a large table. One group argues in loud voices. There are a series of rooms toward the back of the building, divided by a long hallway running between them, but they are dark and appear deserted.

One man is on a cell phone, standing outside the large office. His eyes never leave Chip and Hector, even as he continues to talk on the phone. He is tall and thin, with long brown hair tied in a ponytail. Disconnecting from his call, he smiles and waves as he walks toward them.

"Good morning, gentlemen," he greets them with a French accent. "I am Jacques DuVal, the CIVO on-site supervisor for the cleanup operation and the man with the answers to all your questions about *Denz* and the process." He offers his hand with a smile, which Hector promptly accepts. DuVal's smile fades as he turns to Chip and extends his hand.

Chip locks his gaze onto DuVal's eyes before slowly returning the handshake. There is something about the man he finds unsettling. Maybe his eyes—-their intensity seems to contradict his demeanor, which reminds Chip of Lassiter's bodyguard, Faisal.

DuVal is several inches taller than Chip or Hector. His height gives an appearance of a lanky build, with a small frame and narrow, almost skinny, shoulders. Sunken cheeks present a picture of malnutrition, like he is underfed. DuVal's mustache is gray and ragged. Chip senses an unsettling vibe that the man is not what he appears to be.

DuVal immediately starts talking. His sentences ramble together, only breaking to take a quick breath. He reminds Chip of a car salesman trying to distract from a defect.

"Your team appears to be well trained. Do you have a training facility?" Chip asks.

"Thank you, Mr. Monk," DuVal replies. "As you may well imagine, we have spent considerable time practicing. We have the equipment to train and practice daily—usually four to five hours, sometimes more. After training, our team spends at least an hour a day on in-classroom training. Then we set aside time for physical exercise to keep them fit. That completes their day, giving them a couple of hours to relax."

"Not to interrupt, but how soon before the Desert Rose can be underway?" Hector asks.

"I believe the ship has been sprayed from the air, leaving a few cleanup spots that will be hand-sprayed, but it is free to leave upon completion. The next phase will then be the docks and pier area. After that, we move to the streets where oil has been seeping up through the ground, and then finally, we clean the beach area," DuVal says. His cell phone starts ringing. He pulls it out and turns away to speak in low tones.

"The cleanup of the ship is nearly complete," he says, turning back to them. "We can watch them finish if you want to follow me down to the pier. Please put on a mask, gloves, and shoe coverings."

They walk out into the bright sun toward the pier. In the distance, the helicopter floats above the Desert Rose, soaking the ship in a red mist for the second time before flying back to land in the parking lot. Men with backpacks and spray wands form a line from one side of the ship to the other. Moving from the ship's rear aft to the forward bow, they spray areas the helicopter may have missed. Upon completion of the decontamination treatment, the ship's crew—wearing red coveralls, shoe covers, masks, and gloves—begin loading supplies, making ready to depart.

Hector jumps when the ship's horn gives a loud blast. Billowing clouds of black smoke roll out of the two smokestacks. Giant propellers slowly churn brackish brine-colored water.

DuVal's two-way radio squelches. "Captain, I would pre-fer you wait until we finish spraying and washing off the pier," DuVal says into the radio. There is a pause. Chip can hear a loud voice over the radio but is too far from DuVal to understand the conversation.

"Very well, Captain," DuVal says. "Have a safe voyage." DuVal turns to the red-suited workers. "Spray the ropes!" he yells at them. "The Desert Rose is leaving."

The pink mist is sprayed on the giant mooring ropes as they are removed from the pier cleats. Once unhooked, the mooring ropes, soaked with the red *Denz* spray, are hauled up the side by hydraulic winches with the help of deckhands. Then, with another loud horn blast, giant propellers begin churning up the florescent oil-covered water. Despite the size, four American football fields in length, the ship sits low in the water from the nearly three mil-lion barrels of oil it carries. The ship's bow, pointed toward the open sea, breaks water as the Desert Rose pulls away from the pier.

"At least we got her underway," Hector says, staring at the giant tanker as it grows smaller.

"Where's it bound for?" DuVal asks, not taking his eyes off the slow-moving ship.

"Headed to Bayou Choctaw, Louisiana," Hector says, "one of the larger storage caverns. Denver wants this load delivered as soon as possible. The crew likes that port because it's close to New Orleans."

DuVal nods. "How long will the voyage take?"

"The old tankers could make the voyage in ten to fourteen days. The Desert Rose is new, with a newly designed engine and hull. They'll arrive in four to five days, maybe sooner if the weather holds." Hector says. "I'm guessing the captain is going to haul ass. Time is money to these guys."

One of the red suits walks up. "Mr. DuVal?" The man's face plate is open, and his dark mustache drips sweat. "The pier is done. Next, we move to those areas where oil overflowed into the streets from the rupture of one of the storage tanks. We'll check them out as soon as the military is on-site. I expect we'll be done here by the end of the day."

A shriek from a red-clad worker echoes up and down the pier. Activity halts as workers stop and turn toward the sound. A man has fallen to the deck, grabbing his ankle. He begins squirming, rolling back and forth, and screaming in pain. Taking their eyes off the departing Desert Rose, Chip and Hector rush toward the moaning man, followed by DuVal.

"Stand back," DuVal orders the gathering crowd. Chip noticed DuVal made sure his hazmat helmet was securely fastened before leaning over the injured man. There is a large rip in the metallic coveralls near the injured man's ankle. Pink spray covers the torn area.

DuVal pulls out his radio. "We need an ambulance immediately where the Desert Rose was docked. Hurry!"

Chip looks down at the man withering in agony, pain etched on his sweat-laden face. "What happened?"

DuVal ignores him. Taking off the belt from his red suit, he straps the man's leg above the rip but below the knee and pulls it tight. Moments later, an ambulance, lights flashing, speeds down the dock toward them.

Two men jump out of the emergency vehicle, both clad in red suits. One pulls a gurney out of the back while the other bends over the sobbing man on the ground. With the assistance of several other workers, the man is lifted onto the stretcher and slid into the ambulance. Lights flashing but no siren, the ambulance races down the pier, disappearing around the corner.

Chip turns to DuVal. "Where are they taking him?"

"We have a facility just past the warehouse for any injuries that might arise," DuVal answers. "Our doctors are trained to treat sprains better than the local doctors." DuVal turns away, rapidly speaking into his phone.

"I want to go to this facility—I want to check on this man's injuries," Hector tells Chip.

Overhearing Hector, DuVal turns and says, "I don't think that's a good idea. Why don't we just let the doctors do what doctors do and not interfere?"

Ignoring DuVal, Chip and Hector make their way back toward their vehicle. "That guy has much more than a sprain," Hector says. "I think he was contaminated by *Denz*. I want to see its impact on unprotected people so we can advise our crew."

Chip pulls out his phone as they head toward their jeep.

"Dan, is Kim done with her meeting?"

"Hey, Chip. Yeah, we just left the hotel and headed to the northern suburbs, where the oil spilled from the tank farm. You would not believe what a mess this is."

"Hector and I are headed over there, but first, we're stopping by the hospital on the pier. One of CIVO's crew ripped his suit and got exposed to *Denz*. We want to check up on him. This shit has a mean bite to it and works quickly."

"Jesus," Dan whispers. "I'm looking at the tank farms. One of the storage tanks has a large rupture. Oil overflowed the berm and ran down into the streets. People are out with buckets scooping it up. Don't know what the hell they'll do with it, but it's a muddy gooey mess."

"A spark could set that off. We need to clear the civilians out of that area," Chip warns.

"There's some military here, but not nearly enough. Someone needs to update Jesse," Dan says.

"Hector will call him after we get to the hospital. It's the middle of the night in Denver. Let's check in every thirty minutes. We're going to the tank farm after the hospital. We'll meet you there," Chip says before disconnecting.

CHAPTER 10
D.C.

It is dark when the phone call wakes me. With my eyes still closed, I automatically reach for my phone and squint to see who's calling.

"Hector, what's up?" I mumble, still half asleep.

"Hey, Jesse. Sorry to call so early, but I'm afraid we have a problem."

Late-night phone calls. It never fails. I crack my eyes open. It's not early; it's the middle of the night and still dark outside. I wrestle with the urge to hang up, knowing he wouldn't call unless there was a problem. A surge of adrenaline jerks me fully awake. I put my phone on speaker and abandon the warm bed. "What's going on, Hec?"

"Lassiter lied."

The room suddenly feels hot. "A few more details would be nice," I say, frustrated by his lack of specifics.

Hector seems reluctant to continue. "*Denz* is designed to eat oil. The problem is, it doesn't stop there."

"What the hell do you mean, 'it doesn't stop there'?" My irritation is growing.

"I think it's dangerous to people. One of the CIVO people got some on his ankle. They had to rush him to the hospital." He pauses. "His leg had to be amputated."

The words are like needles of fear jabbing into my skin. My stomach does a flip-flop, and I swallow the heartburn that tastes like vomit.

"What are CIVO people saying?"

"They clam up when I start asking questions. Someone mentioned it was the African heat."

"I'm headed back but stopping off in D.C. and won't be back in Lagos until late tonight or tomorrow morning. Is Lassiter there yet?"

"Not yet. I was told he'll be in Lagos sometime tomorrow."

"Let CIVO know I want to meet with him."

"I think that's a good idea. I'll keep you updated. By the way, Chip and I are headed to the farm tanks where a storage tank ruptured. Dan and Kim are already on-site. Kim will probably call you after we check it out. Any updates on John?"

"Nothing new on John. I spoke with the doc, who said a full recovery is uncertain. We're just waiting until they can start running some tests on him. Tell Kim to get me some pictures of the tank farm area. See you in a couple days."

Disconnecting, I dial Libby's number, intending to cancel, but then pause. I need to get back to Lagos to see how bad it is. But maybe I should just let Hector and Kim handle it. An image of Libby flashes into my mind. I hesitate, then disconnect the phone. I want to see her.

***

It is late morning when the Gulfstream's wheels lift off the Denver runway.

"Ron, let's make a side trip to D.C.," I say into the cabin phone. "It will only be for a couple of hours."

"Yes, sir. Good idea. We can top off our fuel tanks before crossing the pond."

It is late afternoon when the Americo jet lands at the Washington Dulles International Airport's private jet section.

The taxi drops me off at the address of the restaurant Libby had texted me. I am early, so I grab a seat at the bar. Located in Chinatown, the restaurant is in a dark, out-of-the-way place just off a Washington side street—the kind of restaurant Libby loves.

I'm working on my second drink when I hear steps behind me.

"Hey, sailor, you with anybody?"

Turning, I stand and give her a grin.

"Hi," We both speak at once and hug. She kisses me lightly on the lips. I touch her elbow as the maitre d' escorts us toward a cozy corner in the back.

"You look good," she says, "except those worry lines are starting to etch a little deeper."

"Um, yeah. A few problems," I acknowledge, rubbing my hand across my face.

The faint dusting of freckles across the bridge of her nose gives Libby a feisty look I always found sexy. She has lost weight, and her smooth olive skin glows, a gift from her mother's Spanish-American heritage. The top two buttons of her fitted bodice are unbuttoned, revealing a peek of cleavage.

A wide leather belt cinches her narrow waist, and her shoulders and arms are defined and firm. Her dark hair is different—shorter, with blonde highlights. "You look pretty damn good yourself." I smile.

Her brown eyes twinkle. "I've lost a few pounds—exercise and watching my diet. I spend a lot of my free time working out. Nothing else to do these days," she adds, looking sideways at me.

After we order drinks, a Cosmo for her and the usual Jack and Coke for me, Libby reaches across the table and takes my hand. "I'm so sorry about John," she begins. "Have you seen him?"

"Yesterday. He's tough, but it sounds like he'll have a rough road to recovery. I miss him, especially with all the bullshit going on now."

Libby looks around the room. "Jesse, there's a rumor floating around—nothing solid, mind you—that the oil facility in Lagos was sabotaged. There's also a rumor that big money, like Middle East money, is behind Henshaw, the driving force behind the legislation to ban drilling." She leans forward, staring into my face.

"When you say, 'The Middle East,' do you mean a government, a rich sheik, a terrorist group—what?" I ask.

"Henshaw is cozy with a large assortment of lobbyists, many known to have connections in the Mideast, including Iran. Of course, everything in D.C. is based on rumors and innuendos, but in this crazy place, where there's a rumor, there's usually a grain of truth."

I frown. "I understand why the Arabs want the Henshaw Bill passed, increasing our reliance on their oil, but—"

She reaches out and touches my hand, interrupting me. "What's going on with this oil spill? I've done a little research on this CIVO company. . .."

I started to shake my head. "I really don't want to get into it."

Her dark eyes flash. "Oh, come on, Jesse, it's no secret what's going on over there."

I exhale. She's right. It was no longer a secret; I don't want to keep her in the dark, secret or not. "We have some problems," I admit reluctantly. "This company, CIVO, has developed a virus they call *Denz* that is supposed to eat oil."

I stopped talking when the server came to the table. Holding up two fingers, I ask for another round.

"Well, that sounds like a good thing," she continues.

"Yeah, except for one little detail—after it eats the oil, it's supposed to die off. It doesn't." I think about Hector's phone call about the injured worker. *Denz* was designed to eat petroleum, not people.

Libby bites her lower lip. "Not dying? You mean a little virus that's like a—zombie?"

My laugh is half-hearted. "Hope not, but I don't know. Hector called me last night. A CIVO worker was infected. So I'm headed back to get some answers."

"Damn," she whispers. "That stuff sounds potent. If it doesn't work, Americo could risk losing the Nigerian oil rights. That would kill the company, especially if drilling on federal lands is banned."

"We still have our reserves in the ground." I try and sound confident, but in truth, I'm not.

"Yeah, but in the U.S., much of that oil is on federal property. So you may not have access to it if the Henshaw Bill passes."

I lean back and run my fingers through my hair. "We knew this was coming years ago. Most of our domestic oil is still in the ground—for future use and not going anywhere. We haven't exactly been sitting back on our money doing nothing. We have a few things cooking."

"Like what?" she asks, looking at me over the rim of her glass while sipping her drink.

"Well, let's just say we're preparing for the future. Hector has been working on some experimental . . . well, it's best if I don't talk about it. Libby, you're not helping me relax any. I'm tired of talking about work."

She impishly flutters her eyelashes. "Come on, baby, you can tell me." She grins. I look at her. God, she is beautiful. Then, putting the most severe look on my face I can muster, I say, "Can I trust you? I mean, really trust you?"

She squeezes my hand, serious now. "You know you can. Jesse, rest assured that if you tell me something in confidence, it remains in confidence. Remember, I also went to law school. I understand confidentiality. You know, 'trust me, I'm a lawyer.'"

I want to trust her. I do trust her, and I feel like talking. "Okay, remember that TV show from the sixties, Star Trek? What does the phrase 'beam me up, Scotty' bring to mind?"

She thinks for a second. "Well, wasn't that when the starship's captain used a machine—the teleporter, I think it was called—to shift from one place to another?"

I respond with a nod.

Her eyes grow wide. "You're kidding. A teleporter?" She slaps my arm. "That's the stuff of science fiction."

I shake my head. "Not anymore."

"So, tell me about it. How does it work? Can you actually beam people from one place to another? God, Jesse, that would be a game changer."

I sit back and watch her excitement build. "I try and stay on top of it, but it is too complex for my little brain. With the help of Artificial Intelligence, Hector has developed a 'quantum computer' that is so far beyond anything out there I can't even begin to describe it. We haven't teleported a person yet, but we are close," I admit.

"Just imagine," she says, with a whimsical sparkle in her eyes, "I could work in DC, transport back to Colorado for lunch, and be back in DC post-lunch break. Then, after work, beam back home, wherever that might be," she says peering at me over her glass. When are you leaving for Lagos?"

"Tonight. I want to be there in the morning. A problem with the cleanup. I need to be there."

"My apartment isn't far," she says, blinking her eyes.

"There is nothing I would love more than to spend the night with you, but I can't. In fact, I nearly canceled so I could go straight back to Lagos."

"Well, I'm disappointed but not mad. I understand. You have a lot of responsibility with John out. I'm happy we got a chance to be together for dinner."

"I promised I would be here, and I am. But now I promise I will make it up when I return."

She leans over the table and kisses me. "That's one of the things I love about you, Jess. You keep your promises."

CHAPTER 11
THE FARM

Lagos. The fifth-largest city in the world, with a population estimated to be over fourteen million, is a city that pulsates with life, energy, and contrasts. Within its boundaries, Africa's millionaires coexist side by side with the most impoverished slums.

Where the tree-lines asphalt ends, the ghettos begin. Towering skyscrapers, the homes of the rich, loom over ramshackle dwellings only steps away—a stark reminder of the inequalities of life between the rich and the poor.

While Chip maneuvers the jeep around potholes, Hector studies the GPS, struggling to pronounce street names and guess directions. The drive from the hospital to the tank farms began on a four-lane paved highway but is now reduced to a single-lane dusty dirt road. They have entered the overcrowded ghettos where the neverending struggle for survival continues. An eye-watering smell permeates the air and washes over them, mostly smelling of sewage but occasionally mixed with a whiff of fried bean cakes, a local favorite.

Chip has both hands on the steering wheel, fighting to keep the jeep out of the canal of raw sewage lining the road. Garbage covers the ground outside the corrugated tin shacks. Residents walk narrow paths made of wood planks toward their homes, hopping from board to board to avoid stepping in the slime.

Located near the heart of downtown, where opportunities and jobs are abundant, real estate in this area for both the ghetto residents and the rich is at a premium. Here, ghetto residents, encouraged by the demand for land and overcrowded conditions, have learned to construct unconventional and risky high-rise megastructures towering hundreds of feet into the air. Built vertically from a jumbled assortment of weathered materials salvaged from the remnants of former structures, they are connected by precarious walkways that stretch high into the air.

Distracted by the multi-storied towers, Chip struggles to keep his eyes on the road while dodging ruts and craters. Hector clings to the safety grips of the jeep, staring upward in awe at the stares of the people looking down who rarely see a vehicle venture into the ghetto, let alone with two white men.

"I've never seen anything like this," Chip says to Hector. "It looks like a movie set for a post-apocalyptic sci-fi movie."

"They don't look safe. I don't see how they can stand the smell," Hector replies, pulling the leftover mask from the pier over his nose. "Too many people."

Chip shakes his head. "I don't think they have much choice. If you're not rich, this is where you live. There are worse places, but not many."

"Look over there. You can see the storage tanks." Hector points to the gigantic petroleum storage tanks in between the soaring towers. Each tank holds millions of gallons of black crude only blocks away from the poorest of the poor.

The oil smell becomes sharp and piercing as they approach the tank farm. Hector begins to gag. Chip's eyes start to water. The aroma triggers a memory from his teenage years when he and his buddies used garden hoses to siphon gas for their cars, a scent, and a past he despises. That was the last time he was arrested.

They pass people walking on the grimy road as they near the storage tanks. Chip honks his horn to make a path through the street. Some respond with a cold glare, while others wave and ask for a ride. Each person carries a bucket or container. Some push wheelbarrows. Most are barefoot with handkerchiefs wrapped around their nose and mouth. The smell of the oil grows stronger.

"What in the hell are they going to do with those?" Chip asks, pointing to the buckets.

Hector shrugs. "I . . . don't know. Maybe scoop up the oil-saturated dirt and use it for cooking fires."

A barrier blocks the road as they round a corner. Chip brings the jeep to a halt when a soldier steps in front of the jeep and signals to stop with a raised hand. Behind him, another soldier holds a rifle across his chest.

"They don't look friendly," Hector says.

Chip hands his weapon to Hector. "Take this and hide it."

The soldier eyes the men in the jeep. "No further—danger," he says in broken English.

"Yeah, we know. It's okay," Chip says. "We're with the cleanup company."

The soldier nods. "Cleanup? ID." Chip and Hector hand over their Americo identification.

The soldier examines them. "American?" he asks.

Chip nods. "Yeah, we're Americans."

Not moving, the soldier stares at them.

Chip stares back as he reaches into his pocket and hands the soldier a U.S. twenty-dollar bill. The soldier smiles, returns their IDs, and steps aside, waving them through the blockade.

Just past the roadblock, Hector points to Dan's parked Land Rover. Dan and Kim stand near the vehicle, silently watching people scoop up the oil-soaked dirt. Kim, a scarf across her face, turns and waves, motioning them over. Dan has a mask from the pier across his nose and mouth, which does nothing to alleviate the powerful smell of oil.

"Can you believe this shit?" Kim says, shaking her head in disbelief. Hundreds walk through the gooey street, scooping up the oil-soaked mud. "I feel so bad for them."

Many people are coughing. Some bend over, vomit, stand, wipe their faces, and continue filling buckets.

Kim turns to Hector. "This is terrible. We need to do something. Call Jesse and see if he can use some leverage, money, or whatever it takes to get these people out of here. One little spark . . ." There was no need to finish.

Chip looks up the street toward the storage tank on the hill. A tsunami of millions of gallons of oil had overflowed the berm around the tank. The overflowing oil had cut a gully through the ridge, flooding the dirt streets and houses below. A slight trickle still flows as they watch.

"So much for the container berm," Chip says. "What happened to the tanks? We heard it was an explosion."

Dan frowns. "That's bullshit. If there'd been an explosion, this area would still be burning. I spoke with a government engineer who told me the tank was either too full and ruptured or rusted from the inside and burst open."

Hector, who had been silent, now says, "Maybe when the valve was shut off to stop the overflow into the Desert Rose, it backed up, increasing the pressure in the tank and causing the rupture."

"We'll have time to figure that out later, but right now, we need to get rid of this gooey shit," Kim snaps.

"I called DuVal and told him to get some road graders and backhoes over here pronto," Dan says.

"When?" Chip asks.

"The ship and pier area has the highest priority. By tomorrow they should start moving equipment in here."

Chip looks around. "They could at least block this area off. That roadblock is useless. They let everyone through. No one should be allowed in here. We shouldn't be allowed in here."

"I contacted the oil minister's office," says Dan, "and asked for more military to get these people out of here, but—" Screaming on the street interrupts him.

As a group, they turn toward the screams further down the street. A cluster of people is pointing and screaming at a man lighting a cigarette. Then, as one, the crowd scatters in all directions, scurrying away from the cigarette man.

Fear grips Chip. "Get outta here!" he yells, grabbing Kim's arm and pulling her back toward the parked vehicles.

The white flash of light is followed by the hot demon breath of a fireball rolling toward them. The world burns red. Chip pulls Kim to the ground, narrowly managing to shield her from the blast. But the force of the explosion is too strong. The shockwave hits them with a deafening roar, throwing them toward the sky. Chip tumbles through the air losing his grip on Kim.

Falling toward the ground, Chip sees Hector's contorted body in a grotesque position suspended in mid-air. A pressure wave from the explosion violently rips away the air creating a vacuum that silences Kim's scream. She is hurled to the ground as projectiles whiz overhead, resembling missiles in flight.

Chip crashes to the ground with a sickening thud. Pain shoots through his body, and he can taste blood in his mouth. His ears feel like an ice pick has pierced them, and there is a loud ringing from the sound of the explosion. Slowly, the ringing goes away, replaced by silence. Dimly now, he begins to hear the sounds of screaming and the hissing and crackling of fire.

He lies still, his eyes open but not moving. Above him, a plume of smoke rises in the otherwise clear blue sky. Slowly, his hearing is returning. Fiery paper and debris curl in the air, drifting back toward the earth like snowflakes. His skin stings as though rubbed by gritty sandpaper.

Confused, he rolls over on his right side and leans on his elbows. Then, lifting himself on his knees, his SEAL training kicks in. The first concern is to check on his people. Chip shakes his head, staring at the ground. He picks himself up in a series of slow moves, checking to see if there are any broken bones. His left side and back are burned and painful. Wiping his eyes and mouth, Chip ignores the pain and searches for his companions.

The landscape is an inferno. Farther down the street, the ground is on fire. The heat is intense. People are screaming; some are on fire, madly running through the streets, waving their burning arms, or falling to the ground. The few not injured are trying to put out the flames on the burning victims.

Kim lies on her side. Blood oozes from a large gash on her arm. Only semi-conscious, she moans while struggling to sit up. Chip staggers over to her. Squatting down, he pushes her back to the ground and examines her arm, wiping the blood away from the wound.

"Don't move, Kim." He looks around, making sure there is no fire nearby, pulls off her scarf, and wraps her arm tight to stop the bleeding. "Wait here. I'll be right back. Going to check on Hector and Dan."

Nodding, Kim lies back on the ground, her eyes wide, staring aimlessly into the smoke-darkened sky.

Chip staggers over to Hector, dreading what he will find. Then, kneeling, he turns him over. Hector's face is caked with dirt and oily mud. The outer layer of skin on his right arm is bright red, swollen with blisters, and shiny, wet-looking skin.

Maybe a second-degree burn. Not too bad.

He removes his shirt and wipes Hector's face, cleaning the mud out of his mouth and eyes. Hector begins coughing and gagging, but with eyes still closed, he reaches for Chip with his hand. "Chip," he calls out. "Help me, Chip," he whispers.

"I got you, Hec. Don't move. I'll be back. I'll get some water from the jeep to clean your eyes."

Walking is painful. Chip feels like he has been hit with a wrecking ball. However, the jeep is in better shape, and aside from some blistered paint on the front end and a blown-out windshield, it does not appear damaged. Reaching the back seat, he grabs two water bottles and heads back to Hector. He lifts Hector's head, pours water on his face, then wipes it off with his shirt.

A blood-curdling scream slices through the smoke-laden air. Chip instinctively swivels toward the sound and sees Kim; her body doubled over something on the ground. She screams again, raising her blood-stained hands to her face.

Dan's unmoving body lies on the ground, partially covered with dirt mixed with oil. Chip hands Hector one of the water bottles, telling him to rinse his mouth. "I'm going to help Dan and Kim. I'll be back."

Chip rubs his ears, trying to get his hearing back as he stumbles toward Kim. He stops when he sees Dan's body. Dan's clothes are still burning. Chip tries to remove his burning shirt, but layers of blacken skin are stuck to the clothing, peeled back in layers.

"Oh no," he whispers.

A piece of corrugated tin from a shanty roof is buried in Dan's neck, leaving his head attached, but only by shredded muscle and skin. Blood is spurting out of the wound.

Kim is on her knees next to his body. "No . . . please, God, no," she gags in between sobs.

Chip kneels beside her and puts his arm over her shoulders. "He's out of pain. It was quick for him," he whispers in her ear.

He helps her stand. Wrapping his arm around her waist, he helps her drink from the remaining water bottle as they limp back to Hector, now sitting up.

"Where's Dan?" Hector asks.

Chip looks over at Dan's body, then down at the ground. He shakes his head.

The wail of sirens can be heard in the distance.

CHAPTER 12
THE PIER

I step out of the hatch of the Gulfstream to see Hector looking up at me. His right arm is covered in gauze wrapped by medical tape for the burn. Reaching the bottom of the stairs, I give him an unexpected hug and tenderly pat him on the back.

After the fire, I am constantly on the phone with either Hector, Kim, or Chip. Dan's death is a blow to the company and a loss to his friends and family. His intellect, humor, and down-to-earth solutions to problems are missed.

Arrangements have been made to transport Dan's body back to his hometown in Greeley, Colorado, for the funeral and memorial service. After a long and animated discussion on the pros and cons of Dan's funeral, it is agreed that with the ongoing CIVO cleanup, Kim will fly back while the others remain. She promises to convey the sympathies of those remaining in Lagos unable to attend the funeral.

Dan's parents still live in Greeley, a fast-growing front-range community an hour north of Denver. Because they live nearby, they were regular and well-liked visitors at the Americo head-quarters. The Denver office will shut down so those who want to attend the service can do so.

The entire Lagos team takes Kim to the airport. After hugs

and a promise to explain why they could not attend, she boards the Gulfstream.

"Any idea when you'll be back?" I ask as I walk Kim up the air stairs.

She shrugs. "I'm not sure. I need a little time off."

I understand. "Take what time you need, but not too long. I need you back here."

She smiles but doesn't look at me. "I know you do." She hugs me and, with a kiss on the cheek, disappears into the plane.

On the ride back to the hotel, Chip says, "Let's have a wake. Good ole Dan loved his whiskey. I think we owe him one . . . or two," he says with a sad smile on his face. "Meet at the bar in an hour."

No one objects.

The following day at breakfast, Hector gives me a devastating update in a detached, lifeless tone. His eyes are bloodshot and filled with weariness, reflecting the weight of the tragedy. "Over a hundred people died in the fire. Some of the injured won't make it."

I find myself staring into my coffee cup, lost in my thoughts. Seeking a momentary distraction, I absentmindedly stand the spoon upright in the thick brew, reminiscing about a peculiar cup of coffee I had in Russia so thick the spoon would stand up on its own. I've never been able to repeat the stunt.

"Any news from Lassiter?" I ask, staring at the coffee cup.

"Nothing," Hector mumbles. "I don't know if he's here or still in Paris. DuVal called and offered his condolences. He and Dan spent time together getting CIVO set up."

"I want to go to the pier and see the operation firsthand. Are you up for that?" I ask, still stirring my coffee. "How's your arm?"

"I'm not looking forward to going back down there," Hector admits, "but you need to see it." He lifts his arm. Most of the injury is in the bicep area. "The arm is better. Pain pills help."

I look around for Chip to see if he wants to go, but there is no sign of him.

"Let him sleep," suggests Hector. "He got pretty toasted last night. I doubt if he will be up before noon."

I grunt in agreement. "We all got toasted. I should probably still be in bed myself." I look at Hector and sigh. "Let's hit it."

***

"You know as much about the micro virus as anyone," I tell Hector as we drive toward the pier. "What are your thoughts on why *Denz* isn't dying?"

"I've been trying to get that answer from CIVO, but whenever I pin them down, their eyes glaze over," Hector replies in an aggravated tone. "Everyone's in cover-your-ass mode. They don't want to talk to me about it."

"They're going to want to talk to me even less," I say, frowning.

The jeep skids to a stop at the entrance of the CIVO warehouse on the dock. A dozen people are gathered near the building in small groups. I jump out of the jeep even before it rolls to a halt. Some outside turn to stare at us, but most don't make eye contact.

The air conditioning inside the warehouse is a relief. Red hazmat suits hang on the walls beside the computers and monitors where a group of men have gathered, engaged in an animated conversation. They go silent when Hector and I enter the building.

A tall, thin man with long hair tied in a ponytail approaches us with his hand out. "I'm guessing you must be Mr. Ford," he says, nodding toward Hector. "I'm Jacques DuVal."

DuVal looks down at the ground. "Please know how truly sorry I am about Dan. We got along well, and I liked Dan. Dr. Lassiter sends his condolences, also. I know you have questions about *Denz*, and I will try and answer them. But please keep in mind, the results are only preliminary."

I shake my head. "Why is it reproducing? I thought that was impossible?"

"*Denz* is doing exactly what it is designed to do. It metabolizes the petroleum, allowing the virus to convert the oil to a non-hazardous substance in the form of an environmentally friendly powder. In other words, it eats the oil and shits it out," DuVal says, followed by a quick chuckle.

I stare at him. He's not telling me anything I haven't heard before. "You left out the part about it being hazardous to humans," I say, feeling the anger rise. I take a step toward DuVal, who backs up.

"Uh . . . well," DuVal stutters, "conditions are different here in Africa than in the lab. But to get a more scientific answer, you will need to speak with Lassiter. We are seeing *Denz* consume triple the amount we expected.

"I think that's a line of bullshit. I want to know why it isn't dying. And what happened the other day to your technician at the pier? I know he was rushed to the hospital."

DuVal gives a nervous laugh. "We need to give it more time. Samples indicate the virus is more concentrated than when we first sprayed. But it's too early to be concerned. We are looking at problems caused by heat. In the lab, *Denz* was never tested in a temperature this intense."

A technician hurries over to us. "Mr. DuVal, you need to see this," he interrupts, pointing with gloved hands to the microscope at his workstation.

In two strides, DuVal is at the workstation, peering into the microscope. Hector and I are close behind. DuVal stands up. "Shit." His face is pale, drained of color.

Hector shoves DuVal aside and looks into the lens. After thirty seconds, he stands and gestures to me. I bend into the microscope. There are thousands . . . tens of thousands of red spiral-shaped structures outlined in a thin black band, all in a golden hue. The technician enlarges the image a thousand times. Jagged-shaped tail-like shafts appear to grow out of the main structure, each shaft with thorn-like shapes. A shiver of fear flows through my body when the tentacle shapes begin to move and wiggle. At the tip of the tentacle, an opening like a claw opens and closes.

I take a step backward. "I saw this at the CIVO lab. What's different?"

Hector stoops over the microscope a second time. "Look," he whispers, "they're multiplying, not dying." He stands up. "Where did this sample come from?"

"The pier," answers the tech, looking at DuVal.

Hector peers into the microscope once again. He stands, now agitated, and stares at DuVal. "This is like a fucking petri dish.

They're multiplying at an unbelievable rate. Does Lassiter know about this?" He pauses, not waiting for an answer. "Why wasn't this disclosed to us?"

There are beads of sweat rolling down DuVal's neck, even though the temperature is pleasantly cool in the building. When I turn to him, he backs away from me. "DuVal, you . . . we have a serious problem," I warn. "Is there an antidote to kill these things?" Except for the whirring of computers, there is a tense silence.

DuVal looks around. The CIVO people studiously keep their eyes glued to computer screens. "We may have a problem. We're seeing abnormal behavior that wasn't exhibited in the laboratory. But I'm just not technical enough to give you a simple answer. Dr. Lassiter will be here tomorrow. Ask him."

"Oh, I intend to." In frustration, I turn to Hector. "Let's go," I snap. "I want to take a look at the pier."

In silence, DuVal watches us go, not bothering to suggest we wear protective clothing. I climb into the driver's side of the jeep, hooking the mask's straps behind my ears.

Leaving the asphalt road, the jeep's tires cross the wooden deck of the pier leading out to the docking station for the ships. In the distance, we can see red-clad figures walking.

Spills from years of loading and unloading the giant oil tankers have saturated the wooden dock and turned the wood black. The last time I saw this area, it had been covered with black sticky goo and had a nauseating smell. Even the street leading down to the dock had been covered in oily tire tracks. Now it is amazingly oil free.

The smell is still present but not as overpowering as our earlier visit. Any oil that may have been on the deck of the pier is nowhere to be seen. As we approach the end of the long pier, the workers in the red suits are no longer visible, and we are alone on the dock. A fine layer of black powder with a greenish hue under the sun's rays blows across the pier in the gentle ocean breeze. As the jeep passes through the powder, the dust swirls in twisting spirals behind us. The usually bustling port is eerily quiet, making me uneasy. I grip the steering wheel with both hands, cautiously driving toward the end of the pier. I cast a sideways glance at Hector, noticing sweat droplets shimmering on his forehead—from the heat or anxiety, I'm not sure.

The pier runs a quarter of a mile in length out into the ocean, where the water is deep enough to accommodate even the largest tankers and cargo ships. The black dust coats everything and drifts in the air. It reminds me of lava dust from an erupting volcano. I adjust my mask so it fits snugly on my face.

"What the hell is that?" Hector says, pointing. I slam on the brakes, staring.

Lying on the ground is a large black rubber hose, ten inches in diameter and about thirty feet long. This type of hose connects to a ship to drain its sanitation system. The hose looks shredded. At first, I notice nothing unusual, but as I continue to watch, the hose appears to move as though alive. We both exit the jeep and walk cautiously toward the hose, stopping a few feet away.

Hector squats down on his haunches for a closer examination. Before our eyes, the shredded remains of the hose are disintegrating, turning into black powder, giving the illusion of a moving, living thing.

Without thinking, Hector reaches down with his burned right hand, touching the hose with his index finger.

"Careful," I warn. At the spot where Hector touches, the hose dissolves into a swirling black powder.

"Son of a bitch," he yelps, jerking his hand back. "I think I just got bit."

I crouch down next to him, looking at what is left of the hose. Before our eyes, the hose continues to disintegrate . . . changing from solid matter into a fine powder in a matter of seconds. Hector wipes his index finger on his pants.

"That means . . ." my voice trails off.

"That means Lassiter's little virus is doing its job, going after anything with a petroleum base, like this rubber hose." Hector brushes the black powder away with his foot.

I spot a crowbar lying on the pier. Picking it up, I scrape away part of the pier's wooden deck. It dissolves and crumbles as I pry the wood back. I strike the timber with the crowbar, surprised at how easily it gives way, as though rotten.

We both peer into the newly created hole. Thirty feet below us, the slate-blue waves churn. We exchange glances, realizing the entire pier is unstable. Suddenly there is a loud crack, followed by a tremor through the dock.

"I think we'd better get the hell outta here," I yell. My pulse is racing as we both bolt toward the jeep. A shudder follows another loud cracking sound, the dock lurches, and a section of the wooden surface behind us detaches, plunging into the sea and leaving an enormous chasm.

"This whole pier is going," Hector says in alarm. He keeps wiping his finger on his pants.

We turn and sprint toward the jeep. I am turning the ignition key when another crack sounds, much louder than the others. The deck underneath the hose we were just inspecting splinters and crashes into the ocean.

The jeep engine sputters, then dies. I stomp the gas pedal twice, then turn the key once more. There is a loud crack, and the Jeep starts to tremble. At first, I mistake the vibration for the engine and shift into reverse, but nothing happens. The engine is dead. Hector yells after another crack. The jeep gives a sickening lurch forward, and the right-front tire drops through a newly formed opening in the deck.

"Jesse, you better get this sucker fired up!" Hector cries out. He starts to jump out, but I reach over and grab his arm.

"No!" I shout. "Stay in the jeep."

"Come on, baby," I beg, holding my breath as I turn the key again. The engine coughs and roars to life. I slam the gearshift into reverse and floor it. The spinning rear tires begin to smoke, and a mixture of wood splinters and black dust covers the jeep. With a lurch, the jeep catches traction and backs up. I do a quick U-turn, pointing us toward the shoreline, and floor it.

The spot the jeep had been parked only seconds earlier is now vaporizing, leaving the black powder in its wake drifting slowly to the ocean below. Oil-soaked timbers fall, disappearing into a cloud of black dust on their way to the water below. Tires screeching, I give the jeep full throttle as we speed toward the distant shore.

I stare through the windshield. From this distance, the far-off shoreline looks normal. We're going to make it.

Beside me, Hector is rubbing his right hand back and forth on his pants like he's trying to extinguish a fire. The skin on his hand is inflamed, and blisters are forming on his fingertips. The more he rubs his hand, the worse it looks. Sweat trickles down his forehead, carving rivulets into the dust on his face. His eyes are wide with excitement or fear, probably both.

We are halfway back to the beach when the right-front tire explodes. The jeep swerves to the right. I crank the wheel to the left and jam on the brakes. The jeep stops with the right-front tire hanging over the edge. The water is still about twenty feet below the deck of the pier.

I gingerly step out on the pier deck. It seems firm. Hector is already out inspecting the blown tire. There are only shreds of rubber left on the metal rim.

"It's *Denz*," Hector says, holding his right hand with his left. "The tires are rubber and have a petroleum base."

I give a disbelieving grunt. "Not that fast . . . it couldn't have eaten a tire that fast."

"We've been driving around on this stuff all afternoon," Hector points out, wiping and shaking his hand.

Hector has my full attention now. "Let me see your hand." I take his arm but do not touch the red area. His right hand is now covered in a rash up to his wrist. The earlier pus pockets have erupted and are bleeding.

Hector closes his eyes and squints in pain. "This shit burns. It looks like it's spreading up my arm."

I struggle to keep my voice from shaking. "We need to get you to the hospital." Hector's eyes are like saucers, and his skin is pale and clammy.

"Remember, DuVal told us his infected man on the pier recovered, right? So Chip and I went to the hospital to check on him. Yeah, he did recover." Hector swallowed hard before continuing. "But they had to amputate his leg."

"We need to get you to a hospital," I repeat. "It's spreading."

I run around the jeep, checking the tires. The right front is gone. Only the metal rim remains. The two rear tires are going flat as I watch, and the remaining front tire is not far behind. "Let's walk. The jeep is done!" I shout.

We set off toward the end of the pier, walking at first, then breaking into a slow jog while watching where we place our feet. Hector holds his hand as he runs, grimacing in pain. The cracking and groaning noises from the pier are magnified over the water and grow louder. Every so often, we could feel the pier quiver and shake. We cast wary glances behind us but do not slow down.

With only three hundred feet to go, the sound of cracking and popping increases. The deck is swaying under our feet. In unison, we break into a hard sprint toward the shoreline.

I hear a shriek from Hector behind me and turn. His left leg has fallen through a gap and is buried in the deck up to his knee.

"Jesse!" he screams, a look of terror on his face. "Help me. I think my leg is broken!"

CHAPTER 13
DENZ

I instinctively grab my friend's outstretched hand and try to pull him out of the cavity in the crumbling pier, but it's too late. His trapped left leg is securely wedged in the crevice. Hector clings to me and leans backward, trying to use his right leg as leverage to pull out the trapped left.

With a crack, the wood under his right leg suddenly gives way. Now both legs are captured in the decaying pier. Twisting and turning, he fights to escape but only slips closer to the water, pulling me toward the gap in the unstable deck. At the last minute, I release his hands to avoid getting pulled into the fissure with him. He stares at me with his mouth open. Hands waving in panic, he reaches for me.

"Jesse, help me!" he screams. Losing control, he begins flopping and squirming like a fish out of water, but the effort only causes his legs to wedge tighter in the hole. Finally, exhausted and out of breath, he stops. Both legs are buried in the pier up to his waist.

I crawl on my hands and knees toward him, locking my fingers under his armpits, and pull with all my strength, but the weight of his body is too much for me. Hector cries out in pain. The deck under me snaps and begins to tilt. Pieces tumble into the water below. In desperation, I lean back in a last-ditch effort to pull Hector out. No good. Both of Hector's legs are wedged tight.

A loud crack from the pier sounds like a gunshot, and the deck disintegrates into a rain of timber. I start to slide over the edge. Struggling to stop my slide, I am forced to let go of Hector. In desperation, I claw for something, anything, to anchor myself. As gravity pulls me toward the water, I reach out to grab him. We touch fingertips, but my hand is torn loose. Unable to stop my fall, I tumble forward into the heaving ocean.

The deck above collapses with Hector still trapped. I raise my arms to block the wooden fragments as they fall like bombs around me, watching in horror as Hector tumbles into the choppy ocean. The taste of the oily water and smell disgusts me, and I begin to gag. Fragments of wood fall on me, a large piece striking me on the shoulder. Taking a deep breath, I dive for protection. The oily water burns my eyes, and I immediately surface, gasping for air.

Frantically, I search for Hector, but he is nowhere to be seen. Panic sets in as I realize he may be trapped under the pier, unable to escape. I take a breath and dive again. My eyes burn so bad I have to close them. I can't see under the water, so it makes no difference.

I kick my legs toward the spot where Hector hit the surface. A feeling of helplessness creeps over me. Even though I am virtually blind under the water, I reach out with my arms and legs, hoping to make contact with the injured scientist. Finally, my lungs are ready to burst, and I am forced to resurface. Gasping for breath, I call Hector's name. I turn a complete circle using my feet and arms—no sign of him.

Another breath, and I go down again, knowing it might be too late if I don't find him this time. Under the water, I am blind. I hold my breath until my lungs are ready to explode. Then, in despair, I finally kick toward the surface, realizing I have lost him.

In the murky darkness, my foot strikes something soft. It must be Hector. I am on the verge of passing out but may never find him again if I resurface. Stopping my ascent, I turn, reaching out, searching—still nothing.

Instinctively, I open my burning eyes. Fighting a silent scream, I see a shadow to my left. Stretching out, a piece of cloth touches my hand. I pull it close, grabbing it while kicking for the surface. Spots are dancing under my closed eyes when I feel the cool air on my face. Gasping for breath, I pull Hector's face out of the water.

"Hector," I pant, breathing hard, "it's okay now. I got ya." I look toward the shore for help, but it is deserted.

Unresponsive and barely breathing, Hector's olive skin is pale. I put my lips on his and blow with all my might. Hector's chest rises, and he coughs and sputters. His eyes are closed, and there is an ugly gash across his forehead just above his left eye, but he is breathing. Relief sweeps over me. Hector's coughing gives me a renewed sense of energy.

Fragments and slivers of rotten wood litter the water's surface. Except for the metal pylons, the pier has nearly disappeared into the ocean. I grab a floating board with my free hand, brushing the smaller chunks away. Wrapping my arm around the board, I pull it snugly into my armpit while holding Hector's face above the water with my other arm.

"Hector . . . Hector, can you hear me?" I cough out. There is no response. I struggle to stay afloat while holding Hector and kicking my feet toward shore.

As a wave washes us closer to shore, I scan the beach for help. It is still deserted. Too exhausted, I can no longer fight the tide flow as it pulls us back out to sea. I put my left arm around Hector's neck. I must keep my free arm wrapped around the board. Otherwise, all is lost.

I nearly lose my grip at the thought of *Denz* infecting me the way it did Hector. The dock disintegrated because *Denz* did what it was designed to do: eat petroleum. I give my life-saving board and hand a close examination, looking for any sign I might be infected. The wet board looks normal, and so does my hand. No rash, no itch. Maybe the saltwater neutralized *Denz*? My mind begins to drift. I am exhausted. It feels as though I've been in the water for hours.

A wave peaks, lifting the board and offering me a view of the distant beach. It seems a thousand miles away. I know I do not have the strength to swim to shore—not with Hector in tow. My legs burn just from the effort of staying above water. A flood of doubt sweeps over me. Is this how I die? Forgive me, Hector.

I stop trying to fight the water, watching the rhythmic pattern of the ebb and flow of the surf. A wave builds, rising higher as it breaks toward the shore, nearly tearing the board from my hand. I pull the wood plank close and wrap one arm around it while holding my unconscious friend with the other. As the wave surges to its peak, I am able to throw a leg over the board, straddling it like a surfboard. Reaching behind me, I grab Hector by his shirt collar. With a loud grunt, I pull the upper third of Hector's body out of the water.

The swelling wave breaks. In seconds, we are halfway to the beach. As I watch the approaching shore, my hopes rise like the crest of the wave. I grab Hector tight, prepare to release my grip, and swim for shore. But it's too late; the wave breaks too soon, and we are being sucked back out to sea.

I do a quick calculation as another wave grows and surges toward us. I maneuver the board's angle to catch the crest of the wave. The swell peaks at the perfect spot, lifting the board while the beach gets closer. I slip off the board, and my feet touch the sandy bottom. As the wave recedes, I lean into the rushing water, falling to my knees.

The greasy taste and smell of the oil gag me. Coughing, I lean over and vomit but grateful to be on land. Wiping my mouth with my hand, I stagger to my feet. The sun is blistering hot. Searching for Hector, I put a hand over my still-burning eyes to shade them. I spot him lying face down on the beach but still in the water.

Stumbling over to his body, I roll him on his back. There are no signs of breathing. I check his mouth for any obstruction in his airway; there are none. Rolling him over on his back, I start chest compressions. Using my body weight, I apply firm pressure directly in the center of his chest and press straight down about two inches, as rapidly as I am able. After about thirty compressions, I pause to check for any sign of breathing. Nothing. I squeeze his nose and blow into his mouth to raise his chest. Still no breathing.

Once again, I start the compressions, but it is quickly becoming apparent I am getting too weak in the hot sun. Sweat pours off me, and I am ready to give up; when his chest rises, he gags and begins coughing up water.

I turn him over on his side and pat his back. "It's okay, Hector . . . it's okay. We made it."

First, I examine his right hand. It is still bright red, with small blisters beginning to form. I grab him under his armpits and pull the limp body onto the sandy beach. His eyes are closed, but he's still breathing. Falling to my knees, I bend over him and wipe goblets of oil and sand out of the corners of his eyes, nose, and mouth. A glance up and down the beach tells me what I fear; we are alone.

A short distance away, a clump of palm trees offers what little protection from the sun there is on the beach. I drag Hector toward the shade. Sweat is pouring off my brow by the time I reach the trees. I would give anything for a big glass of ice water. Laying Hector down, I try to make him as comfortable as possible. His right leg is bent at an unnatural angle. The rash, clearly visible on his swollen right hand, appears to be spreading toward his forearm. I fear I don't have much time to get him medical attention.

He moans, and his eyes flutter, then open.

I lean over him, wiping hair out of his eyes. "Welcome back. It's okay. We're safe now."

With a groan, he lifts his hand. ". . . hurts."

"I'm going to find a set of wheels . . . don't move, okay?"

A ghost of a smile crosses his face as he whispers, "Don't worry."

I remove my shirt and arrange it into a pillow under his head. He drifts back into unconsciousness. I stare in the direction of the CIVO warehouse—no sign of life.

I reach into my pocket and pull out my phone. Time to see if it's waterproof as advertised. The phone beeps and lights up. The warehouse is not more than a mile away, but I don't know the number. I could call Lassiter, whose number is on my contact list, or I could call Chip, but he is probably still sleeping, and it would take him at least an hour to get here, or there is Kim, but she is still in the air heading back to Denver; or, finally, I could call the office in Denver.

In Colorado, they would just be starting their day. I hit the number, listening to the phone ring three thousand miles away.

"Good morning. Americo Oil." Deirdre Croft's voice answers, sounding as sweet as water in the desert.

"Deirdre, this is Jesse. I'm at the oil terminal dock in Lagos. We've got a serious problem. Hector is hurt, and I need to get him to the hospital. Our jeep is . . . wrecked, and this area has been evacuated. No one's around."

"Do you need an ambulance?" she asks, sounding confused.

"No. That would take too long. I believe you have the phone number for the CIVO warehouse in Lagos. Find that number, call them, and tell them to send a vehicle to pick us up. We're at the end of the pier, on the south side of the beach, under a palm tree."

"Oh, that sounds rough. It's snowing here. Okay, I'll call you back," she says, disconnecting.

Mumbling, Hector fades in and out. No way can we walk. I collapse in the shade of the palm tree, too exhausted to stand.

My cell phone chirps. "Hello, Deirdre?" I ask hopefully.

"I called them. They're on the way. I'd give them about ten minutes."

"Deirdre, you're a lifesaver. Thanks."

Deirdre pauses. "How's Hector?" She sounds worried.

"He's in rough shape. We need to get him to the hospital as soon as possible."

"If you need anything, call."

"Gotta go. Thanks."

As I disconnect, I hear an engine starting from the direction of the CIVO warehouse. I stand, and as the sound gets closer, I see a jeep with two men in the front seat. I wave my hands, and the jeep flashes its lights.

I recognize one of the men as DuVal.

"Damn! What happened?" DuVal asks as the jeep comes to a sliding halt. His gaze shifts between Hector and me.

"Your little virus got hungry and ate the pier. We were on the dock when it began to disintegrate. Hector touched something with his finger and got infected. It looks like a reaction to his skin. Whatever it is, it is spreading fast. He may also have a broken leg. Strange, because I grabbed onto boards from the pier while in the water but never saw any sign of the infection. Does salt water neutralize *Denz*?"

DuVal looks nervous. Ignoring my question, he hands me a bottle of water. "Wash your eyes out," he orders.

While being loaded into the jeep's back seat, Hector cries out, rubbing his hand. After pouring water onto my face, I wash out Hector's eyes, wiping off specks of oil and sand from around his nose and mouth. Then, putting my arm around his shoulders, I try to comfort him.

A small one-story bungalow serves as the oil terminal hospital. DuVal calls ahead, and two nurses with a gurney meet us when we pull under the ER canopy. I help get Hector out of the jeep and onto the gurney. My arm rests on his shoulder as we wheel Hector down the hallway.

"This is modeled after a mobile army surgical hospital. We got it from the Army but made improvements," says DuVal as he walks behind the gurney.

In a moment of clarity, Hector grabs my sleeve. "Man, I need something . . . the pain . . . is getting intense," he whispers, dropping his hand back on the gurney.

I turn to a doctor speaking French to DuVal. "Hector needs some pain meds. Can you give him something?" The doctor pauses, looks at Hector, then hurries off, returning within thirty seconds. A second doctor in surgical scrubs follows him.

"Mr. Ford, this is Doctor Kenneth Okoro. He works with CIVO," explains DuVal.

Doctor Okoro nods as he examines Hector's hand and leg. Then, turning to me, he says in a heavy French accent, "Mr. Ford, your friend has a fractured leg, which is not a problem, but he is also infected by what appears to be the *Denz* virus, which is feeding on the oil in his skin. Once it is introduced into his blood supply, there is nothing we can do to stop it. It must be . . . isolated now, within minutes. If not, your friend will be eaten alive."

I shake my head, not believing what I am hearing. "How? He touched a rubber hose with his finger. This stuff can't be that deadly. It only eats petroleum. Can't you stop it? Isn't there an antibiotic or medicine?"

"It has spread too far," says the doctor, closely examining Hector's arm. He holds a small monitor, moving it up and down Hector's wrist. After reviewing the image on the screen, he looks up at me. "I'm afraid there's only one way to save this man's life. We need to amputate his arm above the infection."

"You've got to be kidding me," I exclaim in disbelief. "Can't you give him a drug or radiation treatment? There's got to be something?"

"Mr. Ford, we are in the middle of Africa. That might be an option in Paris, New York, or the Mayo Clinic. But here . . . it's a choice between living and dying." His voice trails off as he looks around. "You must decide within the next few minutes, or it won't matter anymore."

I wipe the sweat off my forehead. I have no right to make this decision. Hector's wife, his children . . . I don't know how to contact them, and we don't have the time to do it. If I authorize the amputation, it will haunt me for the rest of my life, and Hector will hate me every day.

"Isn't there something else we can try . . . anything?" I plead one last time.

"I wish there were. But unfortunately, we've seen this before. There's no time to try anything else." Dr. Okoro raises his eyes toward DuVal, who gives the doctor a stern look.

I hesitate. Silence hangs over the room like a black cloud. Every eye watches me while Hector moans, drifting in and out of consciousness.

I touch Hector's shoulder. "Hector. Can you hear me?"

"Jesse . . ." Hector twists and turns on the bed. ". . . it fuckin' hurts."

"Hector, they must cut your arm off to stop the spread. If not, you will die. They want me to decide. I can't. You need to make that call."

Hector squirms, looking up through bloodshot eyes. He tries to speak, but no sound comes out.

I turn to the doctor. "Do it!"

CHAPTER 14
LAGOS

I rise to my feet when the twin doors of the operating room burst open, followed by Dr. Kenneth Okoro. His eyes search the nearly empty waiting room before resting on me. As he approaches me, I search his face for any sign of optimism, but it remains as unreadable as a blank slate. A surgical mask dangles below his chin, and his gown is splattered with blood.

In a hollow voice, he tells me the hand was infected by a virus feeding on his body. "We had no choice but to amputate just below the elbow to stop the spread. If not, he wouldn't have survived more than a few hours."

"How is he? Did you get it all?" I ask, returning the doctor's stare.

The doctor hesitates. "He lost a lot of blood during the surgery, so we had to give him a blood transfusion. Other than that, the surgery went fine. The break in his leg isn't that bad, and we got it set.

"How was he infected? He merely touched a hose on the pier. Is that how he caught this?"

"We're testing the virus but can't discount the possibility it spreads by contact," the doctor answers.

"What do you mean, 'by contact'?" I ask.

"As I said, we're still testing, but the virus seems fond of the oil on human skin."

"Is there an antidote, a vaccine, anything?"

The doctor's eyes drill into me. "Ask Dr. Lassiter."

Startled by his answer, I take a step back. "Are you saying Lassiter has an antidote?"

"There is a rumor he has developed one."

"Do you know if he has it here in Lagos?"

"I hear he . . ." The doctor stops talking when he spots DuVal walking toward us. DuVal takes a sip of a soda, his eyes shifting back and forth between the doctor and me.

"So I hear the Mexican is doing well?" he says, avoiding eye contact with me and looking only at the doctor.

Mexican? My eyes narrow, and I feel the rage building. Turning, I take a step toward DuVal. Without thinking, my right-hand makes a fist, landing a beautiful right hook squarely in DuVal's face below his left eye. DuVal starts to fall, and his soda flies through the air, striking the wall in an explosion of fizz and foam. I step toward him and grab his shirt, pulling him close.

DuVal cowers against the wall, with me only inches from his face. A low growl comes from my throat, sounding like a wild beast ready to kill. "Don't you ever call my friend a Mexican again!"

I push him to the floor and stand over him. "Is he doing well? He lost his arm, you inconsiderate asshole. How do you think he's doing? You knew about *Denz* all along. Why didn't you tell us?"

174

DuVal puts his hands in front of his face. "I'm sorry. I meant no disrespect to Dr. Ramos. All the research on *Denz* was done in Paris. I had no part of that. They delivered it and told me to spray the oil with *Denz*."

"When is Lassiter going to be here?"

DuVal's eyes bulge and disengage from me, looking left and right. "Not sure. I think today or tomorrow."

I grab his collar and stand him up. "I think you're a lying asshole. Get out of here while you can, and tell your boss I want to talk to him."

Glaring at me, DuVal turns and walks down the hallway, not looking back.

Doctor Okoro remains silent, warily watching me. He shuffles backward, catching my attention.

"I want to see Dr. Ramos . . . now!" I growl, looking him straight in the eye.

The doctor quickly nods, his eyes wide. "Come with me. I need to check on him, anyway."

I follow Okoro to Hector's room. The monitor alongside the bed beeps a steady rhythm. Hector's eyes are closed, and he is reclining on a pillow covered with a light blanket. There is white gauze covering his right arm. I can't keep my eyes off his arm . . . or where it should be. Even under the bandages, it looks stunted compared to the left arm.

Hector blinks his eyes and slowly turns to me. He lifts his left hand a few inches before it collapses on the bed. I give his hand a squeeze, which is softly returned.

"I hate oil," Hector whispers, bringing a quick smile to my lips.

After a quick examination, the doctor cautions, "He's waking up but will be groggy for a bit." He turns to me, "Mr. Ford, let me give you some free medical advice. Go home, clean up, and get some rest. You look and act as if you could use it."

"As soon as I can, doctor," I answer. "A moment, please."

As he leaves the room, I reach out to stop him. "Where do they keep the antidote?" I quietly ask.

The doctor's voice drops to a near whisper. "I am told it is kept in the warehouse on the pier. That's all I know, Mr. Ford. Please don't say anything. I don't trust these people. I have a wife and children. . .."

I nod. "Thank you, doctor, for saving my friend's life."

After the doctor leaves the room, I turn to Hector, who has been watching us.

Looking into my face, he shakes his head. "Don't . . . don't do the guilt thing." He speaks slowly, pausing in between words to breathe. "You made the right call. I would be dead or eaten alive if they hadn't . . ." Another pause. "I would have made the same decision if you were lying here. You saved my life, Jesse. I'm just happy to be alive. Now, when can I get out of here? I want to go home."

"Soon as they release you, we'll have you on the jet." My throat grows tight, and I swallow. As I look down at my friend, I can feel a tear begin to form in the corner of my eye.

In a husky whisper, I say, "Hector, I am so sorry,"

"I know you're going to see Lassiter. Make sure you take Chip with you and get that fucker. He lied to us. But first, get some rest . . . and take a shower. You smell like shit." Hector cracks a smile that turns into a grimace when he starts coughing.

***

The late afternoon sun reflects off the hatch as it opens on the sleek silver jet with a black-and-red CIVO logo on the empennage. DuVal watches the plane, restlessly shifting from one foot to the other.

Lassiter is the first one off the plane, dressed in a custom-fitted white linen suit and matching white fedora. He stops at the bottom step, slides on dark sunglasses, and turns to watch two women follow him, one blonde and the other brunette. Both are dressed identically in white linen pantsuits. Lassiter and the blonde woman wear dark wraparound sunglasses. Faisal, the bodyguard, is the last person to exit the plane.

Eyeing the women as they descend the stairs, DuVal extends his hand to Lassiter, who ignores it. Lassiter turns and walks quickly toward the black Land Rover parked near the plane as DuVal trails behind him.

"They know about *Denz*. Dr. Ramos managed to get his arm infected, which had to be amputated," says DuVal while holding the door open for Lassiter. "Ford wants to see you tomorrow. He mentioned the antidote. Be careful of him. He's pissed and violent." DuVal rubs his swollen face.

"Close the door, please, Mr. DuVal. I need to get out of this heat."

The blonde woman climbs into the driver's seat. "I'll drive," she says. The brunette follows Lassiter into the back. DuVal sits in the front passenger seat.

Lassiter leans back inside the air-conditioned Rover, removes his hat but leaves the sunglasses. He wipes his glistening forehead. "Faisal is going ahead. We will meet him at the house. I want him there when we meet."

DuVal nods, not wanting to be in the room with Lassiter's bodyguard and Ford.

***

". . . and guess who the Board is blaming?" John Hammer's voice sounds weak on the phone. Hammer had recently been released from the hospital and was already back at work, much to the dismay of his cardiologist.

I hesitate before speaking, "Do they want my head?"

Hammer balks before answering. "If only your head." He sighs. "Not only your head but every other square inch of you. After they learned about your side trip to D.C. to see your girlfriend, and now this fire in Lagos with hundreds of people dying, Vernon Sheldon was screaming at me to fire you on the spot until Marci Stone stepped in, but it was ugly."

"Are you letting me go?"

"The White House is pointing the finger at us, blaming Americo for the spill and using that as an excuse for the high gas prices. Riots are popping up at California gas stations, and it is starting to spread to cities nationwide. The EPA wants to know what we're doing to clean up the spill. I'm under a lot of pressure here, Jesse."

My grip tightens on the phone. "Brace yourself—I'm afraid there's more bad news. *Denz* goes above and beyond what it was supposedly designed to do. The virus is not limited to just

178

oil but seems to enjoy any material with a petroleum base." I take a deep breath. "Here's the scary part. It has a special taste for the oil on human skin. Once infected, it spreads throughout the body. The only way they could stop the spread in Hector was to amputate his arm. Without that, it would have eaten him . . . alive."

"Holy shit!" exclaims Hammer. "What a nightmare. Why oil on human skin? That's not a petroleum base."

"Hector has had some time on his hands in the hospital, so he has been researching the same thing. It turns out the agriculture industry uses petroleum-based ingredients in fertilizers and pesticides on crops that we eat. These ingredients are ingested and accumulate in human tissue, even at the cellular level."

Hammer is silent on the phone. Then he asks, "Anyway to stop the spread? Is there an antidote? If you can get a sample, we can duplicate it."

"Hector will be released and on his way back home tomorrow. Lassiter arrives in Lagos this afternoon, and Chip and I will pay him a visit. I suspect he has an antidote for *Denz*. But if I meet with him and he finds out I've been dismissed, he'll ignore me."

"What about that ship, the Desert Rose? Where's it at?" Hammer asks.

"On the way to Louisiana. That ship hauls ass. The new design and engines should cut crossing time in half."

"Is it contaminated with *Denz*?"

"Don't know. It was sprayed. Maybe we should call it back to Lagos before it dumps its load."

"Hold on a second. Let's think this through. The politicians drained the Strategic Petroleum Reserve. The SPR is designed to be used by the military, not to buy votes. But now that card has been played, prices are down now but will be shooting back up, but now our reserves are depleted. By replenishing the reserves, Americo could come out of this looking like a hero."

I can almost hear Hammer's mind working. "Send the ship a message," he says. "Tell them not to unload the oil; that will cover our ass if things go south. Make it clear to the captain that he is not to unload. Leave the oil on the ship for now. You get the antidote; we can treat the oil and crisis over."

"Good plan," I reply, "but a lot could go wrong,"

"Not if you get the antidote. Shit rolls downhill, Jesse. I hate to admit it, but this heart attack kicked my butt. I'm tired. I just dumped my problems on you. Get that antidote. Officially you're released. Unofficially you're a consultant . . . doing a special job for me. That job is to get the antidote. The future of Americo is on the line here. The antidote is the key to neutralizing *Denz*. Make this happen. Do whatever you need to do, understand me? Fix this, or neither one of us will have a job. Time to go off the reservation."

***

"Chip, you up for a little reconnaissance work?"

The former SEAL sits up straight and turns his bar stool toward me. "Oh, hell yes. You know the answer to that."

We sit in the dimly lit hotel bar while soft lounge music plays in the background. I nod toward the back of the bar, and we take a booth in a darkened corner. Often a popular place for visiting foreigners, the hotel bar is nearly deserted at this late hour. We sit hunched over our drinks, leaning into each other. I explain the plan, Chip occasionally nodding and asking questions.

"Weapons?" Chip asked.

I shake my head. "I'm more comfortable with a knife. Now, tell me about this guy Franklin. What do you know about him? Can he be trusted?"

"I know his older brother, a fellow SEAL. He mentioned his younger brother many times. He always hoped his little brother, Franklin, would follow in his footsteps, but little brother became a computer geek instead. I can't believe he's now working for CIVO. He's staying in this hotel. I will pay him a visit."

I stand, looking down at Chip. "Okay. Breakfast in the morning. We have a plan. Tomorrow night."

CHAPTER 15
BAYOU CHOCTAW

Elias Mutombo, captain of the Desert Rose, clenched his fist and glared at his executive officer. It was no secret the captain hated his XO. The captain is shrewd and savvy but realizes he is no match for his senior officer's intellect. Nevertheless, he is still the captain, which gives him the luxury of bullying and intimidating anyone on the ship, including his XO.

At two hundred fifty pounds, he outweighs his number two by seventy pounds which, coupled with the fact that he is the senior officer, gives him the advantage of intimidation. If that isn't enough, he has been known to use violence and force when necessary.

"When did you get this?" Mutombo demands, waving the printout with the Americo Oil logo in his large hand.

The bridge of the ship is hot in the late afternoon. The muggy and sticky air is still. The executive officer's forehead is dripping with sweat, but not because of the heat. He is well aware of his captain's legendary temper.

The executive officer has been to the Strategic Petroleum Reserve at Bayou Choctaw on past runs and hates the swampy, alligator-infested Louisiana bayou. Swatting a swarm of mosquitoes away from his face, he wipes burning sweat from his eyes, longing to be back at sea again where there are no bugs and he can avoid this psychopath standing before him.

"It came in last night," the XO replied.

After rereading the communique, Captain Mutombo issues a stream of curses directed at his executive officer.

"I tried to reach ya, but you never answered your phone," the XO says defensively, stepping back.

Thanks to the futuristic design of the ship, powered by turbocharged diesel engines, the Desert Rose arrived at the Bayou Choctaw site days early. The final stretch had been spent navigating the sultry Mississippi River, recently dredged to make the storage site more accessible for even the largest oil tankers.

Seeking to take advantage of the early arrival, Mutombo put his XO in charge of unloading the oil into the SPR. Once the off-loading was underway, the captain hired a car to take him to New Orleans, some eighty miles southeast. The last day and a half had been spent snorting cocaine and drinking whiskey with New Orleans whores. He remembers the cell phone ringing in the middle of a l'amour encounter on Bourbon Street, but he was too busy to answer and too stoned to care. He reread the fax:

"Captain Mutombo: Do not, repeat, do not unload oil at Bayou Choctaw. Cancel all other deliveries. Call immediately to confirm."

"You sure you didn't tell anyone about this?" he growls.

"No, Cap'n."

The Desert Rose had already unloaded three hundred thousand barrels of Nigerian crude at the Bayou Choctaw storage site. There was no taking it back. Even if they wanted to, the engineers at the reserve facility would not let the oil go. The giant salt dome was capable of holding seventy-six million barrels of oil. The engineers told the executive officer they had drained the site to less than one million barrels, and the government was pressuring them to get the newly delivered crude to the nearby refinery and out in the market as soon as possible.

Mutombo's fist tightened, and his dark eyes pierced his exec. His was as bleak as the storm clouds overhead, made worse by the lingering hangover. Sweat-drenched sour clothes clung to him, making the sweltering ninety-degree heat even more intolerable.

"Y'all never got this . . . understand!"

The XO quickly nods, reading the threat.

Mutombo begins to walk away, then stops and turns back toward his second.

"Why'd you keep unloading after ya got this?" he asks, waving the fax in the face of the senior officer.

"Cap'n, you're the only one with authority to stop unloading. I couldn't reach ya."

Mutombo gives a satisfied grunt. He would have killed the man had the unloading been halted. His commission is $10,000 from this drop. No idiot sitting in an office on the other side of the world is going to screw him out of it. Ignoring the fax, he crumples it up and tosses it over the side into the murky water. He never got it.

Mutombo stalks up the ladder to the bridge. Stopping, he turns and screams at the XO, "Are we done unloading!?"

"Yes, Captain, about thirty minutes ago. We're ready to get underway."

"Make it so . . . immediately." He can still smell and taste the whiskey from the night before. It had been a memorable night, but now he wants to puke. The rancid smell is made worse by the hot, clammy air, which smells of rotten swamp water. His roiling stomach churns—even worse after reading the fax. Why would the company want him to cancel all deliveries? He shrugs inwardly. Too late now. It's no longer his problem.

The captain leans over the side of the bridge railing, watching the executive officer bark out commands under the direction of the site's maritime pilot. Finally, the dock workers on the pier cast off mooring lines, and the ship pulls slowly away from the dock, maneuvering out into the Mississippi waterway for the journey back across the Atlantic. Once underway, he will call Africa.

He scratches the burning itch on his arm. Probably caught something from one of the whores.

CHAPTER 16
ANTIDOTE

Chip and I sit in the comfortable chairs in the lobby of the Lagos Continental Hotel, people-watching and pretending to read newspapers. A group of people enter the hotel's lobby, letting in the outside traffic noise and heat—some head for the elevator, but most detour toward the bar.

Chip leans toward me and says in a low voice that blends with the background noise, "That's him, with the blue shirt and glasses."

I spot him right away. Tony Franklin has that "American" look about him, overweight with a button-down blue shirt that fits too tight, a mustache, short-trimmed brown hair, and wearing baggy jeans, even though the temperature outside was in the high nineties.

He looks longingly at the bar for a few seconds, hesitates, but keeps walking toward the elevator. Earlier in the day, Chip checked out his room for any bugs or cameras and announced it was clean.

The bronze panel that shows which floor the elevator is on indicates the elevator is headed down from the seventh level. When it arrives at the first floor, the doors slide open with a swoosh, and Franklin steps into the empty lift. The doors are nearly shut when

Chip sticks his hand in the gap between the closing doors. They pause with a jerk, then reopen. Chip and I step inside, not looking at Franklin. I see him glaring at us out of the corner of my eye. With a huff, he pushes the fifth-floor button on the panel. Chip and I stare straight ahead, neither touching a floor button.

Inside the enclosed area, I smell his sweaty armpits. No one looks at anyone else, and there is silence except for the lifting cables. I can see Franklin in the distorted reflection of the shiny walls. He rubs his hand through tousled hair and leans into the mirror image, pulling down the skin below bloodshot eyes.

As the floor indicator light passes the third level, Chip reaches over and pushes the STOP button, bumping the elevator to a sudden halt.

"Excuse me! What're you doing?"

Chip turns to face the man, only inches apart. I stay in the corner, watching.

"Tony, my name is Chip Monk. I'm a friend of your brother, Wyatt. We were SEALs together."

"Oh, lucky you." Franklin tenses up, backing against the wall with clenched fists, his narrow eyes darting back and forth. "Now, Chip Monk, will you be so kind as to push the fifth floor?"

Chip looks down at Franklin's clenched fist, a hint of a bemused smile playing on his face. "Relax," he assures the man. "We're not here to harm you. We have something to discuss. This seems like a good spot to introduce ourselves. Meet Jesse Ford, Vice-President of Americo Oil."

I nod but remain silent. We want to instill a thread of fear, to let him know we're serious.

"This is about CIVO, isn't it? I recognize your name," Franklin adds, looking at me. "My boss doesn't much care for you."

"Who's your boss?" I ask.

"DuVal."

"That asshole is not your boss."

Franklin's eyes open wide. "Oh, you mean the big man."

"I mean Lassiter."

Franklin turns to Chip. "You say you know my brother? Where is he?"

"Last time I saw Wyatt, he was at Fort Benning. I think he was about to get laid and feeling no pain."

Franklin frowns. "That sounds typical of him." He pauses, looking both of us up and down. "So I'm guessing with this cloak and dagger visit, you want something."

"We want the antidote," I tell him.

Franklin stares at us. "Let's go to my room. I have something you need to see. Fifth floor, please."

***

Room 540 is a tastefully decorated corner suite. I stand while Chip casually strolls around the room he was in only hours before. Franklin offers a drink, but both of us decline. Pouring a tall scotch and water, Franklin takes his laptop out of the canvas briefcase, lays it on the coffee table, and pops it open.

"This is a computer simulation I constructed on how *Denz* will spread. The red dots represent *Denz*. My model is based on the assumption that *Denz* starts here in Lagos.

We stand behind Franklin, looking over his shoulder. On the screen is a map of Africa. There is a red dot on Lagos.

"This is twenty-four hours after introduction." The area north and south of Lagos is beginning to fill in with red dots.

He hits the tab key. "This is forty-eight hours." The red area around Lagos becomes more solid, spreading inland and northward.

"Five days."

No one says a word. There is no need. The entire west coast of Africa is nearly solid red, all the way north to the Kingdom of Morocco.

"Now, ten days." Franklin's voice is low and raspy.

The northern coast of Africa and southern Europe are now solid red.

"At fifteen days, I assumed the oil tanker that left Lagos has delivered its load into the U.S. reserves." Franklin expands the map further, showing the U.S. mainland. Parts of the South along the Gulf Coast are red.

"Now I jump out to thirty days." Most of the Middle East, the Saudi Arabian Peninsula, and Iran are now smothered in red. There are a few spots of red in Israel. The red is spreading to the Russian oil fields and population centers. Both the east and west coasts of the U.S. are red. There are red lines across the continental United States.

"What's that?" Chip asks, pointing to the red lines across the U.S.

"Those are interstate highways," I tell him. "You can assume state and county roads are also contaminated."

"That's as far out as I took it," Franklin breathed.

"I didn't realize it could spread so fast," Chip says, still looking at the screen.

Using a small printer on his desk, Franklin prints out a screenshot and hands it to me.

"Based on my data, *Denz* will double its reproduction rate every twenty-four hours. It has a frightening ability to spread but can only spread through physical contact with petroleum or any substance with a petroleum base." Franklin's face grows noticeably pale.

"Has Lassiter seen this?" I ask in a low voice.

Franklin stands and pours himself a second drink. "Not only has that psycho seen it, but the man was ecstatic when I showed him."

There is a glance between Chip and me as Franklin downs the drink.

"Think about it, gentlemen," Franklin says, taking his seat. "Anything containing a derivative of petroleum that *Denz* comes in contact with will cause the virus to multiply, doubling in size every day. Roads have asphalt, rubber hoses on planes, cars, and tires, insulated wiring on electrical generators, plastics, fuel, gas and diesel, propane, kerosene—there is virtually no end to it."

Chip quietly asks, "What about the oil on human skin?"

Franklin nods his head slowly. "That was the tipping point for me. I think you know the answer to your question. Even though the oil on human skin has no petroleum hydrocarbons, per se, that is not entirely true. Humans consume processed food products that contain petroleum derivatives from plants sprayed with fertilizers and insecticides." Franklin stands to mix another drink. Having heard this from Hector's research, I nod and am ready to join him for that drink.

190

"Look at the labels on food products," he continues. "Now, I'm not a health food junkie, but that shit is in our bodies. To *Denz*, human skin is like a dessert. Look at what happened to your Dr. Ramos. His hand got infected, and his arm below the elbow had to be amputated within hours of contact. We also had an incident with one of our workers. *Denz* loves to cannibalize human skin." Franklin stands and nervously paces the room, stopping to face the two men.

"There's something else. The makeup most women use has an oil base derived from petroleum. It's creepy, but *Denz* can't get enough of it. After it consumes the makeup, it moves into the skin, dissolving it. Anyone infected dies a gruesome death. I can't stand by and do nothing. If Lassiter even finds out I am talking to you . . .." There was no need to finish the sentence.

I stare, my mind lost in thought. Libby uses makeup. "What about the antidote?" Franklin shakes his head. "I don't know much. That's not my area. I'm just a tech guy, but I hear it's a fairly simple compound."

My eyes are glued to the computer screen. "Is there any here in Lagos?"

"I know a few bins in the back of the warehouse were brought here from Paris to test in a live environment."

I stand, looking down at Franklin. "I want a sample of it."

Franklin looks at me, then Chip. "I want to help. You're going to need me."

***

Chip and I spend two days gathering equipment and finalizing details. After faxing the Americo office a copy of the printout we got from Franklin, I speak with Hammer and Kim, letting them know what our plan is.

"Good God," Kim cries out. "This can't be happening. Don't let that bastard get away with this," she pleads with me.

"Stop using lipstick, eye shadow, or any kind of make-up," I warn her. "Tell all your friends. Now, let me speak with Hammer."

"Why do you want my approval?" Hammer demands after I explain the plan. Never one to mince words, he says, "You don't even have to ask. Get that antidote, and if you get a chance, kill that fucker, but I want you on the plane with the antidote."

Kim gets on the phone again before we disconnect. "You and Chip be careful," she says needlessly. "We'll make sure the jet is waiting for you."

If successful, we will have a sample on the plane tonight and be in Denver thirteen hours after takeoff—fewer with Ron at the controls.

After I hang up from Kim, I hold the phone in my hand, staring at it. I have had a gnawing feeling the situation is spiraling out of control since seeing Franklin's printout. I pick up my phone and memory dial Libby. She needs to know what's going on.

Chip conducts a second surveillance of the warehouse's exterior earlier in the afternoon. By the time he gets back, Franklin, who continues to work, completes a detailed diagram of the interior of the building showing where the antidote is stored. We double-check our gear and go over the plan again. I was planning a power nap before we left, but am too excited to sleep. This is all new for me, and I worry I might screw something up. I wonder if I have what it takes to kill if needed. I think I do, but I've never killed a man.

CHAPTER 17
SKULL AND CROSSBONES

The midnight fog is like pea soup, chilling the night air. In the distance, I hear the sound of breaking waves, occasionally drowned out by a braying fog horn. Chip and I are dressed in black and nearly invisible. The pier is deserted, not a car in the parking lot. The only light is a low-wattage single bulb above the warehouse's front door and a light at the rear where we plan to enter.

We drift through the fog like phantoms in the night, stopping in the shadow of a storage container not more than fifty feet from the front entrance. Chip pulls out the diagram of the warehouse Franklin made, and we take one last look using a penlight.

He leans close to my ear. "You ready?"

I clench my fist and nod. I picture Franklin's computer screen and the gruesome image of Libby and Kim being eaten by *Denz*. Pushing the grisly vision out of my mind, I take a deep breath. We must get the antidote.

Franklin wanted to come with us, but I decided not to use him. He's an unknown, he has a drinking problem, and I don't entirely trust him. But on the other hand, I can't think of anyone I would rather be with now than Chip—except maybe James Bond. For a second, I fantasize I hear strains of the Bond theme.

The plan is simple. We enter the building, grab an antidote sample, and get out. Should be a piece of cake. A company jet is waiting for us at the airport to fly us back to Denver, where it will be analyzed and reproduced in the Americo lab.

I can hardly see Chip in the dark. I crouch to my knees while Chip peeks around the corner above my shoulder. All quiet.

Chip touches me on the shoulder and points. Under the dim lightbulb at the front entrance, two men stand smoking in the shadow of the light. Both are dressed in military-type fatigues. One man has a baseball hat on backward with a short-barrel rifle slung over his shoulder. No weapon is visible on the second man.

"Locals. These guys aren't professionals," Chip whispers. Backing into the shadows, he leads the way around a storage container toward the rear of the warehouse.

Through the fog, the feeble light bulb outside the rear entrance casts an eerie glow on two other men dressed in the same style of clothing. Both carry weapons. They are more relaxed than the guards at the front, leaning against the building and talking in low tones. Occasionally one of the men laughs.

An ocean breeze moves the fog in swirls and waves, giving the air an added chill. Chip makes a fist and holds up his arm. We both stop moving and listen. I feel safe in the darkness. A shot of adrenaline makes me shiver.

"Wait here. This won't take long," Chip tells me in a low voice. He pulls out his tactical knife and disappears into the night.

I see a glimmer of movement in the shadows to the right of the guards. In a move choreographed to perfection, so quick and stealthy I nearly miss it, he strikes. The knife flashes in the dim light. Almost simultaneously, both men drop without a sound. The brutality of it stuns me, but then I think about Franklin's computer simulation.

Chip waves at me. I run low and fast, sweating when I reach the two bodies. Beads of sweat itch as they trickle down my chest.

"Help me pull the bodies into the shadows." I barely hear him, and my mouth is dry. We each grab a foot and pull the dead men deeper into the night. He quickly searches the men, lifts a handheld radio, and slides it into his pocket.

We stoop down below the window level, stopping at the rear door. Chip turns the knob, but it is locked, as expected. He pulls out a long pin-shaped object and sticks it into the lock. I lift my head to peek in the window. When I see movement, I raise my hand to stop him.

"Wait," I whisper. "I have an idea."

Chip jumps when I give three soft knocks on the door. "What the fuck are you doing?" he whispers with a frown on his face. This was not part of the plan.

"I'll take care of this guy," I say. I knew Chip would kill him in all likelihood. But after seeing the two earlier guards with their throats cut, I hope we can get the antidote without any more death.

"I don't like it," he says. "I'll go in."

"Too late," I whisper, shaking my head as I stand. The door opens a few inches. In the dull light, a security guard peeks at me with a hand on his holster.

The outside light is to my back, so my face is in a shadow.

"How ya doing?" I chirp to the guard, who opens the door wider. There is a puzzled look on his face. "Say, is DuVal here yet?"

"At hotel," the surprised guard replies in a foreign accent I cannot place. "Who're you?" His hand grips the butt of the pistol, but it remains in his holster.

"I flew in from Paris this afternoon, and Mr. DuVal told me to meet him here about midnight after my flight arrived." I nod back in the general direction to where the guards are keeping watch. "They told me just to knock on the door." I hold my breath, waiting to see if he buys my story.

The guard checks his watch and shrugs. "Well, he not here yet. Ya wanna come in and wait?"

"Yeah, sure. It's getting chilly out here." I give Chip, who is out of sight from the man, a quick side glance before I step through the door. I can tell by his stance he's ready for any surprises, and by the look on his face, he's pissed at me. The guard slowly opens the door, staring hard. I smile at him as I enter the building, keeping my hands in plain sight.

"You wanna cup?" he asks, starting to relax.

I give a cautious nod. "Sure. I'm just here to grab a sample of the antidote to return to the lab in Paris. I guess they want to make some modifications. Where do they keep it?"

The guard turns to look at me suspiciously. "What your name?"

"My name is Hammer. John Hammer. I'm a scientist at the lab in Paris."

He turns back to the coffee bar. My mind is racing. I slide my knife out of my belt. I'm better with a knife than a gun, but I don't want to kill him. A tap on his head with my knife handle should take care of him until we grab what we need and escape.

There's a commotion and a shout outside the door where I left Chip. I grasp the handle of my knife as the guard turns toward me. Sensing my plan is beginning to go south, I stay focused on the prize. The guard drops the cup of coffee and reaches for his pistol but is too slow. Without thinking, I step into him and bring my knife handle down hard on his head.

He grunts and backs away from me. Reaching up, he touches his head, staring at his bloody hand. "You son of a bitch!" he cries out, lunging at me with curled lips, knocking me backward. The knife flies out of my hand.

I lash out with my fist. He tries to block my swing, but I still catch the tip of his nose hard enough to bring blood.

Jumping back, he wipes dripping blood, saying something to me in a language I do not understand but guess it means something like, "I'm gonna rip your head off." There is a crazed grin on his face.

Taking a self-defense stance, he screams and comes at me. I take another swing while backing up, aiming for his ribs, but I miss. He grabs my arm and flips me across the room. I crash into a metal desk, then roll onto the floor. My left shoulder has a flash of burning pain, causing me to gasp for breath.

I struggle to my feet as he rushes me with a furious bellow bordering on a scream. When he gets within reach, I grab his left wrist and pull it toward me. Caught by surprise, he loses his balance and falls into me. I turn and sidestep him, and as he drives past me, I smash my fist into his ribcage with all my strength, feeling a bone crack. He yelps and falls to his knees.

His bloodshot eyes are filled with hatred as he struggles to stand. "I'm gonna kill you." Red spittle spews from his mouth, and he holds his side. I hit him with an upward blow to his nose with the palm of my right hand, a killing blow. He's done. His eyes roll back in his head, and he collapses in a heap.

Breathing hard, I lean down to check for a pulse. Not feeling any, I stand over him. Then it dawns on me—I have just killed a man.

Stepping to the back door, I open it slowly. Chip is lying on the ground. Next to him is a guard surrounded by a pool of blood with Chip's tactical knife buried in his chest.

I stop and look, listening for any sound. In the distance, I hear running footsteps growing fainter. Is this one of the guards from the front? Kneeling beside Chip, I touch his shoulder. His eyes are closed. There is a bloody lump on the right side of his forehead, and blood trickles down his face. "Chip," I call softly, "are you okay?"

He groans, and his eyes flutter, focusing on me. "You're still alive?" he says as though surprised. "I was headed in to help when this guy sucker punched me from behind." Then, turning toward the body next to him, he says, "Looks like I got him." He struggles to sit up and turns to me. "Are you okay?"

"Yeah, I'm good, kinda," I answer. "I'm going to get the antidote. Wait for me." I help him stand, but he staggers and is still groggy.

I stand and listen—nothing. The fog muffles the usual night noises. Walking back into the building, I step around the dead guard on the floor. According to Franklin's diagram, the antidote is stored in a back room at the end of the hallway.

I pause again, listening for any sound from the front guards—still nothing. I'm surprised they didn't hear all the racket, but it's a big building. Maybe the fog muffles some of the sounds. Too late to worry about it. I've come too far to stop.

I move through the hallway toward the rear room. Franklin said there were two rooms at the end of the hallway. The antidote is in the first. He didn't know what the second room was used for.

I stop at the first room door and feel around the door jamb, looking for wires. Chip taught me that—no sign of any security system. I try the door handle. It's locked.

Walking back to the guard on the floor, I check his belt, then his pants pocket for keys. No luck. Glancing at the wall, I see a key rack above the coffee pot. About ten keys hang on hooks. Grabbing them all, I head back toward the locked door. The seventh key opens the door.

The room is pitch black. My penlight cuts through the darkness, resting on a row of green cylinders stacked upright in the far corner. Each cylinder is small, about the size of a home fire extinguisher. I pull one of the cylinders out of the middle row, surprised at how heavy it is. Shaking it, I can feel liquid sloshing inside.

I shine my light around the room. This has to be it. Nothing else even comes close. There is a label on the cylinder: skull and crossbones, but no writing.

My left shoulder is painful and stiff from the scuffle with the guard. It feels like it's dislocated, which I have had before. It takes both arms to lift the cylinder onto my right shoulder. Flipping off my flashlight, I move toward the dim light at the rear exit. I try not to look at the guard lying on the floor, but can't help it. I'm surprised there are no regrets. I have what I came for.

I open the back door a crack and peek out. The guard's body is still lying on the ground, but Chip is gone. I start to call his name but stop. If he's not here, there's a reason. I hear nothing but silence, broken up by the deep, reverberating warning of that damned fog horn.

The single bulb lights up the immediate area outside the door. Opening it, I creep into the night air. I can hardly believe my good fortune but feel anxious about Chip's disappearance. Chip would never leave me unless it were for a good reason. Something's wrong, I can feel it, but I need to get the cylinder to the airport.

As I turn to close the door behind me, I sense rather than hear movement in the shadows. Thinking it's Chip, I turn. From out of the night, a searing pain explodes in my head. I fall forward, losing my grip on the cylinder. Someone is holding me down. I hear a familiar voice say, "Give him the shot." The last thing I remember before the prick in my arm is Chip telling me, "It never goes according to plan."

Then nothingness.

CHAPTER 18

COAST GUARD

Lieutenant James Ford, Jesse's brother and the copilot of the HH-60 Coast Guard Helicopter, wrestles with the joystick as he fights the thirty-mph wind gusts. The white-capped Atlantic churns its displeasure a thousand feet below at the oncoming storm.

Even though Lieutenant Ford outranks the pilot, he considers himself fortunate to be the copilot for Master Chief Randy Reeves. Reeves is regarded as a legend in the Coast Guard, with over eighteen years of experience as a helicopter pilot and hundreds of rescues.

"So what's going on here, Chief? Is this a Medevac or a rescue?" asks the lieutenant.

The chief has been strangely quiet since the phone call from the EPA. "Could be both," he says. "The lady at EPA told me a ship, an oil tanker, might have hazardous material on board." A worried frown crosses his face. "They've been unable to contact the vessel since it left Louisiana."

Lt. Ford jerks at the controls as a gust hits, dropping the copter twenty feet and sending the crew into free fall. "Jesus, I bet that one was at least forty," the radarman yells into the cockpit at the two pilots.

The chief adjusts his headset from the drop. "Rad, how far?" he asks the radarman.

"About three miles to the ship, Chief. You should be able to get a visual in the southeast any minute. According to radar, the tanker is dead in the water."

"Well, fuck. That sucks. How's the weather?" the chief asks in his usual colorful language.

"Shitty, and getting shittier by the minute. Winds are picking up. Seven to ten-foot swells on the surface. A tropical depression is headed in our direction, so it's going to get worse."

"How long do we have?" the chief asks as another gust hits the helicopter broadside.

"Maybe an hour before we're in the thick of it."

"There it is," says the chief to his copilot, pointing to a speck on the roiling gray water below.

"Sparks, we have a visual. Any luck raising them?" calls out the chief.

Sparks, the radio operator sitting just behind the pilot, has been trying to raise the ship on various radio channels, including emergency frequencies, since leaving the Miami Coast Guard base.

"Nothing, Chief," replies Sparks, gripping a handrail to steady himself. "The fact that the tanker is failing to respond to a call from the Coast Guard is unusual unless they are in a dire emergency or drug runners. However, the stationary position rules out the latter," Sparks pointed out to the Chief.

"Well, shit. That's not good." The chief looks at his copilot. "This vessel is supposed to be state of the art with the latest communication equipment."

It is not unusual for a ship to be set on automatic pilot while crossing the Atlantic. But even on automatic pilot, there will be an officer of the deck monitoring communication.

As they approach the oil tanker, it is clear the vessel has a problem. It's bobbing like a cork at the mercy of the angry sea.

"Sparks, call Miami. Tell them we found it. We're going to circle, then drop down and pay them a visit."

"Aye aye, Chief," the radioman answers, going to a different frequency. He is silent as he listens to Miami's reply. "Hey, Chief, some lady from the EPA is on the horn and wants to speak with you," he calls out, leaning forward to tap the chief on his shoulder. He switches the radio to a privacy channel and hands the headset to the chief.

"This is Chief Reeves." For two minutes, he is silent, then says, "Yes, ma'am, I understand."

Handing the headset back to the radioman, the chief keys his headset for the entire crew. "Listen up," he announces. "We're approaching a ship in distress. There are no communications, and the vessel appears dead in the water. We've been ordered to board and check it out. There are ten-foot swells and getting bigger. With the pitch and roll, it is too risky to land on their platform. So we're going to hover and use the rescue strop. This is a high-risk operation, but you guys are well-trained and know your job. We've done this before. Look sharp."

A rescue strop is a critical tool every Coast Guard helicopter has that performs search and rescue operations. It allows the team to extract people from dangerous situations. They constantly practice rescues. The strop is designed to wrap around a person's chest and under their arms to lift them, usually off a distressed boat, to safety.

"Get ready, boys," Chief Reeves says. "We'll circle her a couple of times to wake them up."

What had been a speck on the horizon has now become a large oil tanker, riding high in the water, swaying from side to side. Waves are breaking over the lifeless ship.

"Get the rescue strop ready," the chief says. Lieutenant Ford and Martinez will go down. Any questions?" None of the five-man crew answer. They know the drill, having practiced countless times.

The chief calls Lt. Ford aside. "I want you to take sidearms. Officially for defensive purposes only. Unofficially, use if you feel the need. Wear hazmat suits. This whole thing sounds weird, but I don't want to take any chances. Stay in constant radio contact and report everything you see. Don't touch anything; you got it? Not a damn thing."

The tension level on the helicopter matches the increasing wave size on the raging ocean below. Ford retrieves two standard-issue Beretta M9 nine-millimeter semi-automatic pistols, a reliable and accurate weapon. He straps one on his hip and hands the other gun and holster to Larry Martinez, the Second-Class Petty Officer going down with him.

The crew watches the two men in silence as they don their hazmat suits, including helmets. Each man has a portable oxygen tank strapped to his back, special boots, and gloves.

"Sparks, you sure there's nothing on the radio from the ship?" the chief asks again.

"Still trying but getting nothing, Chief."

They are close now and begin a final circle, looking for the best spot to drop the cable. As they cross the stern, they see the ship's name, Desert Rose. Large waves pound the ship's side, rolling across the deck, causing the vessel to list forty-five degrees on the leeward side.

"Try hailing them with the loudspeaker," Chief Reeves tells his radioman as they make the final circle. The dual speakers mounted underneath the helicopter are designed to be heard above the wail of the wind and the chopping noise of the engine. The helicopter circles once more, calling out over the speakers. Still no sign of life. It starts to rain, and off to the south, the radarman sees a dark band of clouds building.

"Son of a bitch," curses the chief as he fights to keep the helicopter steady and level. "Brace yourself. This is going to be a rough one. Okay, boys, get strapped in. We'll lower you on the windward side of the aft deck. Stay on the deck or the bridge. Don't go inside unless it's something—exciting. Good luck."

"Aye, aye," both men say in unison.

***

As the officer in charge, Lt. Ford goes first. He slips the nylon rescue strop under his arms and around his back while Petty Officer Martinez clips the cable to the winch. Ford gives an inward sigh of relief that Martinez, the most experienced man with the strop onboard, will be his second. He saw Martinez in action one night at a bar in Pensacola and knows the man can take care of himself.

Ford wraps his arms around the oxygen tank and gives the crew a thumbs-up. He has done this over twenty times, both in practice and actual rescues, but never in a storm of this magnitude. One of the men slides the side door open. Grabbing the cable over his head, he leans out, looking down at the shifting deck below him.

After a brief hesitation, he breathes and steps out into nothingness. The air seemed to hold its breath until it didn't. A gust of wind shoved the helicopter toward the deck of the oil tanker, rolling in the furious ocean below. Suddenly Ford was falling in zero gravity over a rolling ship in a stormy sea, not halting until he was about ten feet above the ship's deck.

On board the helicopter, the men watched Ford fall with their hearts lodged in their throats as Lieutenant Ford fell dangerously close to the ship's deck below. But then, with a rev of its engine, the helicopter began to climb upward. A cheer erupted from the men as the tightened cable secured Ford from a potentially life-threatening crash onto the deck.

Ford's boots hit the deck with a jarring thud. He staggered but managed to regain his balance and unhook the line so the winch could pull it back up for Martinez. Before stepping off the bird's deck, the radioman does a video check with the built-in helmet camera.

"Read you four by four," Ford says, his voice tense but steady. "How me?"

"You both look good. I feel like I'm at an IMAX theatre," Sparks joked, his voice a grounding source amid the chaos. The visual feed from both men filled his screen, which was being forwarded to the Coast Guard base in Miami.

Fighting to stand upright on the tilting deck, Ford looks up at Martinez as he swings out of the helicopter. As he is lowered, another gust of wind hits, causing the aircraft to drop again. Martinez comes down hard and fast, hitting the deck with a bone-jarring crash, his body slamming against the metal surface. A wave hit the ship's broadside in perfect harmony with Martinez's impact on the deck. A raging wall of water rushed across the deck, nearly dragging Martinez over the side. Ford lunged forward and grabbed the harness. With a grunt of effort, Ford yanked his comrade back, pulling him from the edge of the ship's deck.

"You good?" Ford yells, not sure if Martinez can even hear him over the noise of the helicopter in combination with the wind. Martinez's face is pale. He nods and begins to stand. Suddenly his face grimaced in pain, and he reaches down to grab his left foot. Limping, he falls back to the deck.

"You need to go back up?" Lt. Ford asks, concerned.

Martinez shakes his head. "No way, Sir. I can shake this off." Martinez hesitates, then says, "Thanks for saving my life."

Ford gave him a thumbs-up and unhooked his cable.

The chief boomed over their earbuds. "Martinez, you okay? Let's do a video check," he orders while the bird continues to hover over the ship. Then, getting a confirmation that the landing party was good, the helicopter backed off to a higher altitude.

Seeing Martinez fingering his gun, Ford orders him to leave it in the holster. "We only use weapons in self-defense."

The two men scan the deck of the ship to get their bearings. There is no sign of life, and the only noise is the distant helicopter and wind and waves crashing into the ship.

"Let's head to the bridge. Be alert." The Lt. warns unnecessarily.

They climb a nearby ladder to the next deck, several times holding onto the railings as the combined water and wind attempts to toss them over the side. Battling the elements every step, they lean into the wind and rain as they cross the second deck, at times holding on to each other as they move toward another exterior ladder going up to deck three.

"Hey, Lieutenant," calls Martinez. "There's a hatch. Why don't we go inside and get out of this shit?"

Despite the chief's warning to stay outside, they realized the mystery of the vanished crew would not be resolved from the outside. Both men were soaked and tired of being beaten by the wind and water. Plus, inside, there was no worry about being washed overboard.

"Good idea, Martinez," said Ford, "but put your mask on and turn on the oxygen. Stay toasty."

Ford wrenched open the hatch, revealing a pitch-black passageway. Both men peeked into the blackness.

"Lights on," Ford commanded, his voice competing with the howling wind behind them as they stepped inside the ship and slammed the hatch door shut.

Martinez stops, shining his light on a life buoy hanging on the bulkhead. "Hey, Lt., check this out." The ship's name, Desert Rose, was stenciled in red letters across the bottom. The lifesaver hung in shreds. "Damn, looks like something ripped this apart." Martinez reached out to touch what was left of the life buoy.

"Don't touch that!" Ford barked, causing the petty officer to jump back. "Don't touch anything, even with gloves on."

THE SPILL

They climb up a starboard ladder to another pitch-black deck which appears to be the mess hall in the darkness. Still no sign of life, no bodies, nothing. On the far side of the mess hall is another ladder. Pushing open the hatch at the top of the ladder, they step onto the bridge. Both men are silent, and still no sign of the crew.

The bridge is large, elevated so as to provide an unobstructed view of the surroundings. Bridge wings extend on either side, and large windows made of reinforced glass to withstand the impact of waves and provide an unrestricted view.

"Hey, Lt.," Martinez exclaimed, "check this out," says Martinez, nodding toward the far side of the bridge near the helm and navigational equipment. Both men make their way toward the captain's chair. Seated in the chair, a man with a hat has his back turned to them.

Lieutenant Ford calls out to the man. "Sir . . . Sir, we are the United States Coast Guard. Are you okay?" His hat has a captain insignia.

There is no response from the motionless figure. They approach the silent man slowly, hands resting on their sidearms. Suddenly a massive wave strikes the ship, causing water to surge and engulf the bridge windows. The vessel lurches, tilting forty-five degrees to the port side. The man in the chair is thrown from his chair, crashing onto the deck with a sickening thud.

Both men stare at the flesh and muscle hanging off the man's face, in some places revealing the cheek and jaw bones. The only thing left of his left arm is the humerus bone, with shreds of muscle tissue hanging off it. It is a grisly sight. Martinez takes a step back and gags but keeps it down.

"We need to hold it together," Ford warns, giving Martinez a concerned look.

"Chief," Ford says, swinging his helmet camera in a 360 around the bridge, with a final close-up shot of the semi-decomposed man lying on the deck. "Are you seeing this? Looks like something ate the captain."

The chief's response is silence, then the radio crackles to life. "Lieutenant, I think it's time for you guys to get your asses back here. We got what we came for. We need a hazmat crew here." A brief pause follows before the chief's voice continues. "You guys didn't touch anything, did you?" The tension is evident over the headset.

"The only thing we've touched is the deck with our shoes and the climbing ladder handrail with gloved hands. We're coming back out on the deck," Ford said.

Martinez, still visibly shaken, clings to the helm for support. "Sorry, sir," he says to Ford, "I've seen some shit in my life, but I ain't never seen anything like this. That smell makes me want to puke."

"Don't worry about it, Martinez. Chief wants us to head back. Let's get out of here," says Ford. Taking a camera out of his side pocket, he kneels and takes some close-up still pictures of the captain while Martinez wanders around the bridge.

"Hey, Lieutenant, check this out." He points to a room off to the back side of the bridge. A sign on the door says "Radio Shack."

Both men move toward the door, which is slightly ajar. Martinez cautiously pushes it open to the sound of grating hinges. The room inside is dark. Both men turn their helmet lights on, searching the small room before entering.

210

"Well, now we know why they didn't respond to radio calls," Martinez says grimly.

Electronic equipment lines a wall. Copper wires, stripped of their insulation, hang loosely from the radio, radar, and sonar equipment. Bare cables swing gracefully back and forth to the ship's movement.

Sitting on a chair and hunched over a desk is a man's body. On the desktop is a NAVTEX transmitter maritime radio, partially torn apart, wires shredded of insulation.

Ford approaches the body slowly, his helmet light cutting through the darkness reveals a gruesome scene. The man's arms and hands have been stripped of skin, muscle, and tendons, leaving only bare bones.

Martinez jabs the body with his gun barrel. Suddenly the lifeless body jerks and moves. A freakish moan comes from the man, who lifts his head, revealing pain-filled, bloodshot eyes fixated on nothingness. Martinez's scream pierces the air as he jumps back as if bitten by a rattlesnake. He instinctively raises his weapon and discharges a single round.

Startled by the sudden movement and loud retort of the gun in the small room, Ford quickly moves backward. He stares at Martinez, anger and confusion on his face. "What the fuck, man" he yells, his voice filled with a mixture of frustration and disbelief.

Despite being struck by the bullet in the shoulder, the man whispers a plea, "Help me . . . please, pl . . . please just kill me," he stutters in agony. "The pain . . . I can't stand the pain . . . please, kill me."

"Poor bastard," Martinez mutters, his voice filled with sympathy. "Hey man, I'm sorry for shooting you." He slowly backs away.

Ford braces himself, angling his helmet's video camera. "You catching this?" Ford says to the chief.

"Yeah," is the terse reply.

Suddenly the ship is struck broadside by a large wave. The ship lurches to the port side. Caught unexpectedly, both Martinez and Ford lose their balance and fall into each other, becoming entangled and falling on top of the partially decomposed radio-man. They scramble to regain their balance, but not before the radioman's groans increase, broken by his whimpering cry of "Kill me."

"Motherfucker! This is too much!" Martinez yells. "I'm getting out of here."

The radio helmet crackles, causing both men to jump. "Lieutenant, you and Martinez get your asses back on deck now. That's an order! I'm coming overhead to lift you off. Don't touch anything. When you get up in the air, kick your shoes off and get rid of your gloves and mask—anything that came in contact with anything, understand?"

Ford turns to Martinez. "We're out of here. Follow me."

Ford opens the hatch to the bridge wing, thinking they could avoid the gruesome interior of the ship to the pickup location at the stern. Ford grips the railing, looking toward the rear of the ship. The waves are violent, reaching the bridge level and beyond, and the wind is gusting and howling like a pack of wolves. Both men hesitate at the top of the ladder, recognizing their grim odds of getting to the stern of the ship from the outside creates a high risk of being swept overboard, almost certainly resulting in death.

"This won't work," says Ford into his radio. "We're going inside."

As they reenter the bridge through the hatch, the chief's voice crackles through the radio. "We're tracking wind gusts in excess of seventy. That makes this a category-one hurricane. Do not, repeat, do not go on the exterior. We'll figure out how to extract you once you reach the pick-up point."

Ford looks at Martinez, who is nodding his head in agreement. "We may get to spend the night on this boat," Ford remarks, a half-ass smile on his lips.

"No fucking way," retorts Martinez. "I'd rather take my chances in a cat one hurricane."

Walking back through the bridge, they skirt the captain's chair. Dropping one deck, they open a hatch onto the mess deck. Neither man says a word above the creaks and groans of the ship being twisted by the power of the waves and wind.

On the other side of the mess deck is a hatch. Ford, who is in the lead, opens it and shines his helmet light down a long passageway that disappears into the darkness. Snaking their way down the walkway, they use the bulkhead walls to keep their balance as the ship sways back and forth.

"What's that?" Martinez halts abruptly, pointing to what appears to be a body lying on the deck. Next to the body is a door marked "Sick Bay" stenciled in red lettering. As they approach the body, both men slide to the farthest side of the narrow deck, putting as much space between themselves and the body as possible.

The man's face is horrendously disfigured; his nose and lips are nearly gone.

As they edge past him, his eyes fly open. Groaning, he reaches out and grabs Ford's ankle. Tilting his head up, he says, "Get out. They'll come for you." His voice is nearly unrecognizable as human.

With a jerk of his foot, Ford backs up, then bends toward what's left of the man. "What happened here?" His voice trembles.

"Invisible. . . can't see them," the man whispers, then closes his eyes.

"Sir, we need to move." Martinez's voice is on the edge of hysteria. He reaches out to touch Ford's shoulder.

Ford is shaking from the encounter, and he needs no encouragement. They continue their journey through the dark, not knowing what will be around the next corner.

"I think I just peed my pants," Martinez says, embarrassed.

"Don't worry, I won't tell anyone," Ford says over the headset.

Reaching the pickup location, Ford opens the hatch, but the wind tears it out of his hand, slamming it against the bulkhead. "Chief, we're at the hatch by the drop site," he shouts into his helmet.

The chief's voice in our heads sounds steady, in control. "If any piece of clothing came in contact with—whatever it is, ditch it. In fact, from what I saw, get rid of all your uniforms, strip everything—skivvies, weapons, everything. Before you hook onto the cable, I want you both naked as newborn babies. Understood?"

"You want us to strip?" Martinez asks in disbelief.

"I don't want you bringing anything onboard except what your momma gave you when you were born."

***

Back onboard and wearing dry coveralls, Lieutenant Ford settles into the cockpit. Thanks to the crew's professionalism, he and Martinez have been hoisted up into the chopper, despite the wind, without incident and are now headed back toward Miami.

"So what was it like?" the chief asks, looking sideways at Ford.

"The captain is dead; his skin dissolved," Ford's voice quivers, recalling the sight. "The radioman was still alive, barely. He begged us to . . . kill him . . . it wasn't necessary. He didn't last long."

"It sounds like there was nothing you could do for him, and I'm not going to jeopardize the crew by bringing a body onboard with some infectious disease. We need a special hazmat team out here," the chief says grimly.

"Yeah, and to clean up Martinez's pee. I'd sure hate to have that job," chirps Sparks. The entire crew, including Martinez, breaks out in nervous laughter.

"Lieutenant," the radioman says over the headset, "Some lady on the phone from the EPA wants to talk to you. You can take it through your headset."

"Lieutenant?" the female voice on the phone asks. "This is Libby Burns with the EPA."

"Yes, ma'am. I remember you. We met at my father's funeral in New Mexico."

"I remember." There is an awkward pause. Then, "James, I saw your video. Did you see anything other than what was on that video? What about the crew?"

"Well, ma'am," says Ford in a slow, measured tone, "it was worse than I expected. The captain's body on the bridge looked like it had been shredded."

There is silence on the phone. "Did you touch anything while onboard the ship?"

"Tried not to after what we saw."

"If you see any rash on your skin, get to sickbay immediately. We'll get some decontamination people out to the ship. Please make out a full report as soon as you land in Miami. It is critical that you be as complete as possible."

"Yes, ma'am."

"Oh, and Lieutenant, there is one other thing. Have you heard from your brother, Jesse?"

"Ah, no, ma'am. Last I heard, he was in Africa—Nigeria, I believe."

There is a hesitation on the phone. "We're working with him and Americo Oil on the spill in Lagos. Unfortunately, Jesse is missing."

***

The President signed the Executive Order in the Rose Garden Wednesday morning. By three o'clock that afternoon, U.S. Strategic Petroleum Reserve oil flows into the nation's refineries. News pundits on the nightly talk shows agree it is a masterful stroke, virtually ensuring the President's re-election. By Thursday morning, customers are pumping gas refined from the petroleum reserves. By noon Thursday, gas at the pump has fallen a dollar per gallon, the first decrease in three months. Friday's poll numbers show a five-percent increase for the President, short-lived though it is.

CHAPTER 19
LIBBY

Libby Burns sits at her desk at the headquarters of the Environmental Protection Agency, within walking distance of the White House, resting her chin in her hands. Her heart sinks as she watches the video from the Coast Guard. The computer screen goes blank, but she continues to stare at it. A wave of nausea washes over her.

"Son of a bitch, SON OF A BITCH!" she exclaims with clenched fists to no one in particular but loud enough to be heard in nearby cubicles.

Fred Shard, the balding, overweight supervisor walking by her cubicle, hears the outburst and stops. "What's going on, Libby?"

"Sorry, sir, for that," Libby says, embarrassed now. "Remember you asked me to check with my contacts at Americo Oil about the oil spill in Nigeria? Unfortunately, they lost contact with one of their ships, the Desert Rose, after it dropped off a load at the Bayou Choctaw reserve site."

Shard, a lifelong bureaucrat, adjusts his glasses. "Yeah, I remember. What's the news?"

"So I called the Coast Guard and told them a ship might be in distress. They located the ship but were unable to communicate with it. They sent a helicopter out to investigate. I just heard back from them. It's not good."

"Who authorized the helicopter?" Shard asks, looking at Libby over the tops of his glasses.

"It was the Coast Guard's decision—well, I guess I encouraged them," Libby admits, "but you wanted me to check my contacts in Denver. The rescue copter was the Coast Guard's idea." She follows up with a summarized version of the Coast Guard report but fails to mention she first gave the Coast Guard Commander a thorough briefing on the *Denz* virus, with a final warning to the crew not to touch anything on the ship.

"I admire your initiative," Shard says, "but you clear everything with me next time. The last thing I need is a 'Lone Ranger.' So what's next?"

"I was going to call Americo and advise them of the situation."

"Wrong." Shard scoffs, shaking his head. "The next call is to the Director. He'll advise the President."

Libby balks. The Office of the Director of the EPA has a well-deserved reputation for leaking to the press. "I don't like blindsiding them like that. I used some sources deep inside the company. Those bridges will be burnt—forever if we call the Director before informing Americo of what we found on the ship."

Shard, the consummate politician, hesitates. He understands how essential sources are and is also well aware of the Director's reputation for leaking to the media. "All right. Call Americo and update them. I'll hold off on informing the Director until I get a full report from you, but I want it on my desk by the end of the day," he says over his shoulder as he walks off.

Libby breathes a sigh of relief. She picks up the phone, memory dialing the Americo office in Denver.

A female voice with a Southern accent answers the call.

"John Hammer, please. This is Libby Burns with the EPA calling."

There is a pause, then a faltering, "Mr. Hammer is unavailable. Would you care to leave a message?"

She must be new, thinks Libby. "Sure. Tell him the EPA is aware of the oil spill in Africa. We know about the micro virus, and I'm trying to warn him that the shit is about to hit the fan. It might be a good idea to make Mr. Hammer available."

Miss Southern accent hesitates, then says, "Could you hold a moment, please? Let me see if I can locate Mr. Hammer." Libby imagines the alarm bells going off behind the phone.

Thirty seconds later, a female voice abruptly answers the phone: "This is Kim Carson. Mr. Hammer is out. May I assist you?"

Libby is surprised to hear Kim's voice. They met years ago at one of the Americo Christmas parties, but most recently in New Mexico at the funeral for Jesse's father.

"Kim? This is Libby, Libby Burns. With the EPA."

Kim's voice is cool and indifferent. "Hello, Ms. Burns. Yes, I remember you. Is there something I can do for you?"

"Unfortunately, Ms. Carson, " Libby follows her lead, switching to a formal tone, "I'm calling about the spill in Nigeria . . . an unreported spill, I might add. I just received a report from the U.S. Coast Guard about your oil tanker, the Desert Rose, you know, the one that just dropped its load at Bayou Choctaw. Have you heard from that ship?"

"How do you know about this, Ms. Burns?"

Libby admires Kim based on the few times they met and what Jesse had mentioned about her, but something about Kim makes Libby feel uncomfortable. She fights the urge to disclose that the source of her information was Jesse himself.

"How I am aware of this is irrelevant. The fact is, the crew of the Desert Rose is dead—eaten by a flesh-eating bacteria or virus, or whatever it is. This ship was hauling oil for Americo from Lagos. And now, you should know that everything I've just told you is being reported to the Director of the EPA, who will report to the President and likely leak it to the press."

There is silence on the other end. Libby can almost feel the sweat through the phone.

"What I don't know," Libby continues after Kim fails to respond, "is if the oil on the Desert Rose was contaminated when it was dumped into the Strategic Petroleum Reserve because if it was Ms. Carson, we all have a problem."

"Ms. Burns," replies Kim, sticking with the formality, "you apparently know more than I do. You said the crew on the tanker—what was it, Desert Rose—is dead? How did they die, if I may ask?"

"I will soon have a hazmat team onboard the ship. They're bringing bodies back and will perform autopsies. Based on the Coast Guard report, the crew of the Desert Rose was attacked by something that devoured most of the flesh from their bodies.

Whatever it is, it has gone astray and mutated into something pretty nasty."

Kim's voice is flat. "I will have to check with our company officials in Lagos to see if we've ever used that specific ship. We use many tankers, and I'm afraid I don't memorize all their names."

Libby sighed. "Kim, I know you view me, at least professionally, as the enemy. I will do everything in my power to work with Americo to avert what could potentially be the biggest disaster this country has ever faced. Unfortunately, some here at the EPA would love nothing more than to damage the oil industry, and right now, their sights are set on Americo Oil. I assure you I do not fall into that camp."

"Thank you, Libby," Kim answers after some thought. "I appreciate that. As you probably know, Jesse is currently in Lagos dealing with this. We expect to get the situation resolved shortly."

"Kim, the President has signed an Executive Order releasing the oil in the reserves. It is flowing into the marketplace as we speak. Have you thought about what that means? Is Jesse the point man on this?" Libby asks. "I've tried to contact him, but he seems to have vanished. Have you heard from him?"

Kim's voice chokes for a second. "We've been trying to reach him also." Kim pauses to gain control of her emotions. "The last we heard, he was getting a sample of the antidote for the *Denz* virus. No one has heard from either him or Chip since then."

"Kim, please keep me advised. I will do the same if I hear anything on this end. No one will ever know we spoke about this."

CHAPTER 20
CHIP

Ade towers over the body of the white man lying in a pile of dirty blankets in the alley. The man's yellow hair is covered in dried blood, and Ade is unsure if the man is unconscious or dead.

His companion, Kuno, squats down to take a closer look at the man. He reaches out and touches the bloody forehead. It is warm. He's still alive. Kuno gently shakes him, but there is no response. A large contusion on the man's forehead is covered with blood.

He is clothed in black—a shirt and pants—with blood stains on his sleeves. The man is lean and muscular with tattooed arms. Around his chest is an empty shoulder holster. On his belt is a sheath with a knife holstered.

Kuno stands, looking at Ade. "Where's the gun?"

Ade hands a pistol to Kuno, who examines it and ejects the magazine. There is one bullet missing from the clip. "Help me take him to Bemdoo," he orders.

They help the man—who mumbles incoherently—to his feet. He sways and nearly falls. With one man on each side, they drape his arms across their shoulders, but after a few steps, the man stops and removes his arms from their shoulders. "I can walk," he whispers in English.

It is the early morning dawn of another busy day in the Lagos market area. Vendors are busy setting up their outdoor stalls with a colorful array of fresh produce, spices, handmade crafts, and souvenirs in preparation for the rush of locals and tourists that will soon flock to the marketplace. The aroma of cooking lamb fills the air.

Despite few people giving them a second glance, Kuno takes his baseball hat and pulls it on the head of the white man, telling him to keep his head down.

They make their way to a quiet corner of the marketplace where a woman with a weathered face is selling steaming cups of tea. Brushing aside a heavy blanket, they enter a covered enclosure behind a stall selling wooden knickknacks and tribal paintings. The woman watches with curious eyes as they lay the semi-conscious man on a makeshift bed, who immediately passes out.

Her long gray braids brush across his chest as she bends over him to examine his wound. It looks like he was hit with something blunt and hard. Her face, weathered by the sun, is covered with an elaborate pattern of scarification. She squints at him with bright dark eyes mixed with approval and pity.

His head wound is mixed with blood and dirt and smeared with sweat. She wipes his head, cleaning off the area, and presses a cloth against the injury to stop the bleeding.

"Sir, can you hear me?" she says in English, gently shaking his shoulder. The man groans, his eyes flutter, and he tries to sit up. "You safe," she says, pushing him back down.

His blue eyes are bewildered as he looks around the patchwork of blankets and cardboard walls.

"Where am I?" he whispers, staring at the woman. His voice is weak, and he speaks with difficulty. Swallowing, he rubs cracked lips with his tongue.

"Get some water," Bemdoo orders, turning to Kuno.

"We found you in an alley. You have a wound on your head," she tells him.

Touching his forehead, his eyes begin to focus. "I'm thirsty," he croaks in a raspy voice.

Kuno offers him a bottle of water. He struggles to lift his head, takes a small drink, then falls back on the pillow, closing his eyes.

"Who are you?" Bemdoo asks, running her eyes up and down the man lying in front of her. For a white man, she thinks him quite attractive. She reaches, running her fingers through his tangled yellow hair—so silky and soft. She squirms, becoming uncomfortable when he turns his intense blue eyes on her.

He gives a heavy sigh, relaxing on the blankets. "My name is Chip. I was at the warehouse by the pier, owned by CIVO, when I got jumped. I had a friend with me. Another white man. I need to find him."

The tall black man steps forward. "My name is Ade. I work at the warehouse as a janitor. This morning I saw a white man tied up in a back room. Does he have dark hair?"

Chip fights to sit up, all the while watching Ade. "How is he? Is he still alive?"

"He looked—unsteady—lost. There were many guards around him."

"Did you see DuVal or Lassiter?" Chip asked, leaning back on his elbows. "I need to get him out of there."

Bemdoo's eyes grow wide, staring at the rippling muscles in Chip's arms—arms as big as her thighs. The right arm had a tattoo of an eagle at the top, an anchor in the center with a pistol, and a trident tightly interwoven. She had seen the emblem on other Americans but did not know the meaning.

"I know DuVal. He was there," Ade continues, shaking his head. "I don't know this 'Lassiter,' but there was a man today I have never seen before, dressed in a white suit. He seemed to be boss—giving orders to DuVal. Two women with him—beautiful women. Not African. Arab, I think."

Chip falls back on the bed and drapes his forearm over his eyes, remaining silent.

Bemdoo goes into a small kitchen area. Despite her gray hair, she moves smoothly with a spring in her step. Returning, she hands Chip a stoneware cup filled with a steaming liquid.

"Here," she says. "Drink this. It will help your head."

Chip lifts his head off the bed, smells the cup, then hesitates. Bemdoo nods and smiles. "No worries. It is not poison. It will help your head," she assures him.

He cautiously takes a sip and makes a face. The liquid in the cup is bitter. Bemdoo nods. "Drink."

Chip holds his breath and drains the cup, then lies back on the bed and closes his eyes.

Kuno, mostly silent in the background, steps forward. "Excuse me, Mr. Chip. I know how we can get your friend back."

But Chip is already drifting off.

The potion Bemdoo gave Chip works its magic. Minutes later, he is in a deep sleep. "He will sleep all night; then we talk," she tells the two men as she dresses the head wound.

Kuno takes Ade aside. "I think those bastards are the ones that killed my supervisor, Washington, and my brother, Fanan," Kuno swore. "I want to make them pay. I want to clear my name. I think this man can help me. I have an idea."

***

Chip doesn't stir from his sleep until midmorning the following day. Rubbing his puffy eyes, he surveys the unfamiliar room, still disoriented. The events from the past days are foggy and distant.

The room is hot, and his clothes cling to his skin, damp with sweat. He rubs the tender bump on his forehead, waiting for the wave of dizziness to pass before getting up from the bed. I feel pretty damn good, but could eat a horse.

He turns when a woman calls his name. "Mr. Chip, how do you feel?" A contagious smile lights up the dark olive skin of her face. At first, he doesn't recognize her but recalls the braided hair and that god-awful drink. His eyes shift to the scarring on her face. She notices his stare and turns away in embarrassment.

"Stop," Chip says, reaching out to touch her arm. "It's okay."

She turns back to him, her eyes glinting with anger. "A gift from my tribe when I was a young girl."

Chip gives her a weak smile in return. "You helped me. That makes you beautiful, as far as I am concerned. I'm sorry, ma'am, but I forgot your name."

Bemdoo laughs, blushing. "I'm no 'ma'am.' My name is Bemdoo," she says, smiling. "You look much better than yesterday."

"How long did I sleep?"

"We found you passed out on the street yesterday morning, almost twenty-four hours ago. You had a bad bump on that head of yours. Kuno and Ade brought you here."

Chip rubs his forehead, recalling the explosion of pain. It still hurt, but the lump was smaller. "Thank you for taking care of me, Bemdoo."

Bemdoo turns a light shade of crimson and looks to the ground. "Oh, it be nothing."

"I need to go. Can you tell me how to get to the big hotel, the Continental Hotel?"

The eerie gentleness behind her dark eyes masks a cunning sharpness. "Before you go, we have come up with a plan to help you get your friend back. It is Kuno's idea, and he can tell you. It won't be long when he returns. Please wait. I fix some food for you."

Chip shrugs. Nothing to lose, and he is starving. Besides, at this point, he really doesn't have a strategy. He remembers one of the men saying he worked at the CIVO building. It might be smart to listen to what the man has to say.

The flap to the shanty opens, and Kuno walks in. After greetings, the two men sit cross-legged on the rug-covered floor. Bemdoo stands in the background, listening to the men talk, occasionally interjecting her thoughts.

"The other man with you, what was his name?" Chip asks.

"Ade. He works in the CIVO building. A janitor. He will be here soon."

"Can you or Ade get some guns and ammo, pistols or assault rifles, Russian AK?"

Kuno gives a quick smile. "Oh, yes. Ade was a soldier in the civil war. He was taken as a child from his village by the rebels. They train him to fight the government—for five years. He knows guns very well." Kuno is apologetic for his halting English. "I am not used to speaking your language—English. Ade speaks English, too."

Chip laughs. "Don't worry about it. You speak better English than a lot of Americans I know."

Ade walks through the door flap, looking haggard. "I just get off work and run all the way here." He went into the kitchen, filled an empty water bottle from a bucket, and drank long and deep.

Chip views Ade in a different light after hearing about his childhood. He is familiar with the brutal existence rebel child fighters were forced to endure in the so-called civil war with the government. He heard stories of the boys taken from their villages, some as young as eleven and twelve—usually after their families were brutally murdered.

"I have a plan to get your friend. I learn his name is Jesse Ford. He is a big shot for the American oil company. They are taking him to Paris tomorrow morning."

CHAPTER 21

JESSE

The harsh glare of the fluorescent light above me blinds me when I first open my eyes. What happened? My thoughts are fragmented into bits and pieces. I remember walking out the door of the warehouse with a canister under my arm when my head exploded.

The metal table I'm lying on is cold, and my head throbs with a killer headache. My mouth is parched, making it nearly impossible to swallow—the stench of sweat and urine clings to my clothes. A chilling dampness lingers in my crotch area. I must have peed my pants while unconscious.

Lifting myself on my elbows, I search for a wash basin and water faucet, but the room is too dark. I start to roll over on my side but am stopped by the straps around my hands and feet.

Shivering, I lie back on the cold metal table, waiting for the spinning to stop. I hear the creaking of a door open at the far wall. Turning my head, I see a figure silhouetted by a backlight. He steps into the room, followed by a second person. Their features are shadowed, and I don't recognize them. The squeaking of their shoes on the floor gets louder as they approach me.

"Greetings, Mr. Ford." The voice is familiar, but I can't place it. "I hope you had a nice rest." I lift my head and stare at the smirking face of Lassiter.

"I'm thirsty," I tell him in a raspy voice. "I need to use the bathroom."

Lassiter nods to his companion, and a plastic cup with water appears before me. I lift my head and drink the tepid water. "Thank you," I respond, lying back on the cold table.

"As for the bathroom, Mr. Ford, I see you have already done what you had to do." There is a mocking tone in his voice. "You will not be released."

"Why are you doing this?" I ask in a gravelly voice.

"Why, you ask? Because I haven't been paid, Mr. Ford and you are trying to steal from me, that's why. And not only are you trying to steal my money, but you are also trying to steal my virus. Is everyone in your company a thief?"

"I don't believe you. If you release the antidote, we will pay you."

Lassiter snickered, a smug look on his face. "Mr. Ford, you are either very naive or believe I am. I'm afraid your money is no longer relevant. It is not mere money I want. I have plenty of that. What is it you say in your country? 'It's not the money; it's the power?'"

"So what do you want?"

An arrogant look of contempt settles on Lassiter's face. "The answer to that question has many possibilities. I stand in the unique position of maybe a half dozen people in history. You see, Mr. Ford, I will reshape our world. Think of it: I control the very lifeblood of your existence. Who has ever had that power? No one! Do you think I would surrender that for mere money? Not likely. I think it's fair to say my price has increased to more than your company can pay."

"What are you trying to do? Destroy the United States? Think of the millions that will suffer and die if *Denz* is released. Do you want to go down in history as a depraved psychopath?" I try to appeal to his humanity but know it is futile.

"Ahh, Mr. Ford, I will go down in history as a savior. Millions are controlled by the arrogant rich. I will consider it an honor to destroy that source of evil in our world. History will portray me as a hero, an equalizer of the classes. I will be another Mohammed, another Jesus. I will save the world." As he speaks, his voice becomes louder.

I turn my head toward him. "You are a psychotic asshole." I wanted to say much more, but it would have been wasted breath.

Lassiter answers with a sneer, "You will never get out of here." He leans toward me and whispers in my ear, "You have become an expendable obstacle. You and your kind are about to be . . . readjusted to the new world." He starts to walk away, then stops and turns.

"I misspoke," he adds with a laugh. "You won't be around to see the new world." Then he glances at his companion, "You know what to do."

As Lassiter leaves the room, the other man moves into the dim light. It is DuVal.

"DuVal," I plead, "your boss is a madman. Help me get out of here."

DuVal walks over and looks down at me. "Save it, Ford. Most men of vision probably are mad, but you're not going anywhere."

"How long have I been here? What's going to happen to me?"

"Let's see. You have been our guest for about two days. Dr. Lassiter wanted to keep you . . . subdued while we took care of a few chores." DuVal walks over to where I am strapped down. "But now I will unstrap you so you don't piss your pants again. Dr. Lassiter plans to keep you contained for a while. After that," he shrugs, "who knows."

The door opens, followed by one of Lassiter's women proteges carrying a tray. Without a word, she sets the tray on the metal bench and removes my straps. She leaves the room without a word or so much as a glance at me. What a cold, mindless bitch.

"Now, why don't you just eat and get some rest? You're going to need it. Tomorrow, we go back to Paris," says DuVal as he closes and locks the door.

As the door locks, I slowly stand. My muscles are stiff and sore as I explore the room's exterior. A cot is in the corner with a blanket thrown haphazardly over it.

A wave of fear and confusion washes over me. I'm trapped. I collapse onto the cot, overwhelmed with despair. Dan Farmer is dead; Hector is injured and nearly died; Kim is injured and back in Colorado; last I saw of Chip, he was injured and may be dead now. And here I am, captured and facing death. Added to that is the fact I have failed to get the antidote. The weight of my predicament settles heavily over me.

Grabbing the blanket, I drape it over my shoulders, still chilled from the steel table. I make use of a rusty toilet and sink in the far corner. After cleaning myself as best I can, I walk to the door and inspect it. Solid metal. I pick at the food on the tray, which reminds me of nothing more than a cold tortilla.

Hopelessness settles over me like a dark cloud. There is nothing I can do but wait and bide my time. I lie back on the cot, staring at the ceiling, vowing to take my revenge on Lassiter—somehow. I wonder about Chip.

***

The sound of the door unlocking wakes me. A man slowly enters the room. He hesitates in the dim light, then softly calls out my name. "Ford?"

I stand but don't answer. There is a familiar silhouette of a second man behind him. My heart leaps at the sight of Chip, and I rush over to him.

He holds a finger to his lips. "Easy, boss. Damn, you smell like shit," he says in a typical Chip greeting.

I feel like giving him a big hug. "Oh, man, am I glad to see you."

"You okay?" A frown replaces his smile.

"Good enough to get the hell out of here," I say. "But first, we need to get the antidote."

"By the way," whispers Chip, "I met some new friends. This is Kuno," he says, nodding at the shorter of the two men, "and this is Ade."

I shake Kuno's hand and tilt my head to Ade. "Thank you," I say, knowing I would hear the whole story later. "Now, let's get out of here."

We step through the door into a dark hallway. The body of a guard is sprawled on the ground next to a wall.

We start toward the rear of the building where the antidote is stored. Hearing a noise, I turn. Out of the shadows, DuVal steps into view. Startled, I crouch down, ready to kill if need be, but Chip reaches out his hand to stop me.

"Wait," Chip says. "He's with Israeli Mossad."

Shocked, I stop in my tracks. "You're shitting me." I turn to Chip in disbelief, then to DuVal.

"I know, I know," DuVal says, holding up his hand with an amused look. "I know you think I'm an asshole, but I have been undercover for two years and had to maintain my character. We've had our eye on CIVO for some time. It's a long story, and I'll explain later. First, let's get the antidote." He puts his finger to his lips, motioning us to follow.

I hesitate only a second, relying on Chip's judgment. DuVal waves us against the wall. "They have security cameras in here," he whispers, pointing at a tiny camera near the ceiling.

We continue creeping down the hallway toward a door at the end of the hallway. I recognize the entrance to the room where the antidote is stored. Chip and his new friends wait out in the passageway keeping watch, while DuVal and I go inside the room. DuVal closes the door and turns on the light, dim though it is.

He walks straight over to the bin containing the antidote cylinders. A blanket is lying on a nearby chair. Grabbing the blanket, he removes one of the cylinders with a skull and crossbones label from the storage bin and loosely wraps the cylinder in the blanket, which he carries under his arm.

"Ford, your people need to understand he was never going to release the antidote to stop the virus. He only tested it in Lagos to see if it worked. But let your people know the antidote does not—I repeat, does not—stop *Denz*. They were not able to perfect it in their lab. Your people will have to tweak it."

He leans in closer to me. "Lassiter's plan all along was to contaminate your Strategic Petroleum Reserve. *Denz* was never designed to die. When your President released the oil from the reserves, that was just an unexpected bonus to speed up the process.

"Our people have been working on an antidote that will neutralize *Denz*, but so far, had no luck." DuVal continues. "We thought we had an antidote, but we were mistaken. The antidote side effects proved to be . . . well, let's just say the side effects were unpleasant. We are counting on you, Americans. We'll share our research with you, but," he stops and turns to me, "you are our last hope against this expanding chaos. I don't mean to sound dramatic, but civilization as we know it teeters on the brink."

His words stir a surreal terror from deep within me. Whether the antidote succeeds or fails, the world as we know it has already been irreversibly altered.

Before turning out the light, he pulls out a handgun. "Take this," he orders. "Do you know how to use this? It's a Glock Seventeen—a weapon you can trust."

I nod, ejecting the magazine to ensure it's fully loaded before shoving it into my belt.

"I can get you out of here, but once you're out, you're on your own," DuVal says. Shutting off the light, he opens the door back into the hallway. All is quiet. Chip is standing next to the door, waiting for us.

Kuno reaches out and touches DuVal's arm. "Do you know who killed my brother, Fanan?"

DuVal stops, turning to look at Kuno, and shakes his head. "I'm sorry about your brother. Lassiter brought in some of his thugs from Saudi, including the woman your supervisor, Washington, took up to the terminal that night. The plan was to kill Washington and let you escape, then blame you for the murder and the spill. You were to be picked up later and made to disappear, but you vanished. They went to your brother's home looking for you. I heard there was an argument with Fanan. I'm sorry."

Kuno hangs his head. "I will get even with them," he vows.

"Not that it will help, but the facts have been reported to the Nigerian police by my agency. They no longer blame you for Washington's murder, or the girl's, for that matter."

"They kill my brother because of me."

"I understand how you feel, Kuno. All I can say is, do what you need to do. These people are cold-blooded assassins, the worst kind," DuVal says with empathy, patting Kuno on the back. "I'm very sorry."

With grim determination in his eyes, Kuno shakes DuVal's hand.

"Take this," DuVal turns to Chip and hands him the antidote cylinder. "Be careful. I cannot get any more. I need to disappear now."

I shake his hand.

He smiles at me. "I owe you a punch from the hospital."

"After this is all over, we'll meet up, and I'll give you a free shot," I reply, shaking his hand. "Thanks, DuVal."

"Go through those doors," DuVal says, pointing to the rear entrance to the warehouse. "Watch out for the military types. There will be at least two guards outside the door. Lassiter has brought in some Arab special forces. Stay low and slow. The door is unlocked and will get you outside. After that, you're on your own."

DuVal stops and snaps his fingers. "Oh, and one more thing. Have you caught the weather report? A haboob, an African dust storm, is blowing in. It should help hide you after you are outside." DuVal says quickly. "Go . . . now!" With that, he disappears back down the hallway.

As they approach the exit, the blowing wind rattles the door, but there is no sign of any guards. The men, led by Chip, crouch low in the shadows. Chip opens the door a crack. Waves of dust blow across the floor. Two men wearing fatigues with face masks and goggles with their heads down stand outside the door.

Chip lifts his pistol. "Wish I had a silencer," he says, just before pulling off two quick shots. Both guards drop. In the howling wind, no noise can be heard.

CHAPTER 22
THE LAB

Dr. Adams takes a deep breath, allowing Hector to absorb the news. Despite his professional demeanor, he couldn't help but feel sympathy for his patient.

"There's no easy way to tell you this," the doctor says in a somber voice. He places the printout on his desk, clears his throat, and continues. "After reviewing your medical records from Lagos, the symptoms you complained of prompted me to do some blood work. I have the results and compared them to your last visit," he said, indicating the printout.

"When your arm was amputated, you were given a blood transfusion during your surgery. The blood you were given in Lagos wasn't properly screened or may not have even been screened at all. I'm seeing signs of the HIV virus in your blood now."

Hector sat dumbfounded, staring at his doctor. The silence is punctuated by the ticking of the office clock.

"I'm truly sorry, Hector. I'll double-check it, of course, with a second test, just to be absolutely sure," Dr. Adams continued. "After that, we'll begin antiretroviral therapy to suppress the virus. It's important to understand that this is a manageable condition."

Hector felt sick to his stomach. In the last few days since his return from Lagos, he and his wife had made love several times. Have I infected her?

"What about my wife?" he asks his doctor.

The doctor sighs. "HIV is primarily transmitted through sexual contact with an infected person. We better get Maria in here to test her."

Hector groans at the thought of telling his wife. They have kids and grandkids. Everyone will know. Everyone will blame him.

Guessing his thoughts, the doctor says, "Hector, this is not your fault. That surgery was required to save your life. You had no control over what happened. There are new drugs, even experimental drugs, we will try. Don't give up hope. We have patients living normal, healthy lives with HIV. Get Maria in here. I can help explain it to her."

***

Hector pulls his Land Rover off the single-lane dirt road, gazing with pleasure at the sprawling Americo Research Lab in the picturesque valley below him. Located seventy miles northeast of Denver, the lab is surrounded by wide-open rolling grasslands, broken up by an occasional cluster of scrub brush and hardy trees. To the west, the Rocky Mountains rise over the horizon, providing a stunning backdrop. The snow-capped peaks loom over the prairie, despite the 100-mile distance.

Three towering structures dominate the eighty-acre site, not so much tall as spread out, none more than two stories, but all connected by enclosed, heated walkways to protect against the brutal Colorado winters. The lab is bordered by a formidable ten-foot fence crowned with menacing coils of barbed wire. Vivid NO TRESPASS signs in bold, bright letters are posted every 100 feet, a clear warning to any would-be intruder. A mammoth concrete landing strip stretches across the property, long enough to accommodate a 747. Hector oversees the entire compound, only answerable to Jesse and Mr. Hammer.

Gazing upon the valley below, Hector's thoughts drift back to six years earlier. Then, he and Jesse stood before the Board of Directors, intending to persuade them to fund a modern, sophisticated research laboratory to explore and develop alternative energy sources.

With his practical imagination, Jesse had been the first to recognize that the existing lab had become antiquated and obsolete in the fast-moving world of quantum computers and artificial intelligence.

"I want the most advanced innovative equipment, and I want talented genius scientists to work here; I want people who are not afraid to think outside the box," Jesse declared. "Our primary objective will be the development of alternative energy. The days of fossil fuels are numbered. We are an energy company. Who better to develop a groundbreaking source of new energy?"

"How much?" Hammer had asked dryly when Jesse and Hector presented the idea to him.

"I estimate three billion," is Hector's quick reply.

"For starters . . .," chimed in Jesse. "That's only the initial cost, which includes the land, building, and equipment. After that, there will be ongoing expenses, salaries, maintenance, and especially the equipment."

Hammer looks at the two men. "I agree," he responded. "Now you have to convince the Board."

The presentation began with Jesse's build-up to Americo's Board of Directors of the need to research alternative energy. Next, he called Hector to the front of the room. Hector remembers it well.

"The concept is simple," Hector began. "Ever since the wheel was invented more than 5,000 years ago, people have been inventing new ways to travel faster from one point to another. The chariot, bicycle, automobile, airplane, and rocket have all been invented to decrease the time we spend getting to our desired destinations. Yet each of these forms of transportation shares the same two flaws: They require time and energy to cross a physical distance. We have a solution that eliminates both drawbacks." Hector paused for a moment of silence. The wide-eyed stares that met his gaze were filled with awe. He would never forget it. He glanced at Jesse, who nodded.

"Our preferred choice of energy in today's world is oil," he resumed. "However, the harsh reality is that oil demand is increasing faster than production. We have reached our peak. There are no more large oil fields to be found. Oh, it will take years to run out, but the day will come when we can no longer satisfy the world's thirst for oil."

He now had their full undivided attention. "When that day comes—in the not very distant future, Americo, and all the small independent oil companies, will become obsolete. Then, if we're lucky, we'll be bought out by one of the major oil companies for pennies on the dollar." The Board was now hanging on to his every word.

"We get it, Doctor. So what is it you propose?" Vernon Sheldon says with a tone of impatience. Hector had been warned about Sheldon. Unperturbed by Sheldon's interruption, Hector shifted his focus to Marci Stone. According to Jesse and Mr. Hammer, she would be the most receptive to the idea.

"What used to be science fiction is now science fact. Do you all remember a popular television show from the 1960s called Star Trek.?" There were nods around the room, and now they were curious. "There was a certain phrase," he continued, "the captain of the Enterprise starship used when being transported back to his vessel. Can anyone remember it?"

One of the women on the Board giggled. "Our whole family used to watch that show every week," she confessed. "He would say, 'Beam me up, Scotty.'"

"Teleportation!" Hector declares, sweeping his gaze across the room. "In essence, to transport a material object, its molecular structure is decomposed into atomic elements. Those elements are then transmitted through the cosmos while a replica materializes at the destination location. The process is instantaneous. In the 1960s, the concept was pure science fiction." Hector turned to stare at Marci Stone. "Teleportation is now science fact. We call it Quantum Teleportation."

There were lots of questions—good, intelligent questions. When they started asking about money, Jesse took the podium.

"We're sitting on nearly fifty billion in our reserve accounts. Roughly three billion would be needed to get the lab off the ground. As the facility expands, additional funds would be required. We will hire only the top tier, the best and brightest scientists, and pay them top dollar. We will have the most advanced, state-of-the-art equipment available."

"How long before this teleportation could be commercial and we start seeing a return on our investment?" Sheldon again.

Jesse directed his gaze towards Hector for the answer.

"It's hard to predict," Hector confessed. "There has been a lot of research on teleportation already. We will piggyback on what has already been done. We will recruit experienced scientists with hands-on experience. I would estimate five to ten years, perhaps sooner."

"Are there ways to speed up the process—throw more money into the project?" It was Marci Stone.

Suddenly the entire board seemed anxious to move forward on the Lab—as soon as possible.

A simple billion would have been more than enough to get started. But thanks to Jesse's persuasive skills, they initially authorized the requested three billion. The completed price tag was nearly seven billion. But money talks, and the lab was up and running in under three years. There is nothing like it in the country, maybe the world.

***

Hector's first day back at the lab is awkward for him and the staff. He notices the looks of sympathy mingled with pity and hears the hushed whispers. Hector finally calls the entire team together in the dining hall. Climbing on a table, he discards his jacket and lifts his right arm in the air for everyone to see.

"Take a good look," he says to the silent crowd. "I appreciate your sympathy, but it's time to put it aside. Get it out of your system. My arm below my elbow had to be amputated because it became infected with *Denz*. If it hadn't been, I would be dead now. I can live with this, and I expect you all to do the same."

There is an embarrassed silence until one person begins clapping. Gradually the applause spreads throughout the room. Several female members, overcome by the emotional scene, begin to weep.

"Now, while I have you all together, I'd like to brief you on this deadly infection. This virus, *Denz*, is a game-changer for the world as we know it. Imagine something that can dissolve anything with a petroleum base; rubber, plastic, asphalt, anything."

The room falls silent. "Ladies," Hector continues, his voice deadly serious, "the makeup you put on your face each morning, guess what? It has a petroleum base."

A wave of murmurs and gasps ripple through the room as the women exchange anxious looks.

But Hector isn't finished yet. "*Denz* will go after that and eat it. But it won't stop there. We all eat food sprayed with insecticides and fertilizers containing, in part, petroleum. We eat this food, and our bodies absorb it. So unless you stop eating, exposure cannot be avoided."

Fear and disbelief crossed the faces of those in the room.

Hector continues, "The largest organ in the body is our skin, which is impregnated with petroleum remnants."

People begin whispering, growing louder.

"I know you are afraid. I am, too. I have seen what this deadly virus can do, up close and personal," Hector says, holding up his handless arm. "I want you to be afraid. Our job will be to find an antidote, a counteragent, that will neutralize *Denz*. Hopefully, we will have an antidote sample soon, which should give us a jump-start. But *Denz* is already here, so we aren't even starting to play the game until halftime, and we're behind. We have a lot of catching up to do. However, we have the most advanced equipment and the brightest minds. It's up to us to defeat this scourge." Hector looks around the room at the twenty pairs of wide-open eyes staring back at him.

"Ladies and gentlemen, until we have the antidote, we will split into three eight-hour shifts, working twenty-four-seven. Those currently working on the teleporter will continue. Everyone else will focus on *Denz*." There are some murmurs throughout the room as people grapple with changed plans.

"If this arrangement is unacceptable to any of you, I suggest you go home. I know many of you use the helicopter service to commute back and forth to Denver. Unfortunately, that service will no longer be available due to fuel shortages. Those who live in Denver and commute need to rethink. What gas there is will soon be contaminated or requisitioned by the military. But if you stay, you're going to work. We have lots of room at the lab. Sleeping arrangements can be made for you if necessary."

"Are we good on food?" someone asks.

"We have plenty. If needed, we can buy food from the local farmers and ranchers," answers Hector.

"Now, whoever is leaving, please let me know now so we can make arrangements to delegate your responsibilities."

THE SPILL

The room falls into an uneasy silence. Everyone shares uncertain glances about who's leaving or staying. Hector holds his breath. He can ill afford to lose anyone. But, to his relief, no hands are raised.

"Good," he exhales. "Thank you all for your sacrifice. Now, let's get to work."

CHAPTER 23
CHAOS

Chris Gibson stretches, opens his eyes, and listens to the sweet sound of robins chirping outside his bedroom window. A growing smile crosses his face. He sighs in satisfaction. His first Saturday in retirement. Every day will be Saturday now. He will finally be able to appreciate the endless summer of California. Life is good.

After thirty-five years as a claim adjuster for a national insurance company, he has paid his dues. His retirement income easily provides financial security to him and Glenda for the golden years.

They both still have their health and are looking forward to the two-week European river cruise next week. Then, when they return, they will hit the road in their newly purchased Class A motor home, spending winters in Florida, or maybe even Mexico, and then summers back in Ohio with the kids and grandchildren. He smiles, a satisfied look on his face as he crawls out of bed, smelling the aroma of the breakfast Glenda is fixing.

His biggest chore today is mowing the lawn on his new riding lawnmower, which is more fun than work. After breakfast, he tosses a couple of empty gas cans in the back of his pickup and heads to a nearby self-serve gas station. He spills a few drops as he tops off the gas cans at the pump. In the convenience store parking lot, he sees a woman sobbing, holding her hand while a group of people stands near her. But the gas cans are full, so he lifts them into the back of the truck and heads for home.

He fills the lawnmower with gas on the driveway and starts the engine. After putting on her makeup, Glenda enters the garage and moves the gas cans back into the garage, wiping her hands on her shorts to get the spilled gas off. She returns to the kitchen to clean up after breakfast and notices her hand beginning to itch. She sneezes and rubs her nose and right eye.

A red rash appears on her hand. The itch, irritating at first, becomes more noticeable. Her eye and nose also begin to itch. She is rubbing her eye when Chris rushes into the house, shaking his hand.

"Hon," he says tersely, do we still have that lotion for bites? I think a bug bit me. My hand itches like hell and is starting to swell up." He holds his hand up for her to see. "Damn," he says, "are you okay? The skin around your eyes is really swollen."

"Look at my hand," she says. "I must have got bit by the same thing you did." She's bending over the sink, holding her hand under the running water, then splashing water into her eyes.

"Shit," Chris curses, something he rarely does. "This is all we need—the first day of retirement, and we catch some weird-ass jungle rash. I'm going to put the lawnmower back in the garage. Get in the truck, and we'll head to urgent care. They can give us some ointment."

Glenda gets into the pickup while Chris jumps back on the lawnmower to drive it into the garage, not noticing the gasoline smell or the puddle under it. He turns the starter switch. There is a flash, and the lawnmower is swallowed up in flames. Chris screams in surprise and horror.

His legs are quickly engulfed in flames, and he lets out a blood-curdling scream. Startled by the scream, Glenda spins around to see her husband writhing in agony, trying to put out the fire consuming his lower body. Leaping out of the truck, she sprints toward her burning spouse.

"Chris! Oh my God, Chris!" she cries out as she approaches him. He is still on the lawnmower, slapping at the flames while struggling to climb off.

Leaping off the lawnmower, he starts running but stumbles and falls face down on the grass.

In a state of panic, Glenda searches for the water hose. Chris's agonizing shrieks have gone silent by the time she squirts water on him. The hissing sound of water mixing with the crackling of flames fills the air. The nauseating sweet smell coming from the smoke makes her gag.

Fearful neighbors are standing around the still-burning lawnmower, watching the withering body of Chris when the ambulance arrives seventeen minutes later. The concerned neighbors do their best to comfort Glenda but are unsure why she persists in clawing at her bleeding eyes.

***

Lisa Kelly is a very contented woman. Her beauty turns heads as she walks through the Louis Armstrong New Orleans International Airport. Boarding the Sunday Boeing 737 flight to Los Angeles, she takes her assigned seat in the first-class section.

There have been reports of numerous flight delays from other flights. She is thankful her flight was not one of them.

Finally, her big break. After years of persistent efforts to impress Hollywood producers and directors, rejecting offers of pornographic movies and escort services, and working as a waitress, she has finally landed a leading role in a major motion picture. Despite the promises and lies that come with the industry, she has managed to keep her morals—mostly—and will now reap the rewards for her hard work, night classes, and private tutoring.

As she boards the plane, a friendly flight attendant offers her a drink. Lisa smiles and requests a glass of red as she settles into her seat with a sense of satisfaction.

They are over Texas when the peaceful hum of the jet's engines is interrupted by a skip and shudder, coupled with a quick drop in altitude. The sudden drop causes Lisa's second glass of wine to spill on her dress. Shit, now I'll have to change clothes at the airport before the limo picks me up.

The plane levels off as the captain fights to stabilize the aircraft.

"Ladies and gentlemen," says the strained voice of the captain, trying to reassure the passengers, "please take your seats and make sure your seat belts are securely fastened. We seem to be experiencing a little problem, but no need to worry . . . "

The captain's voice is interrupted by a thunderous explosion, jolting the entire aircraft. The jet lurches to the right as if possessed by an evil force. The once stable plane careens into a stomach-churning dive, hurling unbelted passengers into the plane's ceiling.

Oxygen masks drop from overhead compartments, swaying in front of Lisa. As she reaches out, her attention is drawn to an explosion as the engine nearest her bursts into flames. She is still struggling to put on her oxygen mask when the jet hits the ground at over 500 mph.

***

It's a typical manic Monday morning for Anna Kabobel and her three children. There is the usual mad rush to get the kids up, fed, and ready for school. It always seems worse on Monday.

"Louis!" she yells into the kitchen. "Don't forget your lunch box." Louis Kabobel, a fourth grader, will only eat a cold lunch, refusing to eat the hot lunch provided by the school.

Her fifth grader, Brittany, prefers hot lunches over her mother's peanut butter and banana lunches. Brittany's twin, Jason, buys lunch from the school vending machines.

After a frenzy of last-minute activity, Anna herds the children out the door and into the family minivan. There is a sense of familiarity in the morning routine, even if it is chaotic.

"Seat belts?" she yells, putting the van into gear. The children already have them on. She taught them well, especially after her husband died in a senseless car crash. She sits back, lights her third cigarette of the day, and waits for the expected flood of criticism.

"That stinks," Brittany tells her mom.

"Roll down your window," complains Jason. "If you want to kill yourself smoking, Mom, at least don't kill us, too."

Anna tunes it out, having to hear it every day since her husband's funeral. She cracks the window halfway, holding the cigarette near the window, letting the smoke get sucked out.

THE SPILL

She turns right onto Wilshire Avenue to skip the early morning St. Louis traffic. This morning, she is grateful all the children can attend the same school. This would be the last year. She dreads next year when her two oldest will attend middle school, doubling the commute time.

She glances at her clock. Damn, she thinks, three minutes behind schedule. The kids will get another tardy slip unless she hits all green lights. She takes another drag off the cigarette and steps on the gas pedal harder, hoping to make up the time.

The final light is still green as she approaches. Gripping the steering wheel, she steps harder on the gas, wanting to turn right before the light changes. Just then, a large gasoline tanker truck and trailer pull into the right turn lane blocking her from turning right. She curses the driver under her breath. Of all the red lights to hit, this one is the longest. The long tanker truck extends well past her, half in the middle lane and half in the right turn lane. She takes another pull on the cigarette and curses out loud as the ashes drop on her skirt.

"Mom," says Louis, her youngest, "Mrs. Gilmore says cigarettes are a drug, and you shouldn't smoke."

Anna bites her lip, overcoming the urge to remark about Mrs. Gilmore's family tree.

"Yes, honey. Mrs. Gilmore is right. Smoking is bad." Anna rolls down her window all the way. She will have another after she drops the kids off. But cigarettes were so damn expensive only to smoke half. She takes another drag.

She can hear the music blaring on the gas truck's radio. She casts a sidelong glance at the overweight driver, his baseball cap sitting askew and backward. As she tosses the cigarette out the window, she catches a pungent smell of gasoline. Her gaze follows the cigarette as it lands in a small puddle of liquid dripping from underneath the truck.

Time seems to slow down as she watches in horror as the puddle erupts in a sudden burst of flame. Her final thought before the explosion is of her children. They were right: smoking is bad. A large wall of flame rolls toward the van, engulfing and vaporizing it, along with every car within a hundred feet of the tanker.

CHAPTER 24
ANARCHY

Without warning, an invisible force of annihilation descends upon America. The country is brought to its knees, unleashing fear, destruction, and despair.

Electromagnetic generators powered by turbines that run on diesel fuel—diesel fuel that is becoming more scarce with each passing day—produce most of the nation's electricity. Within three days, the west coast goes dark, quickly followed by sporadic power outages on the east coast. Millions are left without power.

Most major cities, especially those on the coasts, are shrouded in darkness at night. Transportation of all kinds grinds to a halt. Emergency services such as police, fire, and medical providers, at least those reporting to work, are inundated and overwhelmed. The fabric of society begins to unravel, and fear of your neighbor, fear of the government, and the uncertainty of the future spread through every aspect of life.

For some, *Denz* takes on an almost mystic meaning. It is a punishment sent by God, claim some, while others claim *Denz* is one of the seven signs in the Book of Revelation to signify the end times.

Mass transportation comes to a sudden halt. Within a day, most food shelves are empty. The military seems paralyzed, unable ~~able~~ to act. Without power, the internet is down, intermittent at best in some areas. Businesses close their doors, Hollywood studios stop filming, restaurants lay off employees, and traffic jams on typically congested freeways evaporate. During the hours of darkness, people avoid going out—nightlife comes to a standstill. Panic spreads as the lights go out.

MSNBC is the first network to link the contaminated fuel to Americo Oil and a spill in Africa. Americo becomes the focus of blame and hatred. Doing their best to contribute to the overall sense of panic, the news media reports that wealthy areas of the country are not being blacked out, compared to the impoverished regions and large cities where blackouts are common.

Without fuel, the nation's transportation system shuts down, unable to deliver food. America is fast becoming a nation of waiting lines. The military establishes gas stations selling uncontaminated gas to the public in small, rationed amounts. Within days, the nation's supermarkets begin to restrict food purchases. Liquor stores continue to do brisk business when they have their product. Bicycle manufacturers, sensing an opportunity, quickly develop a tire made of synthetic leather when it is discovered *Denz* does not attack leather in any form. Bicycles have suddenly become fashionable and expensive. Concrete roads remain unaffected, but asphalt roads become unusable.

An emergency order from Homeland Security is issued to the news media warning that the sale of all products with a petroleum base, including women's makeup, are banned until further notice. A doctor from the Center For Disease Control used the unfortunate term "zombie effect," setting off an immediate panic among the public—resulting in thousands of reports of rashes, skin disorders, and zombie attacks that overwhelm healthcare facilities.

In a misguided effort to clarify and calm nerves, the Surgeon General issued a special report explaining that the virus known as *Denz* can break down and feed on the skin tissue of its host. The attempted explanation only increased the sense of panic. The media did not help when they labeled *Denz* as the "flesh-eating bacteria."

Riots and violence erupt in the larger cities. The National Guard and Army are mobilized and put on high alert. The most violent cities are put under martial law. No one escapes the impact. Travel stops, and the nation's economy comes to a screeching halt. Chaos spreads throughout the country.

***

The President of the United States, Ronald Coleman, sticks the unlit cigar in his mouth and chews on it, as usual. "Tell me what you know about this Lassiter character," he barks to his chief of staff.

Wallace Smith, the White House Chief of Staff, hates tobacco. After many heated arguments, he and the President reached a truce in the early days of their relationship: The President agreed not to light the chewed-up cheroot in the presence of Smith.

"NSA doesn't have much on Aran Lassiter," says Smith. "He's got a Ph.D. in genetic design and lives and works in Paris, where his company, CIVO, is headquartered. I have no idea what it stands for. They do genetic design work on viruses and microorganisms. Because of the sensitive nature of their work,

French intelligence has been keeping an eye on him."

"Do they think this CIVO is responsible for all this bull-shit?" asks the President.

"One of Lassiter's professors in college did some work on the Exxon Valdez spill in Alaska using genetically designed bacteria to remediate the spill. The French had some of their people reach out to the professor. Unfortunately, he committed suicide about ten years ago, in his office of all places."

"Was Lassiter a student when this professor committed suicide?"

Smith shrugged. "Unknown. Lassiter contacted Americo shortly after the Nigerian spill claiming they had genetically designed a virus to clean it up."

"Unusually good timing," replied the President. "From what I hear, the virus should have checked out after a few days, but something went wrong. Who runs Americo?" asks the President, chomping hard on his cigar.

"A guy named John Hammer is the president. Senator Ben Thompson was his partner at one time."

"Thompson is from Colorado, the same place Americo is headquartered. I remember meeting him. Kind of quiet and laid back. I liked the man. Maybe we should get in touch with the senator and have him come in and visit?" suggests the President.

"You've got an hour this afternoon."

"Make it happen, Wally. I'll meet him in the Oval Office. I want the CIA and the Joint Chief of Staff Chairman present."

"Yes, sir, Mr. President."

***

A look of amused contempt lingers on the face of Saad Kalb,

Aran Lassiter's uncle. Saad sits fixated in front of the TV, watching a smug Al Jazeera reporter opine to his mostly Arabic audience about a deadly flesh-eating micro virus infecting the oil supply of the United States. The picture in the background shows a burning tanker truck to dramatize the story. Finally, Kalb turns off the TV and hits a numbered button on his phone.

"Aran," Kalb speaks in the Najdi Arabic dialect of Saudi Arabia, "assure me once again there is no way *Denz* can spread to the Kingdom." He watches the palm trees on the horizon sway to the tune of the hot desert wind.

"Uncle," Dr. Aran Lassiter answers, "that will only happen if the virus is introduced into the Saudi oil fields, just like what we did to the American Strategic Petroleum Reserve. Even if that were to happen, we have the antidote."

Lassiter has learned that short, simple answers are best for skeptical Arabs like his uncle. Without Kalb's financial backing and connections into the underground of Saudi society, CIVO would not exist, which means his creation, *Denz*, would not exist. But his uncle's need for constant reassurance and paranoia grows tiresome.

"Just in case, how is your supply of the antidote?" Kalb asks with a nervous twitch in his voice.

Lassiter sighs. "For the third time, Uncle, we have plenty, most here in Paris." But it doesn't work on *Denz*.

"My people are watching the news reports out of America and are concerned it might spread. I see there are reports of *Denz* now in Europe. Do the Americans know about your antidote?"

A bolt of fear flashes through Lassiter. "They are asking

questions, but they have nothing. I am avoiding them." Does he know the American escaped? No matter; the antidote they stole doesn't work, anyway.

"We cannot let them get the antidote. Is it well protected?"

"Very well protected," Lassiter assures his uncle. "Thanks to the well-trained security force you have sent me," he adds as an afterthought.

"Good. My warriors are experienced in fighting the Americans and Russians in Iraq and Afghanistan. I have a feeling they may be very useful soon. I nearly forgot to mention. I am sending an additional hundred men to your Paris compound."

Lassiter wants to ask if his fighters are so experienced, why were four of them overcome and killed by two civilians in Lagos, but he stays silent.

"They will be welcomed. Don't worry, Uncle, we are ready," Lassiter snaps, disconnecting the phone. A hundred extra soldiers, in addition to the fifty he already has, might be wise. One never knows what the crazy Americans may try.

Lassiter's next call is to his lab supervisor. "Jahmal, what is the status of the antidote? Did you find the problem?"

The voice on the phone has a whiny tone. "I am sorry, sir. We have tested a new batch of the antidote, but the micro virus refuses to die. I have the entire staff working on it."

"You must come up with an antidote . . . if you want to see your family again," he adds. "I will not accept failure."

"We will, sir. Everyone is working on it."

Satisfied that he had put fear into the man, Lassiter disconnects. What if we cannot make the antidote and *Denz* contaminates the Saudi oil fields? He put the thought out of his mind, an idea too horrible to contemplate. Everything depends on the antidote. It needs to happen before *Denz* gets to the Saudi oil fields.

He picks up the phone again, tapping the speed dial.

"Faisal," he says to his head of security, "is all good?" He nods his head, pleased with the answer. "Be prepared!" he orders. "The Americans may be coming."

He shuts off his phone and turns back to the TV. The destruction of America leaves him with a supreme sense of satisfaction. Even the mightiest armies could not have inflicted such a devastating blow to America. In a matter of days, the entire economic infrastructure of the world's only superpower has been crushed. Without their oil, America will be brought to its knees. He sits back with a satisfied smile. No matter what happens, he has assured himself a place in history.

***

Senator Ben Thompson stares at the new rug in the oval office of the West Wing of the White House. On the rug's border are quotes from famous Americans, circling the presidential seal displaying the bald eagle. In the left claw are arrows, and in the right claw, an olive branch. He wonders what it will be today: war or peace. He has a feeling it will not be the latter.

Unlike Chief of Staff Smith, the smell of a cigar does not bother Thompson. He has known of the President since they were both junior senators but never cared for him then, and his opinion hasn't changed over the years. Also in the room, looking uncomfortable and pulling on his tie, is Richard Monsanto,

Director of the CIA. Sitting next to Monsanto is Army General John Sparkman, Chairman of the Joint Chiefs of Staff.

Thompson has never met the general but is aware of his no-nonsense reputation. He hears through the Washington grapevine that the general's troops would take a bullet for him. He is tall and straight, with a firm military look. His face is tan and weathered, with creases, like most of his life has been spent outdoors in the sun and wind.

"Thanks for coming, gentlemen," the President begins. "We have a crisis that needs to be dealt with. Senator Thompson, I understand you know John Hammer, President of Americo Oil, where all this *Denz* bullshit started. Can you tell us about him?" The President sticks his still-unlit cigar in his mouth and stares at Thompson.

Ben crosses his legs and sits back on the couch. "I spoke with Mr. Hammer and was told Dr. Aron Lassiter came highly recommended based on his college work with the Exxon Valdez spill in Alaska. Americo hired him to help clean up the spill in Nigeria."

"I know all that," the President said impatiently.

"According to Hammer, there were side effects of the micro virus Lassiter failed to disclose. It could have been intentional or a design defect, and the deal went south. *Denz* mutated from what was originally claimed into what we are now seeing. Some of CIVO's staff claim the mutation was due to the hot weather in Lagos. It should be noted that the temperature in Lagos when *Denz* was being applied was well over a hundred degrees."

"A hundred fourteen, to be exact," Smith said.

"Whatever the reason," Thompson continued, "the virus has mutated, is not dying, and doubles in size about every six hours. Lassiter has an antidote that will kill it but won't release it. Based on what we're seeing, I would suggest his plan from day one was to cripple the economy of the U.S."

"Well, he sure as hell is succeeding," said General Sparkman, jumping into the conversation. "Mr. President, I say we send in an assault force, get the antidote, and destroy CIVO."

In exasperation, the President tosses the briefing paper he has been holding on his desk. "If he's got the antidote to neutralize the damn micro virus, why don't we just pay him?" asks the President angrily.

"The price is high," answers Monsanto. "He wants ten billion—"

"So what. Hell, that's pocket change," the President interrupts.

"—and," continues Monsanto, "a fully equipped Nimitz class nuclear-powered aircraft carrier."

There was silence in the room. "You mean fully equipped— planes, weapons, men?" asks the astonished General.

"Fully equipped—without the men. Only then will he release the antidote."

The President sits in the overstuffed leather chair, chomping hard on his cigar. "You think he's got the balls to back up his threat?"

The General gives a dry, sarcastic laugh. "Look outside, Mr. President! This little bug eats gasoline, plastics, rubber, and asphalt on the superhighways. As a result, our transportation system has come to a halt—people are dying—being eaten alive. The guy has already caused more financial damage to this country than the Great Depression and COVID combined. Do I think he's got the balls? Oh, hell yes!"

The President stands and turns to gaze out the window behind his desk. "Are we too late?"

Ben Thompson watches the President. "Sir, I don't think our country will ever be the same, no matter what happens. Without our cars, trucks, buses, planes, and fast food, this isn't the America I grew up in."

The General stands. His face is red. "Let's face it, Mr. President," he snarls, "that little French son of a bitch has taken our energy and broken our toys. When people discover who turned out the lights, they'll be pissed and want revenge."

The President is chomping hard on his cigar. "All right, let's consider the military options."

The CIA Director crosses and then uncrosses his legs, leaning forward. "His compound in Paris employs some stealth technology. Our satellites can't penetrate it. However, we do know he has a security force on the site. On top of that, the French, in their bizarre French way, are proud of this guy. They get a perverse pleasure seeing America brought to her knees. They've always claimed we were too arrogant and wasteful of energy and blamed their high oil prices on us."

"So they won't cooperate? Maybe we should remind them of World War II," says the General.

"I think it is safe to say the French would consider it an act of war if we attacked Lassiter's compound in France," declares the CIA Director. "It's not far from Paris."

With a sigh of resignation, the President capitulates. "Call Treasury," growls the leader of the free world. "Get the ten billion. Don't we have an old carrier in mothballs?"

"The John F. Kennedy is, but it's been decommissioned."

"Call the Joint Chiefs. See what they think," the President looked at General Sparkman. Sparkman started to answer but was interrupted by Senator Thompson. "What about a black op going in to take him out?" Thompson suggested. "It has always been our policy never to negotiate with terrorists."

The President pulls the cigar out of his mouth. "Do we have a Special Ops Team we could get in there? I would love to take that fucker out. But it would have to be a for-sure operation. If it doesn't work, my. . . er, our asses are toast."

"Mr. President," says Wallace Smith, "with all due respect, if you don't do something drastic, your ass is toast, anyway. Unfortunately, I don't see that you have a choice. The American people are pissed. They won't accept anything less than wiping CIVO off the map by whatever means necessary."

The President sits back in his leather chair and rubs his forehead. "Have the Joint Chiefs work me up a plan. I want it on my desk by tomorrow morning."

"One final thing, Mr. President," says the CIA Director, "the Israeli Mossad is telling us this guy is half Saudi Arabian. His mother has blood relations in the royal family."

"Oh, that's just great. So are you telling me we'll have a holy war on our hands if we take this guy out?"

"I don't think we can discount the possibility."

"How deep can the Israelis be involved?" General Sparkman asks.

"The last thing they want is to see the Saudis have that kind of leverage over us. They'll do whatever is necessary," answers the CIA Director.

"I want them on board with us on this operation. We can use their intelligence if nothing else," says the President.

The cigar is back in his mouth. Nervously he takes it out, puts it in a nearby ashtray, then picks it up and lights it. The President glares at his chief of staff. "All right, gentlemen, let's make this happen. Keep me advised."

Senator Thompson rises to leave. "There is a piece of good news. Our petroleum geologists say oil still in the ground is uncontaminated, but the oil companies refuse to pump their wells until the virus has been brought under control. The problem is that the Henshaw Bill prohibits drilling on Federal lands. We're going to need that oil."

"This is a national emergency," says the President, turning to Thompson. "Ben, since your home district is an oil-producing state, and with your connections to Americo, I want you to spearhead the repeal of that Henshaw piece of crap. Call Wally if you need any assistance from the White House.

CHAPTER 25
LIGHTS OUT

I put the phone down while gazing out the Gulfstream window at the awe-inspiring sunset. As the plane drops into Denver, there is a brief glimpse of the spectacular display of the final gold and orange rays as the sun sinks below the mountain peaks. The western horizon is illuminated in a breathtaking range of radiant colors. I find myself in the perfect position at the ideal moment to witness this rare view.

"Are you still there?" Kim asks.

"Just soaking in the view," I answer. Kim and I have been on the phone for the past thirty minutes while I brief her on my encounter with Lassiter at the CIVO warehouse in Lagos.

"Is Chip doing okay?"

"If it weren't for him, I wouldn't be here. He'll be coming home in a few days. A Nigerian named Kuno saved his butt. Chip wants to bring him back. Says he can find a place in security for him."

"Kuno. That name sounds familiar," she says.

"Remember the man in the terminal control room who disappeared? The facts of what happened that night are much different than what we first thought. The people who caused the spill killed the control room supervisor, then tried to kill Kuno, but he escaped. The bad guys went to his house looking for him and killed his brother," I summarized. "Chip can give you all the details when he gets here."

"With the way things are falling apart here, we can use all the security we can get," says Kim. "It's getting worse every day. The media is doing its best to blame Americo for everything. There are daily protests in front of the office building. In fact, there's a protest going on right now."

"Oh, good," I say sarcastically. "We're getting ready to land. See you in about an hour."

"Just be safe," Kim pleads. Her voice is trembling. "There's a lot of anger on the street against Americo. People are pissed, and thanks to the media, Americo has become the target. The country is shutting down. I never dreamed it could spiral out of control so fast." Her anxiety seeps through the connection like an intense physical force. When Kim gets this worried, I get worried, although I have never seen her like this.

"I know, Kim . . . I know," I reassure her, my voice barely a whisper with our shared concerns. "We'll figure it out. We have to." With her level head and balanced judgment, Kim has always been steady in a crisis. I need her help more than ever in dealing with these uncharted waters.

"John's on his way to collect you. I'm sure he'll give you all the gory details. But you and I know if anyone can get us through this bullshit, it's him. Make sure you guys come in through the underground garage. It looks like something is starting in front of the building. People are starting to gather."

"Have you spoken with Hector?" I ask.

"Every day," she replies, her voice composed now. "He's back at the lab, waiting for you to get him the antidote."

"That's good to hear. How's he feeling?"

"Well, he's working his butt off on the teleporter, if that's any indication."

"As soon as I check in at the office, I'm headed out to the lab," I declare.

"You'll need to drive," she suggests. "The helicopter's out of commission because of the fuel situation. Hector's excited to show you what he's done. I guess he's making real progress on the teleporter. I want to go with you. I'm excited to see it. Stay safe."

As the landing gear drops, I gaze into the gathering blackness. I find it hard to believe a vast metropolis hides in the growing shadows below me. A light fog forming on the ground gives the surroundings a threatening appearance. Very few lights can be seen, and Interstate 25, usually congested at this time of the day, is eerily vacant of traffic. The heart of the city, usually bursting with vibrant lights dancing across the glass and steel skyscrapers, is now just a shadow. The towering giants are silhouetted against the backdrop of the blush of a sunset retreating behind the distant western mountains. I am not prepared for the emptiness. A shiver runs down my back as my eyes behold the void I see.

As the plane comes to a halt, I zip up my coat and step through the hatch into the crisp cold air, so different from the hot, humid climate I was in only hours before. John is waiting at the bottom of the stairway, looking up at me. I carry the answer to eradicating *Denz* in a sealed box clutched under my arm. At the bottom of the stairway, we give each other a quick hug. John doesn't meet my eyes. This is the guy who fired me less than a week ago.

"I heard you might need a ride," he jokes, pushing me back and looking me up and down. "You look no worse for wear." He has a sheepish grin on his face. "Did you bring us a little souvenir?" He points at the box I clutch under my arm.

"Yeah, a little gift from Lassiter," I reply with a smile, which fades from my lips as I glance at the box. This 'gift' could be the turning point.

John's eyes turn hard in understanding. He nods, pulling his keys from his pocket. "Well then, let's not keep Hector waiting."

Outside the deserted terminal, I put the antidote sample in the rear hatch of Hammer's Range Rover SUV, now equipped with special tires to drive on the contaminated roads.

"How're you feeling?" I ask John. Better to get the elephant in the room out of the way.

"I'm good," he answers with no elaboration.

"Sorry for the rough ride," he explains. "The tires on this baby are made without any petroleum, but they'll get us there. We're headed back to the office. From there, I'd love to say we take the chopper to the lab, but the mechanics tell me they need more time to rework it, so we're driving. It'll give us time to talk. I want you to get me up to speed on Lagos, and I have a few things to discuss with you."

"Kim wants to go, also."

He nods but does not reply.

I give him the condensed version of the warehouse expedition.

He remains silent, not interrupting. "How's Chip?" he asks when I finish.

"He's lying low for a few days. We met an interesting group, and he's staying with them to keep an eye on CIVO." I tell Hammer about Kuno and what transpired on the night of the spill. "We need to get the jet back to pick Chip up. I need him here."

Hammer turns to look at me. "Jesse, the Board wants you back."

I had to laugh. "Why now?"

Hammer shrugs. "Well, you're a hero for bringing back an antidote sample. The Board realizes you're an asset we can ill afford to lose, especially now." Hammer gives me a sideways glance. "I need you, and Americo needs you to survive. The world is changing. There's no going back to how it was."

I shake my head. Being called a hero feels odd, especially since the Board effectively terminated me. "Sorry, John. All this has given me a different outlook. I'm considering leaving the oil business, moving back to D.C., maybe practicing law."

A look of frustration crosses his face. "Jesse, the oil business is in your blood. Working in a law firm—in D.C.? Hell, you wouldn't even last a month. The world is different, no matter how this turns out. We're on the cutting edge of change here, and you know it."

I sit in silence. He makes a good point. After this, working for a law firm would be . . . boring.

Hammer squints at the empty road. "I can get you a seat on the Board."

"Let's face it, John, I'm largely responsible for all this. So no matter what happens in the future, I will always be associated with *Denz*, the deaths, and the changes."

"Oh, come on, Jesse, that's bullshit, and you know it. If anyone's to blame, it's me. You wouldn't believe all the threats we're getting—I'm getting. I made the final decision to hire Lassiter, not you. So get off your guilt trip. There's plenty of blame to spread around. It's time to move forward—figure out where we go from here."

He turns sideways to look at me. "Jesse, I need you. I can't do this on my own. I went out on a limb for you, but now I need your help," he pleads.

I turn to look out the window. Thoughts swirl in my head like the fog outside.

All the streetlights are out, and even though John is driving slowly on what used to be a busy Interstate-25, we nearly miss the exit ramp. On the side streets, the buildings are dark except for an occasional flicker from flashlights or lanterns.

The headlight beams from the Rover reveal the new harsh reality. Piles of trash and rotting garbage line the streets, a stark reminder of the breakdown of normalcy. The air is filled with a pungent stench, and I grimace, trying to block out the acrid smell. Hammer sees me looking at the garbage and tells me there is an effort to recruit horse-drawn wagons from local ranches to collect the trash, a solution that would have been unthinkable not too long ago. This is not the city I used to know.

Flashing blue lights behind us are the first sign of another vehicle. John pulls over to the side, waiting for a military convoy to pass. The lead vehicle, a military Humvee, has lights on, but the trucks following are dark.

"Most of the traffic nowadays is military. They're the only ones who have gas," he explains.

I turn to Hammer, asking a question that has been in my head since being confined in the CIVO warehouse. "Remember when you called me on the plane while I was flying over to check out the spill—you told me about CIVO?"

"I remember. That's one call I wish I'd never made."

"Who told you about Lassiter in the first place?"

Hammer thinks for a second before answering. "No one. Lassiter called me. Said he heard we had a problem in Africa and suggested he may be able to help."

"How did he find out about the spill?"

Hammer shrugs. "He never said. I had just learned about it and called the Board to let them know. Within a couple of hours, Lassiter called me. That's when I called you."

"I've wondered how he found out about the spill so quickly. You think he's got any connections to the Board?"

Hammer pauses before answering. "Possibly, but so what? Lassiter provides a service we need. I admit his timing was perfect, but it's not unreasonable for any Board member to have connections with a company like CIVO, especially with their experience with the Exxon Valdez cleanup. I have people like that contact me all the time. Of course, most are just looking for Americo to invest money into some crackpot idea, but we did research them, and CIVO sounded legit."

"I keep thinking back to the spill. From what I have put

together, it almost seemed intentional. But if it were, why would someone create an oil spill?"

"Maybe to test a new product. If *Denz* would have worked the way he said, Lassiter stood to make millions," Hammer implies.

"But CIVO had the *Denz* virus ready to go," I recalled CIVO's swift action and couldn't help but admire their efficiency. "Hell, they had planes loaded and flying into Lagos just hours after an agreement had been reached. The speed of their response was remarkable."

I knew—we all knew, that Americo would have willingly shelled out far more than twenty-five million to clean up the spill. The costs associated with a disaster like this could easily have spiraled into hundreds of millions, factoring in remediation costs, potential lawsuits, public relations nightmares, and long-term environmental impact.

The research and demonstration we saw in Paris was nothing more than a well-crafted façade. The virus appeared to devour the oil, then wither away, but in reality, the purpose was far more despicable.

Somehow Lassiter knew a substantial portion of our Nigerian crude would go to the Strategic Petroleum Reserve. How did they know? They had a grand scheme to introduce *Denz* into the SPR.

Hammer gripped the steering wheel, his mouth set in a grim line. "I'm not one for conspiracy theories, but for the sake of argument, you're saying Lassiter had this whole thing planned." Hammer paused to look at me. "But, if true, how would he know the SPR oil would be released into the market? He has connections, but how high do they go?"

I shake my head. "Unknown. He could have just got lucky on that one. On the other hand, the Henshaw Bill effectively stopped domestic drilling, the gas price was skyrocketing, and a presidential election was coming up. The President needed votes. What better way to buy votes than to lower the gas price by releasing the SPR reserves? Lassiter got the best of both worlds—a crippled economy and a weakened military."

Both of us sit in silence, connecting the dots.

Hammer speaks first. "That would make Dr. Aran Lassiter the most powerful person on the planet now. One man controlling the world's oil."

CHAPTER 26
RAMPAGE

Turning the corner onto the street leading to the entrance of the imposing thirty-two-story Americo Oil building, Hammer stomps on the brakes. The Land Rover squeals to a halt, drawing some looks from a large mob gathered in front of the building. The barely visible faces of those we can see are mixed with determination and outrage.

The chaotic flickering of lanterns and flashlights bobbing in the cold night air cast eerie shadows on the steel and glass façade of the building. The building is transformed into a fortress under siege, reminding me of an old black-and-white image of a classic Frankenstein horror movie.

The parallels are vivid and haunting—the furious townspeople, brandishing makeshift weapons and lit torches, storming the castle to destroy the creature they fear and loathe. But in our reality, an unhinged scientist has created a monster worse than Frankenstein.

The enraged mob in front of us mirrors the rampage depicted in the Frankenstein story. Their anger, their fear, is just as real. Only this time, the castle is the Americo Oil building, and those inside are left to confront the curse unleashed upon the world.

Thankfully Hammer had taken steps to secure the building after the threats started coming in. Large concrete blocks have been strategically placed at the entrance to prevent vehicles from breaching the perimeter. He also hired a private security force—fully armed—to protect Americo employees and the building.

A man is standing on one of the concrete blocks in front of the building, speaking to a restless mob, his voice amplified by a bullhorn.

". . . and now we're all paying the price for Americo's corporate greed. This is why we lost our money, lives, and world." The man points at the Americo Building. "They let money control their lives and ruin ours. This company should be punished for the plague it brought upon us."

I scan the unruly crowd; many appear intoxicated—not a good sign. The pungent smell of marijuana is heavy in the air. There had to be at least two hundred people, many giving boisterous cheers, chanting, and waving signs.

Hammer whips out his cell and dials the company number. "This is Hammer!" he bellows into the phone. "What's going on outside?"

His eyes widen in anger and determination as he listens, then says, "No! If anyone is going to talk to them, it will be me. But if they try and force their way into the building, use all necessary force to stop them. Understand?"

Disconnecting, he growls, "These fanatics are not only blaming us for *Denz* but every other problem in the world. They want someone to come out and talk to them."

"John, don't even think about it," I say, seeing the look on his face. "This is nothing but a rowdy, drunken party. At least half this crowd is toasted. You won't be able to satisfy them, no matter what you say."

Hammer waves off my concern. "If I don't, it could get ugly. Maybe I can defuse the situation. They're on my turf. I'll have security beside me. I'll let them vent for a while; then they'll go home."

Hammer calls the building once more. "I'm going to talk to them. I want security to meet me on the front steps. Make sure they're fully armed, and bring a vest for me. I should be on the steps in five minutes, so be ready."

I make one last effort to dissuade him. "John, I don't think this is a good idea. Why don't you give it a few hours? After that, they'll get tired and go home."

Hammer shakes his head as he jumps out of the parked Rover. "Jesse, you stay here," he orders, and with a grim smile, he plunges into the crowd.

Ignoring his request, I follow close behind. The faces in the crowd are wild-eyed and dangerous. They aren't there to listen to reason. Instead, they are angry, focusing only on the evil oil company that caused this upheaval.

The front doors open, and twenty uniformed, armed security guards carrying shotguns and assault rifles appear. The show of force quiets the gathering. The guards form a line on the large patio area at the front entrance. Some in the crowd begin to back away.

Startled, the man speaking earlier stops when Hammer, wearing a Kevlar vest, climbs onto the adjoining concrete block. The security guards, weapons pointing in the crowd's direction, surround the large block Hammer is standing on. One of them holds up a microphone for him.

He stares into the crowd, unafraid. "My name is John Hammer. I'm the President of Americo Oil. You wanted to talk, so here I am." A hush falls over the crowd. They hadn't expected someone from the company to talk to them, especially not the President.

The speaker for the mob is quick to reply. "We demand you vacate the building and cease all business until we figure out how to stop the deadly virus you unleashed upon us."

In a tone heavy with sarcasm, Hammer replies, "Sir, you're in no position to 'demand' anything. As for the virus, you can thank one of our employees for getting the antidote to kill it. Why don't you all go home and go to—"

A shot rings out from somewhere in the crowd. Hammer's body jerks and falls off the concrete block onto the ground. Two security guards begin firing into the air above the gathering. Panicked by the gunfire, other security guards start firing into the crowd.

My heart races as I sprint through the throngs of people toward where Hammer has fallen. I can see him lying on the ground, struggling to rise, his face contorted in pain. Blood spurts from a gaping wound in his neck, and the air is thick with screams and chaos as the mob realizes what has happened.

Hammer tries to shout orders to the guards to cease fire, but his voice is weak and drowned out by pandemonium and exploding violence. Shots ring out from the panicked mob, hitting a security guard who collapses. Another shot sprays me with pieces of the concrete block. I am now in the middle of a war zone. In fear for their lives, the guards crouch down and begin firing indiscriminately into the crowd.

Terrified, the mob panics, stampeding away from the blood-bath, careening down side streets in an effort to seek cover. A mixture of pistol shots and automatic weapons fire echoes through the streets as some in the crowd begin to return fire. One of the guards standing over Hammer crumples to the ground.

I crawl on my hands and knees toward his body, seeking the protection of the concrete block while yelling at the guards to cease fire. The street in front of the building is beginning to empty, most people running for cover, wanting no part in a gun battle with armed troops.

The firing slows, then stops altogether. I peek around the corner from behind the concrete block, full of pock-holes from incoming bullets. Then, satisfied the shooting has stopped, I begin crawling toward Hammer, who is lying in a pool of his blood.

Bodies from the crowd dot the ground in front of the building, some surrounded by blood—silent—others crying out in pain. Security guards pull Hammer and their wounded comrades behind the cover of the concrete blocks. I reach out toward Hammer, but one of the guards steps up and levels his rifle at me.

"Don't fucking move!" he yells.

I freeze and raise my hands.

I see the look of confusion and panic in his eyes. "Don't shoot. My name is Jesse Ford. I work for Americo."

A second guard steps forward. Looking carefully at me, he tells the first guard to lower his weapon. "I know this guy. He works here."

Hammer is lying on his back. I remove my jacket, roll it up, and slide it under his head. Blood is flowing from the wound in his neck. The sight and smell send a wave of nausea rolling over me, but it just as quickly passes.

"I called an ambulance . . . it might be a while before they get here," the second guard says in an unsteady voice.

"Does anyone inside have any medical training?" I yell, indicating the Americo building.

"I already called. They're trying to find someone. The building is mostly deserted this time of night."

Hammer's eyes quiver as his hand grabs my shirt, pulling me close. "Jesse," he mutters, pulling me closer still.

"You're going to be okay," I whisper. "The ambulance is on the way."

"I hope they hurry. I . . . I don't think I'm going to make it." His eyelids tremble from the exertion of talking, but his gaze remains locked on me. "Someone on the Board is trying to bring us down." He pauses to catch his breath, only to be seized by a fit of coughing. "I . . . I think it's . . ." He starts coughing again, and a trail of blood seeps from his mouth.

"Who, John?" I lean over, close to his mouth. "Who is it?"

With the last of his strength, Hammer reaches out with a trembling hand to clutch a small piece of the concrete block. Holding it out toward me, he fights to get the words out, but the effort is too much.

With a heavy sigh of surrender, he lies back against the hard ground; his gaze fixated on the clear sky above. I watch in helpless silence as life fades from him, his body growing still, his eyes losing their spark. I lean close and gently shake him, but it is too late. I am met with a haunting stillness. I grab his wrist, feeling for a pulse. Nothing. His pulse, like his spirit, has faded away. His lifeless hand still clutching the rock.

CHAPTER 27
GUS

The cigar-shaped object resembles a large test tube, inverted and standing upright. Its circular shape stands ten feet and measures four-point-nine feet in diameter. At first glance, the cylindrical shape appears crystal-like, its translucent surface clear and transparent. However, a closer examination reveals a blurry and distorted view when peering through it. A wispy film on the tube's inner surface bends and distorts its contents.

Circular rings with a pale green hue on the interior of the cylinder, spaced at one-foot intervals, begin at the bottom and rise to the top. Outside the tube, high-definition video cameras are located on all four sides, bathing the machine in LED lights from above and below. The only opening is an entry hatch, large enough for a man to enter.

A second tube, although identical in appearance, is located precisely fifty-eight feet from the first. By calculating the speed of the earth's rotation, the solar system, and the galaxy's speed as it moves through space, scientists estimate fifty-eight feet is the absolute minimal distance an object can be transported.

One of the lab techs, also a history buff, suggests renaming 'the transporter.' "That term sounds too formal and lifeless. It sounds like a truck," he points out.

"At the turn of the nineteenth century, a machine called a hectograph was invented, which could duplicate copies from an original. Although primitive by our standards, our transporter is based on a similar concept. Our transporter will duplicate the original and send a copy to a chosen destination. The original will remain with the sender. The result is two identical documents—the original and the duplicate," he explains.

"In the interest of simplicity and to honor the old hectograph," argues the tech, "why don't we give our machine the nickname 'HEC'? Easier to say than transporter, not to mention the first three letters are the same as the inventor of teleportation, Dr. Hector Ramos."

There were nods and a few groans around the room, but general agreement. The two teleportation machines officially became HEC#1 and HEC#2.

The first test uses inanimate material such as a pencil, then plastic balls, followed by an empty glass, then a glass filled with water. After failures, testing, and more failures followed by more tests, repeats, adjustments, recalibrating, and updating software, they begin to see some successes. Each test sees fewer and fewer defects between the original and the duplicated transported object. A fluorescence electron quantum microscope scans the duplicate cells in exquisite detail, comparing the individual cells, molecules, and atoms to the original.

The first organic test is a rat. It takes three days to remove the duplicated remnants of the rat's exploded body and sanitize HEC#2. The original rat remains unharmed after the test. The following six attempts all prove unsuccessful. Parts of the duplicated rats are scattered. One rat has its front legs where the rear legs should be. But with each test, the results improve.

Upgraded computers are purchased, and software is modified, adjusted, and recalibrated. The duplicated rat from test #7 survives four minutes before it collapses dead. The autopsy reveals a massive heart attack. An artery to the heart failed to reassemble in the correct sequence. The original rat remains unchanged and in good health.

***

I hear Hector gasp through the phone as I break the news of John's death.

"He what?" he exclaims, his voice filled with shock.

"John was killed last night," I repeat. "There was a riot in front of the office building. John thought he could talk them down, but someone shot him while he was speaking."

"I hope you're joking," whispers Hector, his voice barely audible.

"I wish I were, my friend," I reply, my voice cracking with emotion.

Hector falls silent as I explain the events leading to Hammer's death.

"I just talked to him yesterday. He was getting ready to pick you up," Hector says, not believing his ears.

"A lot's going on here, Hector. I won't be coming out to the lab today. Maybe tomorrow. Things are rather fluid around here, as you can imagine."

"I understand," answers Hector, still reeling from the news. "Let me know if you need me there. You still have the antidote?"

"It's in a safe place. I'll bring it tomorrow," I assure him before hanging up. The conversation renews the pain I felt from John's loss.

***

Hector sits behind his desk, staring at the ceiling with hollow eyes. He and John Hammer weren't exactly close, but his death will have a dramatic impact on the work at the lab, possibly even halting their research.

He opens his desk drawer and pulls out a half-full bottle of tequila. Putting the bottle between his legs, he begins to unscrew the top with his good hand, then stops. He frowns at the bottle, then slowly screws the lid back on, putting it back in the desk drawer. Hammer's death makes for an easy excuse to drink but now is not the time.

Hector sits back in his chair, feeling overwhelmed by the recent turn of events. He is certain that teleportation will succeed. But his thoughts drift to *Denz*. The *Denz* genie will never be put back into the bottle; it's too late to contain it.

The success of finding the antidote for *Denz* is crucial, as it will provide the necessary clout and influence needed to continue his work on teleportation. It has the potential to revolutionize everything, and he is determined to make it happen.

Hammer had the power, but he was never a true believer, unlike Jesse. Hammer's death is terrible, but maybe some good can come of it. Jesse will have to step up and become the advocate for the research facility.

Hector spreads the word of Hammer's death to the lab. Reactions range from shock and sorrow, followed by rage and vows of revenge. Anyone who wants to return to Denver is encouraged to go—if desired. Hector is pleased no one leaves.

***

It is late afternoon when Christopher Drake, the senior software engineer, and Hector's second-in-command, rushes into Hector's office. "I've solved it," Drake says, breathing quickly. "I understand why the duplicate copies are not reassembling. After teleporting the original object, we now have two; the original and the transported duplicate. The duplicate is prevented from reassembling because it is still connected to the original. This connection creates an error in the software program, preventing the duplicate from reassembling."

"Why?" Hector asks, looking up from his desk.

Drake shakes his head, wiping his unwashed hair away from his thick glasses. "Hector, I'm afraid you don't have the software background for me to explain it to you," he says with an undertone of arrogance. I'm not sure I even understand 'why' myself. But we must do something with the original to get it out of the software before we can reassemble the duplicate."

Drake becomes animated with his hands, removing his glasses and holding them in a clenched fist as he paces in front of the desk, thinking out loud.

"I can rewrite the software. We must purge the original from the software before we can even think about reconstituting the duplicate. We take the essence; the memories, the sum, and substance, the cells, the molecules, the atoms, the DNA—everything that makes up the original—download and copy the original into a separate drive. This download will preserve the original allowing us to restore it whenever we want."

Hector is silent, his mind churning over the radical concept. "In other words," he begins carefully, "we can restart our life again from that point forward. We can hit the rewind button and go back to the way we were at that moment in time when we were first teleported. We could start over, like resetting a video game. It's almost like the legendary Fountain of Youth."

"I hadn't considered that aspect, but yes," admits Chris, "but yeah, you're right. You could teleport when you are thirty, save that snapshot of yourself, and then when you're eighty, you could hit the reset button restoring your thirty-year-old self and live those years over. Of course, you would have no memory of those years after age thirty, and those memories would be lost to you. Your only memories would be those you experienced until you teleported at age thirty. It would be like starting a new life at age thirty."

The remainder of the day and deep into the night, the two men—dreaming of the possibilities and running on pure adrenaline—review, check, and double-check calculations. Because of the implications of this ability to recreate a life backup and restoration of that original could have on society, they agree to keep the process a secret.

"I may share this with Jesse," Hector declares, "but we don't mention this to anyone else, at least for now."

Finally satisfied with their work, Hector regards his fellow scientist with a mixture of respect and anticipation. "You did it, Chris. Can you modify the software before Jesse arrives? It might be later today or tomorrow when he gets here. I want to make sure the bugs are worked out and run a test when he is here."

***

"Get the rat," Hector orders the following moring, his mouth set in a grim line. Someone had nicknamed the rat "Lassiter," a name which did not sit well with Hector. When he learns of the rat's nickname, he looks at the stump on his right arm, "You're shitting me . . . right?" The rat is immediately renamed "Gus."

The entire lab staff is gathered in the large room—even those working on the *Denz* antidote project. Unlike the earlier tests when failure was expected, word has spread that the updated software has solved the reassembly issues of the duplicate. Nervous energy can be felt throughout the testing room as technicians adjust their headphones and controls are calibrated and set. High-definition digital cameras focus on the original HEC#1 and HEC#2.

Hector stands on a platform overseeing and directing the final arrangements. Lights are dimmed except for the LED spotlights on both HECs, giving the lab a surrealistic appearance. Blinking lights on rows of computers remind Hector of the NASA control room.

The countdown begins, with a final hold at twenty seconds. All stations check in with a last "go" or "no-go" response. There is a collective holding of breath as the final station checks in.

"Communications—go." The countdown resumes: ". . . three, two, one." Hector pushes a red button on his console.

The white rat scurrying around the base of HEC#1 freezes. The lab's humming noise of a dozen computers increases in volume.

Then, in the dim light of the lab, a bright circular green light at the base of HEC#1 begins rising, one level at a time, stopping at the top, then reversing and returning to the bottom. The receiving HEC#2 repeats the procedure, taking less than two seconds. Gus, the original rat that was in HEC#1, has vanished. Fifty-eight feet away, a white rodent appears, lying on its side, frozen in place. There is a collective holding of breath and silence. Like a tsunami, frustration builds and sweeps across the room.

A sudden cry breaks the silence. "He's moving." Gus's tail twitches, and suddenly the rat is on his feet. There is a rippling gasp from the wide-eyed technicians across the lab.

Gus scurries around the tube, then tilts back on his hind legs, scratching the walls.

"I think he's hungry!" someone shouts—the room breaks into laughter and clapping. Excited conversations break out.

Two technicians rush to Gus. One reaches through the hatch and carefully lifts him out of the tube while stroking his head and exploring his body. "Initial life signs are good," he pronounces.

Immediately, a half dozen technicians and doctors are beside Gus, squirming like rats do.

There is sporadic laughter throughout the lab. All eyes are focused on Gus. The ten-minute mark comes and goes. No change. All external parts are where they should be, and Gus#2 acts like a normal rat. Life-scanning devices are hooked to Gus#2 that monitor and record every breath and heartbeat. Blood is drawn and sent to the lab to be analyzed and compared to the blood from Gus#1. Fifteen minutes pass, then twenty. Still, Gus seems perfectly healthy. All tests match perfectly.

THE SPILL

"I think we've done it," Hector whispers. Isolated clapping begins filling the lab, then grows into joyous thunder. They have done it; they teleported a living, breathing life form from one point to another, still breathing and no worse for wear.

"I want a complete analysis," says Hector. "Especially brain waves. Does the duplicate have the same brain memories and functions as the original? Backup all data. I want to repeat the test tomorrow."

The original Gus#1 had been taught certain tricks, patterns, and behaviors that rats would typically not do unless specifically trained.

"The brain images from Gus#1 are imprinted on Gus#2. Both behaviors are the same," reports the handler of the two rats. Two hours later, the brain of Gus#2 is imaged with MRIs, followed by CAT scans measuring the brain structure. Both tests confirm the brains are identical in every way.

Hector and Chris look at each other, and Hector nods. Chris sits at the main 'motherboard' computer, his fingers flying over the keyboard. He turns to Hector, giving him an imperceptible nod.

Turning back to the computer, he unplugs a cable from the computer, which is attached to a black box the size of a deck of cards containing the original essence of Gus#1, and slides the small box into a pocket of his lab coat.

Later that evening, alone in the lab, the two men verify the process by reconstructing Gus#1. The procedure works perfectly.

Beyond Hector and Chris, nobody is aware of this feature of the teleporter. There will be time to debate the ethical and medical issues later. Until then, the original DNA replication process is held under lock and key.

CHAPTER 28
THE LAB

I release a pent-up yawn and squirm my butt in the Land Rover's sturdy seat. After two hours, the abrupt end of the narrow-paved farm road was a welcome sight, knowing I only had three more miles to go. My fingers tap on the steering wheel. I'm bored and ready for a break. A muddy dirt road is coming up on my right, and I turn onto it.

Before I left Denver, I called Libby and told her about John and the abbreviated version of my adventures in Lagos the past week. Unfortunately, she cannot return to Denver for John's funeral.

"There's a rumor floating around D.C. the President is planning military action against CIVO," she says with an air of foreboding. "Have you heard about that?"

Surprised by the news, I told her I knew nothing but wished him luck as I glanced at the box on the passenger seat beside me. With the precious antidote in my possession, I had little need for Lassiter. We agreed to arrange a rendezvous after the funeral.

My eyes swing toward the road, coming to rest on the gas gauge. Still more than half a tank, enough to get to the lab and return to Denver if needed, but I will fill it up at the lab. During the construction of the lab, John had the foresight to conceal large fuel storage tanks underground. Additional gasoline caches have been placed at strategic locations throughout the Denver metro area that only the top executives know about. There are certain advantages to working for an oil company.

After three miles on the dirt, the road comes to a halt, blocked by a ten-foot chain-link gate, barbed wire across the top with a warning sign in red letters reading NO TRESPASSING! VIOLATORS WILL BE PROSECUTED! Reading the sign, I had to chuckle. Chip wanted it to read, "VIOLATERS WILL BE EXECUTED." I miss him. He should be back this weekend in time for the funeral.

The gate swings slowly open when I push the remote control clipped to the sun visor. A guard seems to come out of nowhere.

"Afternoon, Mr. Ford," he says when I flash my ID. "He's expecting you," and waves me through. Security cameras have watched my approach since I left the paved farm road. Five security guards monitor the cameras in an underground bunker just past the entry gate. An underground passageway leads from the bunker to the main facility. We can thank Chip for the security at the lab site.

Once through the gate, a quarter mile of hard-packed dirt brings me to the main entrance. The building is neutral in color, and there are no identifying signs. Half of the facility is above ground, but the other half—the crucial half—is below the surface. Hector is waiting for me at the main entrance.

"Mi amigo," I greet him, patting him on the back. "You're looking good."

Hector smiles and grabs my shoulder with his good left arm. He has a prosthesis on his right arm but tells me it is only temporary until the scar tissue heals. "The itching drives me crazy, but docs assure me I will get used to it," he scowls.

"Wait till you see it, Jesse; it's like magic. It takes my breath away whenever we beam something." Hector's excitement is contagious. I can't wait to see this teleporter.

As we cross the main reception area, Hector asks about Kim. I explain she stayed in Denver to deal with funeral arrangements. He nods. "Too bad she won't be here to see this. She would enjoy it."

We enter a nondescript office containing a desk with some open files, a computer, a phone, and a file cabinet. Walking through the office, we enter a second office, small and bare except for a control panel on one wall.

Opening the panel, Hector inputs a four-digit code. The room gives a slight lurch, then begins to drop. There are three elevators in the underground portion of the lab, but this is the only one shown to visitors and VIP types.

"Any problems with the power?" I ask as the elevator descends. There have been some blackouts in Denver.

Hector gives a short laugh. "We're on the Denver power grid, but if we have problems, we have two diesel power generators for backup. You must have seen this coming when you designed this place."

I'm pleased Hector gives me credit, even if undeserved. The lab design had been a joint project between the two of us, with the help of top design engineers. It is so advanced that it would shame any Ivy League university research facility.

Word spread among the science community about the lab. We had scientists, military strategists, and engineers from across the country begging to be hired at the Americo Lab, allowing us to choose the best and the brightest.

The lab itself is dimly lit. Only two people are sitting on computer consoles. I cast a perplexed look at Hector. "Where's everybody at?"

"We're not scheduled for the final test for two hours," Hector says, glancing at his watch. "We have two teams, each working in shifts—one for *Denz* and one for the teleportation. The *Denz* crew is waiting for the antidote, which I hope is this," he says, pointing to the box I carry.

"Let's put this somewhere safe," I say, nodding toward the antidote.

We stop off at Hector's office. His lip curls as he takes the box from me. "I don't even want to get close to that shit," he says, handing the box to his assistant, Chris. "Take this and give it to the team working on the antidote."

The cafeteria is the size of a small restaurant. Hector grabs a couple of sandwiches while I pour two cups of coffee. As we sit at the table, Hector begins stirring his coffee. Hector is strangely quiet. I know what he will ask, and I already have my answer.

Hector stops stirring his coffee and glances at me. He gives me that pleading look, like a kid who wants a new toy. "Jesse, I want to be the one to go."

I shake my head. "I can't, Hector. You're too valuable. We can't afford to lose you if something goes wrong. Plus, now we have the antidote to recreate."

Hector snorts. "We can duplicate that in about thirty minutes. We can keep transporting it through HEC and duplicate it every time."

"HEC?" He lost me.

Hector laughs. "Our new nickname for the teleportation machine. We wanted a shortcut, so they call it HEC."

He looks up at me, wanting to continue the conversation. "Now, first off, nothing's going to go wrong," he says in his most persuasive tone. I start to respond, but Hector holds up his finger. "Second thing is, you're going to lose me, anyway."

That caught me off guard. "What do you mean?"

"In that hospital, in Lagos—when they amputated my forearm—they gave me a blood transfusion contaminated with HIV. I've got AIDS. The doc says it is an especially potent strain of the virus. Our antiretroviral drugs can't touch it. They give me six months . . . a year at best."

Stunned by this news, I stare at Hector in disbelief. My world seemed to crumble around me. My friend is dying. This has got to be a joke the universe is playing, or a nightmare.

"Six months to live . . . I think that's bullshit," I claim. "Are you sure? With the new drugs being developed, people can live a near-normal life. You're going to get a second opinion—right?"

Hector hesitates, giving me a chance to digest the gravity of this news. "When I returned to the States, I was not aware I was HIV positive." He sighs deeply, hiding the pain buried in his voice. "I infected Maria."

Now I am speechless. The initial grief of learning about Hector's condition is now replaced by sorrow for Hector for the torment he must feel for infecting his wife. I hadn't even considered this aspect of Hector's ordeal. Hector and Maria have had rocky moments, but I have always appreciated her. It was always clear she worshiped the ground Hector walked on.

"What can I do, Hector? I'm here for both you and Maria," was all I could say.

"Even if I don't teleport, I'm leaving the lab," Hector continues. "I want to enjoy my remaining days while I still can with my wife, my kids, and grandkids. But since this is my last project, I want to be the first to be transported. No one ever remembers the second man to step on the Moon. Call it pride, call it vanity, or whatever you want." Hector leans forward, and his eyes start to get glassy. "Jesse, you owe me this."

Hector and I have been through a lot together. We are more than friends. We're like brothers. My sight starts to blur as I squint at him. "Are you sure, Hector? I mean, every day new drugs are coming out. Maybe it can be prolonged until something can be developed," I plead, leaning on my elbows with my eyes locked on his face.

But Hector just shakes his head, not meeting my eyes. "Maria and I are taking a cocktail of antiretroviral drugs now. She seems to be responding better than me. The drugs will slow the progression, but nothing can cure it. With all this *Denz* bullshit going on," he chokes up, "it could be years before AIDS research picks up again. I wish I could go back in time to change what's been done."

"But what if something happens to you? What about our research here? We have two big projects that will impact us, the company, the country, hell, even the world for years to come. You're the brains behind the *Denz* antidote and now the teleportation. If you're gone, that research dies with you."

Hector shook his head. "If something happens to me, Christopher Drake has all the notes and has been with me every step of the way. There is nothing I can do that he can't continue."

I wave my arm around the lab. "With all this at your disposal, invent a time machine, cure AIDS, but don't just give up—not yet."

"I'm never going to give up," he says, staring into my face.

CHAPTER 29
MAKE HISTORY

With a heavy heart, I realize Hector's mind cannot be changed. While I understand his desire to be the pioneer of human teleportation, the company could ill afford to lose him. But I would be lying if I didn't admit a pang of envy.

I had no choice but to agree with him. Deep down, I blame myself for him contracting HIV. The memory of my instruction to the doctor in Lagos to amputate his forearm weighs heavy on my conscience. I have no right to deny him this opportunity.

A sense of sadness sweeps over me. Losing Hector will be a severe blow. Not only is he my friend, but he is a leading expert on the subject of teleportation.

I make one last appeal. "Hec, are you sure you want to do this? I'm sure it won't, but what if something goes seriously wrong?"

"All of my notes and data are on my computer. There are a half dozen people here who could step into my shoes and move this project forward. As far as . . . not making it," Hector shrugs, his face grim, "at least this would be quick."

I nod my acceptance and give him a man-hug. "I'm so sorry," I whisper.

He steps back, looks at me, and shakes his head. "Don't do

that, Jesse. Don't lay a guilt trip on yourself. You saved me from a horrible death in Lagos. I will always be grateful."

I can not meet his eyes. He put his arm over my shoulder. "Now, let's go make history." Hector's eyes are bright with excitement.

Hector steps up to the teleportation chamber, caressing the smooth surface. In the future, I have no doubt there will be legends told about this moment. "We're ready," he declares, sealing the chamber door. He flashes me a smile, his eyes sparkling with anticipation and anxiety. "Promise me if things go south, you won't stop the research," he pleads. "Talk to Christopher."

I know he has a certain amount of fear of the unknown. I would. I can't help but admire his courage. "We won't stop," I promise. "Can't afford to. We'll keep trying until we get it right."

Hector Ramos will be the first human to be transported—or killed in the attempt. It suddenly occurs to me there may not even be a body to bury. His atoms would be scattered without a guarantee they would ever be reassembled. I put the gruesome thought out of my mind.

All computer stations are manned. Medical people stand near the HEC#2 machine. Those not required to be at a station are spectators, filming the historic event with their smartphones.

The monitors cast a silver-blueish color, enveloping the room in an otherworldly aura. Hector stands straight and tall inside the transporter, brimming with eagerness. On the other side of the room, fifty-eight feet from the first test tube, the empty HEC#2 awaits his arrival.

I feel frustrated with nothing to do but watch.

Finally, Christopher Drake, Hector's trusted assistant and second-in-command, joins me. "There will be two flashes of light," he explains. "After the first flash, Hector will disappear. Then, following a second flash, he should reappear over there," he points toward the second teleporter pod. "The whole process lasts a mere two seconds."

I turn to Drake with a question. "Hector referred to an original backup and project notes. What was he talking about?" I ask.

Drake shifts his gaze to meet mine. "He didn't fill you in? The teleporter is a perfect duplicator. It will scan Hector, extracting all the data needed to transmit Hector to the second unit, HEC#2, where a duplicate will be reconstructed. But all the data from the original—the DNA, the molecules, the very atoms that makeup Hector—will be archived. We could recreate the original Hector just as he was before his teleportation anytime we want."

My eyes start to glaze over as I struggle to fully grasp the implications of what I am being told.

He looks at my stunned face and smiles. "I know how you feel. It is hard to wrap your brain around. But if something fails, we can recreate the original Hector. When Hector is teleported, we take the essence that makes him up, the memories, the sum, and substance, the cells, the molecules, the atoms, the DNA— everything that makes up the original Hector—download and copy the original into a separate drive and secure it in a facility where it is protected. Then we can restore the original Hector whenever we want to."

Seeing my overwhelmed expression, Drake grins. "I understand your reaction. It's not easy to digest. But the beauty of this technology is that, if anything goes wrong, we can always bring back the original Hector."

As thought seeps back into my swirling brain, Drake drops another bombshell. "And to really twist your neurons, we could theoretically transmit the original Hector to multiple locations. Imagine multiple Hectors all running around at once."

"Is there any limit on how often the original can be transmitted?" I ask, trying to sound like I am keeping up with all I'm being told.

Chris shrugs. "Unknown. We have transmitted up to three original lab rats with no problem. The question of how many can't be answered yet. I, myself, don't believe there is a limit. I see no reason we could not create the original object as often as we want. Hell, we could make an army if we wanted."

"Don't you need a teleporter to receive the original duplicate? You can't just send it anywhere . . . can you?" I ask.

Chris shakes his head. "We discovered we don't need a receiving station. We only need the destination coordinates, which we input into the original teleporter."

My head is spinning with all the talk of thousands of duplicates. The buzzer sound in the background draws my focus to the transporters.

It is time. "I thought we didn't need the second tube?" I say, nodding toward the second machine.

"It's just a safety precaution," answers the nearest technician. "We don't need it, but if something were to happen . . . uh, like, unexpected, we want to have some way to contain things."

"You mean in the event he doesn't make it?" I nod a reluctant understanding. "Well, let's hope it doesn't come to that."

THE SPILL

The technician looks me in the eyes. "It won't." I wish I had his confidence.

The room descends into darkness, engulfed by the ominous hum of the computers. Vast amounts of data are analyzed, calculations made, and instructions sent at light speed. Suddenly, a fluorescent green light illuminates the base platform of HEC#1, rising until it towers over Hector, then slowly descends back to the platform base.

The green light in the tube reflects Hector's wide-open eyes, frozen in fear. His lips move, but the sound is lost in the deafening roar of the machine. Is he praying for salvation or screaming in terror? I can't tell. When the green light reaches the base, there is a blinding flash.

The HEC#1 chamber is empty. Hector has vanished.

Every pair of eyes in the room is riveted on HEC#2. It's now engulfed in the eerie green light rising from the machine's base. Reaching the top, the light begins to descend back to the starting point. Once again, a blinding flash of light erupts, followed by darkness in the chamber, save for the exterior spotlights, which cast the shadowy silhouette of a man in the chamber.

There, amid the contrasting play of light and shadow, stands Hector, eyes closed and mouth slightly agape. He staggers against the side of the tube, regains his balance, and stands upright.

The room is paralyzed. No one breathes, and there is startled silence. My mind struggles to comprehend what I am seeing.

Slowly at first, then growing, a wave of spontaneous applause and cheers swept the room—somewhat restrained, waiting for Hector to emerge unharmed.

"Help him out," orders a technician. Two men open the hatch, speak a few words to Hector, and support him as he steps through the opening. Judging from how he is moving, he doesn't need their help. He shakes his head, looks up at me, and smiles.

I hurry over to where he stands, surrounded by medical personnel and technicians. His assistant, Chris, is asking him a series of questions. Hector nods as he answers.

He holds up his hand in an attempt to slow the questions. "I feel fine," he insists in a loud voice. "Everything seems intact and in the right places."

The group gives a nervous laugh.

Dr. Samantha Park, the chief medical officer clinic at the Laboratory, wasted no time taking charge. "Come with me," she instructed Hector. "I want to check you out before you get too cocky." She leads the way to a fully equipped nearby examination room just outside the central lab, followed by Hector and the entourage of technicians. Here Hector will be given a complete physical, and the results will be compared to the baseline pretest exam.

As Hector departs the lab, a renewed round of applause and impromptu cheering fills the air, growing louder and continuing for several minutes—a testament to the incredible achievement that has just been accomplished.

***

Two hours after the transfer, Hector and I sit in his office, cradling mugs of coffee, as I listen to him describe the experience.

There is still a wild look of exhilaration lighting up Hector's face. As his words spill out, he bounces in his chair, barely restraining his excitement. "I haven't experienced a rush like that in years. Not since my wild college days."

He pauses, his eyes flickering as he recalls the sensations. "I could hear this ringing in my ears, like the sound of rushing wind. It reminded me of the wind noise when I was a kid and stuck my head out the car window, pretending I was flying like Superman. Then for a second, everything just went black. Suddenly there was a bright flash of light, like a starburst exploding on the Fourth of July, followed by a bright green light, and there I was. It was incredible . . . just incredible. Can't wait to do it again."

The doctor gives her approval at Hector's physical check. Except for a headache, there are no apparent side effects. We are ready to move to the next step. Now it's my turn.

"The demand for the teleportation devices is going to be phenomenal," I predict.

"How about you and I starting our own company?" Hector suggests.

I shake my head. "A violation of the work-product doctrine. Anything you create for Americo at your place of employment is a trade secret and belongs to Americo. I guarantee you they would never give up the copyright to the teleporter. They could tie us up in court for years, and legally they have the upper hand." I take another sip of my coffee. "We are better off using Americo's resources and working within the company."

"Who's going to be President now?"

"Marci Stone is the largest stockholder. The Board named her as interim President."

"You think she'll work with us?"

I hesitate, thinking about Marci. "I don't know," I say cautiously. "For now, let's keep news of the teleportation under wraps. There's too much upheaval inside the company. No sense complicating things."

Hector nods in agreement. He had learned several lessons about company bureaucracy as the lab was being built.

"By the way," I ask, "when you were beamed to the receiving station, the proper coordinates had been fed into the computer, right?"

"Something like that. The receiving station can either emit an electronic homing signal which we lock onto, or we can just input the coordinates at some location. We use GPS coordinates, feed the coordinates into the computer, and bang, there you are."

"What would it take to return to the original point of the teleportation?" I ask.

"Simple," answers Hector. "We have the original starting GPS coordinates. We reverse the process to bring you back."

"Could we lock onto a starting point, say in the middle of the desert . . . or a building in France, and beam them back here to the lab?"

Hector pauses, seeing where I am going. "Yeah . . . we could do that, as long as we had the coordinates of the starting point. We've never tried it, but if we brought a person here—from France, for example—I'm not sure if the original would remain at the initiating point or if there would then be two of them— one at the beginning and one at the final destination. That's an unknown."

My mind is racing now. Every answer from Hector opens up a new area of further questions. "But what if there were no receiving station—no coordinates to beam to? Say the object was sent out into space with no programmed destination?"

Hector thought for a second before answering. "If there were no receiving station at the end of the beam, whatever it was you were beaming would keep traveling . . . in a straight line, past the curvature of the earth, into nothingness, until the power source was lost. It'd be a nice way to eliminate something or somebody."

"Yeah," I say, yawning and rubbing my eyes. "Lots of possibilities . . . I want you to beam me to Washington," I say. "I want to see Libby."

Hector smiles. "You're the boss."

CHAPTER 30
TOGETHER AGAIN

Stunned, Libby Burns locks eyes with her boss, Fred Shard. "You want me to what?"

"There's going to be a military operation in France against this CIVO company—you know, that company that released the micro virus. I want you to cover it, but only as an observer on behalf of the EPA."

"Why in the world would you want me to do that? I'm sure there are more qualified people you can send."

"Many more." He now has an annoyed look on his face. As Director of the EPA, he is not used to a subordinate questioning him. "First, I know you have a 'relationship' with that guy at Americo, Ford, who is responsible for releasing that plague upon us, so you have access to inside information no one else does."

"We had a relationship back in law school years ago. I have no 'inside information.'"

"I don't believe you. Ford was in D.C. recently, and you spent the evening together."

"What the hell, Fred? Do you have spies watching me?"

Shard sits back in his chair and raises his glasses onto his balding head. "We will be filing major litigation against Americo Oil for violating the Toxic Substances Control Act. Americo Oil was working with CIVO to release untested microorganisms without the approval of the EPA. We need an on-the-ground representative at the CIVO site. You're the most logical person to go. You recognize the legal issues and the evidence needed for a conviction. You're the lucky winner," he says with a smirk.

Shard leans back and starts clicking his pen, a sound that annoys Libby. He had considered going himself, but a friend in the Pentagon advised him it could get rough.

"When do I leave?"

"I can get you out of this," Shard's voice trembles and lacks conviction. "I'll cancel your trip if your boyfriend agrees to testify against Americo."

Libby's response is instant and sharp, like a verbal blade slicing through the air. "You're a real asshole, Fred!" she spits out, her lips curling into a sneer. "Jesse Ford had nothing to do with the release of 'virus.' CIVO misled Americo and tricked them. He'll never testify against Americo."

Shard merely raises his shoulders in a shrug. "Then pack your bags," he says firmly. "The flight leaves from Andrews Air Force Base on Sunday night, so you have a couple of days to get your affairs in order."

He points a stern finger at her. "Remember, you're only an observer. You're there to gather admissible evidence against Americo. You will not involve yourself in the active military operation, no matter what happens. Is that clear?"

"Thanks for the advice, Fred," she says, her voice dripping with sarcasm. With that, she whirls around and storms out of the room, slamming the door behind her.

"Thank me when you get back. Have fun!" he shouts after her, strictly for the benefit of those listening. Then he shrugs his shoulders. She was never a true believer, he thinks, and if something happens to her, oh well.

***

I blink my eyes and look around, absorbing the familiar chaos. Her apartment is warm and cozy but cluttered, just like it was in law school. Discarded socks and various pieces of clothing sprinkle the living room. Several days of dirty dishes are stacked in the sink. Coffee cups are strewn across the countertops. It's unmistakably Libby. I can smell and sense her presence in the apartment.

I hear the sound of a key twisting in the lock, and the door swings open. She freezes when she spies me, her eyes widening in surprise. She screams my name in shock. "JESSE! What are you doing here? How did you get into my apartment? Oh my God, you nearly gave me a heart attack."

She runs to where I'm standing and throws her arms around me. I squeeze her tight, and a rush of pleasure flows through me at the feeling of her embrace.

"I don't believe it," she says, touching my face. "You're here."

"Well, you said you wanted to attend John's funeral, so I thought I would come and get you." I back up to look at her but can't stop smiling.

"Did you fly in the jet? I thought because of *Denz*, there were no more flights. So how did you get here? I don't understand." She was starting to tear up. "You have no idea how much I've missed you." She wraps her arms around me and kisses my lips.

"Sit down." I lead her over to the couch. "I have something I want to tell you."

"I'm getting a drink." She detours to her small bar and looks at me. "I have something to tell you first."

I am anxious to tell her about the teleporter but can see from her face that she has news that won't wait.

"Fred Shard called me into his office this morning. There is going to be a military mission against CIVO headquarters in France. He wants me to go on behalf of the EPA as an observer. He plans to bring a lawsuit against Americo, claiming you and Americo are responsible for *Denz*, and wants me to gather evidence he can use in court."

My mouth drops open. "Why you?" I ask, my voice filled with disbelief and anger.

"He knows I have connections with Americo through you and thinks he can manipulate me to extract information he can use against Americo. He said he won't send me if you agree to testify against Americo."

I struggle to control my anger. "You know I won't testify against Americo," I tell her, my voice strained with cold fury.

Her head dips in agreement, and her eyes glisten with admiration. "I would think less of you if you did."

"Come over here. I have something to tell you, but you better take a big drink and have a seat first. You're going to need it." I sink into the couch, patting the spot beside me.

She sits and kicks off her shoes, giving me a curious glance.

"Do you remember me telling you about Hector and his research on teleportation?"

"Well, yes," she nods, "but I thought that was just a sci-fi dream of his." She takes a drink while watching me with those blue eyes.

"Not anymore." I went on to explain the successes of teleportation research.

"You're joking, right?"

"It's real, baby. Five minutes ago, I was in the lab in Colorado." Libby sat in stunned silence. "John's funeral is tomorrow," I continued. "I want you to come back with me."

"How?" She hesitates and then scoots away from me. "Oh, hell no, you're not going to vaporize me."

"It takes two seconds and is painless. You're going to love it, Libby." I stand, take one of her throw rugs, and spread it in the center of her living room.

"Stand here, close your eyes, and you'll be at the lab when you open them. It's that simple. Takes literally two seconds."

"Jesse, you know I love you, but I think you're full of shit."

I walk over to the rug and stand on it. "Stand where I am, close your eyes, and when you open them, you'll see Hector's smiling face in front of you." I reach out and rest my hands on her shoulders.

"Trust me, okay? If it doesn't work, the worst that will happen is that I will look like a fool."

She eyes me suspiciously, raising her shoulders in a doubtful shrug. "Sure, why not? Do I have time to put on my shoes?" She gives me a nervous schoolgirl laugh, taking me back to the memories of our law school days. After she steps on the rug, I plant a kiss on her lips. "Trust me," I say again.

312

"Oh yeah, 'trust you' because you're a lawyer." She gives me another giggle. It was an old inside joke between us.

I pull out my cell phone and speed-dial Hector's number. Libby immediately chimes in, concern in her voice. "Hector, are you sure this is safe? I don't want to be lost in the twilight zone forever."

Hector laughs. "It's safer than driving a car," he responds. "Trust me."

"Okay, Hec, you ready? Hit it."

I look at Libby. There is a flash of light. Her mouth opens to scream, but she disappears into thin air before she can utter a sound. My jaw drops open in amazement. Despite having witnessed this before, I can't help it. It's incredible to watch someone vanish in front of your eyes. I'll never get used to it.

Hector's still on the phone. "She's here." I can hear Libby's excited voice in the background. "You ready?" Hector asks.

I close my eyes, waiting for the flash. When I open them, I see Hector and Libby standing outside the tube. I reach out and touch the walls to steady myself. Hector is at the hatch and helps me climb out. In front of me, Libby is grinning from ear to ear and is immediately in my arms, touching my face.

"I don't know what to say—I can't believe it." She is shaking, and her voice quivers. She reaches out to Hector and gives him a bear hug. Everyone is grinning.

Libby is excited and can't quit talking. "I can tell I'm in Colorado. My ears popped, and the air is so different here. It smells thinner, cleaner."

Hector shrugs. "That makes sense. You went from sea level to a mile high in about two seconds."

She walks over to look at the teleporter, which gives me a chance to take Hector aside. "Did you get it?"

He nods his head. "Got hers and yours. You can virtually live forever now. When you get old, we'll recreate your original DNA, and you'll be this age again—over and over."

I shake my head, still trying to wrap my brain around everything. "Now we focus on *Denz*."

***

"Let's go to the cafeteria and grab a bite to eat and relax." Hector leads the way. Libby and I follow. She is holding my hand and can't stop grinning.

My first bite of a chicken sandwich is interrupted by my phone. I almost don't bother to answer, but see it is Chip.

"Hey, boss," he greets me. "I'm ready to come home, but heard the jet isn't flying." I put him on speakerphone.

"Perfect timing," I tell him. "I'm at the lab with Hector and Libby. So, you're about ready to come home?"

"Yes, sir, but not sure how to make that happen. As much as I love Lagos, I don't particularly want to be stuck here."

"Chip, this is Hector. Where are you now?"

"Standing in my hotel room. It's about midnight here, and I am dripping in sweat. I've got a flashlight, but unfortunately, the electricity is out, so no lights or air."

"Can you go down and stand right at the outside entryway into the hotel?"

"Why would I want to do that?"

"Go do it. Call Jesse when you're standing right outside the door."

"You got that teleporter gizmo working, didn't you?" Chip says.

"Get everything you want to bring with you. Go down there and give me a call," I tell him.

"Give me a minute." He clicks off.

"Let's head back down to the lab," says Hector, getting up. I stand, taking one last bite of my sandwich.

Hector is still giving instructions to his staff when my phone rings. It's Chip. "I'm standing just outside the doorway," he says.

"Hang on just a couple minutes," said Hector. "Do you have everything?"

"This won't hurt, will it, doc?"

"Don't be a baby," says Libby into the phone. "You're going to love it."

Chip grunts. "I'm ready."

Hector pushes the red button, there's a flash of light, and Chip is standing in the HEC#1 tube.

CHAPTER 31

FUNERAL

I never cared for funerals, but this one is tough for me. John Hammer was a good man and my friend. His death is a tragic loss. Libby and I stand close together, holding hands. Kim is openly weeping with an unrestrained flood of tears, and I'm pleased when Chip puts his arm over her shoulders, offering comfort.

Even though it is dreary, draped in a blanket of gray clouds, I keep my sunglasses on, shielding my eyes. Small talk and chit-chat is the last thing on my mind, which I do my best to avoid.

Libby stays close to me, a reassuring presence. While remaining mostly quiet, she engages in polite conversation when appropriate. Everyone has come, including John's ex-wife, who, despite their divorce, pays her respects to the man she once loved. The office staff and most of the lab team are present, along with the entire board.

Senator Ben Thompson caught a military jet out of D.C. and is present with his eighteen-year-old son, Tommy Thompson, a student at the Massachusetts Institute of Technology. A hearse loaded with red roses and three limos arrives at the office to pick up the Board members. The rest of us take private vehicles.

Despite the cold, gloomy winter day, the service is outdoors. There are few smiles to be seen. Most in attendance still grapple with the enormity of John's passing.

I am one of the six pallbearers, along with Hector, Chip, Senator Thompson, and two of John's longtime friends.

I recall how John had taken a chance on me. Yes, I had graduated in the top ten percent from a prestigious law school, but being a half-breed Indian was not an advantage in the oil and gas business. I didn't miss the looks and whispers when John first hired me. I have no doubt he caught his share of grief over the decision.

I sit in the front row near the casket, Libby on one side and Senator Thompson and his son on the other. During the service, I catch Tommy staring at me several times, a quizzical look on his face. Before we leave, he approaches me and solemnly says, "We'll meet again someday."

I smile and nod. Years later, I will recall the comment.

Before the casket is lowered into the ground, I walk around it, staring into the pale face. John looks natural, at peace. In the background, solemn music plays—a nice touch. People stand and begin stomping their feet from the biting cold. Finally, the casket is lowered into the ground. With a final prayer, people hurry off toward their vehicles, most left running during the service to combat the single-digit temperature.

A reception is planned at the Americo office building afterward. People are encouraged to enter from the underground garage to avoid potential "unpleasantness."

John would have been pleased with the success of the teleporter. I don't believe he ever felt it could be done, but he had the foresight to realize what a giant leap teleportation could mean for mankind. I'm sorry he won't be here to witness it.

***

The Denver skyline, viewed from the warm office through the double-pane windows, is a welcome sight after the service. The background conversation remains muted, broken up by occasional gentle laughter.

Libby and I stroll over to where Chip is standing with Kim. As they talk, Chip's eyes move across the room. He is not drinking and looks uncomfortable.

"When are you headed back?" Chip asks Libby. I had filled him in about the military operation against CIVO. I think he wants to go, but with all the turmoil, I want him here.

Before Libby can answer, Marci Stone approaches. "Libby . . . Libby Burns? How are you?"

Libby turns toward the older woman, not recognizing her at first. However, Marci's eyes are smiling, and she seems genuinely pleased to see Libby.

Marci hugs Libby like they are best friends, ignoring Chip and Kim. Marci and Libby had only met once at a company Christmas party in Aspen. Libby had been with Jesse, but Marci had captured her for much of the party, quizzing Libby about her job at the EPA. Libby told me Marci had called her once when she had been in Washington, but they never managed to make contact.

"It's nice to see you again, even under these circumstances," Marci says with a friendly smile. "When are you headed back to D.C.?"

"I'm afraid I have to go back tomorrow."

"Oh, so soon. My dear, please go to breakfast with me tomorrow morning."

Seeing Libby hesitate, Marci continues to press. "I insist. I need to know who has been keeping Jesse so occupied. I'm an early bird, so anytime." With that, she gives Libby her cell phone number, kisses me on the cheek, and wanders off.

"Wow," I say, embarrassed, rubbing my cheek. "She has never done that before."

"Yeah, you're the charmer." With a toss of her head, Kim turns and walks off.

***

"Why don't you tell her you can't make it?" I ask Libby the following morning. "I'll fix you some of my 'world famous' pancakes. Then we'll return to the office and call Hector to beam us back to the lab." I was still trying to get used to saying "beam" instead of "drive."

Libby shakes her head. "She's on her way. I think she's sweet and was so insistent on breakfast. I don't want to disappoint her. I'll have her drop me off at the office." A horn outside my townhouse tells us her ride is waiting. A quick kiss and Libby is out the door.

***

A black GMC Escalade SUV is at the curb. Stone's driver, a beefy man dressed in a dark suit and wearing wraparound sunglasses, holds the door open for Libby. Marci sits inside the warm interior, smiling. With a quick hug, she thanks Libby for joining her.

319

Marci is chatty, telling Libby stories of her youth. "Oh, my dear, the things I did when I was young . . ." She giggles. "Makes me blush just to think about it."

Libby mostly listens, nodding respectfully at the appropriate time, but she wishes she had taken Jesse's advice.

"Have you ever eaten at Cold Mountain Restaurant?" Marci asks. "The food is fabulous, and at this time of the day, it shouldn't be too crowded."

"Yes, I have. One of my favorite places," answers Libby.

Dressed in a black tuxedo jacket, the maître d' greets them with a gracious smile at the front door. "Good morning, ladies . . . Ms. Stone. Would you care for the usual table? Marci makes eye contact and nods, following him to a darkened area toward the back of the restaurant.

Two glasses of champagne are served while the women indulge in a lengthy conversation about the Colorado weather; Marci finally asks, "How in the world did you get back here from the east coast? I heard all flights were grounded. Did you hitch a ride on a military aircraft?"

Libby hesitates, her thoughts racing. Jesse had warned her not to divulge anything about the teleportation success. "I tried to. It was a big hassle, but I finally made it," she says, hoping to sidestep the issue.

"I thought Jesse was at the lab with Dr. Ramos. Did you fly into there? I know they have a landing strip. Or did you drop from the sky?" Marci chuckles.

Libby laughs nervously. "Ah . . . no, Jesse picked me up." A true statement, she thinks.

Marci pauses, staring at Libby. "Well, well, aren't you the lucky one?" She fills Libby's glass with champagne for the second time. "What in the world is Jesse doing at the lab with everything going on?"

"I think he and Hector . . . Dr. Ramos are working on the antidote for that nasty virus." Libby is extra cautious now.

"Well, sorry you had to come back at such a sad time. That was a terrible thing that happened to John. We all know D.C. is such a terrible place to keep secrets, but I heard a rumor there are plans to send an assault force against that place in France—CIVO, I think it's called. I don't keep up on stuff like that."

Libby gives another nervous laugh. "You know how rumors spread in Washington. Our country has enough on its plate at the moment." Libby shakes her head, drawing her eyebrows together in a frown. Marci must have good connections.

Marci continues to stare at Libby. "Is everything okay, dear? You look like something's bothering you."

"I'm a little worried about Jesse," Libby confesses to Marci. "He blames himself for this whole micro virus mess and feels he must save the world."

"And just how's he going to do that?" Marci scoffs.

Libby laughs. "I have no idea, and I don't think he does, either." She drains her second glass of champagne, looks around, and excuses herself to use the restroom.

As Libby disappears around the corner, Marci reaches into her purse, takes a packet of white powder, dumps the contents into Libby's glass, then fills it a third time.

Libby returns to her seat with a sigh and takes another drink. The bubbly puts her in a chatty mood, and Marci is easy to talk to. "I need to slow down. I have a flight to catch this evening. So this is it for me," she says with a hiccup.

"I understand, my dear," says Marci, reaching over to pat Libby's hand. "Let's order breakfast, and I'll take you wherever you want."

"I'm supposed to meet Jesse at the office." Her words are beginning to slur.

"I wish Jesse would not blame himself for the virus," Marci says, leaning into Libby. "You know," she says in a conspiratorial whisper, "John Hammer and I were the only two on the Board that voted not to fire Jesse."

Libby nods with a low giggle. "I know. Jesse told me." Libby reaches over and puts her hand on Marci's arm. "And I think that was the best decision you ever made." Another giggle, followed by a hiccup. She puts her hand over her mouth. "Oh my, please excuse me," she says, followed by another titter.

"So what plans does Jesse have to save the world and rid us of that terrible virus?" Marci asks with wide-open eyes.

Libby holds her hand over her mouth and nods. "Oh, they're working on a plan. He and Hector are making rats." Her speech is thick and slow.

"You mean Hector's still trying to teleport rats, like in Star Trek? He told us about that at a Board meeting."

Another hiccup. "Oh, he's beyond trying." Hiccup. "I saw it." A giggle.

Marci's eyes narrow, and her good-natured smile disappears. "Has he done it?"

Libby nods, a silly grin on her face. "Yep." Hiccup.

Marci waves at the maitre d'. "Check, please." Marci helps the intoxicated Libby stand, wrapping her arm around Libby's shoulders to steady her.

"Are . . . we finished? I'm still hungry," Libby stutters. The few customers in the restaurant glance at the two ladies and either smile or shake their heads. With the help of Marci's driver, Libby crawls into the back seat and instantly falls asleep. Stone nods at her driver. "Is the jet ready?"

"All fueled and waiting."

Marci gives a silent thanks for having plenty of uncontaminated fuel in a storage tank at her private hanger. She looks at her driver. "Get us to the airport. Give her an injection before you put her on the plane."

***

I'm at the office waiting for Libby. I glance at my watch for the fourth time in fifteen minutes. She's late. It has been over three hours since Marci picked her up for breakfast.

I tried calling Libby but got voicemail. I scroll through my contact list and call Marci's number. No answer, no voicemail. Now I'm on the edge of being worried. With the world in upheaval, there are a lot of crazies out there.

Although it's Sunday, there are a few people at the office. I ask everyone I see if they have seen Marci Stone or Libby. No luck. I call down to the security guards.

"No, sir," says the guard. "I've been here all morning and

haven't seen either one."

An uneasy feeling hits me in the gut like a fist. It's not like Libby not to show up or, at least, call me. I start to imagine different scenarios, none of them good. Marci has a bodyguard, which alleviates some of my concerns but is no guarantee.

Kim walks through my office door as I disconnect from the security guard. "I called Marci's secretary. She told me Marci would be out of town for a few days. Didn't say where." She pauses and looks at me. "If you're going to the lab, I want to go, too."

There is a gnawing fear in my gut. Something is wrong. I call Chip.

My voice quivers as I update him. "See what you can find out. Libby texted me that she and Marci went to the Cold Mountain Restaurant for breakfast. That was the last I heard."

Next, I call Hector. He answers with, "Where's Libby? I thought she had to be back early this afternoon. Don't forget D.C. is two hours ahead of us." I can hear the worry in his voice.

"Get the teleporter ready," I say without going through the details. "When Chip gets to the office, we'll need you to bring us to the lab." I look at Kim. "Kim's coming, also."

***

Chip's ice-cold eyes stare at me—through me. I've seen that look before. It gives me chills.

His voice is unemotional and monotone as he gives me the details. "I checked with the restaurant. Libby was there with Marci Stone. They were drinking champagne mimosas, then left in a hurry. Didn't even order food."

324

"Champagne at nine a.m. That's not like Libby." I realize Libby was likely toasted by then.

"I tracked down the driver of Stone's car," continues Chip. "At first, he wouldn't talk to me, but I persuaded him to tell me where he took them."

I steal a glance at Chip. I can see worry etched on his face as he recalls the conversation with the driver. I hope he isn't about to tell me there was a traffic accident.

"The driver told me he dropped them off at Centennial Airport, at a waiting jet."

"A jet? What the fuck!" Now thoroughly confused. "To where?"

"The pilot filed a flight plan, and you're not going to believe this, but they're flying to France."

It was like a bombshell dropped on me. I sit down, then look up at Chip.

"Call Hector. Tell him to bring us back to the lab . . . now!"

CHAPTER 32
THE PLAN

"The President is pissed," growls Wallace Franklin, Chief of Staff to the President of the United States. "The French refuse to move against Lassiter. When we asked for permission to put U.S. forces on French soil, their answer was a formal protest to the U.S. Ambassador."

Senator Ben Thompson crosses his legs in the oversized easy chair in the Chief's West Wing office. "What's the plan, Wally? Are we still moving forward?" His brow is creased, emphasizing the grim frown.

Franklin lifts his hand and stares through the window at nothing. Finally, he snorts and lets loose with a sullen laugh while shaking his head. "We had an interesting response from the DGSE, the French Secret Service. It appears they have formed an alliance with the Israelis and have been monitoring Lassiter for some time. They're concerned about his connections with some of the radicals in the Saudi royal family. Surprise, but it seems they have strong links to terrorists."

Thompson shifts uneasily in his chair. As a ranking member of the Senate Foreign Relations Committee, he is no stranger to the covert actions of the Israelis in keeping tabs on Lassiter. He's surprised this news seems to catch Franklin off guard.

"The fucking French," continues Franklin. "They want us to do their dirty work for them while they pretend ignorance. Unofficially, the word has been passed that the French will not be part of—nor will their military be involved in—attacking or defending Lassiter from an American assault. They will do nothing to impede an attack, but they did lay out one condition. . . ." Franklin swivels, fixing Thompson with a piercing gaze.

Thompson sits straight up, unconsciously holding his breath.

"Demolition is their price tag. They want Lassiter and his compound annihilated."

"Damn. I guess they can play rough as long as they don't get the blame. Too bad they depend on us to do their dirty work."

Franklin gives a nonchalant shrug. "No matter. Lassiter is gone, whether the French agree or not. According to the Israelis, Lassiter wants to contaminate the oil fields of the Middle East. This will cripple the economies of both Europe and America. But it looks like we got hit first."

"What about the antidote that fellow brought back from Nigeria?"

"Yeah, well, we're discovering it's not a hundred percent effective. The oil company you were part of, Americo Oil, is working on the antidote for *Denz*, but it tends to mutate. So aside from taking out Lassiter, we want our guys to get another antidote sample."

Thompson scoffs sarcastically. "I hope the President realizes it's too late. *Denz* was contained until he released the reserves. The antidote won't undo that."

Wallace's lips curl, and the scowl across his forehead accentuates the deep wrinkles. "It pains me to say it, but I agree with you. We're pretty much screwed when it comes to the *Denz* virus. Lassiter hit us in our weakest area. The falling energy domino will trigger a spark igniting the collapse of the economy. We need an alternative energy source, but that's years, even decades, away."

Thompson looks at his watch. "What's the timeline for the attack?"

"The assembly point is Andrews Air Force base for the Rangers and equipment. They fly out this afternoon. Considering the flight time and time zones, our boys should be parachuting in, ready to roll by sunrise, Paris time."

Senator Thompson shifts in his chair, verbalizing the taboo subject that hangs over the room. "You know the President doesn't stand a chance in hell of being reelected now."

Wallace drops his head, searching his desk and coming to rest on the photo of his wife. "I know," he mumbles, "and he knows it, too." Wallace stands straight up, turns, and looks at Ben. "But before we go, that bastard Lassiter will pay."

***

Thanks to the teleporter, Chip, Kim, and I are back at the lab within minutes. We have come up with a rough plan. Chip and I are going to France, specifically CIVO headquarters. Hector joins us in the cafeteria as we work out the details.

I lean forward on the table, resting my elbows. "Chip and I have been to the CIVO facility and got the tour, except for the underground basement. No one outside of CIVO knows the layout as well as we do. But you saw the basement, right?" I say to Chip.

"Yep. Even though Lassiter warned me the basement was off-limits, Faisal took me down there. It reminded me of a dungeon in a medieval castle. There was one room full of computers and some geeks sitting at workstations. I peeked in, but that was one room Faisal wouldn't take me to. He claimed it was where they monitored the building security, but it looked pretty elaborate for security."

"That's good to know. Any chance you could draw a diagram from what you remember? From what Libby told me, the military plans an assault Monday night, Paris time. If we can teleport while that is happening, it would make a good distraction. They won't be expecting us. Stealth will be a big advantage."

I look over the edge of my coffee cup at Hector. "Any problem beaming into Lassiter's fortress?"

Hector sits back with a relieved look on his face. "I wondered how long it would take you to get around to that question. I've been experimenting—just rats, mind you. I knew we could transmit you and Libby from D.C., but I wondered if there was a distance limitation. The answer is 'no.' I don't think there is.

"With the help of our GPS satellites, I can preset arrival points to transmit an object—or person to any place on the planet. So we can beam something . . . or somebody . . . wherever we want. I sent a rat to a colleague in Israel. We have a one hundred percent success rate. Sorry I didn't tell you this earlier, but we have been working twenty-four-seven."

Our discussion is interrupted by a "News Alert" on the cafeteria wall-mounted TV playing in the background. Despite the low volume, the breaking news flash on the screen catches my attention.

A breathless correspondent reports that a C-130 Hercules carrying a lethal combination of Army Rangers and Navy SEALs went down near the French and Belgium border. A ham radio operator in Germany picked up a transmission from the plane just before the crash, recorded it, and released it to a local TV station. Despite the German government's attempts to stop it, the final communication of the doomed aircraft was broadcast on German TV.

The TV analysts speculate the cause of the crash is a contaminated fuel supply, with the likely culprit being virus known as "*Denz*." However, the U.S. government remains tight-lipped, refusing to confirm or deny the crash, only admitting that there is a missing aircraft on a routine training flight.

We all stare at the TV in stunned silence. Chip breaks the tension with a sarcastic remark. "Routine training flight, my ass. That was the military operation to snatch the life out of Lassiter." His words hand heavy in the air. *hang*

I nod, feeling the guilt of more deaths, and sink deeper into my chair. "Libby would have been on that flight," I whisper, inhaling sharply. I swallow and stare at Hector. "Could we beam a bomb into CIVO?"

Hector gives me a stern look. "What do you have in mind?"

"Could we send a bomb into the CIVO facility—say, into the computer room Chip mentioned?"

Hector looks uncomfortable. "I don't know. It would be risky at best. Explosives are unstable, to begin with. A bomb may not survive teleportation and could explode at either the transmitting or destination point. We've never tried it—never even considered it."

Chip leans in toward Hector. "Speaking of bombs, is JC here?"

John Claude, or JC as we fondly call him, is the head of security for the lab. I look at Hector, "If I recall, he's an expert in explosives."

Hector's head bobs in agreement. "Yeah, he used to train Navy SEALs in the art of explosives before we hired him."

"We need to speak with him. Can you call him?" I inquire.

Hector looks unsure. "He would be a good man, but I can't speak for him. Not everyone may make it back from this little venture."

"He'll go." I nod confidently. I remember when I first met him. John Claude was applying for a security position at the lab. I happened to be present that day and volunteered to interview the man.

What I saw was a very fit, intelligent, black man who came out of the Louisiana swamps. Only recently discharged from the Navy, he had spent the past ten years as a weapons and explosives expert with the SEALs. When I interviewed him, he worked a dead-end job as a guide for airboat tours through the bayou swamps but was bored and ready to re-enlist.

At the conclusion of the interview, I called Chip and introduced them. "Why don't you take JC to the cafeteria, buy him a cup of coffee, and show him around?" I suggested.

Chip recognized the potential in JC to be a serious contender in a role with the lab's security. I trusted Chip's opinion and wanted his blessing before offering JC the job. They were gone for two hours, but when they returned, Chip gave me a knowing wink. That was all the endorsement I needed. Two years later, JC sits at the helm as the Director of Security for the Americo Research Lab.

JC enters the cafeteria and saunters over to where we're sitting. He nods to Hector and Chip and greets me with a smile. "Hey, Mr. Ford, good to see you. What's up?"

"You want to help Chip and me get some bad guys?" was all I had to say.

His response was swift. "Oh, hell yes, I'm aboard." I knew he would.

Hector, Chip, and I spent two intense hours briefing on the latest information regarding the *Denz* and the antidote, what we knew about Lassiter, and the CIVO lab. Finally, I declared that I intended to find Libby, blow up the lab, and kill or capture Lassiter. JC is all in. I can see the fire in his eyes.

I look seriously at JC. "There's no guarantee of success, but if Libby is there, I won't be leaving without her," I state flatly.

"There is one thing that bothers me," says JC. "When we beam, or transport, to CIVO, what if we reassemble in the middle of a wall?"

"Good question, JC," answers Hector. "You cannot be reassembled in solid matter. The beam will move the reception point, within reason, till there is nothing to disrupt reassembly. I mean, I don't believe we could beam you to the center of the earth. You would never reassemble."

"What about beaming underwater?" I ask.

Hector shakes his head. "Unknown. We've never tried that before."

Chip stands. "JC and I are going to check out our weapon situation. Any particular type of weapon you want?" He looks at me.

"A good knife, and I'll let you decide on guns." Thanks to my younger days shooting prairie rats in the desert, I am comfortable with almost any gun, but very few could match my blade abilities.

Lost in thought, I imagine what I might do to Lassiter should he harm Libby. Gruesome thoughts flash through my mind.

A gentle touch to my arm pulls me back. "Yo, Jesse, you still here?" Hector says, eyeing me cautiously.

I blink, clearing the mental fog, and stare into Hector's watchful face. "He's going to kill Libby."

CHAPTER 33
MARCI

The airstrip was short, just long enough for the Dassault Falcon 6X jet to land but too short for large military aircraft. Before stepping outside the plane, Marci bends over to examine her guest. Libby Burns is still sleeping under the influence of the barbiturate drug. Her hands are cuffed with nylon zip ties, and saliva dribbles from one corner of her mouth.

The pilot opens the hatch, then steps back. Before descending, Stone wraps her head in the Shayla, a blue rectangular scarf pinned in place on her left shoulder.

"Bring her," she orders.

The morning sun is swallowed by the looming storm clouds and a constant westerly breeze. Marci wraps her arm over her head scarf as she hurries toward a waiting van.

One of the men tosses Libby over his shoulder, then throws her into the back of the van. The hard floor of the bouncing van wakes her from the effects of the drug. She regains consciousness and opens her eyes. Despite her blurred vision, she tries to make sense of her surroundings. Her wrists are raw from the zip ties. Where is she? With a jerk, the van stops. The side door slides open, and the man roughly pulls her out of the van.

"Hey! Take it easy!" Libby cries out, wincing in pain. "I can walk if you will help me stand." Two men dressed in uniforms grab each elbow and lift her to her feet. She staggers and sways but, with the help of the men, moves toward an entrance to a large building. As she approaches the door, a cold fear stops her. On the front door is one word: CIVO.

She's in France. There is a sharp jab in her neck, and the world goes black.

***

Libby's eyes flutter open. She emits a raspy groan while trying to lift her heavy head. A blinding light pierces her eyelids, causing pain. Reaching out to the light, she finds herself restrained. Her head falls forward, and her long hair covers her bare breasts. To her horror, she is entirely naked.

She lifts her head, slowly scanning her silent surroundings. She cannot see into the darkness beyond the glare of the light. Her bare feet rest on a damp stone floor, aching from the cold sending jolts of pain up her legs. She has never felt so miserable.

Libby's wrists and feet are strapped to the arms and legs of a cold metal chair with nylon zip ties. A second chair sits to her left but is empty.

Suddenly the sound of a creaking door echoes in the room, causing Libby's heart to race. Marci Stone steps into the light with a slender man dressed in black by her side. Marci's gaze falls upon Libby, and she turns to the man beside her.

"What's this? Why did you remove her clothes?" Marci demands of the man. She scowls in anger. "There's no need for this."

The man turns to Stone. "I've done nothing . . . yet," he snarls while pulling on leather gloves. He moves to the second chair and sits facing Libby. "Ms. Burns, allow me to introduce myself. I am Dr. Aran Lassiter. I take it you had a comfortable trip?"

"You sick bastard," Libby growls. "I don't care who you are. Only an animal would do this."

Lassiter shrugs. "My men may have got a little carried away, but consider it more of a payback."

"I'm thirsty and need to use the bathroom," demands Libby.

Once again, Lassiter shrugs. "I'm afraid you will not have that luxury," he says, ignoring her request.

Libby glares at Marci. "I can't believe you are part of this." Anger builds in her voice.

Marci looks back at Libby. "I must admit, I am more refined than my nephew." She frowns, nodding toward Lassiter.

Libby gasps. "This asshole is your nephew? You have a pretty fucked up family tree," she says through clenched teeth.

Lassiter stands and slams his gloved fist into Libby's nose. The sudden move startles Marci, who jumps backward. Libby yelps and winces in pain but does not scream or cry out. Blood flows into her open mouth, down her chin, dripping onto her chest and stomach.

"Careful what you say about the royal family, you infidel bitch. My mother has the blood of the Saudi Kings flowing in her. Ms. Stone is my aunt—by marriage, of course."

"How do you think I became the largest shareholder in Americo?" Marci gives Libby a smug smile. "My dead husband was the brother of Aran's mother. We have discovered we are . . . compatible."

"What do you want with me?" Libby's voice is weak, barely audible. She looks up at Lassiter. His sunken cheeks make his face look narrow and pale. A defined black goatee has silver streaks accenting the protruding bones of his face, reminding Libby of a skeleton from hell. She shivers as a wave of fear sweeps over her.

"Libby," says Lassiter in a friendly, sincere tone, "I know Dr. Ramos has been working on the teleportation device. While you were having breakfast with Ms. Stone, you indicated Dr. Ramos had made it work. Is that true?"

Libby's eyes open wide, and she shakes her head. "I have no idea what you're talking about. I'm a lawyer for the EPA. So that science stuff is way over my head."

Lassiter shrugs. "It doesn't matter what you tell us. I believe they have it, and you and Ms. Stone will help me acquire this technology. Otherwise . . ." He leaves the sentence unfinished. "It is very simple," he continues. "I get what I want, and you live; if not, you die. But either way, I will get what I want."

"Fuck you, dirtbag," hisses Libby.

"Now, now. Please think about it before you answer. Here, let me give you a little incentive." Lassiter reaches over to Libby's pinky finger, grabs it, and bends it back until there is a sharp snap. Libby screams in pain and withers in the chair.

Marci gasps and puts her hand over her mouth. Lassiter ignores her.

"I am going to call your boyfriend." He glares at Libby as her moans continue. "If you don't do what I ask, I shall break your ring finger next."

He stands. Libby bounces the chair, trying to back away from him. He looks at her with a cruel smile. "Faisal," he calls out. "Set up the camera."

The door hinge creaks with a high-pitched grating sound as a second man enters the dimly lit room. He brings in a tripod and fastens a video camera to it. A small cable runs from the camera to a satellite phone.

He looks at Libby. "Now, no dramatics, please, or I will immediately terminate the call and break your next finger, then we will try it again and again until we get it right. I want the teleportation device."

Lassiter grabs Libby's chin and lifts it, his eyes inches away from her blood-stained face. "Do we understand each other?" he hisses.

She squirms, jerking her head back, but gives a weak nod. "You're going to die for this, Lassiter. The U.S. government will track you down and not stop until you're dead, asshole," Libby whispers between cracked and swollen lips.

Lassiter slaps her across the face with his open hand. "Watch your language when speaking to me," he commands. The blow leaves a red mark on her left eye. "I'm afraid you overestimate the power of your weakling President." He laughs. "Your country has already been brought to its knees."

"Aran," says Marci, "enough of this. There is no need to torture her. I know Jesse Ford. He'll give you the teleportation without this."

Lassiter turns to look at her. "I'm not so sure, Aunt Marci. But," he says, glaring at her, "I enjoy this." He nods toward his security guard. Faisal grabs Marci from behind. She yelps in surprise and struggles but is no match for the security man. Faisal throws her into the second chair, and, like Libby, her hands and feet are bound.

"What are you doing!?" she screams at him.

"Something I have wanted to do for a long time, you infidel bitch. My uncle married you simply because you were young, beautiful, and a good piece of ass. But the family always hated you and your heathen ways. So now I'm using you as a bargaining chip."

With a gloved hand, Faisal gingerly takes a pint-sized silver container and hands it to Lassiter. Both men move slowly and deliberately. The small container has a narrow spout with a trigger at the base of the spout. On the outside of the container is a biohazard warning symbol of three black circles.

He holds the container up for Marci to see. "I would like to introduce you to the world-famous *Denz*, a slightly upgraded version," he says with a sadistic grin. "This edition works within minutes instead of hours."

He holds the container within inches of her face and pulls the trigger. A fine red mist sprays out of the nozzle, covering her face.

Marci's piercing scream is ghastly. She shakes her head and blinks, attempting to back away from the spray, but is held firmly in place by the straps. In between her screams, she begs to be killed.

Lassiter gives a vicious laugh. "You are already dead." He turns his back and walks to the video camera mounted on the tripod. The camera is turned to face Libby.

Lassiter watches Marci's withering reaction with perverted satisfaction. He turns to Faisal. "Start the camera," he orders.

"Now, ladies," he says, addressing Libby and the incoherent Marci, whose moaning is broken up by short gasps of pain. "I am going to call Jesse Ford. Feel free to tell Mr. Ford what happened to you. He must agree to give me the teleportation technology. If not, the next squirt of this will be in your face," he says, looking at Libby.

Lassiter picks up the phone, turns the speakerphone on, and punches in a number.

***

I jump when the phone rings. I answer, only to be greeted by Lassiter's familiar, slimy tone.

"Mr. Ford, I think you know who this is. I have a couple of ladies sitting here you may recognize."

On my phone's small screen, my eyes widen in horror as I see a picture of Libby. She sits naked, strapped in a chair, her face red and swollen. Blood drips from her nose. On the screen, I see Marci sobbing in the background, strapped in the second chair.

Lassiter's metallic voice booms over the phone as the camera zooms in on Marci. "I just introduced my aunt to my virus friends," he continues, "whom you can see are enjoying the banquet they are having." There is a scream from Marci. Her face is inflamed and covered in bright red blisters. Blood drips from both her eyes.

Lassiter is now ranting with a crazed look on his face. "I might mention that I have added a special little touch to this virus . . . without getting too technical for you . . . think of them as *Denz* on steroids. You may wonder why I am showing you this, but I want a trade."

I squirm at the sight of Libby. My fingernails dig into the palm of my hands from my clenched fists. I have to fight to keep silent. Chip is standing beside me. He touches my arm while shaking his head. "Stay cool," he whispers.

"I know you and Dr. Ramos have developed teleportation technology to the point where it actually works. I must congratulate you. Now, I want all the plans, diagrams, research, and a fully operational model of the teleporter in exchange for the lives of these two women. You have ten minutes to think about it. If I don't hear from you, I will spray my little friends onto the face of Miss Burns. You will be able to watch it on video."

Lassiter points his video camera for a close-up of Libby's face. "Imagine the lovely Miss Burns looking like this in ten minutes." He shifts the camera back to Marci's deteriorating face.

"You now have nine minutes and thirty seconds."

"Wait!" I yell into the phone. "I want to speak with Libby."

"An understandable request," says Lassiter, turning the camera back on Libby. "He wants to speak with you."

Lassiter puts the phone next to Libby's ear. I hear her take a shaky breath. Then, she looks into the camera and screams, "Jesse, kill the motherfucker!"

Lassiter laughs, jerking the phone away.

"As you can see, Ms. Burns still has a lot of energy left. But unfortunately, the same cannot be said for Ms. Stone, whom, you may notice, is losing her face, to be followed by Libby in about nine minutes now."

The line goes dead.

***

There is a red haze over my eyes. I want to kill him. Instead, I stare at Chip, who hands me a Glock 17 and holster. Chip has picked out the Glocks for their magazine capacity: seventeen bullets. I do not want a rifle, preferring to use my knife as a backup weapon.

Kim's expression is grim as she helps Chip bring weapons up from the lab armory. JC double-checks them and loads bullets into the magazines. A separate pile of extra ammo is set aside to be sent in if needed. Part of me hopes it won't be needed, but part of me hopes we use every bullet.

I put thoughts of Libby aside and focus on what is sure to come—serious violence. The start of our operation has been bumped up to start in less than ten minutes. We were hoping to wait until it was early morning in France. That no longer matters.

Chip, Hector, Kim, and I assemble with JC in the lab, finalizing our plan. We will beam a miniature video camera into the basement to survey the scene and transmit the images to the lab.

If all is clear, it is agreed that Chip will beam into the basement first. Once he assesses the situation, JC and I will follow. I will call Lassiter in a few minutes and pretend to agree to give him the teleportation equipment. Of course, that will never happen, but it will buy us extra time.

Chip, JC, and I will meet up in the hallway outside the basement computer room door. Once the room is secure, Hector wants to send two computer techs back at the same time to download all the info off the CIVO computers, especially data about *Denz* and the antidote. We convince Hector to wait until the computers are secure before sending the techs. One of Hector's computer technicians pulls up a schematic drawing of the CIVO fortress, which we have compared to Chip's basement drawing. All of us have memorized both. Kim will remain in the lab and help coordinate.

"Is everyone good?" I ask. All heads nod. "Okay, here we go."

I pick up the phone and hit redial with the phone on speaker—Lassiter answers on the first ring. I don't wait for him to speak. "We agree. How do we make this exchange?"

"Teleport everything here, along with Dr. Ramos. Then, once we are assured it works, the women and Ramos will be returned. But, wait . . . oh . . . I'm afraid my aunt will not be making that journey . . . it's a little late for her."

"We will need time to gather the equipment and the GPS coordinates of where to send it," I say, fighting to stay in control.

"Put Dr. Ramos on. I will give him those instructions," replies Lassiter.

After giving the coordinates to Hector, Lassiter says, "You have one hour." The phone goes dead.

***

Hector looks at me and nods. "We're ready." He pushes the red button, followed by the customary flash of light. The small miniaturized video camera in the cigar-shaped tube's base disappears.

My eyes grow wide. Everyone stares at the tube. The sight of objects vanishing is still challenging. Every eye watches the image on the monitor. After a few seconds of interference, a shadowy picture appears.

The camera is on the floor of a dimly lit passageway. No movement is seen.

"Go to night vision," Hector tells one of the technicians. The picture shifts to the enhanced night vision image. The camera slowly rotates, transmitting a live video feed to the Colorado lab. There is no sign of life. Coordinates indicate that the camera is on the lower level, a perfect spot. All is ready.

CHAPTER 34
SOMETHING'S WRONG

Our plan is solid, and we have the advantage of surprise. Our immediate goal is to take the computer center. What had started as a search and rescue mission has now morphed into search and rescue, then destroy and kill.

All of us wear the new liquid Kevlar body armor. I adjust the straps, feeling the smooth material cling to my skin. It is lightweight and flexible, allowing me to move with ease. Chip and JC are armed with M4 carbine rifles, handguns, and knives. I check my weapons, ensuring my Glock 17 and knife are secure. Finally, I slide into a backpack containing the micro-laptop on which we will download the CIVO files.

Chip meets my gaze, a spark of excitement in his eyes. I can feel the eagerness radiating off him. He looks me square in the eye. "We good?"

Without a word, I nod and give him a reassuring pat on the shoulder. "Let's do this." He'll be the first to go. "We'll be right behind you," I promise. We are ready.

Hector's eyes narrow as he studies the coordinates on his screen provided by Lassiter. "They don't match the location from where Lassiter made the phone call." He bites his lip. "Logically, he would want us to beam the teleportation equipment into their computer center," he says. "But I think the coordinates from the phone call are where the women are being held."

We all agree that makes sense. Hector does a quick calculation and makes a slight adjustment in Chip's coordinates. "This should put you right outside the computer room in the passageway, which will be the rendezvous point," he tells Chip, "But I want you to confirm this location before I send Jesse and JC."

After the computer room is secure, Chip and I will make our way to where the hostages are being held. JC will remain in the computer room, planting explosives. Meanwhile, Hector will send the tech guys to the computer room, link into the CIVO system, download all the files, and then upload a computer virus that will wipe the CIVO system. We'll then regroup with Libby and Marci, set the timer on the explosives, and beam everyone back to Colorado. Sounds simple.

I am the least experienced member of our team, having never been in actual combat. The thought makes my stomach churn. Chip notices my unease and offers some words of caution.

"Be prepared for anything," he tells me, his voice low but firm. "In the fog of war, anything can happen and usually does. Stay alert."

JC nods his agreement. "Never fails."

Chip is ready. There are still fifteen minutes before our one-hour deadline when he steps into the tube and gives me a thumbs-up. Once he arrives, he will wait for me and JC.

The familiar light flashes and Chip disappears. An instant later, Hector is talking to him on the radio. Hector looks up at me. "He's there." So far, so good.

I wait five more minutes, then call Lassiter. I can barely control myself and want to tell him he only has minutes to live. Instead, I say, "We're ready. I'll be coming first with some equipment. Dr. Ramos will be following me." I confirm the coordinates he gave earlier.

Lassiter sounds anxious. His breaths come in short gasps over the phone. "We'll have people there. How long before Ramos arrives?"

"Don't worry," I say, trying to stay calm and reassuring. "We've got the equipment together. How's Libby?"

"Still sitting here, waiting for her knight in shining armor."

Disconnecting from Lassiter, I go to the teleporter and climb inside. "You ready for this, my friend?" Hector asks. I give him a grim smile but can't resist saying, "Beam me up, Scotty. Let's do it."

As the green rings rise in the tube, I hear a loud cracking noise in the background, an unusual sound. I get a sinking feeling that something just went wrong, a sense confirmed when I hit the ground and open my eyes.

CHAPTER 35
POWER FAILURE

Jesse's silhouette starts to blur in the teleportation device just as a spine-chilling crack rips through the laboratory. Suddenly all sounds cease as the pulsating glow from the computer screens fades, and the entire laboratory is enveloped in complete blackness.

A sense of vulnerability and disorientation permeates the room in the stillness. As if on cue, the emergency lights kick on, bathing the lab in a haunting red glow. The teleporter stands dark and empty.

"Get the backup generators going." Hector's commanding voice pierces through the eerie silence, breaking the tension in the lab. "See if you can find out what happened."

"Power to the whole lab is down," responds a technician. "I got through to Denver. They say the power for the whole city is out. Their power outage must have interfered with our source."

"Great timing," says Hector sarcastically. "How soon can we get the backup generators online?"

"Not long," answers the technician. "Until then, we will have battery power. We can turn on our computers but have no internet and insufficient power to teleport."

"Any luck raising Jesse?" Hector looks at Chris, his top technician, sitting at a computer. "We've got to locate him. He's got a SAT phone, so we should be able to reach him. Did he even make it to the CIVO building?"

Instantly, the technician is on the keyboard moving through the various screens popping up on the monitor while shaking his head. "When the power shut down, it turned off our computers. We need to reboot. That is going to take a few minutes."

Standing on the teleporter's base pad, JC steps away and walks over to Hector. "Did he make it?"

***

I open my eyes and find myself immersed in a pitch-black abyss. Disoriented, I struggle to regain my balance but stumble and crash onto a cold, damp floor. The throbbing pain in my head, a new symptom after teleporting, only adds to my confusion. What the hell happened? I should be standing alongside Chip in the corridor.

Trying to stand, I slip and fall back on the slick wet floor. My backpack is covered in a slimy muck. Cold droplets trickle down my collar, sending shivers down my spine. I fumble for my flashlight, ignoring the smell of stagnant water.

The narrow beam of my light cuts a narrow swath through the darkness. The room is small and bare as if abandoned for years. JC should be appearing, but nothing interrupts the blackness as the minutes tick by.

Speaking softly, I call out their names. "Chip? JC?" My voice echoes in the emptiness. "Anyone here?" Only silence answers me.

Taking a few steps, I lose my balance and nearly fall. My military fatigues are soaked and cold, and I begin to shiver. The knot in the pit of my stomach grows as I realize something has gone terribly wrong.

Fumbling in my pocket, I reach for my cell phone, but to my dismay, there is no signal. The cell phone is worthless here. We planned for this and are all equipped with SAT phones which use orbiting satellites for their signals. I try and call out on my phone, which should be able to connect with satellites in orbit. No luck. Shutting off the SAT phone, I boot it back up, hoping to reroute my signal—still nothing.

I try calling my office number on the SAT phone. Again, the screen tells me there is no signal, and silence is my only greeting. I am trapped in this place. I have no idea where I am, but I take comfort in knowing the lab can track my location on the satellite phone even though I can't call out. Doubt begins gnawing at me. Is this the end of our plan to rescue Libby? There has got to be a way out.

If JC were going to follow me, he would have been here by now. In desperation, I call Chip's cell phone. Surprised when he answers, I fumble and nearly drop the phone.

"Where in the hell are you?" He sounds pissed off.

"I don't know. In some room, but not where I expected to be. I can't reach Hector."

Chip tells me he's also been trying to call the lab but is getting no answer.

The beam of my penlight seems feeble in the oppressive darkness. There has to be a door out of here. At the far end of the room, I spot a dim outline of what appears to be an entryway. When I switch my light off, there is a faint glow of light seeping under a crack in the door.

"I see a door at the far end of this room," I tell Chip. "I'm going to disconnect to save battery power while I check it out. If I get out of here, I'll call you. Stay where you are. I'll find you."

I make for the door, tramping through puddles of foul-smelling water. The room reeks of mildew, reminding me of a tomb. I make for the door, using the faint light underneath as a guide.

The hinges are caked with rust like they haven't been opened in years. I grasp the rusted handle and turn it, but it won't budge. Putting all my weight on the handle, I shake it up and down, then back and forth. Despite the noise I'm making, I grab the handle and pull with all my strength. My heart leaps at the scraping sound, and I feel some give in the door. More light filters into the room through the enlarged opening. Grabbing the handle again, I put one foot on the wall as leverage and pull. The metal-on-metal screech is a loud but welcome sound. One more pull and the door creaks open enough for me to squeeze through. A faint streak of light enters the room.

Stowing my penlight, I replace it with my knife. Hearing no sound, I peek through the half-open door. The silence is so complete all I hear is ringing in my ears. A low-wattage light bulb on a wall reveals a slimy passageway extending in both directions.

I pull the door open farther, wincing at the grinding noise. Hearing no other sound, I scan both directions for signs of life, then step out into a corridor. Taking one last look back into the dark room, I turn to my right, which has a slight incline.

Pulling out my phone, I call Chip. "I'm out."

***

The lights flicker and brighten to their full intensity. "We're back online!" yells Chris, the leading technician in the lab.

Excited shouts come from a man on a computer console trying to locate Jesse's tracking device. "I've got him! He's in the very lowest level."

"Can you reach him?" Hector asks.

"I've got a signal," says the excited technician. "He's not even near the computer room. Thank goodness we had the power to get him that far."

The buzz on Hector's phone breaks the silence of the lab. Hector glances at the screen before answering. "Chip, are you okay?" he asks with a sense of urgency in his tone.

"Jesse got sent to some room where he was locked in," exclaims Chip in a tumble of words, "but we are talking, and he is now out. We need to link up. Can you give us directions?"

"Wait one sec," says Hector as he studies the chart. "He isn't that far, but he is below you. There must be a lower level. I'll give him a call and walk him through it to get back to you. Stay where you're at. There's going to be a change of plan for JC. As you guys enter the front, JC will be coming in from the other side of the room. Give me a few minutes to confirm."

JC heads back to the teleporter. Hector follows him, taking him aside. "This may get a little tricky. We have the coordinates to the computer center where you're going, but Jesse isn't there yet—now, a slight change of plans for you. Instead of going in the door with Jesse and Chip, you'll come in from the opposite side of the room. When they go through the front door, we'll have you appear toward the back of the room, so you can both come in from two directions at once."

JC nods. "That sounds good. Just let them know so they don't shoot me."

JC climbs into the cigar-shaped tube, closes the hatch, and waits for Hector to give him the thumbs-up while Hector calls Chip with the change of plans.

***

As I slip through the silent tunnel, my phone vibrates, startling me. I grab it off my belt hook and hit the talk key, a wave of anxiety washing over me. "Hector, I sure hope this is you." On the other end of the line, I hear a relieved laugh.

"Jesse, you okay?" Hector's voice is strained.

"I'm fine," I say in frustration. "Where in the hell did you send me? Cause it sure wasn't where I was planning on."

Despite the sketchy connection, Hector updates me on the power loss and what's happened since we last spoke. "JC is ready to beam into the computer center, but I want to hold off for a few minutes till you get there. He'll come in from the other side when you and Chip enter the front door. Timing on this is crucial if we hope to catch them by surprise. I see where you are, and you're close. Any sign of Chip?"

"Nothing yet, but I've made contact. He's in position." My frustration is replaced by adrenaline in anticipation of what's about to happen. My palms are sweaty.

"Good. You're close," Hector says. "In about twenty meters, you'll see a stairway on your right. Go to the next floor, turn left, and the computer center should be directly in front of you."

"I'm going to disconnect and may be busy, so don't try and call me. I'll let you know when I link up with Chip."

I pick up my pace through the corridor. The thought of what is about to happen begins to sink in. The passageway abruptly ends with a door on my right. I gently pull it open. Before me are stairs leading upward. Pausing to listen, I start climbing.

The stairway is long and dimly lit, making it impossible to see where it ends. I lick my lips, then wipe them with my hand. Halfway up the stairs, I stop to take a swig of water.

Another door awaits me at the top of the stairs. I listen, then slowly pull it open. The hum of distant machinery greets me. As I step into a dimly lit corridor, a figure emerges from the shadows.

"About fucking time," whispers Chip. He points to the door in front of him and gives me a nod. "You ready?"

I adjust my vest and remove the Glock, ensuring a shell is chambered and the safety off. Looking at Chip, I hold up my finger and speak into the phone. "Hector, I'm here. We're ready. Let's do it."

"Just be looking for JC coming in from the other side. Don't shoot his ass," says Hector. Jesse gives two quick clicks, signifying he got the message.

Back in the lab, Chris's hands fly across the keyboard in a blur of motion. "Okay, here we go. I'm going to send out one focused signal." He hits the Enter key and sits back in his chair, looking at Hector. "We're ready. Give the word."

Hector speaks into his headset, warning JC that Jesse and Chip are going in. JC grimly nods, double-checking his M4 rifle and flipping the safety off. There is a flash of light, and JC disappears.

THE SPILL

I lock eyes with Chip. "Here we go!" I whisper.

He gives a quick nod, lifting his M4. Licking my lips, I hold up three fingers, then two, then one, and reach for the door handle, which is suddenly jerked open out of my hand from the inside.

I find myself face-to-face with a surprised security guard. We both stare at each other, then raise our weapons. Almost simultaneously the two triggers are pulled, and all hell breaks loose.

CHAPTER 36
VICIOUS

In a split second, the triggers of both guns are pulled, unleashing violent explosions. At that instant, JC materializes across the room in a dazzling burst of light. The distraction causes the guard's aim to falter, and his shot finds its mark in my stomach, hitting my vest. I am just as surprised, but my shot hits the guard point-blank in the face, ending his threat.

Gasping for breath, I double over in pain and fall to the ground. My stomach feels like I got hit with a baseball bat swung by a professional baseball player. My Kevlar vest stops the bullet but not the searing pain. The guard is not so lucky. He lay motionless on the floor, his bloody face a mask of shock and surprise.

Chip leaps past me and begins firing at the remaining guards. Amid the chaos of gunfire, flashing lights, and JC's sudden arrival, the remaining guards panic and open fire on JC's shadowy figure. Chip eliminates them with ruthless efficiency, but not before a half dozen bullets tear into JC, who collapses to the floor in a pool of blood.

I'm still lying on the ground, struggling to breathe and process what's happening. When the shooting stops, the room is filled with the smell of gunpowder and smoke.

In horror, I see Chip clutch his chest, stagger and fall to the ground. Our first confrontation did not go as planned. We are all reeling from the violent encounter—JC is dead, I'm shot in the stomach, and Chip is shot in the chest, but thanks to the vests, we are good. JC is not so lucky.

I lie on my back, staring at the ceiling as the pain slowly subsides. The gunshot in my abdomen is painful, and I wonder if I have a broken rib where the bullet struck my vest.

Chip is swiftly at my side, acting as though he is without any injury. After a brief examination, he reaches into his vest pocket and pulls out a handful of white pills. "Here, take three of these," he says, handing me a water bottle. Without hesitation, he tosses a handful into his mouth, swallowing them without the aid of water.

Chip grabs my arm and begins to help me to my feet. I start to get up, but stop and lean down, feeling like I am about to vomit. "You're only going to have some bruising," he says. "You'll be fine. Now, time to harden-the-fuck-up," he smiles, helping me to my feet.

The pain is beginning to subside, and I am breathing easier. Still bending over from the pain, I walk to where JC lies sprawled on the concrete floor. Blood is running out of a head wound. I kneel and touch his shoulder. "JC," I call, "can you hear me?" There is no response. I reach down to feel his carotid artery. It is still.

I painfully pull my phone out of my vest, wondering if Hector is still on the line. "Hector, are you still there?" I gasp in between short breaths. "I'm feeling better," I say, rubbing my sternum, "and Chip is up and moving. But JC took bullets to the head. I'm afraid he is gone. Without him, we aren't able to set any explosives."

Hector hesitates. "Hold on, let me think. Is JC still at the spot where he beamed in?"

"Yeah," I answer, shaking my head. "He never even got a shot off before they blasted him. It was almost like they knew he was coming."

"I have an idea," says Hector, his voice rising in excitement. "I'm going to reverse the process and bring him back to the lab. Don't touch him." Seconds later, there is a flash of light, and JC's body disappears.

***

In the lab, JC's crumpled and bullet-riddled body appears. "Get me the readings for JC's DNA," Hector tells his assistant, Christopher Drake. "Get JC's body out of the teleporter. We are going to send him back. Make sure this line stays open."

Drake's fingers fly over the keyboard. "Ready," he calls out. Hector hits the Enter key on his computer. Another flash of light and a very much alive JC stands in HEC#2 with a bewildered expression.

"No time to explain," Hector tells him. "We're going to send you into the CIVO computer room. Jesse and Chip are waiting for you."

One of the technicians in the lab hands JC an M4 rifle. "Don't get shot this time. Three, two, one." Hector counts down and pushes the red button on his console. In a flash of light, JC disappears and is back in the fight.

The phone line is still open. Over the SAT phone, I can hear the hushed conversation in the lab. I brace myself for the flash of light. When I open my eyes, the sight that greets me is unexpected. JC is back, a silhouette standing in a crimson puddle of his blood, where he had been dead only moments earlier.

A teleporter on the battlefield could offer a lifeline to critically wounded soldiers—no need to draw their final breath in some foreign land's dirty trenches. Thanks to the teleporter that could become a thing of the past. The landscape of war has been redefined. Yet, with all the insanity unfolding around me, it's starting to feel routine.

"Hector, JC is back, alive and well," I am feeling no pain now and, in fact, feeling pretty damn good. Chip's pain pills are working. "You did good, Hector."

"Move him away from that spot," answers Hector. "Ward and Green, the two computer techs, will be right behind him."

Chip grabs JC's arm and pulls him away from his entry point. "You look a lot different than the last time I saw you," Chip says, shaking his head as if trying to make sense of the impossibleo9. JC looks puzzled, not recalling anything since he was beamed out of the lab into the CIVO computer room the first time.

"I feel like I missed all the fun," JC says with a grim smile.

"Trust me," Chip fires back, "you would not have enjoyed it."

No sooner had Chip finished speaking than Nathan Ward materialized. "Got him," I confirm to Hector on the phone.

Ward's eyes are like silver dollars. "Man, what a trip!" His exclamation is interrupted by the sound of a gunshot. We all drop to the floor.

Chip is standing over one of the guards with his M4 still smoking. "The sneaky bastard was playing possum," he growls.

"Hector, we're secure here," I say. "Send in Green to download these files and the virus."

I squeeze my eyes shut as another blast of light fills the room, and Green appears, grim-faced and gripping an M4 carbine rifle. He looks around the room and spies me.

I look at his gun. "You know how to use that thing?" I ask.

"Yes, sir," he replies proudly. "Four years in the U.S. Marines."

I pat him on his shoulder and give him a brief update on the situation. "Guards are all dead. Two of their techs are dead, but the rest are good. We have them gathered in that corner," I say, pointing. "Keep a close eye on them. It might be a good idea to have Hector send you extra ammo, just in case."

I contact Hector, confirming the arrival of Ward and Green. "Send the explosives," I tell him.

There is a collective holding of breath as the lights flash. This time I do not close my eyes but watch in anxious anticipation. Teleporting explosives is a first. The image flickers for a second before solidifying. A plastic container, three feet square, sits before us, containing enough explosives to render the computer room and a good portion of the CIVO fortress unusable.

I wait before I call Hector, ensuring the explosives arrive intact. JC steps forward, his nimble fingers swiftly opening the plastic container and carefully examining the explosives. I watch him intently as he prepares the timer. Done, he looks at me and gives me a reassuring thumbs-up.

"Hector," I say on the phone, "all good here. Another first."

What had been six CIVO computer technicians has been reduced to four. Green has been watching the surviving techs, who sit on the floor with their backs against a wall. One man and one woman lay on the ground in pools of blood.

"Stand up!" I wave my Glock at the remaining technicians. Looking around, they hesitantly get to their feet. "Watch them," I say to Green, who is pointing his rifle. I return to the corridor to retrieve my backpack with the micro-computer and the virus we will download into the CIVO system.

I stand before the silent group of CIVO people, looking hard into their faces. "Which computer is the 'motherboard' that connects all the components of the system?"

No one moves. Green and Chip lower their weapons to stomach level. "You all have about three seconds to answer," Chip growls.

Two technicians both point to the computer in the center of the room. Hector had shown me how to download the CIVO data, but I am no longer needed with Ward and Green here.

Ward connects our computer to the CIVO computer. The CIVO computer screen pauses, asking for the password. Chip turns to the CIVO technician—the one who pointed out the main computer.

"Password!" Chip snaps, shoving his gun into the man's ribs. The tech doesn't hesitate and says a word that sounds Arabic. "Spell it," Chip growls, lifting his weapon.

Ward enters the password and hits the Enter key. He's in. The downloading process should take no more than five minutes.

While waiting, Ward and JC put zip ties on the technicians.

JC scans the fallen guards and frowns, his attention drawn to the French Special Forces insignia on their uniforms. A deep frown forms on his face, and his lips twist in distaste as he notices the disheveled condition of their uniforms. "I know some boys in the French SF, and I can tell you these guys ain't," he declares with conviction.

"The French are very particular about their uniforms, especially the Special Forces. These guys have uniforms with rips and stains, mismatched buttons, and they are faded like they were purchased at a flea market," he says, shaking his head in disgust. "I think these boys are imposters."

He drops to his knees and begins rifling through their pockets, searching for any identification. Finally, pulling out an ID card, he shows it to me. "This dude has a Saudi Arabian driver's license. Wonder who they really are and why they're here."

Meanwhile, the computer beeps, indicating the download is complete. We now have CIVO's files. I take a USB containing the virus and hand it to Ward, who plugs it into a computer port. In a few minutes, the virus has been uploaded, and CIVO's system is wiped clean. Ward pulls out the USB and glances at the CIVO computer screen. It is blank.

Ward looks up at me. "What about a backup? I would be shocked if these computers weren't backed up, either here or elsewhere."

"What about the cloud?" I ask.

He shakes his head. "No. The cloud can be hacked. It's probably off-site somewhere."

I nod and walk over to the one computer tech who has cooperated. "Where's the backup located?"

The tech nervously glances at the dead woman on the floor. "I don't know." He nods toward the body of the woman. "She took care of that. I think there is a place in Riad, Saudi Arabia, but . . ." he shrugs, letting the sentence fade away.

Chip leans against the wall, his eyes darting between the screens and the explosives. "Why are we bothering to upload a virus into their computers if we're going to blow the place up?" His voice is laced with curiosity and impatience.

Ward glances at Chip over his shoulder. "When we upload the virus, it will also be uploaded into the CIVO file on the cloud or any other networked storage site where the program may have been saved," he explains.

"Those files stored in the cloud will infect any system that tries to download them. So the only CIVO clean files left will be this," Ward says, holding up the USB, "the one we just downloaded, and a possible hard copy in storage, maybe Riad. We'll keep ours under lock and key, but we may need to take out the copy in Riad if there is one."

I take a quick look at Ward and Green. "Me, Chip, and JC will get Libby and Marci Stone. Green, can you handle the detonator for the explosives? We might have to improvise, depending on the situation."

Green gives a solemn nod. "This will be easy. But we won't start the timer until you give us the signal. There won't be much left down here after this place blows."

I grab my phone to call Hector. To my surprise, Hector has

remained on the line, hearing the entire conversation since I called him earlier—no need to update him. "Hector, we're about done here. We need to get to where the girls are being held. Would it be better to walk or teleport?"

"Got the coordinates right here. Not far from you. How's your stomach?"

"It hurts like hell, but I'm good," I answer. "So you heard the plan. Any questions?"

"Just remember I only have one transporter. Timing is critical," he reminds us.

Green and JC start to zip-tie the arms and legs of the remaining four computer technicians. "Put duct tape on their mouths," growls Chip. "Let them go meet their seventy-two virgins."

The CIVO computer techs stare in horror at the explosives. They know this place will soon be obliterated, leaving only ashes and rubble.

I look at the cowering technicians. Some may be fathers. I know they were not the real villains here. They had been coerced into this dark and damp cave by threats of Lassiter and his cronies to kill families and loved ones if they refused to help. They had no say in their fate, no chance to escape. I cannot leave them here, bound and helpless, waiting for death.

Approaching the one tech who spoke English and had been cooperative. "We're going to destroy this place," I urgently tell him. "If you stay here, you will die. If we release you, you've got about five minutes to get out of the CIVO building. After that, the whole thing is going to explode." I raise my arms into the air. "Boom!"

Some clearly do not understand me. "Tell them what I just said," pointing to the other technicians. Excited words in Arabic are exchanged.

The tech gazes at me with pleading eyes. "Please, let us go. We owe nothing to Dr. Lassiter. He treats us like his slaves. We despise him."

I nod, then say in an ice-cold voice, "If I ever catch you working for Lassiter again, I will hunt you down and kill you. Understand?" They shiver and nod frantically.

"Okay, but don't cut them loose until you hear from us," I order Green. "We don't want them to warn anyone on their way out."

Chip glares at them, shaking his head, preferring to leave them to meet their fate. "We may end up dealing with these assholes in the future," he warns.

Chip and JC each have a radio they took from the bodies of the slain guards. JC turns one on. Two voices are speaking in French.

"They're trying to reach these assholes." JC points to the bodies of the dead guards. They're starting to get excited because they haven't reported in."

"In addition to being a badass, you speak French?" Chip said, impressed.

"Oh, hell yes! The women fuck'n love it, man. Spent my childhood in the Louisiana Bayou. One of these days, I'll tell you about it."

Chip grunts. "Yeah, can't wait."

JC takes my backpack and throws it over his broad shoulder. We give the room one last look, confirm the readiness of our weapons and gear, and exchange glances with Ward and Green. We're ready.

"We'll be waiting to hear from you," are Green's anxious words as we step out into the corridor.

The moment has arrived. Time to kill!

CHAPTER 37
TIME TO KILL

Libby is transfixed by the gruesome sight that had been Marci's face. Blood drips from both eyes, and the skin covering her cheeks has dissolved into mush, revealing white bones underneath. Thankfully, her shrieks have nearly stopped.

Marci," says Libby, "hang on. Jesse will find a way to get us out of here."

Marci looks at Libby through bloody eyes. "I'm trying." Her voice falters through mangled lips. "Libby, I . . . I can't take this anymore."

Her whisper is mixed with a moan. She turns her head toward Libby. "I'm sorry I got you involved in this." Her head rolls and falls forward on her chest. She is silent. Every few seconds, her silent body twitches.

Libby's tears stream down her face as she whispers a silent prayer that Marci's pain has ended. Even though Libby was betrayed by the woman, Libby feels no anger or resentment toward her, only a deep sense of pity. No human being should suffer such a horrible fate. Yet she can't help but wonder if she is next.

The guards remain silent and still, their faces writhed in discomfort. They avoided making eye contact with the women.

They can feel their stomachs churn and their throats tighten. One of them gags and runs out of the room, only to return a few minutes later, his face ashen. Libby lets out a soft sob, glaring at Lassiter, who is on the radio. Frustrated, he stares at her.

"Your boyfriend is playing a dangerous game," he says in a voice that freezes Libby's blood. "He's going to end up getting you killed." Lassiter shifts his empty stare to Faisal. "Get me the *Denz* container," he orders in a voice devoid of emotion.

***

"Found them," Hector declares. His voice is excited on my phone. "They're only down one level from the computer room." I leave the phone on but turn the volume low. Hector gives us directions as Chip, JC, and I walk in single file down the dim corridor.

The walls are slimy, the floor is wet, and our feet squelch beneath us as we walk under the dim lights. The warm air doesn't move and is suffocating, laced with a foul odor that turns the stomach.

JC wipes sweat from his brow. "It's so damn hot down here, a chicken could lay a hard-boiled egg."

Chip stifles a chuckle, shaking his head. "Where in the hell do you come up with these redneck sayings?"

"Hey, man, I told you, I'm from the Louisiana Bayou."

"Get ready." Hector's voice is a whisper on the phone. "You're close, boys. About twenty feet to go. The entryway is on your right."

Chip stops, holding a fist in the air. He points up. We all look up and see the camera mounted on the wall near the ceiling. "Stay underneath it," he hisses, waving the men against the wall.

We flatten out, sliding underneath the security camera. Chip tiptoes to the door, resting his hand on the latch. He turns back to me and JC, his eyes asking if we are ready. We both grip our guns and nod. JC slithers up behind Chip and pulls a flash-bang grenade off his belt.

With a final glance at us, Chip holds up three fingers . . . two . . . JC pulls the pin from the grenade . . . one. Chip slams the door open while JC tosses the grenade into the room. Chip yanks the door shut, and we squeeze our eyes closed. The explosion is small, but the blinding flash of light is visible through the edges of the door, even with closed eyes.

Chip springs through the door, moving to his right. His M4 carbine spits automatic fire at a guard against the wall taking him out with deadly precision before he can react. JC follows on his heels, veering left. Lying flat on the ground and using a metal table as cover, a second guard fires a burst of gunfire at JC, who unleashes a barrage of automatic fire at the table, shredding the metal top and silencing the guard. I am in awe of the flawlessly choreographed maneuvers of the two men as they storm the room.

The air is thick with smoke and the sound of gunfire as I dive through the door, landing on the floor with a grunt and rolling, ignoring the stabbing pain in my ribs. My eyes sweep the room, stopping on Libby in a chair at the far end. In the chair next to her is Marci, horribly disfigured.

Amid the chaos of smoke and noise, I see two dim figures crouched behind the women's chairs. Squinting to get a better look, I recognize Lassiter behind Libby's chair. Staying low to the ground, I crawl toward the chairs.

A volley of shots erupts from the direction of the chairs; bullets whiz past me, exploding on each side, sending chunks of concrete flying from the floor. I hear a cry behind me but can't spare a glance to see who is hit.

With a tight grip on my Glock, I roll left, staying as flat on my stomach as I can stand from the grinding pain in my rib area. Still lying face down on my stomach, I point the Glock toward the figure behind the nearest chair where Marci sits and pulls off two shots, one on each side.

I am rewarded with a salvo of return fire from two guns. The noise of an automatic rifle behind me comes from the area where Chip is. "Careful," I yell, "don't hit Libby."

I roll left again, trying to get a better angle on Lassiter. My ears are ringing from gunfire when I see a flash and hear a single shot from behind the farthest chair. A bullet tears into my Glock, ripping it out of my hand.

Chip is advancing on my right side toward the chairs. There is no sign of JC. The firing stops, and there is silence in the room.

Lassiter's voice cries out, "Mr. Ford, we have guns pointed at the heads of both Burns and Stone. Drop your weapons or they die."

"Fuck you, Lassiter." Chip responds in a strained voice. "Toss your weapons out here, and we may let you live."

The smoke from the grenade and firefight has largely cleared out of the room. Lassiter is crouched behind Libby's chair with a pistol pointed at her head. She appears motionless, and from where I lie on the floor, I can see a pool of blood gathering underneath her.

Lassiter, still crouching behind Libby, turns his gun on Marci in the chair beside Libby and discharges his weapon. The shot sounds like an explosion in the now quiet room. Marci's forehead erupts with blood and brain matter.

A surge of adrenaline races through my pounding heart as Lassiter turns from Marci's lifeless body toward Libby. He puts the gun barrel to her head and pulls the trigger. The sound echoes off the walls, and Libby's once-beautiful face disappears in a spray of crimson.

"No!" I scream in utter disbelief. My right hand instinctively reaches down and seizes the hilt of my blade. Like a whip, my arm flings the knife with a swiftness that blurs the vision, catapulting the deadly weapon across the twenty feet that separates us, burying itself in Lassiter's right shoulder, eliciting a scream of pain.

Lassiter pivots toward me, his eyes burning with hate. He pulls off one well-aimed shot, driving a bullet into my head. My world goes black.

CHAPTER 38
RENEWED

Despite being hardened veterans, Chip and JC stare in disbelief at the viciousness unfolding before their eyes. Erupting in anger, Chip squeezes off a round striking Lassiter in his uninjured left shoulder. Lassiter spins, losing his grasp of the pistol, which clatters to the floor.

Instantly, Chip is at Jesse's side. "Oh, please . . . no," he whispers, cradling Jesse's head with trembling hands. "Don't you go . . . don't quit on me, you stubborn bastard." Chip lifts Jesse's shoulders off the cold concrete floor.

JC kneels and puts his hand on Jesse's throat, then chest, searching but failing to find a pulse. Finally, he sighs and, with a bowed head, puts his hand on Chip's shoulder.

"Sorry, brother, he's gone."

In the blink of an eye, Chip is straddling Lassiter, hammering at him with his bare knuckles. He rips Jesse's knife from Lassiter's wounded shoulder, pressing the blue steel against Lassiter's jugular.

"Don't!" JC's shout rings out as he pushes himself to his feet. "We need that bastard alive."

An inner battle rages within Chip as he struggles with his emotions. Slowly he eases the blade away from Lassiter's neck.

Chip's eyes shift to Libby, then back to Jesse. Going to Jesse's body, he retrieves the phone. The red light is still on. "Hello? Hector, can you hear me?"

Hector immediately answers. "Jesse, what happened? Is Libby alive? I lost the connection in the middle of all the gunfire."

"Hector, it's Chip. The situation is bad here. Jesse didn't make it, and neither did Libby. Marci is also gone. It's a blood-bath. That son of a bitch Lassiter is still alive somehow."

A sharp intake of breath sounds on the phone, followed by a painful silence.

"Chip, does Jesse still have his backpack? Get it," orders Hector. "There's a pad that will give me his coordinates. Remove it and slide it under him. We need to get him back here fast. After Jesse, do the same for Libby. I want both bodies back here."

Chip's eyes dart around the room, searching for the missing backpack. It was JC who carried Jesse's gear from the computer room. "JC!" he bellows. "I need Jesse's backpack. Now!"

"What about Lassiter?" JC shouts back, his question hang-ing in the air.

"We'll take care of him later," comes Chip's unconcerned reply, his total focus on Jesse.

JC enters the hallway, retrieves the pack, and hands it to Chip, who removes the pad and spreads it on the ground. Together, the two men lift Jesse, gently placing the lifeless body on the pad.

"Stand back," Hector orders, still listening to the conversa-tion. "After Jesse, get Libby and put her on the pad."

"Okay, got Jesse," Hector snaps. "Is Libby on the pad? Tell me about Marci Stone . . . what's her situation?"

"Like her face went through a sausage factory," answers Chip. "I haven't checked her life signs but can tell just by looking that she is gone. It looks like Lassiter sprayed her with *Denz*."

"Stop! Don't touch anything, not even Libby," Hector warns. "In Jesse's backpack is a tiny cartridge that resembles a spray can. That's the antidote."

Over the phone, his tone becomes even more severe. "Before you lay a finger on anything else in that room, spray your exposed skin. I can't stress enough how vital it is to do this. One more thing, leave Marci Stone. Don't bring her back to the lab."

Relief sounded in JC's voice. "Gladly. It would freak me out to even touch her."

"Get Libby and lay her on the pad after you spray your exposed skin with the antidote, then stand back."

With a flash of lights, Libby's body disappears. A few seconds later, Hector says, "Okay, we have both of them. Are you or JC injured?" Hector asks.

"We have a few scratches, nothing serious."

"Good. Do you have Lassiter restrained?"

"Yep. He's not going anywhere."

"Okay, stand Lassiter on the pad . . . then you and JC get your asses back here. Any questions?"

"No," Chip replies. "Got it, except we still have Ward and Green to return."

"Let's get Lassiter back here first. Keep him tied up. Can he stand?"

Chip walks over to the bound Lassiter and kicks him in the head. "Can you stand, asshole?" Without waiting for an answer, he grabs him by his throat and lifts him off the ground like a feather. "Sure, he can stand," he says.

"Put him on the transporter pad. We have security waiting for him," instructs Hector.

While Lassiter sways on the teleporter pad, Chip turns to him. "I almost forgot," He slams his fist straight into Lassiter's nose. "That one was for Dan."

After Lassiter has vanished, Chip tells Hector, "I'm not anxious to get into another gun battle. Two in one day is about my limit. JC and I want to get out of here as soon as possible."

"I hear you. It won't be long. Reach out to Ward and Green. Tell them to set the timer for ten minutes. I can bring them back as soon as you and JC get here. Send JC back first. You're next. Hurry! You guys pulled it off. Thank you."

***

The bright lights stop flashing. I open my eyes to be greeted by Hector's grinning face. He pulls me into a tight hug while slapping my back. I don't know where I am and have no idea how I got here.

"What . . . what happen?" I manage to stammer through my confusion.

"We'll debrief later. First, I have to work on Libby," Hector answers.

"Libby? I ask. "Did we get her? I don't remember. It's kind of a blur."

His face sobers, his earlier smile gone. "Just be patient for now. All of your questions will be answered," he says to me.

A man dressed in a white lab coat offers me a glass of liquid.

"Mr. Ford, I'm Christopher Drake. If you recall, we spoke about the memory loss you may experience after being teleported."

I stopped to think. I did remember that conversation with Christopher just before Hector was teleported. "I thought that would only be an issue when you had to revive a person after a long period," I answered.

"That's true," Drake says, nodding, "or when we must revive someone from their original DNA because they don't survive. Please, take this and drink. It's a high protein-rich mix that will make you feel better." The drink is surprisingly good. I drink it all while watching the activities around me, thinking about what I had just been told.

Swallowing the last of the drink, I hand the glass back to Drake. My mind is beginning to kick into gear now. "Chris, are you saying I did not survive the rescue attempt at CIVO?"

There is a flash of light at the far end of the room in one of the teleportation chambers, and a form begins to materialize—a woman, naked and motionless, covered in blood. I start to move toward her, but Drake stops me.

"Sir, if you could wait a few minutes. Libby will be very confused when she wakes up, just like you were. Let us check her out, and then you can speak with her," says Chris.

I nod and sink into the nearest chair, attempting to sort out the jumbled thoughts running through my head.

There is a second burst of light, and a tall black man materializes, fully conscious, eyes scanning the room. I feel like I know him, but I am too confused to place him. He spies me, and his face splits into a grin. He starts to approach me, but Hector intercepts him. I see Hector shaking his head, and the smile disappears from the black man's face.

Almost immediately, there is a follow-up flash. A second man appears. As he steps out of the chamber, I recognize him. Chip. My mind reels, feeling like it is tangled in webs. He sees me, and a broad smile spreads across his face. Like the black man, he heads in my direction but is also stopped by Hector. After a quick conversation, his gaze swivels to me. However, unlike the first man, Chip brushes Hector aside and moves toward me, but now his face is clouded with worry.

Chip walks up to me, stops, and gives me a long, hard gaze. "Hey, Jess. Are you still in there?" he asks. His eyebrows knit together in worry.

I shake my head, baffled. "I . . . I'm not sure what's going on, Chip," I stammer. "I know I'm at the lab. I remember shooting, getting hit in the chest . . . I think we were in the CIVO computer room. I remember walking down a corridor, an explosion, and we went through a door where Libby and Marci are tied up." I hesitated, struggling to recall. "There were more shots, explosions, then Lassiter shot Marci in the head—and then he shot Libby." I stopped and choked. "Next thing I know, I'm here in the lab."

I shake my head, feeling the emotion rise in me. "Is Libby dead? I . . . I can't focus. I feel lost, Chip. Help me." I fall back in the chair.

Chip puts his hand on my slumped shoulder. "Don't worry, brother. You'll be fine. I'm with you. You just need some rest." He gives me a pat on the back. "Hector's got Libby. She'll be fine but will have some memory blanks like you."

I spent the following hours under the attentive care of Dr. Samantha Park, the chief medical officer at the lab, before being led to a darkened room with a bed and told to get some sleep. Over the next day, in an effort to determine the extent of my recollections before my death at the CIVO facility, I am given an assortment of drugs and quizzed about what memories I recall, some going back to my childhood on the Reservation. Fragments begin to resurface, gradually filling in the blank areas. I'm relieved within 24 hours of being back at the lab, those empty areas are filling in. Thanks to Hector and Dr. Park, I'm born again, feeling good, and ready to roll.

"You two are the first, the pioneers," Hector explains to Libby and me. "We knew we could physically resurrect you after your death by reconstructing the DNA and atomic structure we collected from your last teleportation. Libby, that was when we sent you to Denver for John's funeral. You have no recollection of what happened after that time until you were revived here at the lab. Our objective has been to fill in those blanks."

Hector then shifts his focus to me. "Your last teleportation was when we sent you to the CIVO headquarters just before the power went out here at the lab. You have no memory of what happened after that until you were brought back to the lab. . . technically dead. There was a shorter period of memory loss for you and thus a quicker recuperation period."

Libby, resurrected from the dead like me, has a longer gap to fill in. Hers is more extensive, and there are empty areas in her immediate past that may never be filled. From what Chip tells me, that's a good thing.

After several days of treatment, we are ready to meet with the rest of our group.

I call for a meeting, including Hector, Kim, Libby, Chip, and JC, to decide Lassiter's fate. We have kept him restrained for several days since his capture but are ready to be rid of him.

"We have him thoroughly secured in a room just down the hall," says Hector. "But before we get started, we have a video to show you," he says, directing his comments to Libby and me. "You guys missed this, but when we left CIVO, we planted explosives in Lassiter's little shop of horrors as a parting gift. We had all previously agreed not to leave the building standing. I recorded the event and thought you two would be interested in seeing the results of our handiwork."

Hector points at the wall-mounted monitor on the wall. "We had a drone hovering above CIVO with a bird's-eye view."

In the video, we can hear Hector doing a countdown. "Brace yourselves," he whispers. From the aerial view, a seismic shock-wave can be seen rippling across the earth, radiating outward from the epicenter at CIVO headquarters, followed by a silent eruption of smoke and fire. It is eerily similar to watching a volcano erupt. Smoke climbs steadily into the air, higher and higher.

We watch the video screen, transfixed by the explosion ripping apart the CIVO headquarters. Chip breaks the silence with a low whistle. "Just as good the second time. Those were some kick-ass explosives. Looked like a mini-nuke going off."

The group grows silent, each of us lost in our thoughts of what we just witnessed.

"It's time," I command, breaking the silence. "Go get him."

"Payback time," Chip says grimly.

CHAPTER 39
PAYBACK

Lassiter's swagger remains intact as he enters the lab despite being flanked by two burly guards, each with an iron grip on his unrestrained arms. His arrival casts a freezing silence over the room. He snickers at me, but his eyes widen when he sees Libby.

"Happy to see you recovered so quickly, darling," he taunts her, a sneer on his lips.

"Fuck you," she snaps back, her eyes blazing with rage. She doesn't give Lassiter the pleasure of knowing she has no recollection of what happened at the CIVO fortress but lunges for him anyway. I grab her wrist, holding her back. "Wait! He'll get his."

"Thought you'd appreciate knowing your lab and facility have been reduced to a big crater in the ground," I say with satisfaction. "Oh, and one more thing. We've developed a counter-agent to neutralize *Denz*."

"You'll never stop all of us." Lassiter spits out in defiance. His expression shows no remorse for the pain and death he has caused.

"Oh, I beg to differ," I respond coolly. "It's just a matter of time till we send our calling card to your terrorist buddies in Saudi Arabia, starting with your dear uncle. It's a shame you won't be around to see it." My smile grows when I see the flicker of fear on his face. He begins to squirm in the guards' grasp.

"You wanted a teleporter and were willing to kill to get it. So we've decided to grant your wish. You are about to get your own teleportation journey."

I led the guards and Lassiter to HEC#2. He struggles and curses while being forced through the hatch. Once inside, his eyes, aflame with loathing and pure hatred, fixate on me. He begins screaming in Arabic.

My face is grim as I stand only inches from his face, separated by the hatch. "As you may have guessed, you are about to experience the thrill of a lifetime, or at least, what little life you have left. You wanted to go down in history, and so you shall. Take comfort in the knowledge that you will be the first human ever to be teleported into space," I inform him, my voice icy and barren of emotion. "Unfortunately for you, no one will ever know about it. Your story will be lost in space, just like you."

Hector slides up next to me. "But before you go, we wanted to give you a travel companion." Hector holds up his missing forearm. "The one you created." Hector opens the hatch, sprays a pink mist from a small aerosol can into Lassiter's face, then swiftly seals and locks the hatch.

Libby strides up to the hatch, her blazing eyes fixed on Lassiter. With a savage spit, she adds her farewell message to Lassiter's impending doom. "Have a pleasant journey." She smiles in satisfaction.

By the time the familiar glow ignites at the base of the tube, Lassiter is rubbing his face, his mouth open in a scream. The light travels upward, then back to the bottom. There is a flash of light, and Aran Lassiter vanishes.

A hushed silence hangs in the air. It's Libby who breaks it. "Where did you send him?" Libby asks, her voice echoing in the still room.

"The Sun," I answer.

***

It is well after midnight when the door to Christopher Drake's quarters eases open. Drake peeks out, taking a cautious glance down the empty hallway. Shoeless, his feet clad only in socks, he pads stealthily toward the laboratory—home of the teleporters.

Upon reaching the entrance to the lab, he halts, his ears straining for any sounds of human presence. The silence is reassuring. He tiptoes toward the master computer console.

Drake, never much of a socializer, promised Hector he would shut down the computers and lock the lab. While the rest of the team went to the dining quarters to celebrate the fall of Lassiter, Drake remained. Before he left the lab, he put the master computer in sleep mode instead of shutting it down.

With a cautious touch, he wakes the sleeping computer. With a faint click, the monitor springs to life with a soft hum. From his pocket, he pulls out a small, nondescript black box— hardly larger than a deck of cards. He inserts the box into the computer's front port and holds his breath as the screen flickers revealing the duplicated DNA data from one 'Aran Lassiter.' Drake has a tight smile as his eyes study every detail on the screen—*only one chance to get this right.* After reviewing the readout, he makes an adjustment with the keyboard and reviews the screen again. Satisfied, he presses the enter key. Hector will never know.

There is a soft whirring sound as the computer downloads the stored DNA files into the black box. The rhythmic sound lasts only a few minutes.

His mission complete, Drake swiftly ejects the black box, stowing it safely in his pocket. He then powers down and shuts off the computer. Retracing his steps, he exits the room, securing the door behind him. As he slips back to his quarters, his lips twist into a malicious smirk, hinting at the grim plans unfolding in his head. This is just the beginning.

EPILOGUE

On a bright, sunny day outside Boston, a somber memorial service is held for Marci Stone. I can't help but feel a sense of sadness mixed with irony as she is remembered as an unfortunate victim of a kidnapping by her crazed nephew, Dr. Aran Lassiter, who disappeared and is presumed vaporized in the explosion. Only a select few know the true story behind her tragic fate.

Among the attendees are Hollywood celebrities, dignitaries, members of the Saudi royal family, the Chief of Staff of the President of the United States, Wallace Franklin, and several members of Congress. Marci Stone had cut a wide swath in her lifetime.

After the service, Wallace Franklin pulls me aside. "Walk with me, Jesse. The President wants you to know how grateful he is for what you and your people have done for our nation."

Thanks to Hector and his fellow scientists at the lab, the *Denz* antidote has been perfected. It is being used throughout the country. The treatment will lessen, but not eliminate, the damage from the micro virus. There is no question that the oil supply in the U.S., Europe, and all oil-producing countries has taken a severe blow. The civilized world has changed and is in dire need of a new energy source.

"He is particularly impressed," continues Franklin, "with this teleportation device, and has decided to create a new department,

The Department of Teleportation. He asked me if you would be interested in leading this new department as the first Director of Teleportation?"

I am pleased but not surprised. Senator Thompson had earlier hinted at the formation of this new department to me. "Please convey my gratitude to the President. It's an honor to be considered," I reply. "I assure you I will have an answer for you shortly, sir."

"We have a whole new world to create now. This teleportation thing will have a bigger impact on civilization than the wheel. You can help shape it," Franklin says with conviction.

I nod in agreement. That's precisely what I intend to do.

***

I enter the hallway outside the Americo boardroom, awaiting the impending vote. Since the deaths of John Hammer and Marci Stone, the company has been leaderless, a challenge the Board is attempting to overcome.

I drift over to the window, my eyes soaking in the majestic sight of snow-covered mountains. A sense of tranquility sweeps over me. Behind me, the secretary asks if she can get me anything.

"Mineral water, please." My gaze drops to Interstate 25 below me, running like a ribbon through the city. In the old days, it would be jam-packed with traffic at this time of day. Nowadays, traffic is sparse, and the blue sky seems clearer, the air crisper.

The spill has served as a powerful catalyst, igniting a chain reaction and setting off a series of events that will ultimately transform our fragile planet. In a bizarre way, we may owe our gratitude to Lassiter for *Denz*. Its impact will leave a lasting mark on society and the future.

The lights of the old world have truly dimmed. The days of fossil fuel are numbered. The transition to a new energy source may span several generations but is inevitable. A new age is dawning.

I intend to help shape it, and thanks to teleportation, I now have all the time in the world to do so. I have no doubt the newly named Americo Energy and Teleportation Company will play a major role.

Once again, my gaze drifts westward toward the mountains, their lofty peaks touching the sky. Over that clump of trees is the apartment Libby and I once called home during our law school days. Checking my watch, I note she should be home by now from her new job as a partner with a Denver environmental law firm.

I do not turn when the boardroom door creaks open. Verne Sheldon steps, clearing his throat before he speaks. "We're ready for you . . . Mr. President."

THE END

ABOUT THE AUTHOR

As a young boy, I grew up in the rugged deserts of the Navajo Indian Reservation in New Mexico. After serving in the U.S. Navy, I studied at the University of Northern Colorado in Greeley, Colorado, followed by law school at Ohio Northern University College of Law.

Returning to Colorado after law school, fate stepped into my life, and I found myself in the oil and gas business. Over the next thirty-seven years, my career balanced between the oil and gas industry and my law practice. But, always lingering in the background was my desire to write.

I have been published in The Colorado Lawyer, a magazine of current legal issues. My short story, The 100,000 Year War, was lauded as the "Best Short Story" in the thriller genre. The Spill marks my debut in the world of novel writing and a new chapter for me.

I am a member of several writing communities, including the Rocky Mountain Fiction Writers Association, The Florida Writers Association, The Writers League of the Villages, Working Writers Critique Group, and Pen, Paper & Pals. I now live in Florida.

P	L	
85	23	theory, [it] would
87	9	pressure [to] open
106	26	announcement [on] this
109	10	spacing gap
175	14	spacing gap
197	4	focused [on] the
205	23	spacing gap
227	12-13	"I feel" s/b "he feels"
256	1	unable ~~able~~ to act
311	16	spacing gap
330	16	words ~~hand~~ [hang] heavy
359	19	the impossible~~d~~
370	8	

Made in the USA
Columbia, SC
14 December 2023

27747757R00215